Praise for *An Absolutely Remarkable Thing*

'Fun and full of truth. To be honest, I'm a little irritated at how good the book is. I don't need this kind of competition'
Patrick Rothfuss, #1 *New York Times*
bestselling author of The Kingkiller Chronicles

'An undeniably strange and delightful thing'   V.E. Schwab

'*An Absolutely Remarkable Thing* is perhaps most like a cheerier John Wyndham: a first contact story that, rather than dwelling too much on why aliens have arrived, focuses on how humans react'   *Guardian*

'A fun, contemporary adventure that cares about who we are as humans, especially when faced with remarkable events'
Kirkus (starred review)

'You're about to meet somebody named April May who you're immediately going to want to be best friends with. And bonus, she spends all her time having incredible adventures with giant robots and dream puzzles and accidental Internet fame. *An Absolutely Remarkable Thing* is pure book-joy'   Lev Grossman, #1 *New York Times*
bestselling author of *The Magicians*

'A fascinating look at someone viewing one the greatest events in human history through Twitter'   *SFX*

'Author Hank Green captures what's great about the internet, as well as what's bad about it. The polarising of opinions feels plausible, as online communities spring up both to solve the puzzles and to cook up evil plans'   *SciFiNow*

'This is the book my teen self would have loved, and my adult self immediately obsessed over. I turned the pages of *An Absolutely Remarkable Thing* so quickly the pads of my thumbs were worn smooth by the time I finished it. It provokes the mind, tickles the spirit, and April May is the terribly relevant young protagonist we've been waiting for'   Ashley C. Ford

'Hank Green hasn't just written a great mystery adventure (though he has), and he hasn't just written the most interesting meditation on the internet and fame I've ever seen (but he did that too), Hank has written a book in which the page-turning story and the fascinating ideas inform and support each other. This book expands your mind while taking you on a hell of a ride'

Joseph Fink, creator of *Welcome to Night Vale*

'Funny, thrilling, and an absolute blast to read. I knew Hank would be good at this, but I didn't know he would be this good on the first try'

John Scalzi

'*An Absolutely Remarkable Thing* is both realistic and fantastical, while touching on deep themes, including gender, the internet, fame and humanity. Green's firsthand knowledge of YouTube fame and fortune gives authenticity to the protagonist, twenty-three-year-old April May'

The Herald

'Packed with meditations on the nature of celebrity, social media, and the cultural response to the unknown'

Harper's Bazaar

'[Green's] writing is light-hearted, clever, resonating and funny, tackling socially relevant themes, including the darker side of social media, sexuality, the naivety of youth and media representation . . . Get ready to be absorbed in the story, glued to the book and a little more afraid of Twitter'

Stylist

'*An Absolutely Remarkable Thing* is such a beautiful exploration of what humans can accomplish when we collaborate effectively'

John Green, bestselling author of *The Fault in Our Stars*

AN ABSOLUTELY REMARKABLE THING

HANK GREEN

TRAPEZE

This edition first published in Great Britain in 2019
by Trapeze
First published in Great Britain in 2018 by Trapeze
an imprint of The Orion Publishing Group Ltd
Carmelite House, 50 Victoria Embankment
London EC4Y 0DZ

An Hachette UK Company

3 5 7 9 10 8 6 4

A CIP catalogue record for this book is available from the British Library.

ISBN 978 1 473 22420 9

Printed in Great Britain by Clays Ltd, Elcograf S.p.A.

MIX
Paper from
responsible sources
FSC® C104740
FSC
www.fsc.org

www.orionbooks.co.uk

Thanks, Mom!

CHAPTER ONE

Look, I am aware that you're here for an epic tale of intrigue and mystery and adventure and near death and actual death, but in order to get to that (unless you want to skip to chapter 13—I'm not your boss), you're going to have to deal with the fact that I, April May, in addition to being one of the most important things that has ever happened to the human race, am also a woman in her twenties who has made some mistakes. I am in the wonderful position of having you by the short hairs. I have the story, and so I get to tell it to you the way I want. That means you get to understand me, not just my story, so don't be surprised if there's some drama. I'm going to attempt to come at this account honestly, but I'll also admit to a significant pro-me bias. If you get anything out of this, ideally it won't be you being more or less on one side or the other, but simply understanding that I am (or at least was) human.

And I was very much feeling only human as I dragged my tired ass down 23rd Street at 2:45 A.M. after working a sixteen-hour day at a start-up that (thanks to an aggressively shitty contract I signed) will remain nameless. Going to art school might seem like a terrible financial decision, but really that's only true if you have to take out gobs and gobs of student loans to fund your hoity-toity education. Of course, I had done exactly that. My parents were successful, running a business providing equipment to small and medium-sized dairy farms. Like, the little things you hook up to cows to get the milk out, they sold and distributed them. It was good business, good enough that I wouldn't have had a lot of debt if I'd gone to a state school. But I did not do that. I had loans. Lots. So, after jumping from major to major (advertising, fine art, photography, illustration) and finally settling on the mundane (but at least useful) BFA in design, I took the first job that would keep me in New York and out of my old bedroom in my parents' house in Northern California.

And that was a job at a doomed start-up funded by the endless well of rich people who can only dream the most boring dream a rich person can dream: being even more rich. Of course, working at a start-up means that you're part of the "family," and so when things go wrong, or when deadlines fly past, or when an investor has a hissy fit, or just *because*, you don't get out of work until three in the morning. Which, honestly, I hated. I hated it because the company's time-management app was a dumb idea and didn't actually help people, I hated it because I knew I was just doing it for money, and I hated it because they asked the staff to treat it like their whole life rather than like a day job, which meant I didn't have any time to spare to work on personal projects.

BUT!

I was actually using my degree doing actual graphic design and getting paid enough to afford rent less than one year out of school. My work environment was close to technically criminal and I paid half of my income to sleep in the living room of a one-bedroom apartment, but I was making it work.

I fibbed just now. My bed was in the living room, but I mostly slept in the bedroom—Maya's room. We weren't living together, we were roommates, and April-from-the-past would want me to be very clear about that. What's the difference between those two things? Well, mostly that we weren't dating before we moved in together. Hooking up with your roommate is convenient, but it is also a little confusing when you lived together through much of college. Before finally hooking up and have now been a couple for more than a year.

If you happen to already live together, when does the "Should we move in together?" question come up? Well, for Maya and me, the question was "Can we please move that secondhand mattress out of the living room so that we can sit on a couch when we watch Netflix?" and thus far my answer had been "Absolutely not, we are just roommates who are dating." Which is why our living room still had a bed in it.

I told you there would be drama.

Anyway, back to the middle of the night that fateful January evening. This shitty app had to get a new release into the App Store by the next week and I had been waiting for final approvals on some user interface changes, and whatever, you don't care—it was boring work BS. Instead of coming in early, I stayed late, which has always been my preference. My brain was sucked entirely dry from trying to interpret cryptic guidance from bosses who couldn't tell a raster from a vector. I checked out of the building (it was a coworking space, not even actual leased offices) and walked the three minutes to the subway station.

And then my MetroCard got rejected FOR NO REASON. I had another one sitting on my desk at work, and I wasn't precisely sure how much money I had in my checking account, so it seemed like I should walk the three blocks back to the office just to be safe.

The walk sign is on, so I cross 23rd, and a taxicab blares its horn like I shouldn't be in the crosswalk. Whatever, dude, I have the walk light. I turn to head back to the office and immediately I see it. As I approach, it becomes clear that it is a really . . . REALLY exceptional sculpture.

I mean, it's AWESOME, but it's also a little bit "New York awesome," you know?

How do I explain how I felt about it? I guess . . . well . . . in New York City people spend ten years making something amazing happen, something that captures the essence of an idea so perfectly that suddenly the world becomes ten times clearer. It's beautiful and it's powerful and someone devoted a huge piece of their life to it. The local news does a story about it and everyone goes "Neat!" and then tomorrow we forget about it in favor of some other ABSOLUTELY PERFECT AND REMARKABLE THING. That doesn't make those things unwonderful or not unique . . . It's just that there are a lot of people doing a lot of amazing things, so eventually you get a little jaded.

So that's how I felt when I saw it—a ten-foot-tall Transformer wearing a suit of samurai armor, its huge barrel chest lifted up to the sky a good four or five feet above my head. It just stood there in the middle of the sidewalk, full of energy and power. It looked like it might, at any moment, turn and fix that empty, regal stare on *me*. But instead it just stood there, silent and almost scornful, like the world didn't deserve its attention. In the streetlight, the metal was a patchwork of black-as-night matte and mirror-reflective silver. And it clearly was metal . . . not some spray-painted cardboard cosplay thing. It was stunningly done. I paused for maybe five seconds before shivering both in the cold and in the gaze of the thing and then walking on.

And then I. Felt. Like. The. Biggest. Jerk.

I mean, I'm an artist working way too hard at a deeply uninteresting job to pay way too much in rent so I can stay in this place—so that I can remain immersed in one of the most creative and influential cultures on earth. Here in the middle of the sidewalk is a piece of art that was a massive undertaking, an installation that the artist worked on, possibly for years, to make people stop and look and consider. And here I am, hardened by big-city life and mentally drained by hours of pixel pushing, not even giving something so magnificent a second glance.

I remember this moment pretty clearly, so I guess I'll mention it. I went back to the sculpture, got up on my tiptoes, and I said, "Do you think I should call Andy?"

The sculpture, of course, did nothing.

"Just stand there if it's OK for me to call Andy."

And so I made the call.

But first, some background on Andy!

You know those moments when your life shifts and you think, *I will definitely, without a doubt, continue to love and appreciate and connect with all of these cool people I have spent so many years with, despite the fact that our lives are changing a great deal right now*, and then instead you might as well unfriend them on Facebook because you ain't never gonna see that dude again in your whole life? Well, Andy, Maya, and I had somehow (thus far) managed to avoid that fate. Maya and I had done it by occupying the same four hundred square feet. Andy, on the other hand, lived across town from us, and we didn't even know him until junior year. Maya and I, by that point, were taking most of the same classes because, well, we really liked each other a lot. We were obviously going to be in the same group whenever there was a group project. But Professor Kennedy was dividing us up into groups of three, which meant a random third wheel. Somehow we got stuck with Andy (or probably, from his perspective, he got stuck with us).

I knew who Andy was. I had formed a vague impression of him that was mostly "that guy sure is more confident than he has any right to be." He was skinny and awkward with printer-paper-pale skin. I assumed he began his haircuts by asking the stylist to make it look like he had never received a haircut. But he was always primed for some quip, and for the most part, those quips were either funny or insightful.

The project was a full brand treatment for a fictional product. Packaging was optional, but we needed several logo options and a style guide (which is like a little book that tells everyone how the brand should be presented and what fonts and colors are to be used in what situations). It was more or less a given that we would be doing this for some hip and groovy fictional company that makes ethical, fair-trade jeans with completely useless pockets or something. Actually, it was almost always a fictional brewery because we were college students. We were paying a lot of money to cultivate our taste in beer and be snobby about it.

And I'm sure that's the direction Maya and I would have gone in, but Andy was intolerably stubborn and somehow convinced us both that we would be building the visual identity of "Bubble Bum," a butt-flavored bubble gum. At first his arguments were silly, that we weren't going to be doing fancy cool shit when we graduated, so we might as well not take the project so seriously. But he convinced us when he got serious.

"Look, guys," he said, "it's easy to make something cool look cool, that's why everyone picks cool things. Ultimately, though, cool is always going to be boring. What if we can make something dumb look amazing? Something unmarketable, awesome? That's a real challenge. That takes real skill. Let's show real skill."

I remember this pretty clearly because it was when I realized there was more to Andy.

By the end of the project I couldn't help feeling a little superior to the rest of our classmates, taking their skinny jeans and craft breweries so seriously. And the final product did look great. Andy was—and I had known this but not really filed it as important—an extremely talented illustrator, and with Maya's hand-lettering skills and my color-palette work, it did end up looking pretty great.

So that's how Maya and I met Andy, and thank god we did. Frankly, we needed a third wheel to even out the intensity of the early part of our relationship. After the Bubble Bum project, which Kennedy loved so much he put it on the class website, we became a bit of a trio. We even worked on some freelance projects together, and occasionally Andy would come over to our apartment and force us to play board games. And then we'd just spend the evening talking about politics or dreams or anxieties. The fact that he was obviously a little bit in love with me never really bothered any of us because he knew I was taken and, well, I don't think Maya saw him as a threat. Somehow, our dynamic hadn't fractured after graduation and we kept hanging out with funny, weird, smart, stupid Andy Skampt.

Who I was now calling at three o'clock in the morning.

"The fuck, April, it's 3 A.M."

"Hey, I've got something you might want to see."

"It seems likely that this can wait until tomorrow."

"No, this is pretty cool. Bring your camera . . . and does Jason have any lights?" Jason was Andy's roommate—both of them wanted to be internet famous. They would stream themselves playing video games to tiny audiences, and they had a podcast about the best TV death scenes that they also filmed and uploaded to YouTube. To me it just seemed like that incurable ailment so many well-off dudes have, believing despite mountains of evidence that what the world truly needs is another white-guy comedy podcast. This sounds harsh, but that's what it seemed like to me back then. Now, of course, I know how easy it is to feel like you don't matter if no one's watching. I've also since listened to *Slainspotting* and it's actually pretty funny.

"Wait . . . what's happening? What am I doing?" he asked.

"Here's what you're doing: You're walking over to Gramercy Theatre and you're going to bring as much of Jason's video shit as you can and you're not going to regret it, so don't even think about going back to whatever hentai VR game you're playing . . . This is better, I promise."

"You say that, but have you played *Cherry Blossom Fairy Five*, April May? Have you?"

"I'm hanging up . . . You're going to be here in five minutes."

I hung up.

Several people who weren't Andy walked by as I waited for him. Manhattan is less legit than it once was, for sure, but this is still the city that never sleeps. It is also the city of "Behold the field in which I grow my fucks. Lay thine eyes upon it and see that it is barren." People gave the sculpture a quick glance and kept on walking, just as I had very nearly done. I tried to look busy. Manhattan's a safe place, but that doesn't mean a twenty-three-year-old woman by herself on the street at 3 A.M. isn't going to get randomly harassed.

For the next few minutes I got to spend a little time with the structure. Manhattan is never really dark, there was lots of light around, but the deep shadows and the sculpture's size made it difficult to really understand it. It was massive. It probably weighed several hundred pounds. I took my glove off and poked it, finding the metal surprisingly not cool. Not warm either, exactly . . . but hard. I gave it a knock on the pelvis and didn't hear the bell ring I expected. It was more of a thunk followed by a low hum. I started to think that this was part of the artist's intentions . . . that the goal was for the people of New York to interact with this object . . . to discover its properties. When you're in art school, you do a lot of thinking about objectives and intent. That was just the default state: SEE ART → CRITIQUE ART.

Eventually, I stopped my critique and just took it in. I was starting to really love it. Not just as a creation of someone else, but the way that you love really good art . . . just enjoying it. It was so unlike other things I'd seen. And brave in its "Transformerness." Like, I would be terrified to do anything that visually reflected mecha robots in any way . . . No one wants to be compared to something that's *mainstream popular.* That's the worst of all possible fates.

But there was much more to this piece than that. It seemed to have come from a completely different place than any work I'd ever seen before, sculptural or not. I was pretty caught up in the thing when Andy snapped me out of it.

"What the absolute fuck . . ." He was wearing a backpack and three camera straps and holding two tripods.

"Yup," I replied.

"That. Is. AWESOME."

"I know . . . The awful thing is, I almost walked right by it. I just thought, 'Well, there's another fucking cool New York City thing,' and kept on walking. But it occurred to me that I hadn't heard or seen anything about it, and since, y'know, you're always in search of your big viral hit, you might want to get the scoop. So I've been guarding it for you."

"So you saw this big, beautiful, muscular piece of art and who sprung into your mind but ANDY Skampt!" His thumbs were digging into his bony chest.

"LOL," I said sarcastically. "In fact, I figured I'd do you a favor, and here it is, so maybe just appreciate it?"

A little dejected, he handed me a tripod. "Well, let's start getting this shit set up then. Gotta work before Channel 6 drunkenly stumbles by and steals our scoop."

In five minutes the camera was set up, a battery-powered light was glaring, and Andy was clamping the mic to his lapel. He didn't look as dopey as he had in school. He'd stopped wearing stupid ball caps, and he'd given up on his unruly (or just uncommon) haircuts in favor of a short-wavy thing that complemented his face shape. But despite the fact that he was eight inches taller than me and almost exactly my age, he still looked about five years my junior.

"April," he said.

"Yah."

"I think maybe it should be you."

I probably replied with some kind of confused grunt.

"In front of the camera, I mean."

"Dude, this is your dream, not mine. I don't know shit about YouTube."

"It's just . . . I mean, well . . ." Looking back, I think it's possible, though I've never asked him, that he had some idea that this would actually be a big deal. Not as big a deal as it would turn out to be, of course, but big.

"Hey, don't think you're going to win my favor by giving me internet fame. I don't even want that."

"Right, but you have no idea how to use this camera." I could tell he was making an excuse, but I couldn't figure out why.

"I don't know how to do behind-the-camera stuff, but I also don't know how to do in-front-of-the-camera stuff. You and Jason talk to the internet all day long, I barely have a Facebook."

"You have an Instagram."

"That's different." I smirked.

"Not really. I can tell you care about what you post on there. You're not fooling anyone. You're a digital girl, April, in a digital world. We all know how to perform." God bless Andy for being blunt. He was right, of course. I tried not to care about social media, and I really did prefer hanging out in art galleries to hanging out on Twitter. But I wasn't as disconnected as I made myself out to be. Being annoyed by carefully crafted internet personas was part of my carefully crafted internet persona. Even so, I think we could both feel Andy stretching for a point that wasn't 100 percent there.

"Andy, what is this actually about?"

"It's just"—he took a deep breath—"I think it would be better for the artist if it were you. I'm a fucking goof, I know what I look like. People aren't going to take me seriously. You look like an artist with your outfit and your cheekbones. You look like you know what you're talking about. You *do* know what you're talking about, and you talk it good, girl. If I do this, I'm going to make it a joke. Plus, you're the one who found it, I think it just makes more sense for you to be in front of the camera."

Unlike most of my classmates who graduated with design degrees, I thought a lot about fine art. If you're wondering what the difference is, well, fine art is like art that exists for its own sake. The thing that fine art does is itself. Design is art that does something else. It's more like visual engineering. I started school focusing on fine art, but I decided by the end of the first semester that maybe I wanted to someday have a job. So I switched to advertising, which I hated, so I switched a bunch more times until I caved and went into design. But I still spent way more time and energy paying attention to the fine art scene in Manhattan than any of my design-track friends did. It was part of why I desperately wanted to stay in the city. This may sound dumb, but just being a twenty-something in New York City made me feel important. Even if I wasn't doing real art, at least I was making it work in this city, a long ways away from my parents' literal dairy-supply business.

Ultimately, Andy wasn't showing any signs of giving up and I determined that this wasn't actually that big of a deal. So I ran the mic up the inside of my shirt . . . The cord was warm from Andy's body. The light shined in my eyes and I could barely see the lens. It was cold, there was a little breeze, we were alone on the sidewalk.

"Are you ready?" he said.

"Give me that mic," I said, pointing at an open bag on the ground.

"Your lav is speeding, you don't need it."

I had no idea what that meant, but I got the gist. "No, just as a prop . . . so I can . . . interview it?"

"Ah . . . cool . . ." He handed me the mic.

"OK," I said.

"'K, I'm rolling."

CHAPTER TWO

"**K**, I'm rolling."

You've heard Andy say those words . . . if you're a human who's ever been near enough to an internet connection to hear them. Whether or not you speak English. Whether or not you've ever owned an electronic device in your life. If you're a Chinese billionaire or a Kiwi sheep farmer, you've heard it. Militant rebels in Nepal have heard it. It's the most-viewed piece of media of all time. It's been viewed more times than there are humans on earth. Google estimates that "New York Carl" has been watched by 94 percent of living humans. And by this point, I suppose, a fair number of dead ones.

After Andy edited the video . . . this is roughly what we had:

I'm a mess. I've been awake for twenty-two hours. I'm barely wearing makeup and the dress code at work was basically "whatever looks like you care the least," so I'm wearing a denim jacket over a white hoodie and my jeans have holes in the knees, which isn't helping me keep warm. My black hair is loose around my shoulders, the light is glaring in my eyes, and I'm fighting to keep from squinting, but considering all that, I don't look so bad. Maybe I've just watched the video enough times that I'm over the embarrassment. My eyes are dark enough that they look all pupil even when the sun is out. My teeth are shining in Jason's LED light. Somehow, I seem chipper. The giddiness of lack of sleep has taken over. My voice is croaky.

"Hello! I'm April May, and I'm here at 23rd and Lexington with an unannounced and peculiar visitor. He arrived sometime before 3 A.M. today, guarding the Chipotle Mexican Grill next door to the Gramercy Theatre like an ancient warrior of an unknown civilization. His icy stare is somehow comforting, it's like, look, none of us has our lives figured out . . . not even this ten-foot-tall metal warrior. The weight of life getting you down? Don't worry . . . you're insignificant! Do I feel safer with him watching over me? I do not! But maybe safety isn't what it's all about!"

A couple, headed home after a long night, walk by while I say this, looking over their shoulders more at the camera than at the giant freaking ROBOT.

The camera angle changes abruptly. (This was after a few seconds of me mumbling around for something to say and sounding like an idiot and Andy assuring me that he'd edit out the parts where I sounded like an idiot.)

"His name is Carl! Hello, Carl." Here I hold the dummy mic to Carl . . . standing on my tiptoes. I'm a small person, five foot two— this makes Carl look even bigger than he is. Carl says nothing.

"A robot of few words, but your appearance speaks volumes."

Another cut, now I'm staring back at the camera. "Carl, immovable, solid, and somehow warm to the touch, a ten-foot-tall robot that New Yorkers appear to think is not particularly interesting."

Cut.

"What do they think he is? An art installation? A pet project evicted from his apartment along with a deadbeat tenant? A forgotten prop from a nearby film shoot? Has the city that never sleeps become the city that's too cool to notice even the most peculiar and astounding occurrences? No, wait! One young man has stopped to see, let's ask him what he thinks."

Cut.

Now Andy shares the fake mic with me.

"And you are?"

"Andy Skampt." Somehow Andy is more nervous than me.

"And you can confirm that there is a ten-foot-tall robot standing outside of Chipotle?"

"I can."

"And can you confirm that this is in fact not fucking normal?"

"Uh-huh."

"What do you think it means?"

"I don't know, actually. Now that I'm thinking about it, Carl kinda terrifies me."

"Thank you, Andy."

Cut.

"And there you have it, citizens of the world. A giant, stately, terrifying, slightly warm robot man has arrived in New York City and, through his inaction, has somehow become only interesting enough for a one-minute-long video." All of this is said over close shots of the robot, his immobility teeming with movement, energy glistening just below the surface.

The whole time I was in front of the camera, I was thinking of the artist. A fellow creator who had poured her soul into something truly remarkable that might simply be ignored by the whole world. I was trying to get in her head. I was trying to figure out why she had created this thing and, in the same breath, calling out the world for its callous ignorance of beauty and form. CALLING ALL NEW YORKERS! APPRECIATE HOW COOL SHIT CAN BE! I wanted people to wake up and spend a few moments looking at the exceptional amazement of human creation. Hilarious in hindsight.

"Is that good?"

"Yeah, great, fantastic, you're adorable and smart and the internet is going to love you."

"Oh, just what I've always wanted," I deadpanned. "I am suddenly extremely tired."

"Yeah, well, that makes sense. Why are you even awake right now?"

"Aside from the giant robot? You know, another day, another 'all hands on deck' crisis."

"At least you have a job."

Andy was trying his hand at freelance, which is what you do when you don't have to worry about paying student loans because your dad is a filthy-rich Hollywood lawyer.

And just like that Carl was out of the conversation. Andy grabbed a few close-up shots while I whined about work and he told me about a new client who wanted their logo to look more "computery." I even got on Andy's shoulders to get as close to the robot's face as I could, trying to hold the camera steady for B-roll. But we were just talking about work and life and then it was almost 4 A.M.

"Well, this has been super fucking weird, April May, thank you for calling me out into the chill of the night to make a robot video with you."

"And thank you for coming, and no, I'm not coming over to watch you edit a video. I'm going to bed. If you call me before noon, I'm going to impale you on that spiky thing Carl's got on his head."

"Always a pleasure."

"See you tomorrow."

On the subway ride home I set my phone to Do Not Disturb mode. That night was probably the best night's sleep I had until after I died.

CHAPTER THREE

I woke up at 2 P.M. I hadn't even woken up when Maya got out of bed. She came into the room doing that "knock softly while you open the door" thing, which was somehow both annoying and endearing. She was carrying a cup of coffee. The room was, for my tastes, pleasantly cluttered. A couple items of clothes on the floor, one too many cups on the desk, way too many books on the night-stands.

I don't really understand people who keep everything around them constantly neat. It's way more efficient to do occasional dedicated cleanups than constant maintenance. Plus, my mind likes clutter. It's almost like I need to make the world around me messy to make my art and ideas neat. Simplicity in design, complete disaster in everything else. It was an entire ethos I was working on. Of course, Maya kept me from going completely off the rails.

Maya was far more personally put together than I was, but neither of us were neat freaks, which helped make the roommate thing work. She had clearly been up for hours; her locks were in some fancy updo that remained mostly magical to me. That meant she was probably doing something important later. She'd probably told me about it, but I couldn't remember what it was if she had. Meeting a client for work, maybe? She was the only one of us who had gotten work at a real design firm. It didn't pay great, but it was a foot in the door. Her makeup was already done.

In addition to being a better apartment steward than I, she was also a much better relationship steward. All the weirdness in the relationship stemmed from me. I actively stopped her from talking about serious stuff. If it weren't for my issues, we would have "moved in together" a long time ago.

"I brought you a cup of coffee," she said softly, in case I wasn't already awake.

"And after years of living together, you haven't noticed that I never drink coffee?"

"This is not true." She put the coffee on my nightstand. "You only drink coffee on very, very bad days."

She sat down on the side of the bed. I turned to her with a big ol' question mark on my face.

"April, this robot thing has gotten a little weird."

"You know about Carl?"

"Why did you give him that stupid name?" she asked, exasperated.

"You know about Carl." It wasn't a question anymore.

"I know about Carl—"

"Has Andy been bugging you?" I cut in before she could continue, annoyed that he couldn't leave it until morning. Or, rather, late afternoon.

"Don't interrupt, I let you sleep," she demanded. "Andy has been calling all day and he is freaking out and he needs you to check your email. In there, you'll find a number of important things to read, including several messages from local news stations and entertainment agents and managers. I don't think this is the kind of thing you want to ignore, but I also don't think it's something to rush."

Maya was the most effective talker I knew. It was like she wrote essays in her brain and then recited them verbatim. She once explained to me that she thought this was part of being Black in America.

"Every black person who spends time with a lot of white people eventually ends up being asked to speak for every black person," she told me one night after it was too late to still be talking, "and I hate that. It's really stupid. And everyone gets to respond to that idiocy however they want. But my anxiety eventually made me extremely careful about everything I said, because of course I don't represent capital-B Black People, but if people think I do, then I still feel a responsibility to try to do it well."

I never had any idea what to say when she talked about this stuff. I'm white and I was raised in a very white community. So I just said the thing that I'd heard you should say in situations like this: "That sounds really hard."

"Yeah," she replied. "Everybody has their hard parts. Thanks."

"God, I hope you don't feel like you have to represent all black people with me," I said. "I hope you're not, like, careful all the time."

"No, April." And then it was a long time before she continued. "I'm careful with you for different reasons."

I was too afraid to ask what that meant, so I kissed her and then we went to sleep.

In any case, Maya's efficiency of speech was extremely helpful in the maintenance of a relationship that I was subconsciously keeping on the knife-edge between casual and serious. She was capable of talking with her eyes and her body, but she mostly chose to use her mouth. I didn't mind this.

"Maya," is as far as I got before she put her index finger softly on my lips.

I said, through her finger, "Uh . . . are we gonna make out now?"

"No, you're going to drink your coffee and check your email and not talk again to me or anyone else until you've brushed your teeth because your mouth smells like trillions of microorganisms. I have taken away your phone, you can have it back when you're done with your email."

She stood up off the bed without so much as a kiss.

"But I—"

She drowned me out as she walked to the doorway: "Stop talking! Read!" She closed the door.

Ten minutes later I was freshened up a little bit, sitting on the bed with my laptop. Read messages were blue, unread messages were white—"Important and Unread" was white for five pages. I had no idea what to do so I just searched for "andyskampt@gmail.com" and that cleared things up pretty quickly. One of the fifteen messages he had sent me was titled "READ THIS ONE FIRST" and another was titled "READ THIS ONE SECOND" and a third, more recent email was titled "NO! THIS ONE! READ THIS ONE FIRST!"

Here they are, copied and pasted straight out of my inbox.

NO! THIS ONE! READ THIS ONE FIRST!

I'm sorry all of the emails I have sent today sound as if they were written in a demented frenzy. I value our friendship. Let's try and keep that front of mind.

Andy

READ THIS ONE FIRST

OK, so, whoa. I'm going to give you a quick rundown of everything that has happened in the last six hours. This is everything that isn't conjecture. Carl didn't just show up in New York, there's one in pretty much every city on Earth. There are at least sixty Carls, photos of Carls are popping up everywhere from Beijing to Buenos

Aires. People just stumbled across them, like we did, and people around the world have posted photos and videos on social media, yet somehow ours is the one that's taken off. It has to be some kind of international street art project and you (we?) basically got the scoop. All of them went up without anyone seeing the installers and no one can find any surveillance footage. I'm sure they will eventually but they don't have anything yet.

Everyone is calling them "Carls" because they didn't have anything else to call them. It's not like there's an artist statement on foamcore glued to the sidewalk next to them. They're playing our video on the news (without permission, I'll add). Several news outlets have contacted me to talk about it. The video has already had more than a MILLION VIEWS! People love you!

Don't read the comments.

I've already been back to Carl with a nicer camera to take some daytime footage. I got there before the crowds did, but it's wild out there now. He's a freaking tourist attraction!

I haven't slept since you called me. I feel like a small dog is eating my eyeballs from the inside!

Andy

READ THIS SECOND

Hey, so did you know that my dad is a lawyer? Um . . . this is weird but, like, "our" video has gotten a million views already and it's actually made some money and we need to figure out how to split it.

However, since I don't think there's any way to figure out exactly who contributed what to this video, and it's safe to say that neither of us would have made it if it weren't for the other, I am proposing a

50/50 split on the ownership of the video. I would also like to propose a 50/50 split on the ownership of my YouTube channel "Skamper2001," which I named when I was eleven and am going to regret for literally the rest of my life. Final proposal . . . we should collaborate on future videos about Carl(s), but we can talk about that later.

I had my dad draw up a contract that says that we each own 50% of the video and are entitled to 50% of the revenue from it. It basically also means that I can't do anything with the content without your approval, and you can't do anything without my approval. I know this is dumb, but he's a lawyer, and this is what they do. He would also like for me to propose to you that he represent you as your lawyer when we sue all of the major networks for using our video without permission. I told him to cool his jets, so his jets are currently on ice.

Just so you know, the video has, thus far, earned about $2000. So, basically, we're rich.

Andy

A quick read through the rest of my inbox made me kinda wish I hadn't listed my email on my portfolio website. There indeed were a bunch from entertainment managers and agents. Some people wanted me to know how much they liked my video. Some wanted me to know that, if I was going to be in a YouTube video, there were a number of things I could have done to improve my physical appearance and, really, why hadn't I done that?

There was one that was very clearly creepier than the rest of the normal creepiness. It is amazing how disconcerting a single vile, manipulative person can be even if you have never and (hopefully)

22

will never see them. The power that each of us has over complete strangers to make them feel terrible and frightened and weak is amazing. This was not the first time someone had made me feel this way, but it was the first time it had happened through the internet, and it was enough to make me want to withdraw from the whole thing for a moment. Just a moment, though.

There was a message from my dad. (Really, both my parents— they did this adorable tag team email thing. I swear they sat next to each other on the couch and wrote emails like it was a three-way call. They should make special tablets with two keyboards just for them.) It was sent like a long text message about how they thought the video was great and I sure looked tired and they couldn't wait to see me at Tom's wedding and was I getting enough sleep?

The only message that is long-term important in the story was one titled "You said it was warm?" I'll just copy it directly for you.

You said it was warm?

Ms. May,

My name is Miranda Beckwith, I'm a graduate student in materials science at UC Berkeley. I watched your video this morning and found it both entertaining and fascinating. I was particularly interested when you referred to "Carl" as "slightly warm." Of course, I'm sure your life is ridiculous right now, but knowing a bit about materials, and having seen Carl, it's unusual for something that seems so heavy and shiny to not have a low thermal conductivity.

Basically, Carl looks like he's made of a metal, but it's January in New York, so my guess is it's quite cold and metal at ambient temperature would have felt very cold. Initial reports are that these things are super heavy, so it doesn't make sense that they would be made out of coated plastic. I have no idea what else would not feel very cold to the touch but also be heavy and shiny.

Unless he actually felt warm, in which case there is likely some kind of power source inside of him keeping him warm.

There's a Carl here in the Bay Area, but it's looking less and less likely that I'll be getting my hands on him, so I was just wondering if you could satisfy my curiosity. Was Carl warm like touching Styrofoam would be warm? Or was he warm like touching a mug full of coffee would be warm?

Did you notice anything else about him that would help with this mystery?

Thank you for your time and I totally understand if you're not able to get back to me.

Miranda

That was the only email I responded to that day.

RE: You said it was warm?

Miranda,

Thanks for your message! On the list of peculiar things about Carl, this didn't really stand out, but now that you mention it, it was super weird. He didn't feel warm, he just didn't feel like a temperature. I wouldn't have been able to articulate it without the prompt, but it was very much like hard, smooth Styrofoam. Like he didn't have heat, but all of my hand heat stayed in my hand when I touched him. I did actually give him a good whack with my knuckles and it was like a *thunk* followed by a faint low hum. It didn't give at all. It was like knocking on a painted brick wall.

I imagine I'll have a pretty hard time getting up close with NY Carl again too, so I probably won't be able to be of much further help. Sounds like whoever did this is going above and beyond in the weirdness category.

April

With that, I considered myself done enough.

"MAYA! Phone, please!"

"This is super weird, right?!" she shouted back unseen, before coming into her room.

"So what's the damage?" I asked, gesturing to the phone.

"Um . . . you are suddenly extremely popular. Andy would like to talk. He would like to talk a lot. He would like to talk for at least four years. Your parents also called."

I called my parents—they were fine, if a little stressed. My slightly older, very successful, extremely normal brother, Tom, was getting married in Northern California in a few months and they were helping with a lot of the planning. Tom had studied math and worked at an investment bank in San Francisco. I kept expecting him to move to New York with all the other investment bankers, but he wasn't doing it.

I want to be very clear that whatever hang-ups I have are 100 percent mine. I had a very happy childhood; I just wasn't a very happy child. My parents have always been supportive and without expectations, which is pretty much all a kid can ask for. So we talked about Carl and about Tom and about how much they loved Tom's fiancée and how smooth the planning was going, even if it was still a lot of work. They wanted to know what I knew about Carl, so I told them a bunch of stuff they mostly already knew. They asked about work and hinted that they could give me some money if I needed it, which they always did and I always ignored. They loved the video, and they were proud of me. For what? Who knows. Parents, right?

I called Andy, who sounded . . . unstable.

"APRIL MAY THIS IS GETTING REALLY WEIRD!"

I winced away from the phone. "You're going to need to be calm with me right now."

"The video has had three million views now, people think you're fantastic! You aren't reading the comments, right?"

"I haven't actually watched the video yet."

"You're, like, the only person who has not seen it. The story just keeps getting weirder. They still haven't found any surveillance footage. There's a camera that shows the spot pretty clearly, but at 2:43 A.M. it just cuts out . . . records nothing for five minutes, and when it comes back Carl is just standing there. Military analysts say it's possible that an EMP knocked out all the local electricity for EVERY CARL while they were being installed and they were all installed at the *exact* same time. The thing that makes this weirder is that the static that the security cameras recorded wasn't random. The cameras that were recording audio—every one that the news has gotten their hands on has an undertone of static that is very clearly, if you turn it up loud enough, 'Don't Stop Me Now' by Queen."

"I love that song."

"Really?"

"Yeah, why?"

"No, I'd just never even heard of it. But, yeah, if you listen, it's there. No one knows how it could have gotten there . . . some extremely high-energy radio pulse, maybe?"

"Yeah, this is super weird, but, Andy, it doesn't really have much to do with us, does it? I mean, we made the video, I'm happy to say that we spotted the New York Carl—"

"Just 'New York Carl,'" he interrupted.

"What?"

"New York Carl, that's the one in New York's name. Not 'the New York Carl.' Everyone is calling it New York Carl and the one in Mumbai is Mumbai Carl and there's Hong Kong Carl and São Paulo Carl. Even people who don't speak English are calling their Carls Carl."

"You being picky about nomenclature is not changing my point . . . We didn't make Carl, we just found him. Not even . . . we found like one-sixtieth of him."

"I made this point to my dad, he babbled for like ten minutes about narrative and memetic diffusion and cultural mythology, and he totally convinced me with an argument that I am completely incapable of repeating. Which brings me to the most salient point . . . I just made ten thousand dollars."

There was a long pause, and then I finally said, "Um . . . neat?"

"News stations would very much like to interview you, but they took me instead because I'm the best they could do at the moment. Pundits and experts are blabbing about Carl for about five minutes every hour, but there's only so much they can say to keep it interesting. They can't interview Carl, but they can interview you. My dad says he can get us a ten-thousand-dollar licensing deal with all the major networks if you agree to do interviews."

"Wait . . . total? Or per network?"

"Per network! They're totally fucked because they already ran the footage. Dad has them by the balls."

My head wasn't working super fast, but I did recognize that $10,000 multiplied by the number of news networks I could think of would eliminate a sizable portion of my student loans. I could quit my shit job. I could have time in the evenings to do things that were *my idea*.

"I would have to go on TV?"

"You would *get* to go on TV!"

"What am I supposed to say on TV?"

"You just answer their questions!"

"Do I have to do my hair?"

"April May, it's gonna be like fifty thousand dollars."

"OK, fine, I'm in."

Within the next thirty minutes, I had two network news interviews scheduled for that day, and, figuring that I should probably have something worth saying, Maya and I spent the hours I had free before I had to head downtown reading everything we could about Carl. It wasn't much—Andy had caught me up pretty thoroughly. I was a little bit terrified about going on the news and honestly had no idea what I was supposed to say. "I saw this thing, it was cool, I don't know what it is, my friend and I made a video"—that's like nineteen seconds. Doesn't seem worth precisely $10,000, but I didn't know how TV worked. Turns out, they mostly just wanted to keep using the footage that they'd already stolen from us without getting sued.

I ended up on the Wikipedia page for "Don't Stop Me Now," the barely audible song that bizarrely showed up on all the static-filled security camera footage of areas where Carls had appeared.

> **"Don't Stop Me Now"** is a song by the British rock band Queen, featured on their 1978 album *Jazz* that was released as a single in 1979. Wrtten by lead singer Freddie Mercury, it was recorded in August 1978 at Super Bear Studios in Berre-les-Alpes (Alpes-Maritimes), France, and is the twelfth track on the album.

Weird, I thought, *typos like "wrtten" don't usually make it into Wikipedia*. But, being the good steward of the internet that I was, I edited the page, fixing the typo, then went back and reloaded the page.

"Don't Stop Me Now" is a song by the British rock band Queen, featured on their 1978 album *Jazz* that was relesed as a single in 1979. Wrtten by lead singer Freddie Mercury, it was recorded in August 1978 at Super Bear Studios in Berre-les-Alpes (Alpes-Maritimes), France, and is the twelfth track on the album.

"Hey, Maya, can you bring up the Wikipedia page for 'Don't Stop Me Now'?"

"Yah."

"Do you see any typos?"

"Uhh . . . two in the first paragraph."

"Two?"

"Yeah, 'released' and 'written' are both spelled wrong."

"Fix them."

"Um, yes, master?"

"Just do it, something is weird."

She fixed them and we both reloaded the page.

"Don't Stop Me Now" is a song by the British rock band Queen, featured on their 1978 albu *Jazz* that was relesed as a single in 1979. Wrtten by lead singer Freddie Mercury, it was recorded in August 1978 at Super Bear Studios in Berre-les-Alpes (Alpes-Maritimes), France, and is the twelfth track on the album.

"OK," Maya said, "there is no conceivable way that I didn't see that someone misspelled the world 'album' after you specifically asked me to look for typos. I'm fucking fastidious."

She was.

"I'm going to fix it again," I said.

I fixed all the typos and reloaded the page again.

"Don't Stop Me Now" is a song by the British rock band Queen, featured on their 1978 albu *Jazz* that was relesed as a single in 1979. Wrtten by lead singer Freddie Mercury, it was recorded in Augst 1978 at Super Bear Studios in Berre-les-Alpes (Alpes-Maritimes), France, and is the twelfth track on the album.

"The *u* in 'August' is gone now!" I said, getting more freaked-out. I called Andy.

"Yello!" he said, still clearly delirious.

"Can you go to the Wikipedia page for 'Don't Stop Me Now' right now?" I said, without any preamble.

"Yup!" I could hear him rustling around for his computer. I just waited.

"OK, loading up . . . aaannd . . ." I heard the keys clacking.

"Do you see any typos in the first paragraph?"

"Ummm . . . Yes . . . there's no *i* in 'written.'"

"And that's all."

"Is this a test?"

"What about 'released' or 'album' or 'August'?"

"I have had a very weird day, April, but you are making it considerably weirder."

"Answer the question."

"No, all those words are spelled correctly. You do know how Wikipedia works, right, you can change the page. Somebody probably just fixed it."

I reloaded the page again, all the same typos, no new ones.

"Fix the typo."

"April, we're supposed to be downtown to shoot for ABC News in like two hours. There are a lot of errors on Wikipedia and we aren't going to fix them all today."

"OH MY GOD ANDY DO THE THING," I loudly monotoned.

"I already did . . . I did it while I was whining. It is not fixed. Oh, actually, this is weird, 'released' is now misspelled. Wait, that was one of the words you listed. How did you do that?"

Maya chimed in, "Put him on speaker." So I did.

"Andy, this is Maya, the same thing happened to us, but it didn't require me to make the first change before I saw the second one, probably because April and I are on the same IP address. Every time I fix a typo I see a new one, as well as the one I just fixed. According to the Wikipedia log pages, no one is making these changes. Indeed, according to the Wikipedia log, no one has made any changes, including us, to this page since three hours ago when an editor added a note about the song playing in security camera footage.

"In the time that you two were talking, I tried to fix the final letter, and I didn't see any more typos. It seems as if we have run into a dead end. Additionally, we are not going to figure this out right now because April has to do her hair in the next half hour and then get on the subway to Manhattan," Maya ordered.

"Are we really going to still do this TV thing?" I whined.

"Yes," Maya and Andy replied simultaneously.

"But do you not both agree that this is far more interesting?"

They both did, but then there was the whole matter of the $10,000.

Later, after I had been through a quick rinse and was flat-ironing my hair, I called to Maya from the bathroom, "What were the misspelled words?"

"'Written,' 'released' . . ." She thought for a second before poking her head into the bathroom. "'Album' and 'August.'"

"*I, A, M, U,*" I said.

"Hmm?" she asked as she sat down on the toilet. Not to pee or anything, just because there wasn't anywhere else in the bathroom to sit.

"Those were the missing letters. *I, A, M, U.*"

"'I am you'?" she said.

"Well, I am fairly certain that I wasn't the one ghost-editing Wikipedia from the inside."

"April, this is a mystery we are not going to solve today."

"Uggggghhhh!" I said in frustration. "How can you do thaaat?"

"Do what?"

"Don't you want to figure this out?"

"You're going to be on the national news in an hour, hun. Literally dozens of senior citizens are going to see you, you have to look presentable."

"This is terrible."

She laughed. "You do know what you're doing right now, right?"

"Huh?"

"April, picture this if you will. A young woman who has created some excellent fan art for her favorite band gets an email to ask if she can make some official merch. And then that woman doesn't just not respond, she stops listening to that band entirely. And then remember that you *actually did that*."

"I was already growing out of them, I'm embarrassed I ever grooved to those particular tunes."

"Sure," she said, unconvinced. "The point is that you hate it when money makes you do things, even when they're interesting things. And I get that, it sucks to have money push you around, and maybe you're a little less used to it than the average person."

"That's not fair," I replied, a bit hurt. "Andy is 'freelancing' because his dad can just keep paying his rent while he builds his portfolio."

She laughed. "Yeah, of course there are people who have more than you. Hell, I have more than you. But you still have way more than most people. But whatever. You're you, and you don't like doing normal stuff, and the normal thing when someone offers you ten thousand dollars to do something is to do it. Even if it's stressful and scary."

"I'm not scared of being on TV," I asserted.

"Yeah, you are!" she countered.

I checked, and I found that she was right.

"How do you know?"

"Because it's scary to go on TV. That's not a 'you' thing, it's a human thing. But you shouldn't do it for the money. And you shouldn't do it because you're scared of it. You should do it because it's going to be strange. You're going to see stuff people don't get to see, you're going to know how things work, and you're going to tell me all about it, and I'm going to be fascinated, and we're going to make fun of the weird newspeople together, and then we're going to work on this weird Wikipedia shit.

"Also, in a week you will have fifty thousand new dollars, and that is amazing and I'm really happy for you. You do the things you have to do in the order you have to do them."

Maya has a kind of self-control that almost seems like a foreign language to me. I see her using it and I know it's real, but it never stops feeling like gibberish to my brain.

"And we're not going to figure out the Wikipedia shit right now," I finished for her.

"Nope. I'll be thinking about it and we'll work on it as soon as you get home." She stood up to take a look at my hair.

"Did I do OK?"

"I wouldn't call it an adventurous look. But the good news is that no matter what you do up here"—she gestured to my hair—"all the rest of this"—meaning my face and body—"is just pure genetically in-duced hotness." Her eyes were soft, and not for the first time, I had the sensation that she and I had settled into a rhythm of mutual appreciation that was at once wonderfully comfortable and totally terrifying.

CHAPTER FOUR

That night I discovered that TV interviews are a terrible way to spend time but an excellent way to make $20,000. I learned pretty quick that I didn't have to do my makeup at home because the vast majority of time spent on television news is spent making television news look impressive. This included painting an entirely new face onto my face as soon as I walked into the building. Interesting that, when I did tag team interviews with Andy, he spent the "face reconstruction" time eating free doughnuts on leather couches.

To say that I didn't watch TV news is underselling my position. I actively avoided not just the news but also clips of the news on social media. I believed (or maybe wanted to believe) that I lived in a bubble world unaffected by the kinds of things that happened on cable news.

I was about to get a crash course. Here's the first thing I learned:

TV news spends lots of time and money looking impressive because it is not actually impressive. After I saw it from the inside, the shine immediately disappeared. TV news studios are just rooms with people in them. Some of the people are cool and nice; others are in-secure and loud. It's basically just like every other room full of people you've ever been in, except exactly half of it looks extremely fancy and important, and the other half is just concrete and scaffolding.

It's like a warehouse crashed into the lobby of a three-star hotel and then they just left the mess alone.

It occurs to me that this is a fairly good metaphor for what TV newspeople are like—half boring and normal, half peculiar carica-tures of TV newspeople. They're *so* "TV news" that it seems like they're making fun of TV newspeople. They have a very particular and standardized way of speaking that is *nothing like* the way nor-mal people talk. It sounds natural on TV, but in real life it's basically like "Whoa, wait, stop . . . why are you talking like that?"

We're going to skip around the timeline of the story a bit here, but I have now been on the news a lot, and I have Thoughts.

At first I did the news things for the reason Maya identified for me: It was weird and new, and when someone's offering to pay you $10,000 to talk to them for twenty minutes, you do it. I don't like that everyone has a price, but ultimately you do, and it turns out that mine is below $30,000 an hour.

Even Before Carl, I spent time thinking about what I'd say if I ever had a platform to say it. That's what art is about, right? I mean, not app interfaces, but art.

Much of the best art is about balancing between reflecting cul-ture while simultaneously being removed from it and commenting on it. In the best case, maybe an artist gets to say something about culture that hasn't been said and needs to be said. That's a lofty goal, but not a bad one. I'd spent my four years of art school waf-fling between believing I could do that (or even that I *needed* to do that) and feeling like I should be more realistic and leave art to real artists.

But in those manic moments when I thought I could be some kind of vessel for truth, I'd thought about what I'd say if I someday got a soapbox. That income inequality is out of hand. That all people are pretty damn similar so it would be great if we stopped hating each other. That prison sentences for nonviolent crimes are dumb and that drug addiction is a health problem, not a crime problem.

Well, I finally got my chance and I mostly said, "No, um . . . maybe it's a way of saying, a way to show, that we don't see how much we don't see? Um, just like the news, so many important things happen that, like, nothing seems important. Why do people even watch the news?"

That's an actual quote from an interview I did on cable news. Direct quote. Great game plan, April. I really knew what I was talking about.

Step 1: Stumble around the point and sound like an idiot.
Step 2: Insult the entire institution that is currently giving
        voice to your inane musings as well as the people who
        enjoy it.
Step 3: ????
Step 4: Profit!

Andy's dad called me after that interview to give me some media-relations tips, which, thank god. He literally wanted me to take a class, but I caught on pretty quick. The real trick is to know exactly the one point you absolutely 100 percent need to get across and also know when to shut your mouth. My biggest problem was always the second bit. I always finished really strong and then would say, "uh," like I had more to say, but really I didn't. Listening back, I hate hearing that "uh" so much. It makes me want to smack my idiot face.

Anyway, I did five or six of these chats, and by the sixth I was pretty good. It was four consecutive days of waking up at 4 A.M. to get ready for an interview on *Good Morning America* or the like. Sometimes Maya would be there if she could get off work, and Andy always would (that was part of his dad's deal). It was exhausting and fascinating. It was also distracting and prevented any of us from giving the mysteries of Carl and Wikipedia the attention they deserved. Not that thinking about them more would have helped much.

You can go back and watch a lot of these interviews on YouTube. No one comes out looking anything but dumb because of how completely wrong everyone was about everything. People argued with me that it wasn't about art, that it was, in fact, government spending gone awry. The most prevalent theory (which I couldn't really argue with) was that the Carls were a PR stunt for a new movie or video game, or maybe the launch of a lost Queen album. Seriously. It's so easy to forget being wrong.

It turns out pundits don't want to talk about what's happened; they want to use what's happened to talk about the same things they talk about every day. Eventually, I realized that almost all of these people were talking on the news for free. And they weren't doing it because they wanted to change the world, or because they wanted to do something interesting. They were doing it because it got their face and their name into the world.

But I think I'm being honest when I say that I initially came at all of this fairly reluctantly. At first, I tried to maintain my preexisting distance from the internet. But it didn't take long for it to get out of my control. Here's a story: I was sitting on my bed (the one in the living room) with Maya. We were both on our phones and watching some terrible but also amazing baking show on Netflix. At this point I was still assuming that the attention and notoriety were all short-term, so I had left my email address up on my site. I checked my email and saw this:

Your Cruelty

Our interaction on Twitter today has left me so disillusioned. Judging by your TV interviews and YouTube videos, you seemed like a genuine person. Maybe even a kind person. I now see how wrong I was. I should have known better. I just wanted to let you know that you suck.

Mary

So I wrote back, because not only had I not been mean to Mary on Twitter that day, I also did not have a Twitter account. If this seems completely bizarre, I agree. It can be easy to stay inside your bubble in New York City. It is a world of its own. Instagram was the only platform that meshed well with my strengths (art, design, and being photogenic). I also liked to share photos of whatever I was reading, which was probably Louisa May Alcott but might also have been a biography of a famous artist or something. How else is a girl gonna show the world that she can be irreverent and sophisticated at the same time?!

Anyway, Mary linked me to the Twitter conversation and, indeed, a person pretending to be me had been pretty fucking terrible to Mary.

"How do you get a tweet taken off Twitter?" I asked Maya, who was slightly more social media savvy than me.

"I think you can report it? What's going on?"

"Someone is pretending to be me, I can't figure out how to report them."

She took my phone.

"Oh, hon, it's because you're not logged in. You have to log in."

"I don't have a Twitter, though."

"Well, I guess it's not too much of a surprise that people are impersonating you then."

"Huh?"

"People are going to be looking for you, to follow you or to argue with you or just to see what you're up to. And when they find that you aren't there, some small percentage of them are going to just make a fake account. And since there's no real one, you can't report impersonation."

"So why hasn't anyone else reported them?"

"Because no one . . . cares? I can report them. I don't know if it'll do anything. I think they take it more seriously if the person actually being impersonated does the reporting."

"What?!" I was a little taken aback. "And I can't do that unless I sign up?"

"Yeah."

"So in order to not have people pretend to be me, I *have* to be on Twitter?"

"That's pretty much the size of it!"

"This is not fair," I replied, matter-of-factly.

"I keep wondering when you will notice that that's how everything is," she said with a smile.

So I signed up for Twitter, and we linked to it from the YouTube channel, and I tweeted some things, and by the end of the day I had five hundred real, human people waiting to hear my every word . . . as long as they only came a few dozen words at a time. My Instagram, on the other hand, had been blowing up all week. I had ten times more followers than I had before. It was a weird mix of exciting and stressful. I freaked out a little bit and went through and deleted a bunch of stuff I was less than proud off. Everything that had a border *had to go.* I thought way more about every post, and I felt like I couldn't put anything up if it wasn't really high quality. Suddenly my posts had gotten much better (and required much more work).

Seven days in, I had stopped calling in to tell work I wasn't going to make it, and instead, I just didn't go. Don't do this, it makes it way harder to get another job in the future if you quit by just not showing up, but that's what I did. It helped that, by that time, I had made tens of thousands of dollars. But that income stream was drying up. We weren't being paid for our appearances; we were being paid for the use of our video, which they had already paid for. They were happy to have us keep coming on shows, but they weren't going to pay us. And if they weren't going to pay us, then I had more important things to do.

What eventually became known as the Freddie Mercury Sequence remained a total mystery. I ran through the sequence on Wikipedia dozens of times. Each time, the edits produced the same three additional typos before it reset. A single note had appeared on the Wikipedia page commenting that a persistent typo wasn't allowing itself to be fixed, so at least one other person had noticed.

As the days passed, the search for the artist / marketing firm / shadowy government agency responsible for the Carls got more intense. But knowing that there was more to it was leading me in different directions than the rest of the world.

Googling "IAMU" certainly wasn't helping. It seemed unlikely that this had anything to do with the International Association of Maritime Universities or the Iowa Association of Municipal Utilities. It seemed most likely that it was a hint, just far too vague a hint for us to figure out.

"What if we ask the internet?" This was us, again, on my living room bed. The sun had gone down while Maya and I had been engrossed in our various laptop-based activities, and we hadn't stopped long enough to turn any lights on. Life with no job was wonderful. I could see her mostly by the light of her screen.

"Huh?" Maya replied, hammering away at her computer on some work email. Maya didn't seem to see Carl as a life-disrupting force so much as an event that would someday be a great anecdote to tell at a fancy cocktail party with a bunch of executives while wearing a cute outfit. She had always been as much into the business as the craft, which was extremely valuable and probably why she had the coolest job of any of us.

"I-A-M-U. I could just tweet out the weird Wikipedia clue and let other people try to figure it out. As they say, ten thousand minds are better than three!"

I had been building my Twitter following with posts about Carl and politics. I had also developed a new and voracious interest in growing my number of Twitter followers, which had become a fun game. My brain liked seeing the numbers go up.

"I do not like this idea." She didn't even look up from her laptop.

"Why, because you'd rather I stop obsessing?"

I had been bugging her with a lot of dumb ideas, even though her one-word replies had given me the impression that she was just about done with all this hoopla.

"No, April." She turned to me. "Because it's weird. It's already weird and impossible, but this makes it more weird and impossible. Plus, what if the answer is something big? Do you want to give that up?"

I got the distinct feeling that she added that last part because she thought it would convince me, not because she thought it was a good argument.

"But someone else is going to find it, and they'll talk about it first! It makes sense that the world should know about it, and I want to be the one to tell them."

"Would you rather be the first person to reveal that there is a mystery? Or the person who solves the mystery?" Maya continued to appeal to my newfound sense of self-importance to get me to do what she wanted.

I noticed.

"Ugh, OK, I get it, I'm fully psychoanalyzed. I want to be both, but I have a 100 percent chance of being one of those things if I tweet about it right now."

I tend to get obsessed with things when I'm first learning about them, which had happened with Twitter and was starting to happen with YouTube and even to some extent the news media. There was a part of me that just wanted to tweet about the Freddie Mercury Sequence so I could have more opportunity to use and understand the platform and just . . . see what happened. That's a terrible reason to tweet something, but a pretty common one.

"OK, maybe we need more than three minds, but I don't think we should have ten thousand yet. Who else do we trust?"

"Uhhh . . ." I was somewhat upset to find that no one was coming to mind. We had our three-person team, two people I trusted and me. Adding anyone to the inner circle felt wrong in a way that adding ten thousand did not. My parents? My brother? Some of my friends from college, some of my friends from high school? No one was popping out as a trained puzzle solver.

"Well," I said finally, "there are a few people I've seen over and over again online who seem cool and interested and supportive. It's like they're starting a little community around my video. They . . ." I stopped, not wanting to continue.

"They . . . what?" she asked skeptically.

"They call themselves Carlie's Angels."

Maya's smirk turned into a chuckle and then she just burst out laughing. And then I did too. The constant feeling that she would rather be talking about literally anything else finally washed away.

"I know," I continued. "They seem to be almost all women for some reason. And the guys don't seem to mind the nickname."

"But 'Carlie'?"

"Anything for a pun, I guess?"

She smirked. "Can't argue with that. Do you feel like you know any of them?"

"No, but I see a lot of the same names pop up over and over again. There's a Carlie's Angels Twitter account that they all follow and that I have interacted with. I'm surprised none of them have stumbled across the Wikipedia thing yet. I could DM their account, I guess."

Maya seemed concerned. "Are they fans of you, or of Carl?"

"Both, I guess . . . It's weird to think that I have fans. They get really excited when I tweet at them."

"Yup, that's how Twitter works."

"Do I sound like a complete idiot when I talk about this stuff?" I asked.

"It's just a little surprising how fast you've gone from zero to sixty." She did not seem enthusiastic.

"Because of how slow I was in figuring out other stuff?" This was a not-so-subtle reference to the solid year of living together it took for us to hook up.

I crawled over her laptop and kissed her.

"You are a little manipulative, you know that?"

"Uh-huh, but you? Never."

"Let's make this decision later," she said.

The next morning, I had to get on a flight to LA for a late-night show that Mr. Skampt had booked us on. Even though we weren't getting paid anymore, he thought it would lead to other things, and he wanted us to take some meetings in LA anyway. Maya couldn't just skip out on work, so we had some saying good-bye to do.

I didn't get a lot of sleep that night. Not because I can go All. Night. Long. or anything, but because our flight left at like six in the morning and that meant getting up at 4:30. This was awful because I'm terrible at sleeping on planes. At least, that's what I thought.

So Andy and I got on the plane and went to our seats. We weren't together, and mine was almost all the way at the back. I got there and found someone else already in my seat and no open seats nearby. We did the comparing-tickets dance, and it was 5:45 A.M. and everyone was awake and not asleep *the whole time*, and we all wanted to die, but our boarding passes said the exact same seat. I showed the flight attendant, who was more awake than I have maybe ever been in my life, and with the biggest smile ever he informed me that I was now a first-class human!

So they brought me back up to the front of the plane and I plopped myself down next to a middle-aged balding man, which is what first-class humans seem to mostly look like. I got a mimosa before we even took off, but the little TV built into the seat in front of me was broken and just showed a bunch of numbers and colors. I tweeted a picture of it:

@AprilMaybeNot: On my way to LA and got bumped to business class. My little plane TV is broken though, so I want the money I didn't spend back!

I was virtually a social media celebrity now, and so I had to let the entire world know every time I experienced any inconvenience!

Shortly after liftoff I discovered that I do not have a hard time sleeping on planes; I have a hard time sleeping in uncomfortable chairs. This chair turned into a *literal bed*. Business class was all dreams, baby.

We landed just a few hours before the shoot, so we had to rush through the airport, which became impossible when a group of students came up to Andy and me and every one of them wanted to get a separate photo.

Andy's dad finally dragged us out of the knot of kids and toward the baggage claim. One of those guys in suits was standing at the base of the escalator with a sign. The sign read "Marshall Skampt" (Andy's dad), which was a little disappointing. Still, I definitely snapped a picture of him to Maya, realizing I hadn't yet texted her in all the hubbub since we landed.

The drive to the studio was overwhelmingly composed of Andy being extremely excited. He was just a lot more into this whole thing than I was.

OK, that's not entirely true.

Andy was into the spectacle of it. He believed in entertainment culture in a way I never have. There's an appreciation that stretches beyond enjoying content and into worshipping all the bits that come together to make the content. I still saw it mostly as a necessary chore. I wasn't excited by any of it, but I was interested in what it could do for me. Our different outlooks started to cause some friction.

Here's a scene from the greenroom of that late-night talk show.

"Y'know, you don't have to hate everything, April."

"Have you ever seen the way I look at cheesecake?"

"You know what I mean. Like, this is the only time in our lives anything this cool is ever going to happen, and you look mostly like you need to poop."

"Stop thinking about my poop."

"So many people would kill to be on TV . . . to get to do all the things you're doing. Just look at it objectively, you're getting treated like a VIP and flown around the country and we're basically famous and you're determined to hate it!"

"Andy . . ." I paused to compose myself. "I don't watch TV. I have never watched TV. I do not know anything about this man we are about to talk to. But more than that, I haven't slept more than five hours at a time since Before Carl, I don't like planes, luxuries make me uncomfortable, and my life is so upside down that I fucking forgot I was getting my period so I had to ask a stranger for a tampon just now."

"They didn't have tampons in the bathroom?"

"I didn't even think to check because I'm NEW AT THIS."

And, like that, we were laughing again.

"I'm sorry, Andy, I just don't know what I'm doing. I feel like I'm being asked to be something I'm not. Why, of all people, are they asking me about this stuff? I'm barely anything. But I also like it, sometimes. I like it that people think my opinion matters. It's just . . . I don't know if it does."

Andy thought about this for a long time before he said, "April, I think you're doing a good job."

I looked him in the eyes and almost said something dumb and snarky but then instead just said, "Thanks, Andy."

This was the night it all changed for me. After that conversation, I realized something: I wasn't ever going to love the entertainment industry the way that Andy did, but he was right that it was an amazing opportunity. And my lack of interest gave me a kind of power. I honestly didn't know that there was a difference between being on cable news and being on network late night. To me, TV was TV. I had no idea that what I was about to do was a big deal. For all these reasons—the practice of the week before, my immunity to its power over me and the pull of the power it offered—I suddenly became pretty good at television.

Here's how things went that night. (It's fun to be able to recount some of the conversations I had verbatim because of how there were, like, twelve cameras pointed at me while I had them.)

"Everyone! April May and Andy Skampt, the discoverers of New York Carl!"

We walk out to applause. We had mostly been doing more newsy stuff, so this is a bit different.

"How's life been for the last week?"

I tended to do most of the talking, so I start out, "Pretty weird, Pat. Pretty freaking weird."

"My name is not Pat." Pat laughs.

"Honestly, I've just started calling all the newspeople Pat because I can't keep you all straight."

Andy chimes in here, "April is new to the institution of television. She's spent her entire life being entertained by novels from the 1860s."

Chuckles from the audience.

"Not true, my friend! I have spent a fair amount of my life being entertained by cheesecake." The callback to our previous conversation was intentional. There's some more robust chuckling from the audience.

The host gets back in the game here. "So the saga of New York Carl keeps getting weirder. Estimates are saying that, if it's a marketing campaign, it had to have cost more than a hundred million dollars to pull off."

Andy answers, "Yeah, setting off an EMP to knock out security cameras isn't just expensive, it's illegal."

"There are reports that the Carls in China have been closed to the public. Do you think there's anything for people to be worried about?"

"When you're faced with something you don't understand, I think the most natural thing but also the least interesting thing you can be is afraid," I say. And then I change the subject because I'm bored and pretentious. "Does anyone else think Carl is beautiful?"

You actually do preinterviews with these people. They tell you the questions they're going to ask—they even sometimes prewrite jokes for you so you don't come off looking like a total doof. The hosts are great at improvising, but guests usually aren't, so they want you to keep to the script.

If you look at the tape, you can actually see Andy's eyes get big when I ask that question. He's panicking.

Pat doesn't bat an eye. "Maybe when the light hits him just right?"

The audience laughs.

"I just mean, even if it was done for marketing, they are remarkable sculptures. It's easy to forget how much time goes into things like designing giant fighting robots for movies. It feels cookie-cutter, but thousands of person-hours go into their creation. We love them because they're beautiful, and they're beautiful because of hard work."

Pat nods approvingly before changing the subject: "Has life changed much for you two?"

Andy is so relieved to be back on script and says, "Well, for me it's very weird to be recognized on the street for this video that April and I just thought was a joke. It's not like we've got a nighttime talk show." More chuckles.

"For me, it's the money! The YouTube video has made like five thousand dollars already. Keep clicking on that link, you guys," I say directly to the camera.

Andy is freaking again.

"You've made that much?" Pat asks.

"Oh yeah," I reply. "Also, a bunch of networks ran our video before we gave them permission, so Andy's dad, who is a lawyer, basically got to extort the networks for a frankly embarrassing licensing fee. I paid off exactly 42 percent of my student loans this week." And then I wink at the camera.

We went on to talk, of course, about the mystery on everyone's mind. Pat joked that maybe Carl was sent by space aliens, and because I knew about the Wikipedia sequence and no one else did, I got to confidently say that I knew there was more to the story. But of course I didn't tell anyone what the more was. I looked cocky, but people either love that or they love to hate it, and in the attention game (which I was playing even if I didn't know I was), those things are equally good.

So here's a really stupid thing about the world: The trick to looking cool is not caring whether you look cool. So the moment you achieve perfect coolness is simultaneously the moment that you actually, completely don't care. I didn't care about the gravitas of that TV show, and the freedom and security and confidence that came with that was a *rush*. It took me a while to realize that the feeling I was feeling was power.

Some people found me precocious and entitled, but that didn't matter because those people would still watch, which was all the people doing the booking cared about. Other people thought I was refreshing and clever, and, honestly, I liked it. I liked that I was good on camera, and that people were talking about me, and that I was getting more followers on Twitter, and that people were listening to me.

Most power just looks like an easier-than-average life. It's so built-in that people mostly don't realize how powerful they are. Like, the average middle-class person in the US is one of the 3 percent richest people in the world. Thus, they're probably one of the most powerful people in the world. But, to them, they feel completely average.

Power only does all its business of *empowering* when it's perceived as a difference between the power of those nearby and, even more important, the power one previously had. And I'm not going to pretend that this weird new confidence combined with this weird new platform wasn't more than a little bit intoxicating and already getting addictive. They tell you that power corrupts . . . They never tell you how quickly!

In the squishy, leather, new-car-smelling back seat of the Escalade that was driving us to our hotel, I was obsessively checking Twitter and Facebook for Carl news and Andy was not quite amused and not quite annoyed with me.

"Why can't you just do what they tell you to do?"

"Because that's boring. You were right when you said a lot of people want to be in my shoes, so I might as well be doing something interesting."

"It's like . . ." He was working it out in his head, and then he finally figured it out. "It's like you don't have any respect for any of this."

"Andy, that is exactly it. I don't. I told you, I've never watched any of these shows. I watch almost exclusively 1990s comedies on Netflix. If Pauly Shore calls and asks me on his show, I will be suitably freaked-out, but I just value these things differently than you."

"But can't you just see that everyone else is valuing it and respect it for that reason?"

"No, Andy. I've honestly worked my whole life to *not* think that way. I think that's how a lot of people end up respecting bad things, actually. Not that I think that show we just taped was bad—I'm sure people love it and it makes them happy. I just don't know enough about it to care."

I was starting to feel a little bad, but I also wasn't going to give up on the freedom and the power I'd felt.

"I don't know if I'm necessary . . . Why am I even here?" he said quietly.

I grabbed him by the face, and he blushed slightly. "Andy, don't be dumb. You're here because you're part of this. And also you're here to make the videos."

"Huh?"

"Like you were saying yesterday"—he had been saying it yesterday—"we have a YouTube channel with fifty thousand sub-scribers. We should make more videos. We should be controlling this story."

"You want that?"

"I think I do."

"But . . ." He didn't have to say all the reasons I had already given him for not wanting to make more videos.

"Don't start arguing my case back to me . . . You won."

"A hundred thousand," he said. "We doubled in the last two days."

I leaned forward and said to the driver, "Can you take us to someplace that sells cameras?"

That night we made and uploaded the second April-and-Andy video. It was about what our lives had been like After Carl. I made sure everyone knew that Andy was a partner in the channel. (Every time we did a TV thing, there was some confusion because I had faked that he was a stranger on the street in the first video.) I made some jokes about television sucking, but at least there was free food. I only made very peripheral mentions of Carl and I certainly didn't mention the Freddie Mercury Sequence. Carl wasn't going to be news forever, I figured, so if we were going to transfer this into something that would last longer than that, we'd have to start differentiating ourselves.

I figured we could maybe turn it into a show about art and de-sign. I could do all the talking; Andy could make the camera work and do the editing. We could even bring in Maya to help us write episodes and do illustration. It's weird to look back on how we imag-ined ourselves back then and feel equal parts "Aww, we were so useless and adorable" and "I miss that life so much I would end every panda to get it back."

Sometime while we were shooting that video, the show aired on the East Coast and I got like five thousand text messages. I didn't bother to respond to any of them, not even Maya's. I figured we'd talk soon enough. I was giddy with the attention, with lack of sleep, and with excitement about what Andy and I were doing. I had understood the magnitude of the lightning strike, and we were catching it. Or at least part of it.

But maybe the most energizing thing was that we didn't have anything to do the next morning. Andy's dad wanted to get us into an agency to talk about whatever agencies do, but that wasn't until like three in the afternoon. We were going to get to SLEEP! Really, truly, wonderfully, covered-in-drool, all-by-yourself-in-a-king-sized-bed sleep!

I didn't even bother to stay up and watch the West Coast airing with Andy. I shuffled to my hotel room to take off my goddamned shoes and my goddamned bra and my goddamned pants and drown myself in fancy high-thread-count hotel sheets.

CHAPTER FIVE

*O*f course it didn't work out that way. I looked at my phone, and instead of texting some of the many people who had texted me, I went through Twitter and saw all the things, good and bad, that people were saying about me. And then I opened my inbox . . . like an idiot.

I read and answered an email from Maya and one from my brother, who was proud of me and so excited to see me at his wedding, and one from my parents, who really hoped I was taking care of myself. Then I remembered that email I'd sent to the woman at UC Berkeley. I checked to see if she'd replied. She had, actually, like twelve days ago. I hadn't seen it—her reply had been buried by everything else and I'd totally forgotten about our conversation.

This turned out to be extremely fortuitous because it allowed me nearly two full weeks of blissful freedom from crushing anxiety. I almost went to sleep one last time like that. One more night of normal. Well, not normal, of course, but not this. I've pasted it here completely unchanged (though I did fix some typos because Miranda would have a total meltdown if I didn't).

RE: You said it was warm?

April,

The properties you describe . . . hard, resonant, shiny, heavy, extremely low thermal conductivity, do not sound peculiar, they sound impossible. There are no known materials that have these properties. It is difficult to imagine a material that *could* have these properties. I managed to access the Carl in Oakland and did my own inspection. His thermal properties make no sense. He's showing 0% thermal conductivity. Nothing. All energy that hits him just bounces right back. It's basically impossible, so it must just be that my instruments aren't sensitive enough. I was also in line with a bunch of tourists getting selfies, so I couldn't stay too long without attracting a lot of attention. My research is mostly nonstandard semiconductors, so this is a little outside of my expertise, but I've asked around and no one I talk to thinks this is possible. How energy moves around is what we do in this lab, and we have studied a lot of materials. He's like an aerogel but more dense than uranium. It doesn't make sense.

Anyway, we're left with three possibilities.

1. I have forgotten something very basic about a topic I know a great deal about, and so has everyone else I've talked to about this, including people who are smarter and know more than me.
2. Someone has constructed a new material that behaves unlike anything that currently exists, or should be able to exist, and then put it on the sidewalk for everyone to see.
3. Carl is alien. And I don't mean alien like "weird."

I don't know if you've ever heard of Occam's razor but, basically, it's a principle that the simplest solution tends to be the correct one. It's BS. If there's an objective measure of simplicity (outside of, like, entropic ones), I haven't seen it. Every person will have a different opinion regarding which explanation is simplest. So when I say that the "external origin" hypothesis is the simple one, that's informed by my bias. But I also recognize that it's the least likely, just because so far there have been a lot of things that have happened, and "external origin" has never been the reason.

So, like, external origin has a 0% success rate at explaining stuff, which means it is unlikely. But I do not have a simpler explanation. I am not the only person who will have understood this, but I have also not heard anyone credible saying "external origin." To be fair, I have also not been saying it because, well, it sounds ridiculous and is unlikely.

In any case, I think we can rule out the "art installation" angle, since, even if it were possible (which it isn't), producing sixty-four ten-foot-tall robots out of a completely novel material like this would cost, at minimum, billions of dollars.

Look, I don't know you but I feel like I have a responsibility here since I'm potentially breaking this news to you. There is a very real chance that you made First Contact. In case you aren't a nerd, I'm saying that you were the first human to discover extraterrestrial technology . . . possibly extraterrestrial life. So . . . congratulations?

I'm weirdly honored to have your email address. You should change your email address. You should do a lot of things. This is not something that can unhappen to you. I'm willing to say that there's a 90% chance that I'm wrong and that your life will be normal in a few weeks. But a 10% chance at being the first to meet an ambassador from another world is a pretty big deal. So . . . maybe do a little prep work.

I'm CAMiranda on Skype if you want to chat,

Miranda

I immediately started writing a response, but after half a sentence I opened up Skype to see if she was online. She was. Seconds after I requested her as a contact, a call from her came through. I answered, and her face popped up on my screen.

She was at a desk in what appeared to be an office. Bluish fluorescent light beat down on her wispy, uncontrolled, red-blond hair. Huge brown eyes looked at me with excitement.

"APRIL MAY! This is wonderful!"

"Are you still at work?" My brain was still on East Coast time, but it was after ten on the West Coast.

"The lab, yeah, not really work. Tides and spectrometers wait for no one! You know. I live on campus, so it's barely worth going home."

She was bright and seemed perfectly well rested. Skype is never the most flattering, but she was, like, adorable. Way cuter than I would be interested in. Frankly, I've worked my whole life to not be adorable with only limited success, and two adorable people dating is waaaay too cute for me.

"So, I have to apologize, I only just got your email. And, well . . ." I had no idea what else to say.

"Indeed. I've gone back and forth about six hundred times since I sent the message, but the longer they remain unexplained, the more obvious it seems."

"Obvious?"

"Yeah, I think no one's saying it because everyone's thinking it."

"I mean, I was on a late-night show tonight, it should be on here soon, and the host actually joked about Carl being from space. But, like, just because that's the simple solution doesn't mean it's the solution. Are you sure you're not being . . ." I trailed off. I didn't want to insult her.

"I agree. I am there with you. Like I said in my email, explaining something by saying 'aliens' has a 0 percent success rate. I just think that 'external origin,' which is what I've been calling my hypothesis because it doesn't necessarily mean intelligent others, should be taken seriously because, like, I don't have any others."

"What do you mean, 'it doesn't necessarily mean intelligent others'?" I said, already feeling a couple of steps behind the conversation.

"Well, the only thing I know is that these things are really far outside of how stuff works. I don't want to say 'aliens' because I don't know anything. But it doesn't seem possible that this was done by any man-made technology, and it certainly didn't happen naturally. Like, the Carls didn't grow from seeds. So the vaguest, most general thing I can say is 'external origin.' Meaning, basically, this doesn't make sense."

"So you're not saying Carl is a space alien."

"No, but I *am* saying it looks increasingly likely that the Carls weren't made by humans or by nature."

"So you *are* saying Carl is a space alien!" I started to freak out again.

"No, I . . . I don't know, April! It's exciting, but space aliens are a very specific explanation for a very broad circumstance. There's more to the universe than humans and aliens. Maybe they're made by humans but sent from the future. Maybe they are a kind of projection through space-time. Maybe they're proof that our universe is a simulation and someone is changing the code. Mostly, I don't pretend an explanation is correct just because I haven't thought of any others that fit with current data."

She seemed very sure of herself, even if she looked a little timid and freaked-out talking to me.

"Well, Miranda, speaking of the current data. We haven't told anyone about this, but there's more."

Her eyes, impossibly, got bigger.

I took her through the procedure of the Wikipedia clue.

"This is deeply impossible," she said after we had gone through the whole sequence, "and nonsensical as well. I-A-M-U."

"I know. I've been racking my brain over this for days, so I don't expect you to—"

"Elements," she interrupted.

"What?"

"Elements. I, Am, U—those are all elements. Iodine, americium, uranium."

"OK, that's another lead to add to the fifty-mile-long list of guesses as to what this might mean."

She looked a little dejected, and I felt bad for immediately dashing her first try at explaining it. I mean, of course Miranda would find a sciencey explanation—she did sciencey stuff. So I said, "I mean, that's interesting, though—we hadn't thought of it."

Her smile came back.

"So does this Wikipedia thing make . . . your hypothesis more or less likely? Also, is there a time when we're going to know for sure?"

Her eyes shot around in thought for a moment before she said, "The Wikipedia thing is weird, but less weird than the material thing. But maybe that's just because I don't really know that much about how the internet works. I'd have to talk to someone who knows things I don't know. But the material is not only unknown technology; according to my understanding of physics, it's not possible. And your second question is a great question. I don't know when we will know for sure. Maybe never. Sometimes there are mysteries that linger for centuries. So I don't know. I just can't fathom another explanation."

We sat there and stared at each other for a long time before she got too uncomfortable and just said, "So . . . uh . . ."

"So do you suggest operating under the assumption, privately at least, that Carl is . . . external?"

"It's hard to say, right?"

"It is."

Saying that felt weirdly like cursing in church. I wasn't quite in shock; I was more feeling like I must be an idiot for even listening to this.

Miranda continued. "Sometimes we have to do that. Sometimes we have to go with an imperfect theory and . . ." She got quiet and her eyes unfocused and moved around the room. I stayed quiet because it seemed like if I said something I would be interrupting something intimate and sacred.

"April, what if Carl's asking for something? Like, they want us to bring them things. None of those elements are abundant. Maybe they need something!"

I was, to be clear, completely clueless. For Miranda, things appeared to be crashing into place faster than I even got my mind around the fact that this might be a for-real thing that Carl was doing. That Carl was alive. That Carl was . . . external. I did my best to keep up.

"But, well, we're not going to be able to give Carl uranium."

"Why not?"

"Well, it's uranium. Doc Brown tried to get some and the terrorists shot him."

"That was plutonium, and in any case, it's all a matter of quantity. Iodine is easy—we've got that in the lab. Uranium I don't have, but you can buy unrefined uranium ore on Amazon—it's not dangerous unless it's purified. Americium, though, I don't know much about. It's transuranic, so radioactive and rare. I'll have to do some research. Quantities and purities are the hard part with rare stuff."

She fired this all off at rapid speed, and as soon as she hit "do some research," I could hear her typing while she talked.

"OH! I've got a lead on americium," she said after a tiny pause. "It's in most smoke detectors, so you can literally buy it at Walmart."

"Miranda, is it possible that Carl doesn't want uranium? I've already started to get questions from people who think that they're dangerous. Probably wouldn't be good for their image if they're searching for radioactive materials."

"I mean, I dunno, it was just a thought."

I felt bad for throwing a wrench into her beautiful brain machine, though I did kinda want to slow the conversation.

"I mean . . ." I wanted to encourage her. She was hard not to like, almost like a kid. A genius kid. "It could be. I just thought maybe we should be a little surer before we start stockpiling uranium."

Again, she was typing while I was talking.

"Oh god," she said, seeming scared. And that made me scared. It was the first time I thought maybe the Carls were indeed here to hurt us. Like she had discovered that mixing americium, iodine, and uranium would make a bomb that would destroy the earth.

"Is everything OK?"

"Shhhh." She shushed me. She shushed me like I was a five-year-old who wanted a Popsicle and she was on the phone with a very important client. She was clicking and typing and clicking and typing. I just sat there because, obviously, Miranda was hitting this problem way harder than I had the ability to. After a full minute of me being completely silent, she picked up exactly where we had left off.

"HAH!" she shouted. I startled. "Sorry! Yes! Omigod, April, I am so sorry. I shushed you. Oh god." She was turning red, and then she seemed to remember other things were going on. "April, everything is fine. But Carl definitely meant elements when he said 'I AM U' because everything on this Wikipedia page has reverted to normal except the original typo . . . and about"—and here she started frantically scribbling in pen on her own hand—"nine numbers from the citations. Nine numbers are gone."

She held up her hand, on which was scribbled, "127243238."

"How did you figure that out so fast?"

"I have a proxy IP set up so I can watch BBC shows. I was able to open the page from my IP and a British IP simultaneously. Comparing was easy once I noticed numbers were missing."

"OK, so what is it? It's not enough numbers for a phone number."

"Hah . . . no. They're the most common isotopes of those elements. Iodine-127, americium-243, and uranium-238. Do you know what an isotope is?"

"No, but maybe I don't need to?"

"No, maybe not right this moment. Suffice to say, Carl is asking for elements, and though there are more common elements out there, he's asking for the most common isotopes, which, if we're going to be his couriers, makes our job easier."

"Are you for real right now?"

"In what ways?"

"Did you just, in five minutes, solve a puzzle that has been devouring every ounce of my mental energy for the last two weeks? I can't believe I never looked at the citation numbers!"

"No one ever looks at the citations, don't worry. Sometimes you just need a fresh pair of eyes."

"Yeah, a pair of eyes that have heard of americium." I didn't even know that americium was a thing. It was another few days before I saw it written down and realized it was an element named for America, since it's pronounced like "amer-ISS-ium."

"Eyes can't hear, April! So you're on TV tonight, right? That's exciting."

"OH MY GOD NO IT'S NOT!"

She grinned. "Yeah, I guess not."

"Hey, Miranda?"

"Yeah?"

"You want to go to Walmart with me?"

It was midnight. Our show was on TV, but now that seemed like the least interesting thing in the world. The mystery had eclipsed my obsession with strangers analyzing my performance. I had made a date to meet up with Miranda. She would drive down from San Francisco to meet me at Hollywood Carl after our fancy agent meeting. She was excited to meet Andy as well.

I got into the big, silky, soft, cool hotel bed and turned off the lights and stared at the insides of my eyelids for about an hour before giving up.

Miranda was right: I had had the thought before. When something is impossible to explain, you post the GIF of the guy with the hair saying, "ALIENS." It's just what you do. I mean, "Don't Stop Me Now"? No video footage of them showing up? The fact that none of the Carls had been moved, though no one seemed to have tried super hard? The fact that no one, after almost two full weeks, had taken credit or spoken out about what must have been a massive logistical undertaking?

I think a lot of people thought "extraterrestrial," and of course plenty of people were saying it on the internet. But no one wanted to be the weirdo advocating for the "It's aliens!" theory on cable news. You can't say the word "aliens" without teasing your hair up and bugging your eyes out first.

So the thought had been there, but it seemed like just a normal "my brain is thinking stupid thoughts" thought.

But Miranda didn't seem stupid. She seemed really cool and smart and like she knew an awful lot about material resonance and thermal conductivity . . . things that sounded important and legitimate. She also was clear that maybe it wasn't aliens; it was just maybe not a bad idea to operate, at least privately, as if it were.

I would probably have been more skeptical, but I remembered

what it was like to touch Carl and it did feel weird—like nothing I'd ever touched before, like when I got semielectrocuted when my house got struck by lightning and I unplugged the TV while the wires were still all overjuiced. Not painful like that, just an entirely new sensation.

The only other thought I had was that it was some kind of top secret military thing, but why? What did any government have to gain from putting robots in a bunch of places all at once and then leaving an odd Wikipedia trail to three chemical elements? Just to say, "Hey, we can do this! Scary, right?! Don't mess with us!"? That made some sense . . . but then they would have taken credit, right? I could already feel my eyes bugging out.

While I was unable to sleep in that glorious bed, I figured out the real reason I was freaking out. Not because we maybe weren't alone in the universe or because my life was changing forever and I was going to need a new email address. It was because I needed to make a decision. The kind of choice that you only get to make once and you can't take back and it makes your life totally different, and even if the path is clear, it's still deeply unsettling.

Option 1 (the sane option): I could detach from all this as
   much as possible. Stop doing TV things, definitely do not
   meet a strange science girl at a Walmart in Southern
   California to buy smoke detectors, never do anything on
   the internet ever again, pay off my loans. Buy a big house
   with a gate with the licensing revenue that would, no
   doubt, if this were real, keep flowing for the entire rest of
   my life, and have dinner parties with clever people until
   I died.

Option 2 (the not-sane option): Keep doing TV, spice up my
   Twitter and my Instagram and have *opinions*. Basically,
   use the platform that I was given by random chance to

have a voice and maybe make a difference. What kind of
difference? I had no idea, but I did know another chance
like this wasn't going to come along . . . ever.

Given the laundry list of other potential culprits, it was difficult
to realize that this was the thing that was freaking me out. But once
I knew it, I figured the only thing to do was to make the decision,
which would then maybe allow me to sleep in that mountain of
pillows.

With my brain full of fear and fog and excitement (and far too
impressed with itself), I made my decision. As is often the case, it was
the easier choice to make and the more difficult choice to live with.

Having made that choice, I immediately wanted someone to talk
me out of it, so I called Maya.

She didn't answer the phone.

It's weird looking back on the little insignificant moments that
completely change your life and maybe all of human history. There's
one, right there: Maya Didn't Answer Her Phone That Night. It
didn't go straight to voicemail, so her phone was on—she just didn't
pick up.

I texted her, *I need to talk about some stuff*, and then, with one last
look at that magnificent bed, I grabbed my laptop, walked out of my
room and down the hall, and knocked on Andy's door. And then I
knocked again. The third time, the door opened and Andy stood
there looking like I had just taken away the most beautiful thing in
his life, which I pretty much had.

"I have news," I said.

"This is reminding me very specifically of another time you
woke me up with news."

"And that turned out OK, right?"

"You may be convincing me right now that it didn't. Please,

whatever is happening, can it please, please wait for six hours and twenty-three minutes?"

"No." I pushed past him, turned on all the lights, and walked into his hotel room, which, despite Andy having only been in it for a few hours, was a complete mess. "Whoa, was there a bomb in your bag?"

"I couldn't find my toothbrush," he moaned.

"OK, I need to tell you a few things."

We sat on his bed, and I pulled out my phone and read him the email exchange with Miranda.

He was very quiet after I finished before finally saying, "Carl is an alien?"

"I know, I realize it sounds absurd, and, look, it's probably not aliens. I mean, ALIENS! It's not a real thing that happens."

"Yeah, well, there are obviously aliens. The only question is whether they have the technology and desire to visit."

"There are obviously aliens?!" I said, a little perplexed.

"Yeah, I mean, April, do you have any idea how many planets there are in the universe? Literally more than the number of snowflakes that have ever fallen on earth! Or something. I don't know, it's a really impressive number. The point is that the odds that intelligent life happened just one time are basically zero."

"Oh, so this isn't such a big deal then?" I ventured.

"ARE YOU KIDDING? If this is real, it's the biggest deal in the history of big deals!" He actually yelled at me.

"Whoa, OK, yes, OK, yes. Yes." I almost said "OK" again, but I realized I was starting to sound like my brain had broken. So instead I said, "I know this seems unlikely, but I have more news."

"You're right, it seems unlikely that any other news matters much right now."

"I Skyped with Miranda and told her about the Freddie Mercury Sequence and she figured it out."

"WHAT?! GODDAMN IT, APRIL!"

"Why are you mad at me?!"

"I don't know! I don't think I'm mad! I think I'm having a weird and unpleasant dream. Or, if I'm not, then I'm just overwhelmed and tired. This is allowed to be overwhelming, right?"

"Yes, absolutely. So do you want to know, though?"

"I mean, yeah." But he didn't sound so sure.

I walked him through Miranda's thoughts, her discovery in the citations, and that you can apparently buy uranium on Amazon.

And then I said, "Which is all to say that if you thought we had a scoop before, we now have a very different opportunity and I would like to suggest that we take it."

"What do you mean?"

"I mean, if I made First Contact with an alien life-form, that's a bigger deal than me making a viral YouTube video," I said, using Miranda's term.

"And?"

"And so people are going to talk about this for the rest of time. Maybe we can be a bigger part of the narrative."

"We?"

"Yeah. We."

"April, if, if, IF—and it's a big, huge, Jupiter-sized if—*if* this is real, it's going to be way bigger than us. Every world leader is going to be on the news the moment it breaks. No one's going to listen to you."

"Exactly." I paused. "Unless we work our asses off right now to be out in front of the story. And also, unless we work out and implement the Freddie Mercury Sequence before anyone else."

"Oh, do you think there are other people who know?"

"They're already talking about it on the talk page of the article. If we get to it first, not only are we the discoverers of New York Carl and the initiators of First Contact with an alien civilization, we're the ones who worked out the first system they're using to communicate with humans."

"April, are you sure this isn't a bad idea?"

"No! In fact, I'm fairly sure that it *is*. But I have investigated the other possibility, which is leaving this alone and disengaging completely, and that doesn't sound like any fun at all."

"I can't believe I'm the one trying to talk you out of this . . ."

"ME EITHER! So stop!"

"You know that maybe Carl isn't an alien, right?"

"Yes, but we're going to act as if he is. Make decisions as if he is. We're not going to talk about it, or say it. And if it turns out he's not, we'll have invested in the wrong reality. But if he *is*, we'll be three steps ahead of everyone."

"Is that a good thing to be? Shouldn't, like, the president be three steps ahead and not a bunch of . . . whatever-we-ares?"

"I dunno," I said, honestly. "Let's just walk through the process and find out."

And so we did what we'd been taught to do in school: We built a brand. Branding is something designers think about a lot. You take something like a perfume or a car tire, or butt-flavored bubble gum, and you ask questions about it that you shouldn't be able to ask. What kind of tuxedo would this car tire wear to the prom? What is this perfume's favorite movie? You try to end up in a place where you understand a product as if it is a person.

The reverse of this, where people become brands, should be easy, right? They're already people . . . End at the beginning. Except that really what you're doing when you brand is a process of simplification. You come to understand the *essence* of that fucking tire. And so branding a person also benefits dramatically from simplicity. People are complicated, but brands are simple.

Marketing is a lot more about thinking than doing. We had to figure out what Carl's brand was, what my brand was, and how those identities would be a part of each other. We had to think realistically about the role I would play. I wasn't going to be the president. I wasn't going to be a national security or science expert. But how we defined me would be informed by how we imagined Carl. We decided that Carl represented power and the future and the "other." I would represent humanity and weakness and the world Before Carl. I would balance Carl. For all the "This is huge" and "OMG" freak-outs, I could be a balance. Just a small, unassuming civilian who was handling this new reality fine, so you shouldn't worry too much either. That was an important role that I could fit into, that would be helpful, and that would give us power.

We basically just followed the advertising-campaign handbook all the way through, but this wasn't about designing a logo or picking fonts and a color scheme. In fact, we hardly did any of that. What we did have, after a few hours of work, was a plan and three different scripts. The first two were just there to round out the idea of April May. Who she was. That she was smart, kind, and snarky but open to the beauty and wonder of the world. We'd be able to upload them whenever there was time but, more importantly, they defined who we wanted me to be.

In those videos, we put in little bits about Carl that would be hints to his possible origins. That the Chinese and Russian governments had closed down areas around the Carls rather than moving them, possibly because they were incapable of moving them. But they were mostly about me.

Then we scripted the video we would release as soon as anyone caught on to the Freddie Mercury Sequence. A video that would show us working out the sequence, going to the store to buy smoke detectors, and presenting Carl with the fruits of our labor. Then, of course, the script ended, because we had no idea what would happen next.

People would later accuse me of being a careful and calculating marketer using the situation as an opportunity to get rich and famous. I would deny it, saying it was just a bizarre thing that happened to me, but that was a lie. It was a lie that was part of our careful and calculating marketing strategy. If it looked natural from the outside to you, well, then I guess we did a good job. But we were calculating. I liked getting stopped for photos in the airport, I liked getting paid, I liked the attention, and I was worried about it ending. More than worried, honestly, I think deep down I was terrified. At some point that night, I glimpsed my most probable future. That one day, the most interesting and important thing about me would be a thing that I did a long time ago. That I would go on with my life doing boring UX design and people would say, "Oh! You were April May!" to me at parties and job interviews, as if I was once something but not anymore.

That is the reality I was fleeing from. And I won't say that I didn't consider what I was fleeing toward, because we were pretty careful, and I think that paid dividends. But one thing that I didn't anticipate was that, in creating the April May brand, I was very much creating a new me. You can only do so much pretending before you become the thing you're pretending to be.

By the time we were finished skinning all our social media sites, writing scripts, shooting, editing, writing copy, and eating cold Pop-Tarts from a vending machine, it was 10 A.M.

My phone booped—it was Maya. *What's up hun.*

I was too exhausted to respond. I went back to my room and slept for three hours.

CHAPTER SIX

We still had our meeting with Andy's dad, so we got up at 1 P.M. and our useless bodies dragged our even more useless brains to the car that had been sent for us. We slept through the drive and then walked zombielike into the glass-and-steel building where Marshall Skampt worked. He was a lawyer for an agency, which (as I didn't understand then but do understand now) is a company that turns fame (and ostensibly talent) into money. Agencies have agents, and agents get work for people who are professional entertainers or creators. If you ever meet an agent, here is what to expect (if they're any good):

1. You will never meet a more effective person.
2. If they are talking to you, it's because you can make them money.
3. They're all assholes, but if you get lucky, you might find one who's *your* asshole.
4. Sorry, that sounds weird.

So the meeting with Andy's dad turned out to be a meeting with Jennifer Putnam, who was apparently a huge deal.

The building, like a news studio, was clearly built to impress. The difference here was that it *worked*. I imagine it worked on everyone, but it worked particularly well on me because, after we waited for five minutes in the little lobby drinking cucumber-infused artesian well water, a fashionable young man called our names and we followed him down the hallway and I was trailing the group from the beginning, but about ten feet into our journey I stopped because, half dead and tired as I was, I did not miss the Sherman original in the hallway.

I had some inkling that most great art is in the hands of private collectors, hiding in places where only a few people get to enjoy it. I understand that that is part of how art works, and I have no problem with it; it was just abstract to me at the time. Like, I didn't ever expect to see truly great art anywhere but in a museum or in photos online. But here, sitting right in front of my face, was a photograph that at minimum cost tens of thousands of dollars and was worth every penny.

I imagine agencies make themselves seem impressive to different people in different ways. Maybe some people get off on the in-house movie theater or the embroidered wallpaper. Others might like that every single desk had a large live orchid on it.

This photograph was aimed at people like me . . . to make us think, *Oh, OK, this place is legit.*

Everyone else, of course, kept walking while I froze, staring at the photo. It took them a while to notice I was gone, but eventually the cute assistant guy came back for me.

"April, I'm sorry we lost you." His voice was sweet and soft and made me believe it was legitimately their fault I'd been left behind. "What you're looking at is Cindy Sherman's *Untitled Film Still #56*, part of her *Untitled Film Stills* series. Each photograph is of the artist, but she has set herself into various roles with the goal of making it more clear that our culture has constructed ideas of gender that can control us if we let them."

I knew all this, but I let him finish because I thought it was nice that he didn't just bark at me for standing in a hallway like a dolt. I figured they made everyone learn a bit about the art so that the whole thing could seem more impressive. Did I mention it was working?

"Thanks," I said, because I didn't know what else to say. We turned from the photo and started walking.

"The agency has a large collection, some works given to us by clients, others collected by leaders of the company and loaned to us to display. The Sherman, I believe, was provided by Mrs. Putnam."

As we walked, we passed a number of other extraordinary pieces of art. The walls were gallery white, and every twenty feet or so there was a photograph or painting or mixed-media piece. I estimate that we walked by at least two million dollars' worth of art on the way to Jennifer Putnam's office.

All around us while we walked, the business of contemporary show business was happening. This, apparently, meant mostly phone calls. There was also a fair amount of bustling about keyboards and remarkably little chitchat. We walked by a young woman whom I did not recognize but who was very clearly rich and famous. It's funny how you can just tell, even if you've never seen them before. High fashion is astoundingly different from regular clothes, but I mostly knew because the three people walking behind her had a very clear air of "Don't you dare even think about asking for a selfie."

And that was the state I was in when I walked into the office of one of the most high-powered agents in the world.

"Robin! You found her! Welcome, April." Her voice was not loud exactly, just . . . strong. Surprisingly forceful. She was physically nondescript. Short gray hair, average height, in good shape. Her voice was her most particular characteristic. This was a woman who could cast spells on people.

Her office wasn't huge, but it had a nice view. The shelves were full of books, video games, DVDs, even board games. It read more like a gallery of achievements than a place to store things she liked. Every one of those things was a deal she'd made, and the shelves were full. There was enough room for the four of us to sit comfortably, but a fifth would have been stretching it.

Robin was standing by the door. "She was admiring the Sherman."

"I see you've got good taste! I bought that at auction just a few months ago. Managed to get it a nice place on the walls here, despite the fact that most people couldn't care less about Sherman anymore." I found this to be an odd thing to say considering that she probably paid over $50,000 for that photo, but I didn't say anything. "Anyhow, it's been quite a week for you! I've been following every moment of it. Fascinating, and you're handling it so well! Last night was *fantastic*—you're viral all over again!"

I was confused for a moment, but then remembered the late-night show we had been on. It felt like remembering high school English class.

"Thanks, um . . ." It occurred to me that I had no idea what the game plan was, and I was way too tired to pretend, so I just said it: "So what are we doing here?"

"Well, Marshall"—she indicated Andy's dad—"has been telling me about the two of you and we all just thought it made sense to get you in here and talk about where you want to go from here. There are going to be a number of opportunities, and we want to make sure we go through those doors while they're open."

She talked faster than anyone I've ever heard in real life. Staccato, almost like a slam poem. It was pleasantly peculiar. It was not lost on me that she'd already switched from "you" to "we."

"Well . . ." I looked at Andy, who gave me a little shrug. I interpreted that as "Play it how you want to play it, girl."

So I played it wide-open.

"Last night some information came to light that might change all of this. According to a report that I received from a credible source, it may not be long before people in positions of power publicly confirm that the Carls are not from Earth."

The words hung in the air for a while. Jennifer Putnam looked at Andy's dad, who looked worriedly at Andy, who looked at me. I also would have looked at me if I had been capable of it, but I couldn't because I *was* me. My impulse was to look down at my hands, but I knew that that was wrong, so I just looked at Putnam, who was, by this time, looking back at me.

"Robin, I'm going to need you to cancel all my calls for the next two hours."

"Yes, Mrs. Putnam." If this was unusual, they made no sign that it was. The door closed quietly behind Robin.

"And what information is this?"

"A materials scientist from UC Berkeley that I've been in correspondence with says that the properties of the Carls are impossible. Not weird or expensive or new, but according to everything we know, simply not possible."

"And you trust her?"

"She seems trust- . . . able?" I said, feeling a little bit like maybe I was a complete idiot. But if Putnam was skeptical, she didn't show it. "But also, I have not told you the whole story. I need you to assure me, 100 percent, that you will not tell anyone what I am about to tell you."

"I can have Robin work up a quick NDA if you would like, but if my word is enough, you have it," Putnam said.

So I told her about the Freddie Mercury Sequence, and what Miranda had figured out, and that we were planning to make a video about it. I did not tell her that we thought the sequence was a request for physical material and that we were planning on providing it. Frankly, I knew deep in my heart that that was a selfish and foolish thing to do, and I didn't want them to talk me out of it.

I'm not much older now than I was then, but in a lot of ways, obviously, I'm a different person. So it is easy for me to recognize that I made some good decisions and some bad ones. But it's telling that, with this, I knew it was a bad idea even then but I still couldn't control myself. Knowing something is a bad idea does not always decrease the odds that you will do it. If I had examined my motivations on this one, I probably wouldn't have liked what I found, so I didn't.

After I'd finished telling her about the sequence and that we'd figured it out, Jennifer Putnam said, "Well, then the situation has changed, but the question has not. April, Andy, what do you want out of this? You can, if you're right, have anything."

You hear about Hollywood agents promising young stars *everything*—the sun, the moon, the stars, whatever you want, if you only sign right here! But the way it came out of Jennifer Putnam's mouth, I believed it. The power of the whole thing flooded into me. The Sherman photograph, the confidence on national TV, the knowing of things no one else knew. It was candy, Christmas morning, and a first kiss all rolled into one.

So I gave her the elevator pitch.

"We have already created a strategy. We want the idea of April May to be a counterbalance to the idea of the Carls. Where they're powerful, I will be weak. Where they're terrifying, I'll be cute. Where they're otherworldly, I'll be human. We would like to build the idea of April May to help people deal with the reality of Carl. And, once I have that platform, use it to bring people together and promote simple change and a better world."

I didn't really know what simple change I wanted to promote, exactly—that seemed like the kind of thing I'd figure out once I had the power.

In any case, Putnam loved every second of that, but Mr. Skampt did not. I sometimes imagine what it would have been like if he hadn't been in the room. The thing about getting famous is that, often, the only people who are in a position to be honest with you about the realities of celebrity are the people who will make gobs of money if you go all in. They have no incentive to tell you the dirty truth, which Mr. Skampt attempted to tell me then.

"April, this is a huge decision. Becoming involved with something like this . . . it's going to completely take over. People will hate you for no reason, or for bad reasons, or even for good reasons. People are torn apart by fame, and this is far beyond what most of them deal with. You're talking about yourself like you're a tool, but you're a person too. And an evolving one. This will affect your life forever."

Putnam addressed me, not Andy's dad. "These are concerns that I absolutely share. You will never know what this is going to be like until you do it, and fame is not something that should be sought for its own sake. That being said, I think there are safe ways to approach this, and it is very good that you are here. We need to talk about a lot of things, and you should know that you can back out at any time."

"That's not exactly true, Jennifer," said Mr. Skampt. "Once they're in this, there's only so much that they'll be able to withdraw."

The sea of dopamine and adrenaline enveloping my brain was converting my exhaustion to giddiness. "How can we say no? We're in." I turned to Andy, who hadn't spoken since we walked into the office.

He looked down at his feet for a second before he said, "What she said, no one gets this opportunity, we need to take it."

"OK, we need to do quite a lot of work very fast. How are you two feeling?" Putnam asked.

"Terrible!" I said.

"Like I got fucked by a demon!" Andy added. His dad looked displeased.

Jennifer Putnam did not. "Well, I guess that's what we're working with!" she said.

Over the next couple of hours Robin and Mrs. Putnam built contracts, made phone calls, and quizzed Andy and me. Mr. Skampt made it clear that, in this situation, he was representing the clients, not the company, and argued with Putnam on a number of points that I was far too exhausted to understand. We had absolutely lucked out to have Mr. Skampt fighting like a dog for us. He probably saved our butts (and our dollars) in fifty different ways in the course of fifteen minutes.

The weirdest bit was when they separated Andy and me for one-on-one discussions. They wanted to make sure that one of us wasn't influencing the other, and they asked us about that, and about the deal we'd brokered and about our relationship. I mean, I presume they asked Andy about all the same stuff; if they asked him something different, he never told me. I was as open as I could be. Andy and I were on good standing and it looked as if there was more than enough money to go around and what did I need more than $20,000 a month for anyway?

Then there was the bit I really wasn't expecting.

"Is there anything we should know about you?" Putnam asked.

"Um, I'm a Libra?"

Mr. Skampt chimed in. "April, it's important that if there's anything that might come to light under scrutiny, we know about it now."

"Oh." I hadn't thought about this. "Yeah, um, nothing I can think of?"

"OK, well, we have some prompts." And then he rifled off dozens of terrible things I might have done . . . just in case they'd slipped my mind. Had I ever hit a dog with my car? A person? Had I had a relationship with someone who was much younger than me? Much older than me? Had I ever hired a prostitute? Been a prostitute? Sold drugs? Done drugs? Seen drugs? Killed with my bare hands? Collected the teeth of my vanquished enemies? Carved the bones of children into weapons with which I killed yet more children?

And, if it's not too much to ask, could you please write down the name of every single person you've ever been to first base with?

I answered these questions and did these things, and it was extremely uncomfortable, but I had the feeling that it was a test as well as a practical exercise.

"April, I can't help but notice that there are a lot of names of both genders on this list," Putnam said in a way that both was and was not a question.

"Well, a LOT? I wouldn't say a lot," I said, completely comfortable and *not at all* embarrassed by this line of questioning. (That's sarcasm, by the way.)

"Jennifer," Andy's dad said, "I don't know that that's any of our business."

She replied like he was a child. "Marshall, you know as well as I do that it could soon be everyone's business." Mr. Skampt looked cowed.

"April," Putnam continued, "are you dating anyone at the moment?"

"Yeah, Maya. We were roommates first. It's a little weird, but we have a great relationship." As I said this, I felt a huge wave of guilt wash over me as I realized I still hadn't texted her since she sent that *What's up hun* text.

"So," she continued, "would it be OK if you were just gay? Like, you've had relationships with guys in the past but were gay the whole time?"

"But I happen to not be . . . just gay. I'm gay *and* straight? It's great, I don't even know what it would be like to not be attracted to a person because of their gender. To me, you're the weird one."

It's hard not to be immediately defensive when people challenge you on your sexuality no matter what it is. Some people just can't seem to believe that I feel the way I do, and so suddenly they're off explaining me to themselves with me sitting right there. Is it that I'm greedy, or sex-crazed, or can't make up my mind, or I'm a lesbian but I can't admit it, or that I'm just doing it to get guys' attention because they think it's hot? And if not that, then . . . "Oh, by the way, my girlfriend's bi too, maybe we can [MEANINGFUL PAUSE] hang out some time."

"April, I absolutely understand. But not everybody will. I'm just saying that it would be simpler if you were either straight or gay. I have no issue with bisexuality, and I want very much for the rest of the world to feel that way too, but it would distract from your message. Some people will latch onto this as a way to make you less human. We're looking at this through not just a New York City lens but all of America. Really, all of the world. Your sexual orientation will be a weakness through which you can be attacked."

I looked down at the floor and stayed silent for a full ten seconds. I mean, yeah, it made some sense. We're dealing with fucking space aliens—who gives a shit if I'm gay or bi?

I looked up at Mr. Skampt, who just shrugged.

"I mean, it's not like I'm currently thinking about hooking up with any dudes," I said, sort of lying, since I had just been thinking about hooking up with Robin. But Mr. Skampt's silence sounded like agreement to me, so I caved. "Sure, uh. Yeah, I can just be gay."

That was the first time I got a glimpse of the ways in which Jennifer Putnam sucked as a human being and I didn't even notice it in the moment. I know I'm blaming her when I could just as easily blame myself, but I was confused and out of my depth and she seemed so competent. For her, it was easier to sell a quirky lesbian than a quirky bi girl, so I became a quirky lesbian for her.

Though I'm not sure I'm one to talk, what with the whole staying up until 10 A.M. very intentionally converting myself into a brand. Our goals, most of the time, would align.

After everyone was satisfied that I had never eaten even a single baby, I was released for a coffee break, which I had with Andy at a café across the street. We debriefed and talked war stories. I kept the bi thing from him, and I'm sure he kept some stuff from me. Whatever, neither of us had ever done anything terrible, that was the important thing.

I'd been texting Miranda on and off throughout the day. She had left Berkeley and was on her way to Los Angeles now. We were going to meet her at the CVS (not a Walmart, alas) that was closest to the Carl in Los Angeles (Hollywood Carl). Of course, LA traffic was conspiring against her, but this meeting with Putnam was taking way more time than we'd expected anyway, so it was working out pretty perfectly.

I still hadn't texted Maya. I couldn't figure out how. There was so much to say and so much to do and, honestly, I was afraid of how she'd respond to the day's events. In my mind, I could only hear her on the spectrum from disappointed to livid. I didn't feel like there would be excitement or support on the other side of that conversation, so I just kept not having it.

"Hey, April." Andy had been looking at his phone. "More Carl weirdness. Nobody's saying he's a space alien, but they tried to move the one in Oakland to a slightly more convenient spot because he was causing traffic problems and they couldn't. He broke their crane. The story reads like it was inept city management or crane operators or something. I'm guessing it's more than that."

I stared into my coffee as the magnitude of it all crashed down on me once again. This just kept happening. I'd be living my normal life, being me inside of me the way I'd always been, and then I'd remember. It was a little like how I felt a couple of years before when our cat Spotlight died. You keep forgetting that life is never going to be the same again. But you can only go so long without thinking, "Where's Spotlight? I haven't seen him all . . . oh . . . fuck."

"Oh god, Andy, this is really happening, isn't it?"

"Jennifer Putnam sure seems to think so," he said as I dosed myself with another sip of coffee.

Now, with a better understanding of her business (and of her), I realize that Jennifer Putnam didn't need to be sure Carl was a space alien to go full war room; she only needed there to be a chance. She needed to look like she was all in even if she believed there was only a 5 percent chance we were right, because even a 5 percent chance of making tens of millions of dollars was more than worth her while. In the end, if Carl wasn't an alien, we would still be her client, and she could point to her faith and belief in us. It was a win-win for her.

When we walked back into her office after our coffee break, she said, quickly and carefully, "April, I'm giving you Robin. You need a full-time assistant right now and it's much easier for me to get a replacement than for you to find someone trustworthy. He's fantastic, a little soft-spoken but ridiculously effective. We'll continue paying him, but he'll work for you. He'll be in your email, if that's all right, and possibly doing some social media. We're going to make it clear to him that he works for you, not me."

Mr. Skampt didn't look extremely pleased about this but conceded, "We don't think it would be wise to involve anyone else at this point."

"So you officially have an employee. They make your life easier, but only if you use them. If you are not telling him to get you coffee at least once per day, he will literally feel offended. He is there for you, you need him, and he wants to help."

"Does Robin know any of this?" I asked.

Jennifer Putnam picked up her phone and hit a button.

"Robin, can you come in for a moment?

Ten seconds later he was in the room.

"Yes, Mrs. Putnam?"

"How would you feel about working for Ms. May?"

"I would be honored." He even gave a little bow.

"You would be what?!" I replied. People don't talk like that!

"Ms. May, I've known you for a very short period of time, but you appear to be strong, proud, and driven by good values. More than that, however, you are at the very center of history. If this is real, people will remember it for a very, very long time. I would not"—he paused—"mind being a part of that."

I would also not mind him being a part of it. He seemed really nice, significantly less skeezy than Putnam, and roughly my age, which made it less weird to think about him working for me. The only problem with this was that Robin was . . . attractive.

He was cute enough that Maya would immediately know how attractive I found him. And he was going to be my assistant! This guy would be all up inside of my everything. *Phrasing, April!* He would be . . . very involved in my life. But you can't not hire someone because they're too cute. Can you? That definitely sounds illegal. So there it was. I had an assistant.

"Well, thanks, Robin, it's a pleasure to both meet and employ you. Please help me. I feel as if every page of unread emails removes a year from my life-span. With the following words I give you the power to save or destroy me: My password is 'donkeyfart.'"

CHAPTER SEVEN

We were finally free from the agency at around 7 P.M. The sane thing would have been to go to the hotel, get some sleep, and make a careful plan for the morning. But wc were (or, rather, I was) high on caffeine and feeling invincible. I'd already set up evening plans to visit (and maybe experiment on) Hollywood Carl with Miranda the night before. Going to the hotel seemed ludicrous. Later, Andy would describe it to me this way: "Carl just had too much mass—we couldn't stop falling into his gravity any more than we could jump to the moon."

So we fell.

I assumed we were going to take a Lyft, but Robin seemed to think that would have been a personal insult to him, and also, it wasn't precisely secure to make a video about secret space aliens in a stranger's car, so with Robin driving, we got to film on the way.

I sat in the front seat with the camera. The video starts with me recording myself.

"Hello, and welcome to Robin's car. This is Robin." I turn the camera to Robin, who waves, teeth gleaming. "We have news. Several days ago, Andy and I"—I turn the camera to Andy, who waves—"discovered what we have come to call the Freddie Mercury Sequence. This is a cascade of changes that occur if you attempt to correct typos on the Wikipedia page for Queen's hit song 'Don't Stop Me Now.'

"The meaning of these changes remains something of a mystery. However, thanks to the help of a materials scientist from UC Berkeley, we now believe that we have decoded the sequence. We are headed to Hollywood Boulevard now to meet that scientist and to test a little theory."

Here in the final video, we cut to a screenshot of the Wikipedia page and some voice-over of me talking about the sequence, how we discovered it, and Miranda's later discovery that the citation numbers also changed, and that those numbers corresponded to chemical elements.

Miranda was sitting on the curb of the CVS on Hollywood Boulevard when Robin dropped us off. The moment she saw us, she popped to her feet and ran over to give me a hug.

"This is so cool!"

"It is not not cool!"

She was a little taller than I expected her to be because of how she was not exactly average height. I'm short—I barely came up to her collarbone when she hugged me. It wasn't one of those A-frame hugs either. She smushed our bodies together like I'd known her from kindergarten. Her bright eyes were glinting with excitement. Miranda is a bit older than me, but she looks a little younger. Seeing her was another flood of reality. This was happening. We were going to visit Carl, to give him materials to see what would happen. We were really doing it.

"I'm sorry, was that too much hug?" She looked worried.

"No, that was a perfect amount of hug." She smiled at me,

looking like she didn't quite believe it and would later be chastising herself for her enthusiasm.

"I got some smoke detectors this morning. They don't make it easy to get the americium out, so I'm glad I did it back at the lab." She pulled a box out of her purse and opened it to show a small vial with a couple of silvery metal strips inside.

Andy came from around the other side of the car as Robin drove away to find parking. "Glad you got it out," he told her, "but let's go buy another one so we can show where we got it from."

"Oh!" Miranda's excitement mingled a tiny bit with embarrassment. "I wasn't thinking about the video! Oh, this is so cool! Am I going to be in it?"

"If that's OK with you," Andy said.

He took some establishing shots of the outside of the CVS and then we recorded a quick intro with Miranda.

"We have arrived at the CVS just a block away from Hollywood Carl with Miranda Beckwith, the materials scientist who solved the Freddie Mercury Sequence. What are we doing here, Miranda?"

"We're buying smoke detectors."

"That seems like a really weird thing to be doing."

"This is not a normal day!" Her excitement was fantastic on film.

"And why are we buying smoke detectors?"

"To me, the sequence is pretty clear," Miranda began. "Carl is asking for supplies. And one of those supplies is americium, which is a fairly rare element, but it is used in some commercial products as a source of alpha particles." She had deftly avoided using the word "radioactive."

"Do I need to know what that means?"

"Not really, no. It's interesting, though. Maybe we'll put an explanation in the description. All that's important is that, inside of this smoke detector"—she held up the box—"is about one five-thousandth of a gram of americium."

"Is that going to be enough?"

"Oh, I have no idea! It depends on what Carl wants it for. If he needs it for a catalytic reaction, any amount will probably do. If he needs it to actually construct something, no, this will probably not be enough."

"Do I need to know what *that* means?"

Miranda looked into the lens. "More information in the video's description. Also don't forget to subscribe!"

The placement of the Carls was, of course, a topic of considerable discussion. They were impossible to move, and they invariably showed up in urban areas where they wouldn't go unnoticed. But in every city, their locations seemed nonrandom but also not consistent. For example, they all showed up on a sidewalk, but the part of town they were in was random. Oakland Carl was the only Carl in the San Francisco Bay Area, and San Franciscans were, frankly, offended. Manhattan is a city of somewhat uniform interestingness. New York Carl showed up on a well-trafficked street, but most streets in Manhattan have heavy pedestrian traffic. It's not like he showed up on Fifth Avenue, Times Square, or Madison Avenue. There was nothing particularly special about New York Carl's spot in front of a Chipotle.

Hollywood Carl, on the other hand, showed up in front of Grauman's Chinese Theatre on the Hollywood Walk of Fame, one of the city's major tourist spots and probably the most heavily trafficked pedestrian spot in LA. Not only that, but it's a place frequented by street performers and phony costumed superheroes charging twenty dollars per photo.

Knowing all this about Hollywood Boulevard and America's obsession with fame, I should not have been so surprised when we walked down to the theater and found a line stretching from Carl off so deep into the distance that it might as well have been infinite.

This was, after all, a real-life Carl! People come to the Walk of Fame to get their picture taken with a celebrity's star or their handprints in the cement. These people are the most likely folks in the world to want something for the scrapbook. The theater had even set up some lights so the Carl was more visible for nighttime photographs. They shone harshly on his shiny bits. I don't know why we hadn't assumed that there would be a line, but there it was.

"Oh lord," Andy said.

"Are we going to wait in that?" I replied.

The three of us began to wander down the line, trying to see the end. Eventually, I caved and just walked up to a young woman who was twenty or so people back in the line and asked, "How long have you been waiting?"

Her eyes widened and her mouth became a perfect circle. "OH. MY. GOD," she said, with equal and emphatic weight on every syllable. And then she turned to a friend. "OHMIGAHD ALISON ALISON, IT'S APRIL MAY! APRIL! OHMIGAHD!"

Miranda and Andy just stared.

Every culture has its ways of turning strangers into acquaintances. We don't really think about these procedures; they just exist. And this process almost always begins either by telling someone your name or by having some third party introduce you. Which is why I replied to someone who had just yelled my own name at me by telling them what my name was.

"Hey, uhh, yeah, hi. It's nice to meet you, I'm April," I said.

"OF COURSE YOU'RE APRIL!" the woman replied.

It may be worth saying that usually the second party in the stranger-to-stranger introduction responds to your telling them your name by telling you theirs. And yet this had not happened, which made the conversation even more difficult to have.

I would eventually get used to all this, but at the moment, as the cultural systems for stranger-to-stranger conversation had completely broken down, I had no idea what to say.

Robin appeared out of nowhere, apparently having found a parking spot.

"Do you want to get a picture with April?" He sounded calm and kind and like he really cared.

And then there was much fumbling for cameras and, oh, actually that was a video, and can you take one with me and with Alison and then one with us both? And, oh, Alison's phone is out of space, and don't worry we'll just take it on my phone and I'll text it to you later, and then it was done.

Suddenly there was a hubbub and everyone around us was aware that someone *famous* had showed up. I got the feeling that, even if they hadn't known who I was, every person in that line would have wanted a picture. And Alison and her friends were not like the high school group at LAX; they were freaking out.

The good news was that:

1. Everyone else nearby in the line also wanted a picture.
   And . . .
2. We had now effectively cut in line and were only twenty people back, but nobody was complaining.

We were saved by the existing line. No one wanted to get out of the Carl line they'd been waiting in. Otherwise, I would have been completely encircled and someone may have needed to call the cops.

Luckily, we were able to selfie our way to the front of the line and it only took about five minutes. Once we were up there, Andy (who had been filming much of my fan interaction) made an announcement to everyone within earshot.

"We'll now be making a quick video with Hollywood Carl here. It will only take a few minutes and April will be available to take pictures for a few minutes afterward. Thank you all for your patience!"

Everyone seemed thrilled.

And with that, we resumed the video with both Miranda and me on-screen. I look almost comically short beside her long, thin body, but Carl's chest isn't even in the frame since he's ten feet tall. In the background, spectators are gathering around to watch us film, and behind them, Grauman's Chinese Theatre.

"The line of adoring Carl fans has graciously allowed us to cut"—a clip of the line showed over this—"so that we can get down to the business of giving Carl a little of what he asked for. Miranda, we believe that Carl asked for three chemical elements, right?"

"Yes," Miranda chimed in, confident and on cue. "Isotopes of iodine, americium, and uranium. We have iodine, which can be found in any number of products. I have secured lab-grade, purified iodine crystals and americium, which we carefully and properly extracted from a household smoke detector."

She had done this with pliers and wire cutters.

"And is that americium safe?"

"Not really, no. If you were to ingest it, you might die. Just to be safe, I'm wearing gloves. Definitely don't eat this stuff, though."

"I will keep that in mind."

"We decided, however, that we would not attempt to secure any uranium for Carl. Though nonpurified uranium is safe and available for purchase, it seemed a bit much for this initial experiment."

"What do you think will happen, Miranda?" I asked.

"Uh, I have no idea?" She seemed surprised that I was asking her nonscientific questions.

"What do you hope will happen?"

"That's not really how I think about things. In science, you're not supposed to hope, you experiment and observe. But if anything, I guess I just hope that *something* happens."

"So what do we do now?"

"Let's start with the iodine—put on your gloves."

I put my gloves on. I'll be honest: The realization that we were actually doing this, and what it could result in, never really struck me. We just did it. Like Andy said, we were falling into Carl's gravity. I was making decisions, pretty stupid ones, but it didn't feel like that for me in the moment.

"Is iodine dangerous?"

"No, it's actually used as a nutritional supplement—they put it in salt to prevent goiters. It's also used as a catalyst in organic chemical reactions, which is, if I had to guess, why Carl wants it."

Miranda shook a tiny, silvery-looking flake out of a vial into my outstretched hand. I then held that hand out to Carl.

Andy pulled out into a wide shot to show me, barely breaking five feet, holding my latex-gloved hand out to this ten-foot-tall Transformer. I look pretty much exactly like a confused monkey trying to make peace with a superior life-form.

Nothing happened, of course.

"Try direct contact," Miranda said.

"Cut," Andy said, "I want to get in close on this."

Andy moved in to film me pinching the flake of iodine out of the palm of my left hand, and then, without any visible sign of the fear and anticipation that was shooting through my body, I reached out to press it onto the back of Carl's right hand.

Heat, I felt heat. And then suddenly I was light-headed and nauseated.

"Ohhhnnnnn . . ." I said, staggering slightly.

Suddenly, Robin appeared from nowhere at my side.

"April, are you OK?" Andy said from behind the camera. Everyone suddenly looked quite scared, maybe realizing that we in fact had no idea what we were doing.

But then the feeling passed.

"Yes," I said, shaking my head. "Yeah, I think . . . I think I felt my finger get warm. And then I felt light-headed for a moment." I looked down at my hand. The flake of iodine was gone.

Whether any of that had actually happened or I had just imagined it was immediately unclear to me. There were a lot of reasons for me to be feeling light-headed right then, and the sensation of warmth through a latex glove isn't exactly a precise, measurable phenomenon. And it was a tiny flake—I might have just dropped it.

Miranda immediately attempted the same with her own flake of iodine and reported that nothing happened. Of course, we cut that from the video because . . . boring.

We talked for a little bit about whether we should continue. I felt totally normal by this point, and the fact that Miranda hadn't felt anything made me think maybe I hadn't either.

So the next line in the video is Miranda saying, "Well, I call those results inconclusive, April May. Would you like to try the americium?"

"Seems like the thing to do!"

"This little strip of metal"—Miranda held it up for the audience to see—"contains a tiny, tiny fraction of a gram of americium, a radioactive metal produced as part of the decay cycle of plutonium. April, would you like to see if Carl is interested in it?"

Again, I took the strip in my latex-gloved hand and pressed it firmly to the back of Carl's hand.

"I think I feel a little warmth again, no dizziness." I pulled my hand back, but the little strip of metal was still there.

"The strip didn't disappear like the iodine did," I reported more to Miranda than to the camera.

"The strip is not pure americium, so there was bound to be stuff left over."

"I should have had someone else do it so you could have felt the warmth to make sure I wasn't imagining it," I said.

"That would have been a slightly better experimental design, yes," Miranda replied. "But, honestly, this entire thing has been a travesty of science. Nothing about what we did today would even be considered for peer review."

We stood there for another few seconds while nothing continued to happen. Finally, Andy lowered his camera and said to Robin, "OK, well, maybe time for you to go get the car so we . . . Holy fuck." Andy froze, staring at the place where I had pressed the americium for a tiny moment before frantically grabbing at the DSLR and thumbing the record button. Just in time.

Soundlessly, smoothly, Carl's hand had begun to move. Andy got about two seconds of that movement before the hand disconnected from the body with a soft *click* and dropped to the ground. Stunned silence became sounds of exclamation from the crowd, from me as well. My particular sound we could not include in the final video because we wanted it to be child-friendly.

Carl's hand—as big as a dinner plate—hit the cement, flipped itself over so its fingers touched the ground, and then it ran.

I say it "ran" because that's the closest word I have to what it did, which was that it pushed itself up on the tips of all five fingers and then skittered away, clicking rapidly down the sacred marble of the Hollywood Walk of Fame, causing yelps and leaps of surprise as tourists spotted it. The line behind us rapidly devolved as people rushed to see what was happening or began running in fear.

We spent a precious few seconds staring in absolute shock, which

I think is understandable, before Miranda shot after it just a millisecond before Andy and I had the same idea.

We shoved our way through Los Angeles's only busy sidewalk like perps in a crime movie. I pretty much bounced off a Chewbacca who was posing with a lovely middle-aged couple. I caught a glimpse of the hand as it hung a right on Orange and increased my speed to match my certainty that this was a thing that was actually happening, and also thanks to the complete lack of pedestrian traffic just three feet off the Walk of Fame.

I flew around the corner and saw it, just twenty or thirty feet ahead, but now somehow galloping? Instead of individual steps, it was moving in a leaping gait. Andy stopped as he turned on Orange to film me chasing after the hand a bit before following.

Miranda and I did not stop. We flew past the parking garages and hotels and apartment complexes on Orange. I was not and have never been an athlete. Miranda, on the other hand, showed no signs of slowing down, so I did everything I could to keep up with her.

Orange dead-ends into Franklin, but Miranda and I both distinctly saw Carl's hand head straight across Franklin and then leap up over a small orange retaining wall. I followed a few strides behind Miranda, up a steep, curving driveway, and up to a . . . a frickin' castle?

"What," I said as I gasped for air, "the fuck."

Though it was dark, the building was lit by a number of dramatic sources. It had weird, surprising architectural details like turrets and faux crenellations. After the apartment buildings and shopping centers we had just run past, I had the sudden disorienting feeling that maybe Carl had created a portal and we had been transported to some kind of kitschy Narnia. I looked behind us, and Franklin Avenue was still there, bustling with traffic.

I decided that this was still the real world and marched past the valet parking sign and up to a young man in a tuxedo.

"Did you see a large robotic hand run by here just now?" I said, having caught enough of my breath to speak.

"Hmm?" he said, as if he were just realizing we were talking to him. "Ah. Yes, it just went inside."

"What?"

"Well, it walked up and looked as if it wanted to go inside, so I let it inside. It had not strictly obeyed the dress code, but while the rules are both specific and comprehensive, I thought it made sense to allow an exception in the case of an autonomous hand." He did not seem to think this was all that weird.

Miranda attempted a response—"Um, well, we're . . ."—and she failed in her attempt.

"We need to get in there," I interrupted.

The man, maybe in his late twenties, dressed in a full tuxedo and white gloves, looked us up and down before saying, "Are you members?" as if he already very much knew the answer.

"Um, no. But you just let a robotic hand into the club, why not us?"

"Well, first, you are not members. Second, and I don't mean this as any kind of criticism, but you are not in compliance with the dress code."

"But a robot hand is?!" I said, amazed.

"There is nothing in the rules about robot hands."

"Look," I said, "can we just take a quick peek around?"

"Are you members?"

"No, we are still not members!" I said, losing patience.

"I am very sorry, there is—"

I just pushed past him. I mean, I'm not big, but he wasn't a real bouncer. This clearly wasn't a rough-and-tumble kind of bar, it was some fancy club, and this guy wasn't used to physically throwing people out.

I pushed past, through the door, Miranda on my heels, and found myself in a small room with dark wood paneling, a few small potted trees, and a fair number of bookshelves. Two more twenty-somethings stood behind a desk. The man tumbled in after us. "Nika, I'm sorry, they pushed me!" He sounded astonished.

"Did a robotic hand come in here?" I said, firmly, still out of breath from the run.

"Hello, I'm Nika, welcome to the Magic Castle, are you members?" She was having none of us.

"The Magic Castle?"

"The Magic Castle," Nika replied. "The clubhouse for the Academy of Magical Arts. A members-only club for magicians."

"And this is a real thing?"

She didn't reply.

"And that is why you do not think that it's weird that an autonomous hand just walked in," I said.

"We have seen weirder things."

I decided to put some of my TV skills to work and attempted to pivot.

"Regardless, a robotic hand, about ten inches, came through here several minutes ago, and it is very important that I locate it."

"Ma'am, I'm afraid I'm not authorized to discuss our clientele with nonmembers. Additionally, we cannot allow you admittance as it would be against our policies, which are very clear. This conversation is over."

I decided that pushing had worked last time, so I started to push my way past them into whatever weirdo, freak cult club this was and then realized why this small room was so strange.

"If you would like to push past us," Nika said, "you are welcome to try." She gestured to the doorless room.

"What the frick kind of place is this?" I half yelled. I looked over at Miranda, whose brow was knitted so tightly I thought it might cramp.

"This is the Magic Castle, and I'm afraid I must ask you to leave."

"OK, so, you know how, down the street on Hollywood Boulevard, there is an unexplained ten-foot-tall robot? Well, his hand just fell off and ran into your club. If I can't come in, can you at least go and look for it?"

Nika finally looked at least interested. "We will do that, but first you have to leave."

Seeing no other particular recourse in the doorless room, we left.

As we came out of the castle, I pulled my phone, which had been buzzing for several minutes straight, out of my pocket. Andy and Robin were the culprits. I texted them both to say we were at the intersection of North Orange and Franklin because I didn't want to sound absurd asking them to meet us at "the Magic Castle."

They were both there in less than a minute.

We all piled into Robin's car.

"Why does it smell so good in here?"

"I got In-N-Out," Robin said. "I had to guess preferences. I'm not 100 percent sure that we're even all meat eaters, but there are some animal-style fries for those who aren't."

"You are Jesus!" I exclaimed, realizing that I was starving.

"I'll take those fries!" Miranda said. Of course, the beautiful genius was also a vegetarian. A vegetarian consuming fries brought to me by the man whose job was literally to serve me.

I should text Maya, I thought. But then there was a Double-Double in my lap, so I didn't.

We passed the bags around the car as Robin drove us back toward our hotel while we told Robin and Andy about the bizarre incident at the Magic Castle.

"I can get you in there," Robin said.

"What is it?" Miranda asked.

"Only magicians can become members, and you can only go

inside if you are a member or have been given a guest card by a member. I can probably get one by tomorrow."

"I'm afraid that will be way too late. Besides, we have a lot of video to edit. Also I have tweets to tweet." I got my phone out.

> **@AprilMaybeNot:** Just performed a dramatically successful experiment with Hollywood Carl. His hand detached and ran away. I know that sounds absurd, but that's what happened. We have footage and will be uploading the moment we finish editing.

> **@AprilMaybeNot:** Carl's hand ran to the Magic Castle, where we were denied entry because we were wearing jeans and are not magicians?! ¯_(ツ)_/¯ But, again, we have successfully interacted with a Carl and Hollywood Carl's right hand is now AWOL.

Soon after this, I received about eighty tweets linking me to an AP story with the headline CARL HANDS VANISH ACROSS CONTINENTS. It wasn't just Hollywood Carl. Every Carl had, in the last hour, lost its right hand. The story was just a couple of lines and didn't make any mention of where the hands had gone or show any pictures or video of hands scampering around Mexico City. It was early, so we didn't understand that there was really only one hand loose. We just knew that every Carl that had been checked was now missing its right hand.

"FUCK!" I shouted to the whole car, startling Andy, who had already fallen asleep.

"What is it, April?" Robin said, concerned, from the driver's seat.

"It's bigger than we thought, the AP is already out in front of us." It's almost better to be first than best, but being best is *much* more work, so I was frustrated. I wanted my tweets to be as viral as my first video. I wanted to be in control of the story. The numbers were clicking up fast, but not as fast as if I'd broken the news. Reporters would start calling soon, so at least I would be part of the story, but it wouldn't be *my* story, and so I wasn't going to get all the value out of it I could have gotten if I'd just started tweeting instead of running after the hand.

I figured that the news of Hollywood Carl's hand running off would spread quickly, of course, but if all sixty-four Carl hands had suddenly started roaming around sixty-four metropolises on six different continents, this was already a huge story! And we were behind. I was so scared and frustrated and I didn't even know what I was chasing.

"Andy, get out your camera, let's film an outro and upload now. Robin, can you find us someplace nearby with fast internet?"

"No," Robin said.

"What?" I replied, shocked at the thought that Robin was incapable of something . . . anything, really.

"You don't need to do that. Write an outro, film it tonight, but don't upload tonight. Let the press freak out. If you upload now, you'll be drowned out. You have big news in that camera, but the news has news for today. Tomorrow or the day after . . ."

"They'll be jonesing again," Miranda said.

"Yes, exactly," said Robin.

"But I already tweeted about it," I said, now unsure whether I'd posted too early or too late.

"Then you'll be getting lots of media requests, and we will ignore them until the video goes up and it will just make everyone more excited to see it," Robin said.

Andy added, "This is a good plan because also it means I can not freak out for, like, as many as four whole hours. I can edit on the plane and I can sleep now." And then he added, in a bored voice, "Chauffeur, take me to my place of unconsciousness and away from this ridiculous woman." Then he leaned back up against the window.

"Andy, we are at the crux of history," I said, leaning over the front seat to look at Andy while doing my best American Hermione Granger impression.

"April, I am at the crux of violence." He didn't open his eyes.

"What is the crux, anyway?" Miranda asked.

"It's, like, the center of the cross maybe? Definitely something to do with a cross," Robin guessed.

"You guys, we did that," I said. "And we're doing this."

We all looked around the car at each other. None of us older than twenty-five years old, cruising down Santa Monica Boulevard, planning our press strategy for the announcement of First Contact with a space alien.

We were all a little punch-drunk, so someone began giggling. Within a few seconds it was everyone. Laughing at the absurdity of it all, of that night, of these weeks, of the fact that it was us. We had no right to play this role, but here we were playing it. There was whooping and recapping and fist-pumping, and Andy roused from his grogginess long enough to let a smile take over his face.

Once everybody's cheeks hurt and we had rehashed the whole night one more time, I opened my notes app and started writing a script, which I recorded on that car ride to our hotel while Andy and Miranda slept, Miranda's head lolling on Andy's shoulder.

"We chased Hollywood Carl's hand down Orange and into the Magic Castle, a club for magicians, where we were denied entrance. Staff there, however, reported seeing the hand enter the establishment. It would appear that our interpretation of the Freddie Mercury Sequence was correct, and that presenting Carl with americium or iodine or both either caused or allowed Carl's hand to disconnect and move independently around Los Angeles. We do not know where the hand is now. It's now evident that every Carl on every continent has lost his right hand, but while Hollywood Carl's hand was observed running away, multiple videos show other Carls' hands simply vanishing at the exact same time. We don't know what this means and, honestly, we don't know what we've done. But they asked us for materials, and we provided them. It occurs to me now"—this had only taken so long to occur to me because I had actively prevented myself from thinking about it—"that we took a number of actions today on behalf of all humanity and maybe should have asked for some kind of permission first . . . or let the government decide if this was the correct course of action. I did not do that. I did not think that the result of our experiment would be so substantial or significant. I have no reason to think, however, that the Carls are anything but friendly at this point . . . Well, maybe they are also very, very odd."

And that's how I ended that video. I looked into the back seat. Miranda's head was resting on Andy's shoulder. It looked like the right thing to do, so for the last five minutes before we got to our hotel, I went to sleep, and that was the first time I had the Dream.

I am in the lobby of a fancy office. Shiny and bright and brand-new. Light comes from everywhere, but there are no windows, just wood-paneled walls and gray carpeted floors. There's music playing, but I don't recognize it. No one is around except, at a check-in desk, there's a small robot. Well, not small, human-sized. It looks smoother and sleeker than Carl, blue and white and no chrome at all. It's approachable, so I approach it.

"Hello," it says in a smooth, human-sounding male voice.

"Hello, I'm here to see Carl," I say.

"Do you have a passcode?" the robot behind the desk responds.

"No?" I reply, skeptically.

Then I woke up to find that we'd arrived at our hotel. Discussions had occurred while I was unconscious. Miranda needed a place to sleep, so Robin offered to get her a room at our hotel just to save on driving around. Andy's and my flight was leaving in six hours, so we would actually get to have a solid four hours of sleep in real beds! We were all zombies, but Andy and I more than anyone. Andy was humming a weird little tune as we waited for Miranda to finish at the check-in desk. The song was familiar, but I couldn't quite place it.

We all rode the elevator up together. Miranda was humming the same weird song Andy was.

"God, what is that song? It's so familiar. You've both been humming it," I said to Miranda and Andy.

"Uɪɪɪ," was all Andy could manage.

"Sorry, I didn't even realize I was humming," Miranda replied sleepily.

I looked at Robin since he was good at solving problems. "Sorry, April, it doesn't sound familiar to me."

We all headed to our separate rooms.

I did not take off my clothes, but I did take out my phone. I stared at the gobs of tweets coming in. I'd added more than ten thousand followers since I posted about the hand. I wasn't even interacting, I wasn't learning about my audience, I was just watching it grow. My phone felt like it weighed ten pounds in my hands, and I almost fell asleep, but then I realized I'd been neglecting Facebook, and I hadn't checked my email. I copied my tweets and posted them on Facebook as well, and I watched the post grow there. This whole other audience seemed completely unaware of the situation, and the post grew just as fast there as on Twitter. I checked my email and told my parents I would call them tomorrow. Then I switched back and forth between Facebook and Twitter, checking to see if there was any news, what people were saying to me (and about me.) My phone booped with a text from Maya. *See you tomorrow, I guess*, it read. I was so tired, and that sounded like drama that I did not want to deal with. I swiped it away. And then I kept poking and swiping my phone before sleep finally won its war for my consciousness.

I am in the shiny office lobby, the song is playing, the robot waits behind the desk, I approach it. "Hello," it says again.

"Hi, can you tell me anything about you?" I say, hoping to engage it in conversation.

"Do you have a passcode?" it says.

"No, but . . ."

And I woke up. But at least now I knew where the song was from: It was the one playing in the dream lobby. It sounded a bit like an elevator music instrumental of a sixties pop song. Like "It's Not Unusual," but it wasn't that. It had 100 percent earwormed into my head, though, and would stay there for pretty much the next six months straight.

I must have been singing it in the car, I thought. That's how Miranda and Andy had heard it. I'd gotten it stuck in their heads.

I'd never been one to have recurring dreams. Certainly, there was that one about not going to class all semester and then having to take the test, but everyone had that one. This was the first time I could remember having a dream that seemed so entirely the same as one I had had before.

But if there was a part of me that thought this was weird, it was not a loud enough part to prevent me from going the fuck back to sleep, which I did immediately.

And you know what I didn't do? I didn't open my phone to look at my text messages. If I had looked, here's the sequence of texts I would have seen from Maya over the past twenty-four hours.

> **April 2:00 AM:** *I need to talk about some stuff*
>
> **Maya 9:52 AM:** *What's up hun*
>
> **Maya 12:12 PM:** *April?*
>
> **Maya 7:02 PM:** *Are you OK?*

Maya 9:30 PM: *Poke?*

Maya 12:12 AM: *See you tomorrow, I guess.*

I didn't even see Miranda the next morning. Somewhat heroically, Robin met us in the lobby and corralled us all the way to the airport and then through airport security, and it wasn't until we were boarding that I realized that he had booked a last-minute ticket on our flight back to New York. He had also, amazingly, upgraded me and Andy to first class.

"Did you sleep at all?" I asked him after they'd given us our fancy kooshy seats.

"I did not, I had a lot of emails to send. You're going to want to get a book deal," he added abruptly.

"Why?"

"It will help you sway public opinion. Every person who reads your book will be far more likely to be on your side. Books are the most intensive of all current media. People are willing to spend hours and hours with a book. Additionally, people are still willing to pay for them."

"I'm getting paid for my YouTube videos already," I said as I scrolled through my Twitter. People were freaking out. I started to type out a tweet because I couldn't help myself: "Video coming later today, editing now. Very weird. Very excited."

Robin continued as I typed: "You get paid very poorly for your YouTube videos. You get a fraction of a cent for every person who watches a video. I'd bet we can get you more than five dollars for every person who buys your book."

This made my ears perk up. "And how many people do you think would buy my book?"

"Hundreds of thousands." He paused before saying, "Conservatively."

"I'm going to want to get a book deal," I told him. "I've also been thinking, I'd like to get an apartment on Carl's block."

"Oh! Interesting idea. I like it. You can watch over him, stay informed. I can look into it. Any requirements?"

"Like what?"

"Price range, style . . ." He paused. "Number of bedrooms?"

Oh, right.

"Maya and I," I said to Robin. "It's weird, we're roommates, but we're dating, but we're not really at the 'moving in together' stage. We just already were moved in together when we started dating."

"That sounds difficult," Robin replied.

"Well, I would like your advice."

"I don't know that I can give you any. I know that you're going to have a very complicated life in the next weeks and months, and that you won't have time for much else. But I also know that having someone that you care about and who cares about you might help keep you connected to reality."

"Every time I play the scene in my head . . . I just can't imagine asking Maya to move in with me. It's like imagining dropping a penny through a lead brick. My brain won't do it."

"Just because you can't imagine something doesn't mean you can't do it," he said.

"That sounds like good advice." But still, the thought hurt my head. And I was exhausted.

"So, how many bedrooms?" Robin asked.

"Ugggh, two, I guess." Keeping my options open. And then I pretty much immediately fell asleep.

Of course, I immediately had the Dream again. And again, I didn't think much of it at the time.

You might think it's weird that Andy and I hadn't figured out the Dream yet, but it was a pretty boring dream and, in general, talking about even interesting dreams to other people is dull as hell. I try not to do it under any circumstances because of how much I hate it when other people do it to me. And besides, Andy and I probably had said a total of four words to each other that day.

I did talk a bit more with Robin, but Robin had not slept yet. And so, though he almost definitely had the Dream in his head by this point, he had no way of knowing that. He'd know soon enough, as would at least half of the people on that airplane and a number of others I interacted with at the airport.

You can go ahead and add that to my list of accomplishments:

April May, former pet detective, dairy-supply heiress, initiator of First Contact with space aliens, video blogger, and patient zero for the first and only known infectious dream. And also . . . terrible girlfriend.

CHAPTER EIGHT

By the age of twenty-three, I had already become a master of not being in relationships. Here are some tips if you too enjoy completely isolating yourself from the love of other humans because of deep, subconscious fears that you are unable to recognize even exist.

1. If someone you regularly hook up with serves up an overly familiar pet name, double down on your return. Example:

    "Could you pass me the remote, baby?"

    "Yeah, here you go . . . pookie patchoopie."

2. When conversations head in directions that might result in your relationship being defined as a "relationship," completely disregard all societal rules of conversation. Example:

    "Have you ever felt like this is . . . going somewhere?"

    "I wanna be the very best like no one ever was."

    "Are you singing the Pokémon theme song?"

3. Be prepared, at a moment's notice, to mercilessly and cruelly distance yourself from people who you care about and need more than oxygen. Example:

"So, April, my mom is going to come visit."

"Cool."

"Do you think you should, like, meet her?"

"I live here, don't I?"

Basically, do your best to mock and deride their connection to and appreciation of you because, deep down, you dislike yourself enough that you cannot imagine anyone worthwhile actually wanting to be with you. I mean, if they like you, there must be something wrong with them, right?

This probably seems weird to you, as you are familiar with the April May of video and social media. Always confident, clear, and comfortable. How could that person possibly act so confident and yet be so deeply insecure? Well, if I weren't so insecure, I would have had neither the opportunity nor the inclination to spend every day of my life getting really good at seeming confident.

My relationship with Maya was the longest romantic relationship I'd ever had. I think the fact that she was a great roommate and school partner had probably kept me from completely destroying us, which I had had the impulse to do several times already. But our relationship was mostly held together by Maya's understanding that my ridicule of her feelings for me was a manifestation of my distaste for myself, not her.

The result of this semi-long-term relationship with a beautiful and intelligent woman was that if I even for a moment thought about my life with or without Maya, I would notice how deeply and passionately in love with her I was. The knowledge that I would have to tell Maya about what had happened, and the feelings that gave me (knowing that I'd want her to talk it out with me, being afraid that she'd be disappointed in me, caring what she thought at all, the knowledge that she really knew me), made me want to run like I was being chased by an anaconda. A seventy-foot anaconda that wanted to hug me REALLY HARD.

I'm talking about all this now like I understood it then. I did not. All I knew was that, after that first missed call, I found it more and more impossible to imagine the conversation we'd have once we finally had one. And I'm telling you this because I want you not to hate me. You're probably going to hate me in a couple of pages, and I'm giving you a well-rounded understanding of my psychological turbulence so that you will hate me less.

Our apartment was clean when I got home. Cleaner than I'd seen it in a while.

"Whoa, did you go all mom on me?" I shouted to the empty living room, knowing Maya was somewhere in the apartment.

"APRIL! Oh god, it's good to see you. I've been worried!" she said as she came out of her bedroom. She was in a Wonder Woman tank top and plaid sleeping pants.

"Worried? You *did* go all mom on me." I smirked like it was a joke, but also a little bit like it wasn't.

"You haven't texted me since you told me you had some stuff you wanted to tell me. You might imagine that could cause a girl some anxiety." And she did look anxious, even more than I'd expected.

Two things occurred to me simultaneously. First, that she might have already been expecting a breakup. Second, that it would in fact be a breakup, a real breakup, bigger than any I'd ever had before. How did I let it get this far?

Panic.

"Well, there are some things we need to talk about." This did not lessen her anxiety, and I realized we were already off on the wrong track. I continued. "My trip to LA was very eventful."

"Did you hear that all of the Carls' right hands have vanished?"

I had to laugh. "Yes, well, no, not quite." I'd just watched a video on Twitter that showed a tourist gasping in shock as Tokyo Carl's hand *vanished*. It didn't drop off and run like Hollywood Carl's hand, it just disappeared. Other videos from other Carls showed that the hands didn't run away, they disappeared. All except Hollywood Carl. I explained this all to Maya, though I was a little astounded that she hadn't been following me on Twitter or Facebook.

And then I told her that I was there when Hollywood Carl's hand ran away.

"Oh lord, of course you were!" Her eyes were lighting up.

"Maya, a lot has happened. Um . . ." This was not easy. "Carl is very probably from outer space and Andy and I have—"

"Carl is WHAT?"

"Probably from outer space. Like, a not-of-this-earth, 'E.T. phone home' space alien." I waited to see if this was going to need more explanation, and when apparently she required none, I started back up. "We've already filmed—"

She interrupted again, "Please continue with the space alien thing!"

"Uh, well, right, we solved the sequence. Rather, Miranda did."

"Who's Miranda?"

"She's a graduate student from Berkeley who emailed me about Carl's physical properties. I told her the sequence and she solved it in like six minutes—it was pretty amazing."

Maya was looking uncomfortable with this news. I broke it down for her step by step, hoping to make it seem a little less like I had a new girlfriend.

"The stuff Carl is made of, the way it behaves, how it interacts with its surroundings, it doesn't make any sense. It's not possible. Carl is not a possible thing, and yet there he is, guarding the Chipotle, leading people to conclude that he was not created by humans."

"And?"

"And Miranda figured out that Carl was asking for chemical elements. I, Am, U . . . iodine, americium, and uranium."

"URANIUM?!"

"Yes, that is the reaction most people have. Anyway, we gave Carl some iodine and americium, and his hand detached and it ran away and, good lord, why am I telling you this story and not just showing you the video? Andy is going to make it live any minute now."

I logged into the YouTube account and showed her the video, which was about to be the third public video on the channel. When it was done, she turned to me and said, "She's pretty cute, huh."

Well, that didn't take long. I searched for something negative but also true that I could say about Miranda to make Maya feel less threatened.

"Yeah, she's a weirdo," was the best I could do.

There was a long silence during which I hoped we were going to get back to the more stable ground of discussing how I had found a literal space alien on the streets of New York City, made some videos with him, and become the de facto ambassador to outer space.

"And you're going to make this video public soon?"

"Yeah! No one else has footage of the hand moving independently, it's just us! And we're the only ones who have any idea how or why this happened! No one even knows about the sequence yet! It's just like you said: Now I'm not just the person who uncovered the sequence, I'm the person who solved it!"

She had gotten what she asked for, so at least there's that bit of blame I could properly lay at her feet.

"And you know what happens if you do this?" Her face was like stone.

"I get a platform? I get to communicate simple, positive messages at a time when people need them? It's not that different from advertising, and Andy knows everything there is to know about social media."

"Andy. So this was Andy's idea." It wasn't a question.

"Don't be an idiot, Andy couldn't make me change a light bulb. It was my idea, front to back."

"April." She sat down on my bed, and then stayed quiet for longer than I was comfortable with. "What do you think this is really about?"

She said it like she knew the answer better than I did. Which she did, but that didn't make me hate it any less.

"No one gets a chance like this, Maya! Yeah, there's money, but it's not just that. I think I can do some good here."

I don't know why I've never felt like a totally worthwhile person. I just haven't. It's what drives me. It's who I am. Maya knew that better than I did. She knew that bringing it up wasn't going to help, so she didn't . . . yet.

"And you think you can pull this off alone." Again, not a question.

So I told her about Putnam and Mr. Skampt and that I had an assistant already who was helping with my emails. I didn't tell her too much about Robin because, if there was someone who was going to win my pants, it was more likely to be him than Miranda. I had an agent and maybe a book deal coming, and Andy and I had already built a brand and a launch strategy.

"Did you think at all that it would be a good idea to talk to me about this?"

And here's the moment when a sane person could have healed the situation. It would be very easy to separate all of this. It would probably have been a good idea to put some space between the "We Are Not Alone in the Universe" talk and the "I Want to Grab Power and Do Good with It" talk and the "I Am Terrified of Our Relationship" talk. But I *wanted* to turn the fight into a breakup—the idea of "us" couldn't compete with the idea of "April May"—so I burned it all down.

"What does it have to do with you?" I said.

She was legitimately shocked. She stood up and then froze, still in her pajamas, with her jaw literally hanging open for a few seconds before she understood exactly what had happened. "Oh fuck you, April."

"What? We're roommates, we're friends. I texted you that first night because I wanted some advice, but then we were all caught up in it so I figured I'd just tell you when I got back."

"Roommates. Right."

"Speaking of"—I meant to say this matter-of-factly, but it came out strained and quavering—"I was thinking, for the sake of the story, it would make sense for me to move to Manhattan. Robin found an apartment that has a window that literally looks directly down on New York Carl."

"Robin?"

"My assistant."

"Found you a new place." It came out like fire. "And I assume it's one bedroom?"

"We're just roommates, Maya."

There was a bit of silence then. Her emotions—oh, they were everywhere. Anger, pain, disappointment. Disappointment in me, specifically, not in the situation. I got the impression that she was unsurprised that I had turned out to be exactly what she expected me to be.

All of those strong emotions dissolved into sadness then. Maya was clearly starting to cry as she turned away from me and walked toward her bedroom door. She got there and looked back, her eyes puffy already, and said, softly, "Oh god, April, you really have no idea, do you? You have no idea what this is really about? You're just trying to find an audience who will love you and I'm not enough. Well, this isn't going to be enough either, but I guess you'll just have to go and find out." That was the first time she said "I love you" to me. Or, at least, the closest she'd gotten. She'd known that if she said it I'd freak out.

"I weigh a hundred twenty pounds, and I'm the scariest thing you've ever seen. Call me when you grow a pair." She closed the door behind her.

Thinking back, the only emotion I can remember having as that door closed was relief. I reached for my phone and checked Twitter.

God, I was an idiot.

CHAPTER NINE

Most attributes a person has are, at least in some way, defined by them. They are good at soccer, they are funny, they know a lot about the history of Rome, they have blond hair. Some of these things are things that person worked for, some are just things that they just happen to have, but they are all characteristics of the person.

Fame is not this way.

Imagine if you looked different to every person who saw you. Not, like, some people thought you were more or less attractive, but one person thinks you're a sixty-five-year-old cowboy from Wyoming complete with boots and hat and leathery skin, and the next person sees an eleven-year-old girl wearing a baseball uniform. You have no control over this, and what you look like has nothing to do with the life you have lived or even your genome. You have no idea what each person sees when they look at you.

That's what fame is like.

You think this sounds like beauty because we sometimes say that beauty is all in the eye of the one beholding the beauty. And, indeed, we don't get to decide if we are beautiful. Different people will have different opinions, and the only person who gets to decide if I'm attractive is the person looking at me. But then there is some consensus about what attractive is. Beauty is an attribute defined by human nature and culture. I can see my eyes and my lips and my boobs when I look in a mirror. I know what I look like.

Fame is not this way.

A person's fame is in everyone's head except their own. You could be checking into your flight at the airport and 999 people will see you as just another face in the crowd. The thousandth might think you're more famous than Jesus.

As you can imagine, this makes fame pretty disorienting. You never know who knows what. You never know if someone is looking at you because they think you're attractive or because you went to college with them or because they've been watching your videos or listening to your music or reading about you in magazines for years. You never know if they know you and love you. Worse, you never know if they know you and hate you.

And while I can look in the mirror and know that I'm good-looking, you can never really know that you are famous because fame is not applied equally by all. You fall somewhere different on a broad spectrum with every person you encounter.

Though, weirdly, there comes a point at which you are famous enough that it will no longer matter whether someone has ever heard of you for them to think you're famous. Just learning that you are famous is enough for them to care, to be interested, to want a photo, an autograph, a piece of who you are.

I remember when I was in middle school, I was at the airport and I saw people taking pictures with a guy who definitely looked famous. He had big sunglasses and a ton of sparkly rings and two watches. I went and got a photo with him as well. I later learned that he was a music producer and had rapped on a couple of Lil Wayne tracks. I didn't even really know who Lil Wayne was.

I've had the opportunity to do more thinking about fame than most people, but fame isn't some monolithic thing; it isn't the same for the local weatherman as it is for Angelina Jolie. So let's talk a little about April May's theory of tiered fame.

Tier 1: Popularity

You are a big deal in your high school or neighborhood. You have a peculiar vehicle that people around town recognize, you are a pastor at a medium-to-large church, you were once the star of the high school football team.

Tier 2: Notoriety

You are recognized and/or well-known within certain circles. Maybe you're a preeminent lepidopterist whom all the other lepidopterists idolize. Or you could be the mayor or meteorologist in a medium-sized city. You might be one of the 1.1 million living people who has a Wikipedia page.

Tier 3: Working-Class Fame

A lot of people know who you are and they are distributed around the world. There's a good chance that a stranger will approach you to say hi at the grocery store. You are a professional sports player, musician, author, actor, television host, or internet personality. You might still have to hustle to make a living, but your fame is your job. You'll probably trend on Twitter if you die.

Tier 4: True Fame

You get recognized by fans enough that it is a legitimate burden. People take pictures of you without your permission, and no one would scoff if you called yourself a celebrity. When you start dating someone, you wouldn't be surprised to read about it in magazines. You are a performer, politician, host, or actor whom the majority of people in your country would recognize. Your humanity is so degraded that people are legitimately surprised when they find out that you're "just like them" because, sometimes, you buy food. You never have to worry about money again, but you do need a gate with an intercom on your driveway.

Tier 5: Divinity

You are known by every person in your world, and you are such a big deal that they no longer consider you a person. Your story is much larger than can be contained within any human lifetime, and your memory will continue long after your earthly form wastes away. You are a founding father of a nation, a creator of a religion, an emperor, or an idea. You are not currently alive.

If you look closely at this scale, you might notice that there are two different qualities built into every level of fame: First, the number of people who know who you are. Second, the average level of devotion those people have to you. Cult leaders have Tier 5 levels of devotion but Tier 1 audience size. Thinking of fame in this way has really helped me come to grips with what being famous means, understand where I am at on the scale, and decide what to do about it.

In the weeks after Andy and I uploaded the first New York Carl video, I had squeaked my way into Tier 3 fame. New Yorkers mostly ignored me still, but I'd do selfies if I was close to touristy spots. I had a woman walk up to me and start talking to me like we were friends. After about five minutes I was like, "Do we know each other?" Turns out she just assumed we did because she recognized me and was trying to keep things from getting awkward by telling me about her kids' new school.

Wrong strategy, by the way.

I was making more money than I knew what to do with, but not enough to, like, buy a nice home in New York or LA. And my placement was precarious. Due to the enormity of the Carl story, I would probably always have some revenue from that first video to live off of, but in the time before we visited Hollywood Carl, I could already feel myself dropping quickly to notoriety. Soon, only die-hard fans or, worse, *historians* would care, while everyone else would vaguely remember that I was once . . . something?

The Hollywood Carl video changed this, bumping me solidly into Tier 4. And there is a big difference between Tier 3 and Tier 4. If I had to guess, including bands, artists, authors, politicians, hosts, actors, etc., there are probably thirty thousand Tier 3 famous people in America. At any given time, there are probably fewer than five hundred Tier 4 celebrities.

This was when things started moving fast.

I stopped being some weird anomaly, and I became a part of the story in a very different way. From then on, if I wanted to be on a TV show, Jennifer Putnam could make it happen. I was expected to have opinions, and I had plenty. The Magic Castle became an epicenter of Carl conspiracies, but I was a bigger epicenter. The castle had to drop the illusion for a while and let investigators in, but no one ever found the hand (rather, no one told people when they found it). But I was a person; the FBI couldn't come search me unless there was a crime, and there weren't a lot of laws about this kind of thing. We kept expecting to hear from someone official, but we didn't.

Instead, Robin was in my email getting requests from news agencies all over the world to repost the video. They knew not to do it without asking now. He was pulling in $5K, $10K, $25K per license. He was putting together a media tour, but he didn't want me to do it until there was something we could be promoting, ideally preorders for a book that I would someday have time to write.

The comments on YouTube, Facebook, and Twitter instantly switched from a small, friendly, supportive community to a selection of the loudest, most over-the-top opinions one could imagine. I was a traitor to my species. I was ultra-fuckable. I was a space alien. I was an ultra-fuckable space alien. And so on.

This is going to sound awful, but the breakup with Maya was great timing. That night I went with Andy to visit New York Carl. Everyone there recognized us, so we again got to skip the line and take selfies with people. But now, people were taking photographs of me even when they weren't in them. I felt a bit self-conscious, like I should have been more careful with my makeup that morning (I was a person who never left the house without makeup). But Andy didn't have any problem setting up and filming a bunch of close-ups of the crowd and of Carl for the archive while I kept the crowd distracted.

I had an inkling that we weren't going to have unencumbered access to the Carls for much longer, so I wanted to get as much footage in the can as we could get.

"Are you OK?" Andy asked when we got back to his place to import the footage.

"Huh?"

"Well, I can't help but notice that you didn't go home, and also that you don't seem to be talking to Maya?"

"Oh, yeah, we broke up." These words came out like old, warm soda. "I'm getting a new place on 23rd."

He looked at me like he was surprised, and then like he wasn't.

"And then you just went out with me to film Carl and take like a thousand selfies with strangers and you were just fine?"

"I mean, I guess?" I was keeping my brain from going to the bad place.

"Does it get exhausting?"

For a second I thought maybe he meant "Does being a terrible person get exhausting?" so I was scared to answer.

But he continued. "It just looks like a lot, I don't think I could do it. Person after person, saying the same things, doing the same things. Making jokes, always on, always playing the part."

"Huh, no, honestly it doesn't. It feels natural, fun, like playing a sport you're good at."

"Well, you're very good at it. And you're getting better."

He did something with his computer for a little while and then said, "I'm sorry about you and Maya. Let me know when you want to talk about it."

I remembered again why I liked Andy.

"Thanks, Andy. I don't know. Once life gets a certain amount of weird, more weird just doesn't really matter."

He chuckled and we started watching ourselves on his screen.

I slept at Andy's that night, but that wasn't going to last. I could tell he knew that we weren't going to hook up, and he didn't make any sign that he wanted to, but eventually things would get weird, and then I'd lose my best friend. Weird. Andy Skampt, my best friend.

I needed to get my stuff out of Maya's place. She still worked the nine-to-five, so Robin and I supervised the movers who took my stuff from the old place to the new one on 23rd and I didn't have to see her. Robin and Jennifer Putnam had both strongly advised me not to do any extra media. They wanted people to come to the places I controlled, my Facebook, Twitter, YouTube, Instagram. Those things I could do without traveling around to satellite studios or setting up Skype. They assured me constant posting would help build my following, and also that it would make media outlets even hungrier to talk to me. They were setting stuff up but wanted to wait until it was full-length feature articles in fancy magazines, not just quick interviews focusing on Carl.

My new apartment was not all that impressive unless you live in the bizarro world of Manhattan real estate. You can basically summarize Manhattan living by the number of doors you have. If you only have one door, the one that leads into your apartment, that's not ideal, but at least you're not living in Jersey. Two doors, though—the front door *and* the bathroom door—that's *luxury*!

The apartment Robin got for me had *six doors*. And that's if you don't count closets, which brought the total up to eight! There was the front door, one for each of the two bedrooms, one for each of the two bathrooms, and one to the balcony off the master bedroom. The master had two separate walk-in closets that, together, were about the same size as Maya's bedroom. If Robin had showed it to me, I never would have allowed him to get it for me, which is why he didn't show me. He just signed the lease for whatever ungodly sum they charged and sent me the address. It was way too much space, but the real reason I couldn't say no was the balcony. If I leaned out over the railing, I could look directly down onto Carl across the street. That gave us an amazing opportunity to keep tabs on pretty much everyone who walked by.

So, could I afford a two-bedroom apartment in the Flatiron District with a twenty-four-hour doorman, free valet parking, and an on-site gym? Well . . . kinda . . .

Here's a thing about sudden success: You know it's happened, you see all the numbers on all the contracts, but you don't actually have any money. The YouTube analytics page was very specific. The first video had netted Andy and me more than $50,000 each. The second video was already climbing to match that after only a couple of days. Appearances and licenses had netted us both another six figures. The numbers were going up every day that Carl stayed in the news, which, we were betting, would be for quite a while.

But none of the checks had actually been delivered or (more properly) direct-deposited. It had only been a couple of weeks, and apparently companies pay their bills on very weird schedules, and the contracts have phrases like "up to six to eight weeks after the first full moon and/or when Saturn is in Virgo but only if we feel like it." So, another perk of having an agent, Jennifer Putnam just paid for the apartment with the understanding that the difference would be withheld from some future check. Somehow, the way she told me that it was no big deal and I absolutely shouldn't even consider it a favor made it very clear to me that I owed her one. Another one.

I'm fairly sure that the night I moved in was the first night of my life that I slept by myself. Not, like, in a bed by myself but in a home by myself. Somehow, despite the doorman and the locks and the extremely nice neighborhood, I found myself frightened. I had gone from a tiny apartment packed with the detritus of two cohabitating young women to a bunch of boxes stacked up in the giant living/dining room and a big, empty, open bedroom.

The traffic on 23rd was blocked off and the windows were new and double-paned, so it was eerily silent as well. I've always loved the sounds of the city: honking, engines, jackhammers, raised voices. I wasn't raised with it, but the first night I spent in a real city I knew I was going to love it. That clattering of humanity mixed in all its randomness was as relaxing to me as crickets chirping beside a rushing brook.

The emptiness and silence of this apartment compounded my knowledge that I was, for the first time in my life, the only person sleeping in my home. This forced me to realize that, while I wanted to be fiercely myself, I also wanted someone around to see me do it.

Well, I had my phone at least, and the literally hundreds of thousands of people who wanted to say something about me. I Instagrammed out my new window, letting everyone know I had moved in just above Carl. I figured it was OK for people to know where I lived—I had a doorman now. I thought maybe I should call my parents, or maybe my brother. He'd lived on his own for a while; maybe he had some advice. Then I lay down in my bed and started scrolling through Twitter. I hadn't even washed my sheets. I'd just thrown them in a bag with the rest of my stuff and slapped them right back on the mattress when the movers got everything up here. I rolled onto my side, checking my mentions. A few famous internet creators had just started following me. Then my cheek hit a bit of my pillowcase that smelled like Maya's grapefruity shampoo, and I cried into the silence until I fell asleep.

I was in the dream lobby. Everything was the same. The music, the desk, the robot, the walls, the floor. Except this time I was wondering if maybe I could make it last. Every time I had had this dream so far, it ended when I talked to the robot at the desk. So, instead, I walked past the robot to the door behind it.

I was surprised to find the door open, and that no one moved to stop me. It was an office, fancy and modern. Not like an internet start-up, no weird art or drum sets, but nice cubicles taking up the bulk of the space and conference rooms with frosted glass stacked against the far wall. I looked out the windows and found the area surrounding the office building littered with buildings of all eras. Huts, cottages, and windmills joined colonial homes and brownstones, but no other skyscrapers like the one I was in. The land rolled in hills, and many of the buildings were in architectural styles I didn't recognize.

I turned and walked up to one of the cubicles. A flat-screen monitor, keyboard, and mouse sat on the desk with no wires coming off it.

I sat on the chair and moved the mouse. The screen blinked on. There was one single icon on the pure white desktop, labeled "Game."

I clicked on it, and what appeared to be an image opened. It was a grid, six by four, and one of the blocks of the grid was red. I closed the image and opened it again.

I tried a number of keyboard shortcuts, but I couldn't make the computer do anything else besides open that one image. I inspected the desk carefully, picking up the keyboard and the mouse and looking under the desk and the chair, but nothing seemed out of the ordinary.

I went to another cubicle and repeated the same steps. The image, labeled "Game," was on every computer I opened. This was officially the most boring dream ever. But I kept at it, and on the sixth computer I opened, the image was different. Same grid, but now another block was filled, this time in blue. I went to the next desk, and it was the same, two blocks on the grid filled. I went back to the first desk, and the image showed both the red and the blue block now.

I sat back in the chair. There was a pattern here, but I wasn't seeing it. I did not think it odd that I was having what appeared to be conscious, lucid experiences while dreaming, and I never did feel that way while in the Dream. It seemed weird after I woke up, but never while I was there.

Anyway, I gave up. I decided that this dream was dumb and I was going to wake up and end it. The way I'd done that in the past was to talk to the robot in the lobby, so I headed back. Just as I approached the door, I turned around to give the room one last look, which was when I saw it.

The cubicles were laid out in a six-by-four grid.

From there, it was pretty simple. The grid showed the location of the next desk it wanted me to go to. The orientation was clear from the red-block desk, so I just went to the one represented by the blue block. Voilà, an orange block appeared, I went to the orange-block desk, then purple, then green, then pink, then red, and soon I had visited every desk but one.

So I sat down at it, thinking maybe something fantastic would happen. But it didn't. I just opened up the file, and instead of the grid was a phrase: "Fancy tulip man."

I pretty much ran to the front desk. Was I going to meet Carl? Was the robot at the desk going to give me some grand reward? Had I moved past the first test of the Freddie Mercury Sequence only to solve another test so quickly?

"Hello," it said as I approached.

"Hello, yes," I blurted. "I'm here to see Carl."

"Do you have a passcode?"

"Fancy tulip man."

And I woke up. Pretty furious. Of course it had been nothing— why would it be anything else? It was a dream. I was exhausted both physically and emotionally. My life had been turned inside out and upside down and then blended, spiced, spliced, and rebranded. Of course I was going to have weird dreams. And on top of all that, I was singing that damn song. Except now it had words: "Six, seven, six, four, five, F, zero, zero, four, D, six, one, seven, four."

I went to sleep singing the song, knowing it was absurd, but too tired and disappointed to care.

The next morning the federal government announced that they would be restricting the area around all the Carls in the US, citing a very vague, low-level public health concern. The entire block was to be restricted. The federal government was going to be paying all the businesses there in the meantime to compensate for their losses. Only people who lived on that block would be allowed in (which, hooray, included me).

They did not, however, confirm that Carl was an alien.

Nonetheless, this set off a huge round of speculation, and as I was the closest thing to a Carl expert, my following exploded every time I posted something even semi-sensical about the situation. I was calm and carefully laid hints that I knew more than everyone else, even though, at that point, I had pretty much spilled all the beans . . . all of my beloved and terrifying beans. A piece of advice: When you have beans like the ones I had, you should probably be more careful with them than I was.

But then, suddenly I got some more beans.

Robin came over that morning to try to help me understand why I needed to form a corporation. It was all taxes and liability and in- surance and mortgages, and I hated it all so much. I was humming under my breath while trying to not think about literally anything else when Robin stopped talking and started staring at me like my skin had turned purple.

"Where did you hear that song?" Robin asked. This was unusual for him. He seemed pretty driven to keep our relationship profes- sional, so I was a little taken aback that he'd ask a question that wasn't relevant to work.

"Honestly? I think I made it up during a dream. It's weird, right?"

If my skin was purple before, Robin was now looking at me like it was made of molten lava.

"Are you OK?"

"Can you tell me more about this dream?"

"I mean, yeah, it's weird. I've had a similar one four different times. I'm in the lobby of a weird fancy office building . . ."

And then he finished for me: ". . . and there's a robot receptionist, and there's a weird catchy song playing, the song you were just singing."

"How did you do that?"

"I've been having that dream for days, April. Every time I try to talk to the robot . . ."

And then I finished for him: ". . . it asks for a passcode, and if you don't have one, you wake up."

"If you don't have one?"

"Yeah!" I got excited. I knew more than Robin. "I solved a puzzle in the dream, and it gave me a passcode. I went to the receptionist, and I came away singing, 'Six, seven, six, four, five, F, zero, zero, four, D, six, one, seven, four.'"

"That is . . ." He didn't need to finish.

"Andy and Miranda!!" I shouted.

"What?"

"Andy was humming the song when we were in LA," I said as I was getting out my phone to call. It rang twice before he picked up.

"April," Andy answered.

"Hold on, I'm going to add Miranda to the call." I did.

"Hello?" Miranda asked.

"Hey, guys, have you ever had a dream where you're in the lobby of a fancy office building and there's a robot receptionist and it asks you for a passcode and there's catchy lounge music playing?"

It was very quiet.

"That's . . . ," Miranda said.

And then another few seconds passed before Andy said, "April . . ."

I kept not talking while they processed.

"What the fuck," Andy finally concluded.

"Both of you have had this dream."

"Yes," they simultaneously concluded.

There was a long silence while I waffled between giddy excitement and fear.

"Robin is on speaker with me, he has also had it. Have any of you explored outside of the reception area?"

They hadn't. I told them about the puzzle and the weird string of letters and numbers.

"I suddenly want to go to sleep very, very badly," said Andy.

"April, can you repeat the code you got again?" Miranda's voice came out tinny from the phone's speaker.

"Six, seven, six, four, five, F, zero, zero, four, D, six, one, seven, four." It had stuck in my head so thoroughly that I didn't even have to pause.

"It sounds like hex."

"OK, what's that?" Robin said.

"Hexadecimal. Like, our numbers are in base ten. Hexadecimal numbers are in base sixteen. In computer programming, every number up to sixteen is represented by a different symbol. So, it's like zero, one, two, three, four, five, six, seven, eight, nine, A, B, C, D, E, F."

"What?" I said.

"It's not super easy to explain," she responded. "It's one of the very basic ways computers talk. It's better because sixteen is two to the fourth power, and computers only talk in twos."

"Still not making sense, but we believe you," Andy said.

"OK, I guess the most important thing to ask is, is this just us?" I said.

"Who is most tired?" Robin asked.

"Probably April," Miranda said, at the same time Andy said, "April," at the same time I said, "Me?"

"Right, that was maybe a dumb question. April, can you go to sleep?"

"I mean, almost always."

"OK, that's your job. See what you can find out. The rest of us are going to do a bunch of research and see if we can figure out who else is having this dream and what it means. It all seems impossible."

"I agree it is not possible," said Miranda.

"And yet!" Andy added.

"OK, I'm going to go to bed! Good luck, everyone!"

When I was in middle and high school, I earned some extra money by finding people's lost pets. The town in Northern California where we lived had about fifty thousand people, most of whom lived within a few square miles of each other. It started when I was volunteering at the Humane Society. I would walk dogs, spray out cages, clean litter boxes, and "socialize" (play with) the animals. Pretty great work, but it didn't pay.

With fair regularity, a dog or cat would show up at the shelter and within the day someone would call asking after the pet. It was always a wonderful feeling, reuniting the pet with its owner. But we also got a lot of calls from people whose pets we did not have. I took this pretty hard. The employees at the shelter advised me to not get too involved, but I hated the idea that there was some beloved animal out there, crouched under a porch, maybe hurt or sick but almost definitely scared. And then there were the owners—often kids were involved. These people would do anything to get their pets back, including offering rewards.

Being a pet detective definitely sounds like a fake job, but I googled it and there were real people who did it. I emailed a bunch of them, saying I was doing a project for school, and interviewed them to find out more about their business. One woman was particularly candid, telling me that the real trick of being a professional pet detective was to get paid whether you found the pet or not, and definitely to get paid if you happened to find the pet after it had died. This, apparently, was fairly common. Pets get caught and stuck and starve, they stumble into traps meant for raccoons or foxes, and, more than anything, they get hit by cars.

I was fourteen, so I didn't get paid by the day or anything, but I did always call the number to tell them I was on the case and to confirm that I would get a reward whether I found the pet alive or dead.

For the most part, this is extremely boring work. You learn as much as you can about the pet, its habits, and its fears, and then you walk up and down busy streets hoping to not find that the worst happened.

Most cases were boring, and the success of the occasional live-pet discovery was worth way more than the $200 rewards I'd get. Though, to be clear, the $200 rewards were a pretty big deal for me. But I had a few cases that were actually intriguing—cases with clues and odd characters and some legitimate human drama. It's very important to learn a good bit about the owners. A surprising number of lost pets are actually stolen pets, usually by a friend or family member, often as some kind of retribution.

One of my weirdest cases stretched on for months. I was 90 percent sure that Andrea Vander's Maine coon cat, Bitters, had just wandered off one day and found a different family. This happens occasionally with outdoor cats; they find someone they like better and just stop coming home. Andrea Vander was not a particularly lovely person, and if I were a cat, I probably also would have found a different home. But I'd knocked on every door within a half mile and found no sign of Bitters. I was at Vander's house one day, pretty much ready to give up the case, when some food was delivered by a young woman in her twenties.

I watched as Andrea Vander, with great care, counted out the exact change of her delivery order, leaving zero cents extra for a tip.

"That looks good," I said to Ms. Vander after the delivery driver had gone. "How often do you order from there?"

"Every day," she said.

The next day, I ordered some food from that restaurant. The same delivery driver showed up at my house, and I made her a deal. I wouldn't say or do anything at all if Bitters showed up at my front door in the next twenty-four hours. If that didn't happen, she could expect to see me asking questions around her neighborhood very soon.

"She's just so awful!" the woman whined.

"Shhhh . . . ," I advised her.

Now, look, I know this doesn't sound very high-stakes, but Bitters was home, I got my $200, and everyone was happy.

I tell you this story because, by the age of sixteen, I considered myself something of a talented detective. And at twenty-three, I figured I must be even better. I had solved and implemented the Freddie Mercury Sequence before anyone else even knew it existed. Of course, I did that with help, but that's part of what a good detective does. I was feeling pretty proud of myself.

So when I finally got my ass to sleep after an hour of tossing and turning, I was ready to take the Dream on headfirst. I started out by wandering through the parts of the office building I could explore, avoiding only the receptionist, who seemed to be good at waking you up.

The door to the puzzle room was one way out of the reception area, but there was maybe another: An elevator stood on the opposite wall. I hadn't considered it at first, but if I could go into the office, why not try that?

I pushed the down button and the elevator door opened immediately. It was a normal elevator, nothing special except the number of buttons. They climbed up both sides of the door, higher than I could reach. I thought about going up, but I'd already pushed down, so instead I punched the button for the ground floor. I had already looked out the window of the building onto the peculiar city; I wanted to see if maybe I could get into it.

The elevator opened into the cavernous lobby of a fancy office building. They all look different, but they all look the same. The floor was marble; the ceiling was thirty feet up. There were tables with flower arrangements, a big desk where security and check-in would go, art on the walls, and, in the center of the room, blown up double-sized, towering over the whole thing, was Carl.

Well, that was one mystery solved. Any chance that this was a somehow-unrelated impossible mystery was gone now.

What was conspicuously absent from the whole thing was people. Office building lobbies are central stations of human activity and movement. This place looked like it had been sucked out of reality and put into some kind of museum exhibit: "Here is an example of early twenty-first-century high-rise lobby design and decor. You can see the emphasis on stonework contrasted with meticulously maintained flower arrangements. The hard and the soft, the permanent and the ephemeral, but both costly, giving those who occupied the space a sense of high-class luxury."

In fact, I would later note that the Dream's entire landscape looked like some kind of diorama, constructed as a place to observe, not as one to occupy.

Anyhow, I overcame the desire to explore and instead moved through the giant room and then through the door. Outside was, again, a tremendous stillness, but an assault of conflicting styles. Directly across the street was an Arby's, but not, like, a city Arby's smashed into a row of retail storefronts. A free-standing normal-America Arby's surrounded by its parking lot. Next door to the Arby's, surrounded by a swath of knee-high grass, was a wooden church-looking building. No cross capped its steeple, but the slatted wood and the double doors centered on the front of the building made the sense that it was a house of worship clear.

None of these buildings alone looked weird; they were just dramatically out of each other's context, especially considering the massive marble lobby I had just walked out of. I turned around to look at the building. After a few years living in New York City, you look up less, but now I craned my neck up and found that as high as I could see, there was no end to the height of the building I had just exited. I kept leaning back to try to see farther. Suddenly I stumbled, and then lurched to the side, and then was awake.

My phone was ringing. It was Andy.

"Why did you wake me up, dick! I was out of the building. There's a whole city. There's an Arby's!"

"Yeah, I know. Look, it's not just us, and it's spreading. It's spreading fast."

CHAPTER TEN

The sequence you solved . . . they're calling them sequences . . . the one on the floor with the receptionist, that one's already been solved, but it's pretty cool that you did it on your own."

"What? Goddamn it, Andy, you have to explain things before talking." I was still groggy.

"The Dream, it's full of these weird riddles and puzzles and clues. Somehow we missed it, but there are dozens of communities online talking about it already. The one you solved was the first one that got solved—no one's sure who solved it first. It's weird because it's a dream and it took a while for people to realize they weren't the only one. But now people are out in the city solving these puzzles. There's already a wiki and a subreddit and a bunch of semiprivate chat rooms."

This hit me pretty hard. I mean, not that there was a subreddit, just the realization that I was behind. I had been ahead of the game for so long. The fact that the world knew things that I hadn't figured out . . . that I *should* have figured out! It was unpleasant for reasons that I, in the moment, did not understand.

"Hold on, I'm getting another call." It was Jennifer Putnam. I clicked over.

"Is this about the Dream?" I asked.

"It both is and is not," she said with absolutely no nonsense in her voice.

"I want to get on some shows today—can you talk to Robin about that? I'm also going to need to get debriefed on this Dream."

"Yes, I can make that happen. In the meantime, the president would like to talk to you."

After about ten seconds of silence I said, "The president of the United States?" just to clarify.

"That's the one. She is going to be calling you soon."

"Why?" I suddenly felt *calmer*, which was bizarre.

"I got a call from the White House asking for your phone number and that is 100 percent of what I know. I wish I had more. Best of luck, April. This is a pretty wonderful occasion. Expect a bottle of champagne from me."

"I'm more of a hard-lemonade kind of girl."

"Yes, well, maybe it'll be a chance to develop a taste for finer things. I'm going to clear your line so they can call you. Good-bye, April."

I switched lines back to Andy.

"Tell me everything you know about the Dream," I said. "Quickly."

"Your wish is—"

"QUICKLY!" I interrupted.

"Sheesh, April, OK. Some people have been having the Dream for as long as three days, but most people have only had it once. Miranda and I have been having it for four days, so I get the feeling that it started when we messed with Hollywood Carl. No one knows how it spread, but it starts out the same for everybody everywhere. You're in an office lobby, the same music is playing, the same robot receptionist. Everyone is compelled to ask the same question, though in different languages if they speak different languages, but if you don't have a passcode when you ask the question, you wake up with nothing.

"If you go to sleep right after waking up, you won't have the Dream again. But if you stay awake a while, you will have it again.

"Outside of the office building there are hundreds, if not thousands, of buildings. People are trying to catalogue them all, but it's complicated because the city is so fucking big. There are buildings of all different eras and styles, and at least some of them appear to have real-world analogues. The office building that the spawn point is in definitely doesn't. It's a massive building, over two hundred stories high—bigger than the Burj Khalifa.

"People are guessing that every building has at least one puzzle in it. And some of the puzzles are impossible unless you speak a certain language or know a lot about Shakespeare or the rules to some obscure Iranian sport.

"But if you solve a puzzle you get a passcode, and if you speak it to the receptionist in the building you get a string of letters and numbers that people think is hexadecimal, or hex.

"And like Miranda said, hex is a computer-programming thing. So you know how there are ten single digits, zero through nine, before we put the one in the tens' place and start over again?"

"Uhhh . . ." I said.

"Like, after nine, numbers become two digits long."

"Sure," I said, not entirely sure about my sureness.

"Well, computers don't like ten for some reason and, agh, Miranda should explain this, but basically, instead of going to two digits at ten, hex goes to two digits at sixteen. And the numbers after nine are letters . . . A, B, C, D, E, F. So, zero through fifteen would be zero through F. And then sixteen would be ten."

"Maybe?"

"Whatever, the point is that people think that the bits of information that are being spit out when people discover a passcode are hex code, and that if they're strung together correctly and inputted into the right computer, it will be a program and that program will do something or contain some information. At least, that's the idea."

"How many of these code chunks are there?"

"No idea. Hundreds, maybe thousands."

"Thousands?!" I said. "Thousands of passcodes? If you got one every night, that would be years!"

"Maybe, but people have already figured out a couple dozen of them, and they're sharing. One person—ThePurrletarian is their screen name—has figured out six of them all by themselves."

My heart jumped into my throat, but I didn't make any noise, so Andy just kept going. That screen name was . . . familiar.

"There's no way one person could do this alone. People are taking credit, of course, but there's already a Wikipedia page of discovered puzzles, their locations, and the code they spat out if they've been solved."

"Oh, that's pretty cool of them," I managed.

"Yep, not everybody is as stingy with information as we've been, it turns out."

My phone booped, causing my already-elevated heart rate to shoot higher.

"OK, thank you, Andy, I've got to go." I clicked over.

"Hello?" I said, praying that I had tapped the correct bit of glass on my phone's screen.

"Hold for the president," a female voice said. This was followed by about twenty-five excruciating seconds.

Finally, a little clicking noise, followed by a voice that was absolutely, without a doubt, that of the president of the United States: "April May, thank you for making yourself available so quickly."

"Of course, Madam President," I said.

"Oh, well done, you've got the protocol down." I could hear a smirk on her face. "I'm sorry this meeting couldn't be in person, but time is short for us right now. I'm going on TV in about ten minutes to talk about this whole thing, but I wanted to talk to you first."

"That's very cool," I said, unsure of what else to say.

"Well, I'm glad you think so." Her voice was concise, confident, and forceful. "First, I don't mean to scold you, but I feel it is necessary to say that I'm not 100 percent pleased with how you handled yourself this week."

That was alarming to hear.

"I'm very sorry, ma'am, what should I have done?" I asked, honestly not knowing.

"Well, as odd as this may sound, you should have contacted me."

"What?"

"It's a democracy, April. Our citizens have access to their representatives in government. That can sometimes be a difficult mandate to execute, but I have confidence that you could have gotten through to me fairly quickly. I would have been in your debt."

"For real?" I asked.

"For real," she replied dryly. "It can't be undone now, but in the future, if you are aware of an alien life-form, a message it has sent to the people of Earth, and are planning on taking actions based on that information, that would be a fantastic thing for the government of your country to be aware of before you take any such action. Indeed, if you have any other information, it would be appropriate to share it with me now." She said "appropriate" in a way that made me think that she also meant "legally required."

I stared out my window for a moment, trying to figure out if I did know anything else and coming to the conclusion that I was, suddenly and for the first time, pretty much on a level playing field with the entire rest of Earth. And then my phone booped. Another incoming call. My parents. I ignored them. "Um, I don't know anything that isn't currently public knowledge," I said, maybe lying just a tiny bit. I did know that I was the cause of the Dream since I had had it first, but others were guessing as much and, frankly, I didn't want to fess up to that.

"So you do not know anything about this Dream, how it works, or what it means?"

"I do not. It does not seem like a thing that should be able to work at all," I said.

She did not comment on that before continuing. "April, I believe you are a good person. I think you made some questionable decisions, but I've read a good bit of what you have written about the Carls and I think it is good. I appreciate you being a calm and level voice when you easily could have been dangerously inflammatory. That being said, if you discover anything else, I'm going to send you a phone number that you should call immediately. You appear to be at the center of this. I very much want us to be on the same team."

Somehow, that last phrase sounded simultaneously like a beautiful gift and a very real threat.

"Thank you, Madam President," I said, my voice shaking just slightly. "Can I ask you a question?"

"I can't guarantee an answer."

"Of course," I said. "It's just, is this possible? Is any of it possible? Are you . . ." I wanted to ask if she was afraid. If *I* should be afraid. Publicly, my mind was made up. I'd chosen a course and I would stick to it. But in the back of my brain, I also knew I had been infected by an impossible dream, and that most space alien movies ended with wars. But instead I just didn't say anything.

"April, I'm going to make you wait on my answer. You'll hear along with everyone else. I have to go now. I'd very much like to meet in person. Hopefully that can be arranged sometime soon." And then she hung up.

Andy, somewhat unsurprisingly, was still on the other line. I clicked over.

"DUUUUUUUUUUDE," I said.

"What just happened?" he said, his voice brimming with excitement and confusion.

"Not only did I just talk to the president, I think I just got scolded by the president like she was my middle school principal. I don't know why that seems weirder than hanging out with a space alien robot, but it does."

"What was she pissed about?"

"Oh, y'know, just the whole communicating with aliens and providing them with gifts on behalf of my country and my species and my planet instead of letting someone qualified and authorized make that call?"

"That makes a lot of sense now that you say it out loud. Are we going to prison?"

"Hah. No. But I got the feeling that, if we do this again, we will have some very powerful enemies."

"The most powerful," Andy shot back.

"I suppose that is not an exaggeration," I replied. "She said she was about to go on TV to give a speech about the Carls. I assume it's streaming somewhere." I popped open my laptop and, indeed, people were anticipating the speech, which had been announced about an hour earlier.

Andy and I stayed on the phone together until the speech began. And then we didn't hang up; we just sat there silently together, listening to the other person listening to the speech.

Her points were well constructed. First, she wanted to be clear that there was no danger. All health concerns had been eliminated and the Carls appeared to be completely nonthreatening. The Dream seemed to be a harmless call for people across this planet to work together. Carl's hand was still missing and the Magic Castle was cooperating. She then discussed a little bit of how they had eliminated other possibilities, ending with the kicker that the Carls weren't in fact standing on the sidewalk; they were hovering micrometers above it, completely immobile and unable to be moved by any amount of force applied to them. They had jackhammered under the one in Oakland. It remained there, hanging above the space where the sidewalk had been.

She pitched it as a wonderful moment to be alive, assuring us that the government was hard at work uncovering the mysteries of the Carls, and all of humanity would have to work together to solve the mysteries of the Dream. It was good. It was sudden for almost everyone, but not for me. It was this slow gradual feeling, like your dog dying a year after being diagnosed with cancer. I had a little bit come to terms with it. But still, then your dog dies, and your dog will never not be dead. It happened, it was official, the president of the United States had confirmed it, the scientists had been consulted: The Carls were aliens and we were not alone in the universe.

"Goddamn," Andy said afterward.

"Goddamn," I confirmed.

CHAPTER ELEVEN

OK, there's a lot to tell here. First, let's go back in time about six months. I was walking out of the bathroom and Maya was on my bed with her drawing tablet hooked up to her laptop. I peeked over her shoulder and said, "What are you working on, it looks adorable," as she slammed her laptop shut. "Whoa! Hah, I'm sorry, I didn't mean to peek."

"No, it's fine, I don't know. It's . . ."

This had never happened. Maya had always felt like an open book to me.

"Do you have . . . a secret?" I said, genuinely amused.

She looked at me, at first annoyed, and then I could see her getting excited.

"April . . ." A smile started eating away at her face. "I do."

And then suddenly, six months into our relationship, I discovered that my girlfriend had an *entire alternate life.*

As previously mentioned, Maya is an amazing illustrator. She does fantastic hand lettering, but she's also great at character design and her specialty is cats. Maya can draw thirty individual adorable cats in like fifteen minutes. The first time I saw one, I had no idea that the character design of the little fluff balls had been an ongoing process since she was in middle school. The final product was both elegant and adorable. It was unclear where their heads ended and their bodies began, and each managed to look distinct while clearly using the same visual language.

Sometime during college, before I knew her well, she meshed two of her hobbies (drawing adorable cats and criticizing late-capitalist financialization) into *The Purrletariat*, a web comic about anti-capitalist cats. It had gained a substantial following, and remarkably, through a combination of crowdfunding and T-shirt sales, it was generating enough revenue that she couldn't just stop doing it. But she also, for both professional and personal reasons, liked having *The Purrletariat* be a secret project. Creating content and not taking credit for it, or leveraging it to promote your other socials, is so anti-now, but it was how I used to be, and it was a quality I really loved (and love) about Maya.

Anyway, that's why I freaked out a bit when I heard the screen name ThePurrletarian. It probably wasn't Maya, but also maybe it was.

After Andy and I finished debriefing post-speech, I took out my phone to think about texting Maya. Of course, I didn't. I had tweet storms to outline and Facebook posts to write. Andy was working on a script, but I was sure I'd want to make a bunch of changes. Robin was texting me for yes/nos on interview requests, and while I managed all that, another call from my parents came in.

"Hey, guys." I knew from experience it would be both of them.

"Hi, April." My mom sounded worried on the speakerphone. "Based on when you're posting on Facebook, we are assuming that you never sleep. How are you holding up?"

"Um . . ." This was not something I had checked. "Fine, I guess. I . . . I just talked to the president."

"What?!" they both said, and then my dad added, "Honey, that's amazing. After her speech?"

"Before, actually, I was talking to her when you called me the first time."

"Well, usually we're frustrated when you don't pick up, but this was a good reason!" my mom said, right on the edge of a guilt trip. "What did you talk about?"

"We talked about the Dream, and about how maybe I should have acted a little less . . . carelessly, and she, I think, basically gave me her phone number."

"Wow!" my dad said.

"April, honey, do you think that maybe she was right about you—"

I didn't let her finish. "Yes, Mom, I do. I really do." I was feeling properly chastised. I had crossed a line and I was finally starting to understand that. "I'm sorry, it was a dumb risk. I wasn't thinking. We all got ourselves worked up and excited by the mystery of it all. I'm sorry if I freaked you guys out."

"We're just glad you're safe, April," my dad said.

"Yeah, I know, Dad. You guys are great. It's just all really exciting. I mean, the president! This is pretty weird!"

"April . . ." My mom's tone did not reflect my excitement. "Do you think maybe there are . . . good reasons to be worried about this Dream?"

That slowed me down. I mean, I am not a neuroscientist or whatever, but I was aware that a dream shouldn't be able to be passed from person to person. And people on the news were already talking about how the Carls had clearly altered the brains of humans, which was not a simple intrusion. It was significant. It was scary.

"Have you guys had it yet?" I said.

"No, not yet." There was a little apprehension in my dad's voice.

"It's not scary. If anything, it's fun. I think Carl is trying to give humanity a project to work on together. Maybe they're testing us to see if we can cooperate."

"How long until it's everyone?"

"I don't know, Mom, but it's not something you should be scared of."

"But they're changing our brains. They changed your brain already, right? Like, this Dream doesn't act like normal dreams. What if it changed you more than you think it did?"

That was indeed a scary thought, and hearing it from my mom rather than some internet troll made it seem a lot more real and a lot more worrying.

"I don't know, Mom. I know that if the Carls wanted to hurt us, they probably would have just hurt us. I honestly don't know more than you, but I . . ." I didn't want to say the thing I was about to say, but I had started, so I said it anyway: "I guess I just have faith."

"April," my dad said, "I know you have an awful lot of work to do. And I know that you never stop when something isn't done. That's something I've always respected about you. But take some breaks, honey. Call us. Spend time with Maya, just take a walk sometimes."

"Oh, Dad, Mom . . . Maya and I, we broke up."

And here it was all again, confronting the reality of my idiocy and uselessness. Just in that moment when my dad was being very kind, I had to remind him how screwed up I was.

"Oh, honey." My mom now. "We're so sorry. You don't have to talk about it now."

They knew me well enough that they wouldn't push for the story. They knew what had happened. Not the details, but that I'd cut a string if I ever felt it holding me back. They didn't like it, but they weren't going to fix it.

Eventually my dad said, "Tom's wedding is coming up, we'll have a nice long chat about all of this there. We'll make some time. It doesn't have to all be about him. We love you, April."

And then my mom added, "Call us!"

After that, I lowered myself into the news storm. The president hadn't mentioned me by name in her speech, but there was reference to my work. I was now inextricably linked to this story. Not because I discovered Carl, and not because I was the first person with a following to come out and say he was an alien, and not because I seemed to be the reason his hand fell off and ran across Hollywood, but because I was *all three of those things*.

Robin sent a car for me and I went to a satellite studio. From there, video of me sitting in front of the Manhattan skyline could be beamed to any show anywhere. A producer guy told me whom I'd be talking to and where, and a little earpiece was my only connection to those people. It was a step up in quality from Skyping in, and a step down from being there in the studio. This way, though, I could be on every news program that mattered on both coasts without leaving the room.

As this was the biggest story of all time, absolutely everyone was available to talk, and I got put on panels with them all, whether we had anything to do with each other or not. I talked to retired generals, physicists, sleep psychologists, neurologists, actors who had played aliens in movies, famous science communicators . . . Everyone wanted a piece of this story, and the news shows were building panels out of the biggest names, trying to one-up each other.

So yes, I talked to a lot of fancy and famous people that day and I felt surprisingly comfortable doing it. There was only one interview that was decidedly unpleasant.

News anchor lady: "Joining us today to talk about this remarkable news, April May, discoverer of New York Carl"—I waved—"and Peter Petrawicki, author of Amazon number one ranked *Invaded*"—he nodded.

"Peter, let's start with you. The news about Carl has been out for only a few hours, but you already have a book climbing the charts on Amazon. How did that happen?"

Petrawicki was beamed in from somewhere else via satellite, so he appeared in the little on-screen box next to mine. He looked exactly like every guy I had ever seen walking down Wall Street at lunch: midforties, dark hair, tan, white teeth, gray suit, light blue shirt open a couple of buttons, no tie. If he was going for any particular look, it was "exactly average." Of course, I couldn't see him then. The entire show was just voices in my ear.

"Well, just like April here, I felt it was becoming more and more clear that something odd was going on and the number of explanations that made sense was getting pretty thin. Obviously I don't talk about the president's statement in my book, though I'm already working on an updated version, but this seemed like the story of the century, and I felt like I had an obligation to bring some truth to the table."

"And, April, what do you think of Mr. Petrawicki's assertion that the Carls are potentially a threatening and invading force?"

You can see on the tape that this completely blindsided me. The correct response, now that I know my way around every potential interview environment, would have been to say, "I don't know anything about what Mr. Petrawicki is working on, but . . ." And then I would just say what I wanted to say. Instead, I reacted defensively.

"I think it's foolish." And then I paused to gather my thoughts a bit, but before I could continue . . .

"It's foolish? Is it foolish to consider the security of Americans when a far more powerful force suddenly appears in our cities? A force that has now gone underground and is roaming around who knows where? A force that has not just invaded our cities but now our minds? You think a little caution is foolish?"

If I was supposed to respond, I was not able to. Thankfully the anchor took over for me.

"But, Mr. Petrawicki, what do we know about the actual intentions of the Carls?"

"We know they are wearing armor, we know they came unannounced, we know they've violated international and domestic law, we know they have asked for radioactive materials, one of which was provided for them by our guest here."

I froze up. I wouldn't have been more still if he had been holding a gun to my head. I shot a quick "WHAT THE FUCK IS THIS GUY" glance at Robin, but he gestured to me to keep my eyes on the camera. Looking away makes you look weird.

Again, the anchor chimed in, "Yes, April. That does seem like it was quite an extraordinary step for a private citizen to take."

Thankfully, I was prepared for this question.

"Americium, the element we provided, is a common household product. We purchased it at the CVS just down the street from Hollywood Carl. It's radioactive, but so is the sun. I agree, we got too caught up in the fun, though. We should have presented our findings to the government to let them decide what to do with the information."

This was the talking point we'd decided to go with. If you were watching the interview (which I watched several times in later days), you would have seen Petrawicki with a look on his face like, "Yeah. Duh, you also should not have been an idiot, snotty, shitty little know-it-all brat."

The anchor took over again.

"The president seems to think the Carls pose no threat—"

I was waiting for the anchor to finish her question, but Peter just picked it right up.

"I don't mean to alarm anyone, but you and I know exactly as much about this as the president does. It serves her purposes for us to believe these things peaceful envoys. But why, in the face of this immense threat, would we assume the best? Wouldn't it make more sense to exercise even a little caution?"

"It seems to me," I said, "that if the Carls wanted to hurt us, they're powerful enough that they could just wipe us off the planet."

"So you would suggest, what, that we just lie down in the face of their great power and let them do what they will?"

"No . . . I mean . . . there is nothing threatening about what they've done. They're sculptures, they visited every place equally, and they're providing games to play in our dreams."

"Again, you have no idea. No one has any idea what their intent is, where they're from, what they want with us. But I can tell you that in the history of our planet, advanced civilizations meeting less-advanced cultures doesn't usually end well for the less-advanced people. No, that's not a tendency, it's a rule, a law. The president and every citizen in this country has an obligation to consider this threat."

"And what would that look like?" the anchor said.

"This is America. We have never been scared away from a fight. When we are pressured, that is when we are greatest. That is when we accomplish the most."

"That's all the time we have. After the break . . ." And that was it.

"Next interview, KCKC, radio interview in ten minutes," the producer said.

"Who the FUCK was that guy," I said, tearing my earpiece out.

To save you the scrambling Robin and I did to figure that out before the radio interview I had in ten minutes, here's what we discovered.

Just like me, Peter Petrawicki was in demand. His book, *Invaded*, was more like a blog post with cover art. It was twenty pages long, and he'd update it whenever there was new news. It was only available online, but it was the top-selling book on Amazon. It was three dollars. It was also the only book about Carl in the whole world, so that helped. He'd had guest columns in a few papers, mostly conservative-leaning. He'd been doing the news circuit since his book came out, which was the day after the Hollywood Carl video.

A few politicians had started to use his talking points—that the president was soft; that the Carls were a threat; that if giant robots could suddenly appear in every city in America (somehow the rest of the world was left out), what was to stop giant nuclear warheads from appearing . . . and exploding? Hide your kids, hide your wives! There's a space alien terrorist on 23rd!

Before Carl, Peter Petrawicki was a low-level conservative hawk "journalist," which I put in quotation marks because he seems to have never done a moment of research in his life. He was one of thousands of people who scraped by filtering reality through their ideology and then yelling really loudly at the internet. But his quick thinking (and writing—it took him two days to write the first draft of his manifesto) had made him an instant voice.

This might have stung all the more because I had a fairly similar trajectory. I inserted myself into this conversation when I didn't really belong there. I was pitching a particular ideology that fit for some people but didn't fit for others. It made perfect sense that a different perspective was going to feel more legitimate to people who were more afraid of otherness. A competing ideology was bound to pop up, I just didn't realize that at the time. And so I was legitimately shocked that people were paying attention to Peter Petrawicki. His perspective was ludicrous for a number of pretty obvious reasons. First, if the Carls wanted to destroy us, as we had both agreed, they could do it instantaneously. Just because someone has power over you doesn't mean they're going to use it to hurt you. People who believe that tend to either be:

1. People who have been victims of that sort of
   behavior, or . . .
2. People who, if given power, will use it to hurt you.

Peter struck me as the latter.

In the space of ten minutes of research, my vague understanding of "That Asshole" morphed into a fully fleshed-out mental map of the hairball of hate that was Peter Petrawicki. He was scaring people unnecessarily for his own personal gain, and from that fear was rising a fledgling hatred of Carl that lit a fire in me.

And he'd been on the news every single day since Hollywood Carl's hand popped off. While I'd been breaking up with my girlfriend, moving apartments, answering emails, and replying to YouTube comments, this guy had built an anti-Carl ideology and inspired a growing army of followers. I had even seen them in my comments, but I just ignored them like they were normal haters. But there's a big difference between an isolated troll and a movement. This was a movement, and I had completely misidentified, or willfully ignored, it.

In the days after Maya and I had broken up, I realized, I was just reacting to what was happening. I was trying to keep the jolt of constant attention alive, and who could blame me? There was a lot happening and I was overwhelmed. But I was also running out of fuel and I could feel it. I had solved my mystery, and the new one was far too big for any one person to tackle on their own. I thought maybe I was done. That maybe I could coast forever on what we'd done in two weeks. I was running out of that good ambition fuel, and maybe we had done all we could do.

Talking to the president was temporary fuel. The importance of the Hollywood Carl video was as well. Even knowing that I would go down in history as the person who made First Contact with an alien, that was somehow fleeting. Those things felt good, but they couldn't keep feeling as good as they had felt when they first happened. And as they receded, even in the moments immediately after they happened, I felt the hole they left behind growing inside of me.

But this was different. My annoyance became frustration, which became anger, which became hate, and hate is a long-burning fuel. Peter Petrawicki refilled my tank.

This was excellent for my short-term mental health and productivity but terrible for absolutely everything else.

Peter Petrawicki also gave me a bunch of strategies. I took his playbook and turned it right around on him, except I had a bigger audience and a better message.

As soon as I was home from the satellite studio, I had Andy come over to make a video pulling Peter Petrawicki apart at the seams. I read and watched everything of his that I could get my hands on. (I even shelled out the three bucks for his book.) Then I took his arguments one by one and shoved them right back down his throat to rejoin the fetid lump that spawned them. Another thing I learned from him was to take what his supporters were saying as if it was what he was saying. He was fanning flames that ought not be fanned, and highlighting the worst of his audience was an easy way to show it.

And, of course, I had no idea of this then, but by engaging with him, I was affirming him and his wackos. Their ideas were getting more exposure through my larger audience, and I (and, of course, every news channel out there) was confirming the idea that there were two sides you could be on. It was a huge mistake, and also great for views.

It was a pretty dramatic shift for my channels. We had been informative, sure, but mostly wholesome, endearing, witty, and pretty lovey-dovey with the whole thing. The brand was happy, excited, interested. Now, suddenly, we were adding snark and bite and, yeah, politics. We went from being a thing that everyone knew about to a thing that everyone could have an opinion on.

If Peter had opinions about why the Carls were here, then I had to have opinions as well. I started being more overt with my suspicions that they were watchers, sent to observe how humanity reacts to the knowledge that they are not alone. This fit in well with the Dream: They were giving us a task that none of us could accomplish on our own. If we could accomplish it, that would show that we were a global, cooperative species.

The consequences for failing the test that Carl had put to us could be dire or they could be nothing at all. The consequences for passing, though, might be the end of poverty and disease. Whoever made the Carls obviously had technology far superior to ours, and if they wanted to, they might offer us everything from interstellar travel to immortality.

Of course, I was pulling this all straight out of my ass. I didn't know if the Carls were dangerous or if my mind was being controlled. Who cared as long as my made-up shit wasn't as poisonous as Peter Petrawicki's made-up shit.

In the end, my brand was *me*, so whatever I said became something I believed.

CHAPTER TWELVE

And that's how I came to spend months of my life being exactly the thing I hated most in the world: a professional arguer, a pundit. Not because I was good at it or because I needed the money but because I was mad and scared and I didn't know what else to do. The Carls had become more than my life; they were my identity. I used to be good at TV because I didn't care and that irreverence was something people enjoyed. Now I had to be good because I did care.

And that's what I try to take away from this period. Whatever I did, I did it because I cared. I believed Carl was a force for good in the world, and humanity's opinion of Carl mattered because I came to honestly believe that the Carls were here to judge us. It didn't even matter if I was right, because that was the world I wanted to live in; that was the world that made sense to me. And even if I was wrong, I believed the world would be better off if we just acted as if I was right.

Every person who joined the loosely defined international (and mostly online) movement that Peter was part of (which of course became known as the Defenders) was a vote against humanity.

We just went through about three weeks of my life and it took almost half of this book. Now things are going to get a lot more spaced out. I hope you don't mind. I am not proud of these months, but more importantly, they were mostly boring and you know that we're still a ways away from July 13 and you're wondering when the heck we're going to get there. So I think I can give you a pretty good idea of what went down during those months with some vignettes and I'm going to start each one with a tweet I posted that day. Like this:

February 12

> **@AprilMaybeNot:** Pauly Shore is the hero we deserve.

I'm sitting in the studio/office that Andy and I built in my apartment's second bedroom. It's a complete mess except for the area behind my desk that Andy and I have made look respectable so that I can make videos easily. There's a semi-impressionist portrait of Carl on the wall behind me that we commissioned from a friend at SVA. One of the best things about having money is paying people to do good work.

Another good thing about money is that it makes problems go away. For example, Robin has brought us not only pizza but also a second phone for me, dedicated entirely to April May, the internet persona. We can pass it around so that Miranda or Andy or Robin can all tweet as me, while I can keep my personal phone dedicated to actually being a normal human.

The camera and lights are all facing me, but they're off. Robin is sitting in the swivel chair Andy usually sits in while we make videos.

We're both eating the pizza he's just brought up from Frank's downstairs. I've been trying to write the thing that would become *My Life with Carl* for about a week. So far it's terrible, but I need to get something out. Putnam said we were losing a lot more than money. She feared we were losing a stake in the world. "Every time someone says 'bestselling author Peter Petrawicki' without being able to say 'bestselling author April May' is a day that we lose credibility" were, I think, her exact words.

"Robin, is ghostwriting really OK?" I asked with a mouthful of pizza. I had gotten extremely comfortable with Robin.

Andy was in the living room, which we had set up as his in-apartment office, probably editing an episode of *Slainspotting* (yes, even after all this he was still making his dumb podcast with his teammate Jason).

"It's standard industry practice," he said, looking a little uncomfortable.

"Look, Robin," I said, turning to him, "I like you. I think you're smart. I need you to be helpful and useful to me and that is going to require you to be honest. I appreciate you not outright lying like Putnam does, but I need you to be totally straight with me whenever possible."

He looked even more uncomfortable. "Jennifer has not been lying to you."

"Oh, really, what about when she told me that no one thinks ghostwriting is skeezy anymore. I didn't even know what ghostwriting was, but when she explained it to me, *I* thought it was skeezy, so obviously someone does."

"She's trying to make you feel better about the easiest and best path forward."

"Do you think having someone else write a book and then putting my name on it is the best path forward?" Traffic was still closed on 23rd, so it was eerily quiet.

"It is certainly a path, but to me it does not seem like the kind of thing April May would do."

"Oh god, even my friends think of me as two different people."

He blushed a bit there, which I didn't get at the time. "It's how you talk about yourself, it's hard not to pick up the habit." He smiled.

I was still April May, the snarky BFA grad, but that's not who I wanted the world to see. That wasn't the person who would establish First Contact with an alien race. So I was also April May, the surprising, quirky, unassuming, but passionately intelligent speaker for the Carls.

"So you don't think I should have it ghostwritten."

"It does not seem like the sort of thing April May would do," he repeated.

"UGH! I *completely* agree with you and it is *so* annoying. How long are books? How much do the NaNoWriMo people write?"

"I'll look it up." He started to get out his laptop.

"Fifty thousand," Andy shouted from the living room without missing a beat.

I turned back to Robin with a smirk. "Always use all the tools at your disposal. So that means I only need to write one word fifty thousand times. I mean, not the same word over and over. How many words are in the average tweet? Like twenty? So that's just like twenty-five hundred tweets. I can tweet twenty-five hundred times. Oh god, I probably have. Can we just publish a book of my tweets?"

"No, but there are degrees of doing this on your own. You don't have to sit in here by yourself for a month straight doing nothing but writing. I think what we need to do is get you a great editor, someone who has worked on books like these. If they end up writing a significant part of the book, you can credit them as a coauthor because that's the sort of thing April May would do." He smiled at me.

Robin had a narrow frame and bright, bright blue eyes. He didn't smile much, so when it happened it felt good.

I leaned toward him a bit. "I'm glad you think so highly of me."

He leaned away, pulling his laptop onto his lap. "I'll email

Jennifer about getting you some meetings with editors. You'll have your pick, I think."

I watched his hands move over his keyboard and thought to myself, *We should put him in videos more.*

February 19

> **@AprilMaybeNot:** What do you think is the best profession for your spouse to have?

> **@AprilMaybeNot:** Everyone is saying "Masseuse!" or "Doctor!" But I think it's "Political Pundit" because that way you can shake them awake tomorrow morning and tell them that you're going to divorce them if they don't quit their terrible job that is destroying America.

> **@AprilMaybeNot:** And yes, I am aware that I am a political pundit.

I'm sitting in a Pret A Manger in midtown. Because of the constant stress of being April May, I have forgotten what sleeping a full night is like and I am now a huge fan of coffee. I usually get an Americano with two shots, no room for cream. But I dump sugar in it because it makes it taste like hot chocolate.

At the table with me are Robin and Sylvia Stone, who is the second editor we've met with. The first guy was sure he knew exactly what I wanted to do with my book and got frustrated when I disagreed with him. I hated the meeting so much I pretended like I had diarrhea to get out of it. Sylvia, in her midthirties, dressed in a black silk button-down and jeans, with dark glasses around her gray eyes, was fitting my image of whom I wanted to work with a lot better.

"You've got two big problems with this story," Sylvia was saying. "First, it's too big. The whole world is in it, and people will be looking to you for a full story. You can't just crank out some piece of slop because the whole world will want to read it. There's an obligation, and that can be a lot of weight."

Robin looked at me. I nodded, knowing that this was at least part of the problem I had been having.

"Second, it's not over. You're in the middle right now. If the Dream had never happened, there would be a clear narrative arc of this thing. It would end in some mystery, but in an appropriate amount of resolved mystery. Instead, there are millions of people working hard every day trying to solve the puzzles in the Dream and more of them are indeed getting solved every day. We can't even endeavor to tell the whole story because we're in the middle of it."

"OK, I think you've put your fingers on at least two of the many problems I have," I said to her. "That doesn't necessarily help me, though."

"You have to define a timeline and you have to decide what you want to get across. What are your goals with the book? What do you want everyone to think when they finish it? Do you want them to understand you? Do you want them to understand your story?"

"Honestly I just want them to come away feeling like this is an opportunity for humanity and that the Carls are a good thing, not some alien nightmare."

"Oh, that's really good, actually. Say that again but more."

"Huh?"

"Oh, sorry, I . . ." She looked a little flustered. "I was editing you. I'm sorry, it's a habit. I just mean, tell me more about that idea."

I laughed. "That's pretty great, actually. That was a good note.

I'm honestly worried, because I think we're just starting to get used to the impact that the social internet is having on us culturally and emotionally and socially. It wasn't exactly bringing us together before this, right? But now I'm worried we have this whole other massive change to get used to. If we keep driving wedges, if we keep getting more and more scared . . ." I trailed off because I didn't actually know what that would mean; I just knew it would be bad. "It's like when winter comes and it sucks outside and the sun starts going down at 4:30 and you can look at that and get pissed and sad and grumpy. Or you can invite some friends over and make hot chocolate and share blankets and light candles and tell dumb high school stories. Both of those are natural ways to respond to it getting fucking gross outside, both fit really well with winter, but one is great and one sucks. It's like that, except with space aliens instead of winter.

"Did I take your note well?" I asked, finally taking a breath.

"April, I want to help you write this book. And the good news is that a manifesto is probably the easiest book for you to write. You can put in moments of your story, but more than anything you're making an argument. That's a very traditional format for a book, and one that does not have to be long. You talk to experts, who will all take your calls. You quote them, you build an argument, and you publish the book. I could write the outline for that book this afternoon. Probably faster if you helped me."

Robin had said this lady was no-nonsense. She had bylines in every major newspaper and magazine in the world and had several books as well, the most popular of which I had downloaded on Audible and listened to a bit of, called *Luck Be a Liar*. It was about how people are fooled by imagined or insignificant patterns into believing things that are very wrong. I liked it.

"OK, let's do it," I said.

"OK," Sylvia replied, "your place or mine?"

"Why not right here? Let's build an outline," I said, not really knowing what that meant.

Robin said nothing. I think he was terrified of showing me how pleased he was because he thought maybe I'd notice and change my mind just to spite him.

In an hour's time, we had built a book. It wasn't written, but it was constructed. It had an introduction in which I talked a bit about me, but other than that, the chapters were basically arguments against being afraid of the Carls and that was that. Easy! I took the outline home that night and I fleshed out some of the sections. Sylvia sent them back to me with some comments and ideas for whom we could talk to to get quotes and more robust backing for my ideas.

March 10

@TheCADDY95: April May is pretty cute, but she completely ruins it by being so full of herself.

@AprilMaybeNot: I mean, definitionally though, what else am I supposed to be full of? It's just me in here. Well, me and an embarrassing number of Doritos.

I've been so stressed that I injured myself. I'm twenty-three years old and my back has flipped out, maybe from sleeping weird, maybe from staying up late working on the final revisions of the book, maybe from stress. Let's be honest, it's from stress. I've been interviewed for TV, radio, magazines, and newspapers for two months straight. First I was telling my own story, then I was defending Carl, but before long, I was defending the president, the Constitution, and freedom of speech. Robin had hired tutors specializing in press relations, government, and international law to try to make it sound like I knew WTF I was talking about.

The scary part was that I had started to actually know WTF I was talking about. And I passionately believed it.

Robin also booked me this appointment at a day spa. Just some alone time to get my whole body rubbed by a stranger, get my toes fancied up, and maybe come out of it feeling a bit more like a human. The people at the place were all deferential and nice. They knew who I was and they would have been happy to talk, but they also knew when a client didn't want to and, honestly, I didn't want to.

This is going to sound weird, but, like, it was nice to just have someone touch me. Flirting with Robin was like flirting with a statue. He kept it so professional that we didn't even hug. Sometimes I'd lie in my bed at night and fantasize about someone *lying on top of me*. I just wanted to feel another human. I'd been so cooped up working on the book, staring at it, talking to Sylvia about it. It was like my body had stopped existing.

Anyway, I came out of the massage feeling slightly refreshed. The silent time was a good opportunity to put myself in check and make sure that I was working on all the things I wanted to be working on—that the not sleeping and stress were worth it. I thanked the ladies in the lobby as I left and they looked a little nervous, which I just put down to them not quite knowing how to behave around April May.

It became apparent that it was more than this when a woman came out of the back, having finished her spa day as well. She was in her fifties, she looked as pampered and primped as could be, and she was using that voice that some rich people in New York use that says, "I'm only talking to one person, but I would nonetheless like everyone in the world to hear me."

". . . and her nerve! She gets on with Rachel Carver and thinks she can go toe-to-toe on international relations. She's a *child*! It would be funny if it weren't so disgusting." She was accompanied by the massage therapist who had been working on her.

Hah, that's funny, I thought. *I was on the Rachel Carver show like three days ago.*

Everyone in the room knew what was going on way before I did. Everyone wanted to stop it; no one could. Her therapist tried to change the subject rapidly, glancing in my direction. "I really hope your IT band is feeling better, ma'am, it really seemed to loosen during the session."

"Yes, well, it's probably all of this drama. I just hate that that thing is in my city and there's nothing I can do about it. And people like that child—" And that's when she saw me. She immediately went silent, which was the moment I *finally* realized that she'd been talking about me.

"Well, let's just get you checked out so you can be on your way," the therapist said to her.

Robin had already paid for me, so I just turned around to leave the lobby, heading into the hallway and then the elevator, which blessedly arrived before the woman came out of the spa studio.

This dumb little moment was the first time I heard a stranger hating me in public. I knew then, for real, that thousands of people were having that exact conversation all over the world every moment of every day. Those people were real, and their thoughts were formed by overblown or just straight made-up stories about me that I could never adequately defend myself against.

People all over the world whom I had never met and would never meet hated me. *Hated.* And what they thought about me was completely out of my control.

At this point in my life I was tweeting about pretty much everything of note that happened to me. You can never stop creating content, both because it feels nice to have people listen and because you have to keep people's attention. And I had become accustomed to measuring my life in likes. I did not tweet about this encounter. I didn't even tell anyone about it. I just texted Robin to tell him how wonderful my spa day was and how great he was for thinking of me. I knew that if I stopped being mad at that lady (and at all her compatriots all over the world), I would have to experience some feelings that were much worse than rage.

So instead of talking to any of the people who could have helped me at that moment, I went home and read blog posts about how I was awful, ugly, and a traitor.

March 17

> **@PrimePatr1ot:** Sometimes I wonder how much people like April May are being paid to shill for the government.

> **@AprilMaybeNot:** They pay me in PopTarts. So. Many. PopTarts. Why did I sign this deal? I have a problematic number of PopTarts.

I'm leaning out over my balcony, watching, with Andy standing next to me. He's filming as they remove the tent from over Carl and reopen 23rd Street. Thank the lord, the noise will be back. Also, now I can truly look down on Carl and see him there beside the phone booths that, for some reason, are still taking up valuable street real estate in Manhattan.

My book is in the hands of a legion of copy editors trying to find every mistake and mislaid argument. There's nothing I can do to help it at the moment, which is wonderful because I'm fucking sick of the book. Also, we've got videos to make.

The army of experts who had been flowing into the tent they had erected around Carl had figured out more or less absolutely nothing in the past few weeks. Did they deliver uranium to Carl to see what happened? I don't know, but I'm pretty sure someone somewhere did, though it didn't seem that there was any immediate effect. If they did discover something new about Carl, they didn't tell anyone.

What we knew was that he wasn't standing on the sidewalk; he was hovering very slightly above it, latched onto space somehow. He was not at all thermally conductive; it seemed that the atoms of our world didn't even interact with the atoms of his body. He couldn't be moved or damaged. It was as if we could see him, but he was not actually in our space. Except for Hollywood Carl's hand, of course, which still hadn't been seen since it disappeared into that weird magicians' club.

Suddenly, Peter Petrawicki was there, down on the street, followed closely by a young guy holding a camera. Some police started harassing him—I couldn't hear what was happening. He looked indignant; he was gesturing to Carl, and to the building behind him. The police looked like they really, really didn't want to be in the video, but they also had instructions to not let anyone near Carl right now. Besides, the street hadn't been opened yet, so how did he even get in?

"How can anyone look at that guy and not immediately get that he is the worst thing that ever existed?" Andy said.

"There are people who say the same thing about me," I mused.

Peter posted the video later, and of course Andy and I watched it. It's mostly Peter saying, "What have you found out? Is it safe? You clearly thought there was enough danger to block off the street last month, what have you found out that makes it safe now? The people deserve to know!" That kind of thing. But then he cuts from the street to him sitting in a small but chic office.

"Eventually, a time comes when we must take some action. I am calling on the Defenders to begin collecting data from the Dream privately. I know that many of us would rather not interface with the Dream at all, that we wake ourselves up immediately to prevent it from further infecting our minds. But while hundreds of passcodes have been uncovered already, hundreds remain, and if someone . . . reckless is the first to decipher what the code means, that could put the entire planet at risk. We must decipher the code first. We can and must work together to play this game so that we can control the outcome, and I am linking to several spaces online that we have created for that purpose. We have information that several governments are already putting personnel to work to attempt to solve the code before anyone else, but I don't believe governments should be trusted with this either. While we can work together, when a code is deciphered, we must put that information in a central and secret location. I have created an encryption code and am including below instructions for how to use it. If you find a code, please send it to us, encrypted, and we will check it in the Dream for accuracy, and add it to our proprietary list of codes only Defenders will have access to. With the size, passion, and intelligence of this community, I believe we will be the first to understand what the next chapter in this story is, and I know we are the only ones I would trust with that information. Thank you, and stay safe."

"Thank you, and stay safe" was how he ended all his videos. Pretentious and subtly menacing . . . Peter Petrawicki all the way!

"We're going to have to do that now too," I said after we'd finished watching the video.

"Fuck that, we're above his shit." Andy was pretty pissed. "This is something the Carls want humanity to do together. Pitting us against each other, that's what Peter wants."

"No, he just made it impossible for people to feel like we're investigating some great caper as a species. I want that as much as you do, but I can't encourage people to post discovered codes publicly. If he has access to all the secret ones they have, plus all the public ones everyone else has, the Defenders really will decipher the code first, and be in control at that point."

"Maybe that's a race that it's OK to lose."

"Fuck that," I parroted back to him. "I'm not letting him win."

"Let's take some time to think at least. Assemble the brain trust."

So we did. We got Miranda and Robin on Skype and explained Petrawicki's plan.

"That is not good," Miranda said. "This is a genius move on PP's part. Not only does it give them a chance at winning, just framing it as a competition instead of a collaborative effort helps their cause. It slows everyone down and it pits us all against each other."

"Yeah, I get it, dude's a genius and he sucks. So what do we do?" I asked. No one said anything for a moment.

"Well, I have no idea," Robin said, which must have been physically painful for him. Not being able to help was his least favorite feeling in the world. "To be honest with you I don't even know very much about the Dream."

"Me either," I replied. Everyone looked surprised.

"Really?" Robin said.

"Yeah," Andy added, "I would have assumed you'd be all over it. Mysteries are your thing! You were a freaking pet detective."

"What?" Miranda and Robin said simultaneously.

"I'll tell you guys about it later. It's just . . . It's weird when there are billions of other people on the case. I just feel like my efforts are better spent elsewhere. The chances of me uncovering a unique passcode are, like, nil. So, Miranda, I guess you're the only one of us who spends much time in the Dream."

"Uhhhh . . . no, it stresses me out. Once I start on a puzzle, I can't stop, and then I stop having normal dreams. You still wake up rested, which doesn't make any sense and is probably impossible, but I don't like waking up frustrated. I just wake myself up and then go back to bed and sleep like a normal person for the rest of the night.

"I've felt like my time is better spent working on the output. The passcodes are spitting out hex code, which people have figured out can be compiled sensically into a vector image. That's, like, an image that is made up of math."

"Hah, yeah, Andy and I are VERY aware of what vector images are."

"Oh, right, designers!" Miranda said. "Well, anyway, the problem is that every time a new string of code gets added, the image changes shape completely. It's basically a big mess of interrelating math, so whenever anything is added, everything changes. No piece of code is at all useful without all of them."

"Do they know how many there are?" I asked, genuinely surprised that I didn't know any of this yet.

"Probably," Miranda said. "There's no way to know if it's actually following the image format perfectly, but if it is, then there are 4,096 total fragments of code. But, again, I don't know anything about the Dream itself, only about what it's been spitting out."

"OK, so none of us spend time in the Dream. Do we trust anyone who does?" Andy asked.

There was an active Wikipedia page of completed puzzles. So far more than five hundred had been solved. I kept tabs on it both because I wanted to see how it was going and because the list contained the names (or screen names) of people who had assisted in solving puzzles. If you sorted by that number, the top ten names or so had become fairly well-known among people who even peripherally followed the Dream. At number three, with sole or shared credit on eleven confirmed passcodes, was ThePurrletarian.

"Um, well," I said, "never mind."

"OK, that's not how sentences work," Andy said. "Once you say 'um, well,' you've committed yourself to finishing the thought."

"I think Maya may be ThePurrletarian."

"What?" Andy almost shouted.

Robin and Miranda were quiet. They knew *of* Maya, but they'd never met her.

"And why do you think this?" Andy asked.

"It's a secret?"

Robin broke in here from inside the computer. "Do you want to contact her, to ask what she thinks about this situation?"

"Is she online?" I asked.

"Um, yeah, should I go chat with her?" Andy was hesitant.

"Good god, she's my ex, not a hell demon. Just add her!" I half shouted in a loud monotone.

And then there she was. She was sitting on her bed in our apartment. Or, rather, my old apartment. I suddenly worried about how she was paying rent. Had I screwed her over? I hadn't even thought about it. Sweat leapt out of my skin.

She was leaning on the same big blue pillows with the same Hundertwasser print hanging up over her bed frame. It was just so . . . *the same*. I wondered if she had a new roommate. I wondered how things were going at her job. I wondered if she was bitter that Andy and I had gotten rich and she hadn't. I wondered if she hated me. Then I realized, of course she did, and wondered how much.

"Hello?" she said, looking around at all of us with a mix of concern, skepticism, and maybe a bit of resignation. It was the first time we'd talked since I left her apartment. She didn't look angry; she did look annoyed.

"Hey, um," I replied, unable to think of what else to say.

Andy took over for me: "Are you ThePurrletarian?"

"Goddamn it, April," she almost whispered. "What did you tell them?"

"That you might be ThePurrletarian, that's all." If weakening her secret identity was what she was going to be mad at me about, I felt like I was getting off *very* easy.

She looked resigned, not angry—at least, not at that moment.

"After . . ." And then she had to restart. "I got the Dream before almost anybody. The first night I had it, I solved four sequences. I knew it wasn't just a dream. It's . . . It's amazing in there."

I felt a little guilty that I had spent so little time exploring the Dream then. I spent all my time defending it, but also I avoided it.

"Are you going to introduce your friends?"

"Oh god! I'm sorry. Maya, this is Miranda, a materials scientist at UC Berkeley who we've been working with, and Robin, who is my assistant," I said.

Andy then cut in, "It's really good to see you, Maya."

"It's good to see you too."

If you want yet another example of what a shit I am, I hadn't even considered that I'd basically made Andy choose and that he had chosen me. Another wave of heat and sweat hit me. Luckily, Andy took over and told Maya the situation with Petrawicki.

"Oh, yeah, do not give into that rat-faced shit. Seriously, if every person got a nickel every time someone else thought something nasty about them, that guy would be the richest man on earth."

"Right, no one wants to give in, but we have to do something or he's in control."

"First of all, no, he's not. All the more complicated clues require collaboration now anyway. Yesterday there was a passcode uncovered and the key was to have someone who spoke a particular dialect of Hindi and had knowledge of their region's creation myth working with someone who knows abstract mathematics. I was following the whole saga and I still don't really understand. It was something about circles, both geometrical and mythological. It really shows an amazingly detailed understanding of human culture. And, for all their

strengths, the Defenders don't necessarily seem like the most culturally aware group of people."

There was a round of agreement.

"But more importantly," she continued, "we can fuck with them."

"Oh, I like the sound of that," I said.

"It takes time to check a passcode to ensure that it's real. You
can't just pop into the Dream, say the passcode, and get the data. You
have to go through the whole puzzle sequence, get the password in the
Dream, and then deliver it. Some of the puzzle sequences take hours."

"Oh, this is delicious," I said. "So we just have to set up a racket
of people who send Peter Petrawicki fake puzzle sequences and hex
codes hundreds of times a day."

"No," Maya said, "*you* don't need to do anything. People active
in the Dreamer community are already working on it. When I say
'we' can fuck with them, I mean us, not you. No offense, but I don't
think you could come up with a convincing fake puzzle sequence to
save your life."

I did not take offense. I saw myself as a leader of the community,
not a member. I had no idea what a messed-up perspective that was
at the time. "Oh, so, we don't have to do anything. This problem will
solve itself."

I saw frustration bloom on Maya's face. "No, April, this problem
will get solved by people who just happen to not be you."

Everyone got a little wide-eyed with that rebuke. Miranda blushed
bright red, while my guess is that my face went a shade whiter.

"Right," I stammered. "Of course. God, I'm sorry, that was a
dumb thing to say."

Maya just made that face where her lips disappeared in conster-
nation. I hadn't been called on my bullshit in a while. It was unpleasant but also a little refreshing.

"If you don't mind me asking," Robin said, "how did you get so
involved in the Dreamer community?"

"Well, the first night I solved the forty-ninth-, fiftieth-, and fifty-first-floor puzzle sequences. The forty-ninth floor, that's the floor you started on, was solved by hundreds of people by the time people realized that it was a shared experience. I had worked out those three and even a few outside the building when the first Dreamer communities started popping up. It made me a bit of a celebrity in those communities. It also didn't hurt that I had the connection to April." She nodded at me. "Now, I just like it, and the people are amazing, and from all over the world with different ideas and worldviews, all working together toward a common goal. It's a pretty beautiful thing. In fact, you all should spend a little time in the Dream. Just look up one of the solved sequences on Wikipedia and go through it. It might give you a better appreciation for the Carls. I know it has for me."

Then she sat there for a few moments with a thought on her face before saying, "And, yeah, I dunno, I probably wanted to stay involved in this stuff in some way. It wasn't as easy for me to leave it behind as I thought it would be."

I could tell she was looking right at me. I couldn't find any words to say, and I was worried that, if I said them, she would be able to hear the lump in my throat.

"Speaking of which, I didn't originally want to ask, but there's something you guys could maybe help us out with, if you wanted to."

That night, after mulling over Maya's proposal, I decided to take her advice and spend some time in the Dream. First, though, I read through some of the more recent puzzle sequences that had been worked out. The one I picked was one of the last ones ThePurrletarian had credited, though there were two other names I didn't recognize listed beside hers. They didn't uncover it simultaneously, I found; they did it together.

When I fell asleep and found myself in the Dream's lobby, I turned around and punched the down button on the elevator. The door opened, and I walked in and pushed the button for the lobby. I walked out, past the massive super-sized Carl, out the door, and onto the street. The Dream's streets were not on a grid like Manhattan; they would spur off in diagonals, coming together in three-way or five-way or even six-way intersections. Alleys shot off in surprising locations, and none of the architecture made any sense.

I looked back to see the office building where the spawn point was located—so high that, from my vantage point, it looked like it went on up forever, more than two hundred stories. It's weird to talk about these things as if they are fact since they were in a dream, but the fact that everyone experienced it in precisely the same way made it feel concrete. What is reality except for the things that people universally experience the same way? The Dream, in that sense, was very, very real.

Directly across from the exit of the office building was the Arby's. This magnificent dream location was the best branding Arby's had ever gotten; they'd become the unofficial fast food of Dreamers everywhere. Next door to that was the old wooden church and on the other side of the Arby's was a train car that was definitely not modern, but I couldn't tell you when it was from. Maybe the 1920s?

I headed straight across into the Arby's. It was empty, as everything in the Dream was. This sequence relied on a fairly detailed knowledge of how the equipment in an Arby's worked. Maya had worked at an Arby's in high school and was also one of the first people to try this sequence.

On the counter next to the cash register was a Chicken Bacon & Swiss sandwich, a large drink, and one of those folded apple-pie things. I went behind the counter and punched the corresponding buttons on the cash register to ring up the meal. The cash register tray opened, revealing a bunch of money that I would not have recognized but knew from reading about it online was from Pakistan.

The money, to my eyes, was useless, but a Pakistani Dreamer who Maya had found online determined that a number of letters were missing from the notes. Those missing letters spelled out the Urdu words for "floor" and "under." This remained a mystery for a couple of days until another Dreamer had the idea to bring a pry bar from a nearby auto shop and start prying up floor tiles. Just by the cash register, where you would stand if you were ordering, they pried up a tile where, underneath, a passkey glowed in bright blue letters: "Double picture day."

I didn't need the pry bar. If you knew which tile it was, you could just lift it with your fingernails. I had the passcode now, but I didn't see any reason to go and turn it in. That would just wake me up and give me a hex sequence that everyone had known for weeks. Instead, I started walking around the city. I recognized the styles of about one in every three buildings. There was a craftsman home, a brownstone, a bunch of churches—some old-looking, some very old-looking, some new. There was a strip mall and an Italian villa, and there were temples and mosques. I did my best not to go in a straight line. I got myself well and truly lost. I turned down alleys and wound through streets both narrow and broad. Eventually, if I did this all night, I would just wake up.

So that's what I did. I walked and walked and walked until I hit the end of the city. It was abrupt; it ended in grass, grass that went on forever. I walked out into the grass. There was no path, no trees, no hills, just an infinite flat plane of close-shorn grass. Like the most boring golf course of all time. I looked up at a noise in the sky. A jet plane was coming down for a landing. Was there an airport in the city? I didn't know where you'd put it, but I also didn't see why not. It was odd, the first moving object I'd seen. The eeriness of the Dream city was mostly its lack of occupants, but there was also no weather—no clouds, no discernible temperature, even. The sun was locked, unmoving in the blue sky. Nothing moved. Except that plane, I guess.

I set out into the grass and kept walking until I woke up. It was morning. My feet felt fine, I was well rested, and more than anything I wanted to talk to Maya.

The Dream, this creation of the Carls, it had been there for me to enjoy and I'd been ignoring it because I didn't feel like I was going to get anything useful done. So what, though? It was marvelous. Just working through what other people had done gave me a feeling that this was all actually worth it. When you get stuck fighting small battles, it makes you small. Hopping from cable news show to cable news show to discuss controversy after controversy had made me small. I thought only about the fight, not why I was fighting.

I opened Skype. Maya was online. I clicked on her name and then closed my computer and, instead, recorded a video about how we weren't going to let the Defenders' tactics close down the open discussion of the Dream, and that we were going to be working with some well-known Dreamers to create a tool that would help with just that effort.

The month of April, generally

> **@AprilMaybeNot:** What if there was a place designed for Dreamers by Dreamers to help solve through sequences, what would your top feature requests be?

By this time, there were millions of people active in the Dreamer community, and keeping track of not just the solved sequences but also which were unsolved or in progress was a lot of work. There were also hundreds of message boards where people went to seek out people who might have useful skills or information for in-progress sequences. Some of these sites were built on existing platforms like Reddit, Facebook, and Quora; others were hacked together from forum or chat software.

All these efforts were duplicated across literally hundreds of sites. Maya had the idea that I (and Andy) had two things no one else had:

1. The attention of far more Carl aficionados than anyone else in the world, as well as the credibility to go with it.
2. A huge pile of cash.

Of course, there were tons of developers and engineers and coders who were happy to try to cobble together something useful for the Dreamer community in their spare time. But as long as no one was getting paid, everyone wanted to be in charge. Maya had identified this problem, but Miranda (along with money from me and Andy) was the one who solved it.

Miranda kept telling me she was a shit coder, and honestly it really wasn't her area of expertise, but as we tossed around this idea, it was Miranda, over and over again, who would say, "No, that's not feasible" or "Yeah, that will take like fifteen minutes." She knew the difference between a hard problem and an easy one in a way that perplexed the rest of us. And when we brought on our first programmer, Andy's roommate, Jason, Miranda was the person who understood both the vision and the practicality enough that it made sense for her to be managing Jason.

And that's how we (and by "we," I mostly mean Maya, Miranda, and money) created the Som.

The Som was a centralized location for Dreamers to share their skills, their projects, their theories, their failures, and their successes. It started out just as a website, but Jason coded it so that it could easily be integrated with an app. We started poaching people from my old job.

Soon, a Som app could be set to notify a user instantaneously if someone was looking for their skill set or if a comment was added to a theory thread they were following. By the end of a month, the whole thing was so interconnected and bloated with features that it was impenetrable to the average user. But it wasn't for average users; it was for hard-core Dreamers, and it may have been a little glitchy, but it was better than any of the other cobbled-together solutions by a wide margin.

Plus, we just kept throwing money at it as the user base grew. Every time I mentioned the Som in a video, the influx bumped exponentially. And whenever that happened, we needed more help to keep the site running, not to mention just the cost of the servers. Luckily the cost didn't matter much. Robin and Jennifer Putnam had landed me a ridiculously large advance for my book and I got a quarter of it on signing.

As the Som got bigger (and it got bigger fast), Miranda just kept being in charge. She was managing Jason, and then she was managing Jason and a couple of app engineers, and then she was bossing around user interface people, data engineers, stack developers, database designers, graphic designers, mobile app developers, and even a couple of accountants. Miranda, it turned out, was not one to focus her expertise. She knew a lot about a LOT.

Whenever I hung out with Miranda, she never felt like a very confident person. It wasn't that she was shy; it was more that she was deferential. So the fact that she somehow wrangled this mess together, becoming the twenty-five-year-old CEO of a pretty large tech start-up, astounded me even more than it astounded her. When she was dealing with people who weren't me, she was friendly and thoughtful, but she was also firm and authoritative. Turns out, she could manage the fuck out of a project. And by working closely with Maya—who was extremely well respected in the Dreamer community and had a huge amount of insight into the kinds of tools they'd need—the Som became the most-used hub for Dreamers within weeks. Peter Petrawicki's pathetic plan to wrangle secret sequence solutions was also constantly messed with from within the Som. Whenever people were bored, they just went into a private chat and churned out a fake sequence solution.

By the end of March the Dream had taken over so much of our life that the Carls mostly dropped off our radar. But we rented office space across 23rd from Carl to keep an eye on him anyway. It was amazing how fast we spent money. We weren't really in danger of running out, but it also didn't take long to realize that "rich" is very relative. I maybe had $2 million in the bank at that point, and we burned through a full $300,000 of that in the first month of development. The money was officially going out faster than it was coming in, but everyone seemed confident that that would change as soon as the book came out, so that's most of what I was focusing on.

The good news was there was a solution to the money problems just on the horizon.

April 24

> **@AprilMaybeNot:** When did "makin' love" become
> "makin' love" because they talk about makin' love in lots
> of old songs and I don't think they're talking about fuckin'.

My brother has gotten me and two hundred of his closest friends to fly back to Northern California so we can watch him get married. I wanted to drag everyone with me, but the development of the Som has become more than a full-time job. Only Robin came with, as it is his job to make my life easy. He is good at it.

To tell you the truth, I resent this wedding. It's beautiful, picturesque, even. They've rented out a venue in the woods surrounded by old-growth trees. Tom has made a lot of money at his job, so it doesn't seem they spared much in the way of expenses. I've only hung out with his fiancée a couple of times, but she's lovely and I'm honestly very happy for them, but I have work to do back in New York.

I know that makes me sound like an ass, but I'll remind you that there was a space alien and it had infiltrated our dreams. In fact, you probably don't remember this, but this is the week when we found out a bit more about how the Dream worked and everyone freaked out.

I was one of the bridesmaids, so I had to be there for the rehearsal, and of course there was a rehearsal dinner and there were toasts and it was really touching but took a really long time. Halfway through the rehearsal, the news broke. The US government had found some people who hadn't been exposed to the Dream yet and begun to study them under quarantine. They had determined that the Dream did indeed pass from person to person exactly as if it were an airborne disease. More than that, the infection (they tried to not let this word be the word everyone used, but it was the one that fit best) was being spread by a physical thing. It could be filtered out. And the thing made measurable changes to people's brains; fMRI scans of people with and without the "infection" were distinctly different.

I was trying to be a good sister, so I didn't look at my phone for like three straight hours, and when I picked it up, all hell had broken loose. I went to the bathroom and stayed there for a full half hour during the rehearsal dinner trying to catch up.

Robin texted me, *I assume you've heard about this "infection" nonsense. Otherwise, do you need me to get you some laxative?*

I feel like I need to do something. People are looking to me to say something but I don't know how to frame it, I texted, still in the stall.

There were tons of tweets from Defenders like,

> **@BadApple24:** It seems that @AprilMaybeNot is
> suddenly, very loudly silent. Nothing to say about this
> news, eh girly?

And Peter Petrawicki himself tweeted:

> **@PeterPetrawicki:** Don't expect folks like aprilmaybenot
> to talk at all today, they don't want to engage with the
> reality that scientific study has concluded definitively
> that we have been infected with a mind-altering
> contagion.

This was a thing they did to draw you into the conversation they wanted to have. Which is not to say it didn't work. There was so much frustration and fear already that people were forcing themselves to stay awake so they could avoid the Dream, some taking amphetamines. But you can't not sleep. A couple of people had died . . . They had died of the fear that Peter Petrawicki was peddling.

> **Robin:** *April, your family is out here and they know what
> you're doing.*

Frustrated, I pocketed my phone and made my way out.

"I'm sorry," I said to Robin when I got out into the room. "You're right. Is there any way you could prep a couple of talking points on this for me for later?"

"Of course."

"You look fantastic in that suit, by the way."

"Thanks, it was not cheap."

"I'm not going to be able to stop thinking about this. It's such bad optics. Everyone is saying 'infection.' Maybe if I had been there a few hours ago, I could have molded that language a bit, maybe called it something more technical."

"April, your brother needs you."

"I know, thank you, Robin. You're a good friend." He blushed a bit. Then I went back to pretending I wasn't completely distracted and attended my brother's wedding with 25 percent of my mind, max.

May 19

> **@AprilMaybeNot:** "My Life with Carl: A Memoir and Manifesto" is in stores now! But who are we kidding, you're ordering it on Amazon just like me because we care more about saving two dollars than the continued prosperity of our country! http://amzn.to/2ElGwTL

I am standing in a Barnes & Noble; my book is on the shelf. The cover looks abstract, but it's actually a close-up shot of Carl's shoulder. The publisher wanted my face on the cover, they said it would sell more books, but I couldn't imagine having my face staring out from every airport bookstore in the world. I picked it up and opened it to a random page and read words I wrote that were now sitting on the shelf of a bookstore.

> It seems likely that the iodine was necessary for the creation of the Dream. Harvard biochemist Alan Reichert writes that iodine, of the chemicals asked for, "is the only one commonly used in biochemical processes." It's a necessary compound for the creation of multiple thyroid hormones. While we still do not understand the mechanism of

the Dream's spread, when I touched the iodine to Carl's hand, a wave of dizziness came over me. Soon after, everyone who had been exposed to me was also a carrier for the Dream. However the Dream is carried, it must have required raw materials that Carl had available, in either in the air or in the concrete as well as iodine.

Did you spot it? A friend of mine once told me that, no matter how much you proofread, the first time you open the final version of your book, you will find a typo on the very first page you look at. Ugh.

But I'd done it. I wrote a book. There it was. Hardcover, tens of thousands of words, and I wrote them all. Sylvia, of course, gave me a lot of nudges, but ultimately, it was a thing I made. It felt very different from any of the other art I had done. So much of me was in it, and now here I was on the shelf. People were going to read it and, I hoped, maybe some minds would be changed. Ultimately, almost everyone who read that book was already on my side, and the only thing it served to do was make people like me angrier.

June 1

> **@AprilMaybeNot:** I've only been on tour for like a week, but I already feel like maybe I've lived my entire life on this bus and everything else was an illusion.

I'm on a stage in Ann Arbor, Michigan, in front of two thousand people. They've all bought tickets to see me read from my book and then to have me, Andy, and Miranda answer questions after the show is over. The space is not a traditional auditorium; it's just a big carpeted box in a hotel that someone set up a couple thousand chairs in. The event sold out in less than a day. Every person had to buy a book—even if they already had one.

The tour has actually been a blast. The three of us and Robin (and occasionally others—Andy's dad, Jennifer Putnam, Sylvia Stone, publicists, marketers, etc.) are on a tour bus with bunks and a Nintendo and a shower and a refrigerator. It's close quarters, and occasionally we grate on each other, but mostly it's goofy, silly fun. Miranda and Andy actually have been spending a bunch of time together, which has given me time to write and hang out on the Som and yell at Defenders on Twitter.

We've been answering questions for about twenty minutes. Most of them are about the Dream or about what I think about the cult in New Mexico that will shoot at anyone who approaches for fear of contracting the Dream or this or that crackpot theory about the Carls. We have a deal: I handle crackpot theories, Andy handles people who make "jokes" about me and Miranda being cute, and Miranda handles anything technical. Miranda often resents the time we have taken away from her work on the Som, but she agreed to come as long as there was really good Wi-Fi on the bus. Throughout the entire tour I have wished that Maya was there with us to handle questions about the Dream.

Like this one:

"What's the weirdest thing that's ever happened to you in the Dream?" This was asked by a twelve-year-old-girl.

"Well, of course, it is all very strange," I said, stalling, "but it's such a silent and still place, the plane always catches me off guard."

"The what?" Miranda asked from the chair next to me.

"The plane. When you get to the edge of the city, it comes in to land somewhere. I've never found where it lands."

There was a shuffling in the room.

"Have you never been to the edge of the city?" I asked.

"No, I've been," Miranda said, "but there's no plane. Nothing in the city moves. Ever."

"Raise your hand"—Andy took charge—"if you've ever seen a plane flying in the Dream."

No hands went up.

"Oh," I said.

There was a fairly long silence and then I said, "Well, I guess that really is the weirdest thing that's happened to me in the Dream then!" There was some laughter and we moved on to the next question.

It was a guy in his thirties. He was wearing a sport coat and had neat, well-styled dark hair. His voice shook a little as he asked his question.

"Yes, this question is for April. How does it feel to be a traitor to your species?" Now there was some loud grumbling in the audience, and the guy spoke louder into the microphone because he was worried we couldn't hear him over other, nonamplified people talking. "How does it feel to know all the things you know and to go on pretending that there is no threat here? How does it feel to sell your planet and your country short for a few dollars"—here he held up my book—"and some notoriety?" His voice was trembling a bit and he sounded nervous. A few of his friends (whether they actually knew him or were just sympathetic Defenders who had come to cause a ruckus) whooped and shouted "Yeah" back in the audience.

"Look, we disagree." This kind of confrontation had happened before, and I'd gotten OK at dealing with it. "I am willing to accept that you have the best interests of the planet at heart, and it hurts me that you cannot accept the same thing about me. I have no evidence indicating that the Carls want anything other than to bring humanity close—"

"FUCK YOU, TRAITOR BITCH!" someone, not the guy at the mic, shouted from the back.

Suddenly the entire auditorium was involved. I looked to Andy and Miranda, who seemed startled and scared. People were standing up to look for the guy who had shouted. Things were officially out of hand. I was shouting into the mic, but no one could hear me—either that or they weren't paying attention. People were in the aisles now. I looked up from my chair and saw Andy in front of me. He grabbed my hand and pulled me up. I didn't want to leave the stage. If we couldn't calm the room down, this would be all over the news tomorrow: APRIL MAY BOOK TOUR CANCELED BY PROTESTERS or some such. Things were not calming down in the room, though. Andy and Miranda physically removed me from the stage.

June 6

> **@AprilMaybeNot:** You'd think that if space aliens built me from scratch to help them conquer a planet I would be coordinated enough not to close my boob in a door.
> And yet . . .

I'm back at my apartment on 23rd sitting in front of my computer. I know what I have to do, but I can't do it.

The book tour was canceled after the Ann Arbor debacle. Since they've existed, the Defenders have been harassing me online. Their conspiracy theories just kept piling up on each other until I was literally nonhuman. Maybe I was the anti-Christ, maybe I was a demon, maybe I was an alien. Dehumanization is usually a metaphor, but for a certain segment of folks, it had become reality. I was not human.

I'm going to be honest with you: It was horrifying. That moment in the hotel, when things got out of control, that was scary. But worse was diving down the rabbit hole of people's delusions and knowing that I was at the center of it, knowing that there were thousands of people in the world who would be happier if I died—they told me so all the time. I was constantly anxious, which in turn made me moody and distractible, and led to me catastrophizing. Publicly, I played it cooler than James Dean.

My address wasn't a secret. The NYPD had been called a dozen times by people claiming to be held hostage in my apartment, an online harassment strategy called "swatting." The hope was that the police would take the threat seriously and send the SWAT team to literally bust down my door. Lucky for me, Robin had, in his first week, called the NYPD to add me to a list of potential targets so I would never actually meet the SWAT team face-to-face. I did, of course, watch videos of it happening to people. It often happens to people who are livestreaming gameplay. It's terrifying. The door crashes down, everyone is yelling, these huge guys in body armor point assault rifles at everyone. One plus of the Dream was that if I stayed in it all night and didn't wake up, I'd stay out of my nightmares.

There were ten thousand moments in a hundred days when I wanted to hang it all up and hide. The Som had become mostly self-sustaining when Miranda added a premium subscription tier that cost five dollars per month. *My Life with Carl* had sold more than a million copies, and I made a ludicrous seven dollars for every one that sold, so, like, you do the math. I could retire now, and it would have been safer and nicer if I had. The only things that kept me in the game were:

1. I hated Peter Petrawicki and the Defenders, and I was going to do everything in my power to defeat their message with the truth, which I believed we were close to figuring out.
2. Giving up because people were harassing me would have been letting them win.
3. I was really, deeply, honestly, and truly infatuated with having people pay attention to me.

I did promise you honesty.

I've gotten off topic. I was sitting at my computer in the second bedroom in my apartment. No one was there. It was 8:03 P.M. I had, earlier that day, texted Maya to ask if we could Skype. She said sure, 8 P.M. would work for her. I had now been just sitting there with my mouse hovering over the button for three minutes.

Of course, she just went ahead and called me. I answered.

"Hey," I said, trying to sound normal.

"Hi, April. How are you?" It was so good to see her.

"I don't know, honestly it's very hard to check in with myself these days," I answered, way too truthfully.

She nodded with a mix of concern and frustration. "Yeah, that's . . . Yeah, that's not surprising. I'm really sorry about what happened in Ann Arbor, that sounds terrible."

"I'm getting used to it," I lied. The only thing I was getting used to was pretending like I was getting used to it. Since I knew Maya knew I was lying, and she knew I knew she knew, we just gave it a pass.

"Look," I continued, "something else weird happened in Ann Arbor and it's stuck with me. You know more than anyone else about the Dream, so I wanted to run it by you."

"Shoot."

"Every time I walk out of the city and into the grass, I can hear and see an airplane landing somewhere nearby. I can only track it until it goes below the buildings, but it's definitely landing. I mentioned that and everyone in the audience seemed to think I was making stuff up."

Maya sat there still as a stone, head crooked very, very slightly to the side, lips open, eyebrows just a little bit furrowed. There was something in her face that made me think that maybe she felt just a tiny bit like throwing up.

"Maya?"

"Nothing in the Dream moves unless you move it," she said.

"The receptionist moves," I said.

"Yes, OK, aside from that." She brushed it aside. "This is a well-known thing. There's fabric in the Dream . . . flags hanging on flag-poles, but the wind never stirs them. There are plants, but they never get bigger or lose their blossoms. This is a well-accepted and known thing. Nothing moves in the Dream."

"Well, it's happened to me every time I've been to the edge of the city. The airplane comes in and lands somewhere."

Maya groaned a long, low, quiet groan. She leaned her head forward and her locs fell over her face.

"Did I do something wrong?" I asked. Not defensive, but concerned. I was getting a feeling from Maya that I screwed something up.

"April." Maya looked up at the camera, and then her face flickered through like twenty different emotions. Frustration, fright, excitement, back to frustration, curiosity, excitement again, and then yet more frustration.

"Maya," I said, after it seemed like she needed to be snapped out of it.

She threw her arms up in frustration and then literally facepalmed.

"OH MY GOD WHAT?!" I was actually a little scared, like I had some kind of dream cancer or something.

"Nothing moves in the Dream, April. But weirder than that, worse than that, nothing is different for anyone in the Dream. The receptionist moves, and the receptionist speaks the native tongue of the dreamer, but other than that, everything is exactly the same. EXACTLY. People have counted the number of blades of grass in a house's front lawn. It's exactly the same for every person. Every person on earth.

"So when you say something happens in your dream that doesn't happen in anyone else's, it is a mixture of extremely exciting and extremely frustrating. Exciting, because you and I are going to work on this mystery, which may very well be the last puzzle the Dream has to offer, as we're quickly reaching 4,096. And frustrating because, good lord god almighty, I know that you are a good person, but the last thing you need is some other sign from heaven that you are special." She sighed.

That pissed me off a little. I put on a stern face and said, "Maya, I didn't ask for any of this."

Maya took a long moment to think before she said, "Is it OK with you if I retract my previous statement and we keep this conversation to business?"

"That might be a good call." I was annoyed that she was avoiding the fight, but I also didn't want to fight. "I'm just going to be someone with an unusual Dream problem, and you are the expert who needs to help me. Let's role-play!" I immediately regretted that joke. But Maya, courteously, laughed.

"OK, it frustrates me to no end that I cannot be in your brain to figure this out, but here's what you are going to do. The moment you spawn, you are going to make a beeline for the edge of the city. The fastest way to get there is probably to run straight down Broadway— that's the street that you exit the tower onto. The moment you see the plane, you're going to run—DO NOT WALK—toward it. If you see the plane, or if you're able to get on board, here's what you look for.

"First, anything unusual. You need to spend the next few hours and maybe the next few days learning everything you can about airplanes. Try to figure out what kind this is in your first go. Is it a Boeing? An Airbus? A CRJ? You can start broad and narrow it down doing research between sleeps. You might just have a sensation that something is a little off. Dream clues are often omissions, things that aren't there that should be, but you might not be able to spot them if you don't know what the plane's cockpit is supposed to look like.

"Second, any broken repetition. Usually repeating units in the Dream are identical, so anything that makes one thing different from others of the same type is probably important. If one of the seats isn't in its full, upright, and locked position, or one of the windows is single-paned, or one of the bathrooms smells weird. It could be anything.

"Third, don't try to do this on your own. Talk to me. I'll get together a few people I trust who might have relevant knowledge. I know that it can be really appealing to you to win independently, but there haven't been any puzzle sequences solved by a lone Dreamer for over a month now. These things are complicated, and it's clear to me that the Carls want us to be working together. Find what you can find and report back to me. I know what I'm doing."

I had been taking notes. I tabbed over back to Skype. "Any other sage wisdom, O Guru of the Dream?"

"Yeah," she said. "Don't mock me or I will leave you alone with this mystery and your failure to solve it will eat you alive."

"Right!" I said.

That entire conversation had the feeling of a pleasant stroll inches away from the edge of the Grand Canyon. It was really quite nice, wonderful, even. But it was impossible to forget that I was one stumble away from some serious unpleasantness.

"I will report back in the morning," I said.

"If you're lying to me about any of this, I will set fire to your apartment building," she said.

It was not particularly easy to fall asleep that night. Anticipation always negates grogginess, even if you've become the kind of person who is perpetually groggy like I had. But I kept reading a biography of Rodin that I'd been working my way through for the fourth time until I finally found myself in the lobby. I did just what Maya told me to, and soon I was running toward a plane that was headed for a landing somewhere in the city. After having done some preliminary research on airplanes, I could tell that this was a big plane but not a huge one. It didn't have two stories like a 747 or an A380, which meant it was, like, one of twenty-five different types of planes that all looked practically identical.

As I ran toward where I thought the plane was landing, I noticed that I wasn't getting tired, I could run at full speed for as long as I wanted to. I guess that's not weird for dreams, but being in control and aware the way I was in the Dream made it a thrill. So I let my feet carry me as fast as they could, which was about as fast as I could go in real life. Which is to say, not particularly fast.

After I lost sight of the plane, I had to make an educated guess at where it landed. It would keep moving after it touched down—planes did that—so I headed off roughly to where I thought it might end up.

I failed. I got lost, wandered the city for forty-five minutes, had a thought, and then slammed my head hard against a tree. On purpose, of course. There were a number of ways to wake up from the Dream, but the easiest was to try to hurt yourself. It never actually hurt and you found yourself lying in your bed.

Getting back into the Dream required that you spend some time awake. If you just went straight back to sleep, you'd have normal dreams all night.

So I groggily checked Twitter, read a couple of top posts on the Som, and then, judging it to have been long enough, went back to sleep.

This time, I headed toward the edge and then walked around a bit until I found what I was looking for: a building that was taller than most. It was maybe seven stories high, some dope Japanese pagoda. It was only a few blocks from the edge of the city, and it was higher than the vast majority of buildings around it. I scouted it and found that the stairs indeed led all the way to the top story.

So I went all the way to the edge of the city, saw the plane, and then ran like mad to the pagoda and up to the top floor. I still couldn't see where the plane was ending up, but I got a much better idea of some nearby landmarks. It dropped below the skyline in front of the main skyscraper, so it was in my part of town. An experienced Dreamer would have been able to walk straight there, but the city's winding, angled, narrow streets still baffled me.

But I got there.

To this day I don't know how it's supposed to have landed, but the plane was there, nestled into a little park that now looked to clearly have been made for a plane to fit into it. Apparently, it didn't need a runway. I mean, obviously these things don't have to make sense. That was emphasized as I approached the plane and some-thing felt really off about it. Maya said that that might happen, some-thing might be missing, except that this wasn't subtle. The plane's landing gear wasn't down. It was floating, its belly six or seven feet off the ground, the engines just a couple of feet. I could walk right up to them and touch them. Overcoming some seriously irrational fear, I put my hand into the jet engine and spun the giant fan inside.

It was painted to look like it was owned by an airline, but I didn't recognize the logo. It was a gray horizontal bar with a lighter gray circle overlapping it. Like a sun rising behind an ocean, except the circle was in front of the horizon. The image's intense simplicity made it look more like a country's flag than a corporate logo.

The fuselage was wrapped entirely in a honeycomb pattern with randomly placed red hexagons among the white ones.

I finished walking around the plane and could find nothing else of interest. It was way too big to even think of trying to get up to the door. I could reach up over my head and brush the underbelly of the plane while I walked under it, but the only places I thought might be a hatch I could open wouldn't open. There was no landing gear to climb up, so I tried to climb up the engine. I started on the front, but that definitely wasn't going to happen. The engine was twice as tall as me and there was nothing to hold on to.

I went around the back and started trying to climb. I'm not super in shape, but at least I'm light. I wedged myself between the engine's outer and inner levels and tried to shove myself up. I managed to wiggle my way up to the point that the engine was curving back toward the plane and was almost on top. Now I just had to get my hands spun around so I could get a grip on the engine's outer casing.

As I tried to do this, my butt slipped, and suddenly I was toppling a full fifteen feet, out of control and panicking. I woke up before I hit the ground.

The next day, when I debriefed Maya, she had a couple of suggestions for me, the biggest of which was that I wasn't going to solve this whole thing on my own and that I really needed to stop pretending that I was the only hero of this story. Her argument was that it wasn't just slowing us down; it was dangerous. The more I made it look like I was the center of this story, the more people who hated me would hate me.

My argument in reply was that those people were unstable douchebags, so we shouldn't listen to them. Maya's argument was that they were cray . . . so we should.

July 8

> **@AprilMaybeNot:** Today I met a literal billionaire and he gave me a prompt and thorough critique of the way I introduced myself to him, so . . . fuck that guy.

I just went to the fanciest party of my life. Miranda, Andy, Maya, and I had been interviewed in this documentary film a very famous guy made, and we got invited to the premiere. We got to buy extremely expensive clothes that made us feel (if not look) like movie stars. And then we walked down a literal red carpet while hundreds of professional photographers took pictures of us.

By luck, the movie premiere also fell on the day when the 4,096th (and, as far as we could tell, final) sequence in the Dream was solved, though we didn't know that at that point.

We watched the movie in a historic theater and then went to a bar that the movie people had rented out. It was dark and all the lights were red-tinted and the bar was giving away free Carl-themed cocktails.

Of course, as with any party like this, the invite list was narrow but deep. Lots of people who weren't involved in the movie but were nonetheless A-list celebrities had decided to come because it was a social event.

They all wanted to talk to me.

And that was great, except I really had to pee and there was a line for the bathroom that was about forty people long. You'd think they would have planned for this . . .

Robin and the rest of the gang had all set up shop at a booth, being significantly less in-demand for selfies than me. Miranda was wearing a dark green cotton affair. It was half knitted, half flat. The sleeves hugged her arms tightly all the way down to her wrists and the dress flared out above her waist and ended just above her knees.

Cute. Cute. Cute.

But Miranda's cute isn't my kind of cute, I reminded myself.

Anyway, I started to walk toward them before getting swept back into the glory and adoration, and the filmmaker introduced me to a literal billionaire.

The majority of my interactions that night were cool people telling me they thought I was cool, while I had three drinks, which put me very near to out-of-my-comfort-zone drunk, but not quite. There were a couple of other people at the party who mostly created for the internet—I could actually have conversations with them, and I did. The traditional Hollywood people just had absolutely nothing in common with me.

So, basically, it was extremely fun, but then time passed and eventually I was in my hotel room and it was over and I didn't know what to do. I was still drunk. I didn't want to go to sleep. The only thing that was waiting for me there was an unsolvable mystery plane that I'd been working on for almost a month. I'd explored every inch of the exterior of that plane. Maya's efforts to help within my limitations had been fruitless, but I wouldn't let her spread it any further than that. I didn't want to watch hotel TV. I tweeted about the party a bit, but it didn't give me anything. It all seemed deeply, deeply normal and that wasn't supposed to be me anymore.

My feel-good brain goodies had been going all night and now it was over. You'd think I'd peacefully cuddle into my fancy hotel bed and drop off to a delicious sleep, but no. This is what rock stars feel like after their concerts . . . This is why they have after-parties with groupies and cocaine. You want to keep the high going, but you can't rock forever, I guess.

I picked up the phone and dialed the operator.

"Can you connect me to Miranda Beckwith's room?"

"One moment please."

And then Miranda was on the phone.

I was well aware that hooking up with Miranda would make my life more complicated. I wasn't even that attracted to Miranda, but (and I realize I was coming at this from a position of extreme privilege) I was terrified of the aching loneliness of this cold hotel bed.

"Hello?"

"Hey, it's April, are you still up?"

"Yeah, I mean, why didn't you just text me?"

"I thought this was more fun, I had the *operator* connect us!"

"Oooooo," she mimicked my faux enthusiasm.

"So, I know you've been doing some research on what I've told you about the 767 Sequence." I'd shared this with Maya, Andy, Robin, and Miranda and sworn them all to secrecy. I figured Miranda would have some ideas by now. "I thought maybe you could come by my room and we could go over it before I go to sleep."

"Yeah! I've got a couple ideas!" She sounded absolutely oblivious to the fact that there might be an alternate interest in my asking her over, which worried me. She was obviously a little obsessed with me, but maybe that didn't go beyond "April May, Discoverer of New York Carl." Maybe I'd misread her. Maybe she was super straight or just not attracted to me!

This was the kind of fear-based excitement I was looking for.

"Cool, 606," I said.

"Oh, that's funny," she replied.

"What?"

"Nothing, I'll tell you when I get there."

I went to the bathroom and brushed my teeth. I had taken off my fancy dress, of course, but I freshened up my makeup just enough that hopefully she wouldn't notice I'd done it. Then I put on a tank top that was a little too small and sleeping pants that were a little too big. I looked at myself in the mirror and thought, *I'd do me,* and then she knocked. I swear I caught her checking me out for just a millisecond before her eyes hit mine.

She looked adorable as always in a gray T-shirt fabric skater dress. The waist of the dress was high, almost an empire waist. It was tight across her slight bust and then flowed out to only hint at the shape below.

This was the evening I needed.

We sat down next to each other on the bed and chatted a bit about the adventures of the evening before settling into Dream interpretation. "The hexagons? I have no idea, that could be encoding anything. It could be binary, it could be some numerical pattern, I don't know, April, I've worked through it a dozen ways and nothing makes any sense. But I do have a couple leads on the airline logo thing." Since the hotel room didn't have much in the way of chairs, we sat together on the end of the bed, our laptops in our laps.

"It felt familiar to me in the Dream," I said, "but nothing we've gone through has turned anything up."

"Well"—she lifted her laptop and leaned it gently on my upper thigh—"it probably looks familiar because it has the vague look of a flag. If you filled in the top, it would be a rectangle with a circle in it with bars of color. That's, like, flag design 101. But not only is this definitely not a flag of an existing country, it just seems more likely that it's representing something else."

"Why?" I tried to make as much eye contact with her huge brown eyes as I could.

"I don't know, it just doesn't seem like the Dream to be referring to a specific country so blatantly. Usually it's more abstract than that."

She seemed both excited and nervous.

"I think it's more likely that it's either symbolic or representative. The symbolic feel is like the sun in front of the ocean, which might mean something to someone, but it doesn't mean anything to me. But I've been thinking about it being representative. What if it's not a single symbol, but two? It could be one dot and one dash of Morse code. If it's just a dot and a dash, that would be just the letter *A*. But if it's broken into two letters, that's"—she checked her computer—"*E* . . . and *T*."

I lifted up my finger to her. "E.T.?"

She lifted her finger up to mine. "Phoooone hoooome."

We laughed and she blushed and I reached my hand out to grab hers as if that were a natural thing to do when sharing a laugh with a friend. Just a little extra physical touch. She tilted her head down and looked up at me, her smile gone, her face flushing red. I dropped her hand and put mine on her shoulder. As soon as my hand hit the fabric, she leaned into me with a kiss that was, ultimately, a bit of a mess.

I didn't mind.

About an hour later (sorry for leaving out the fun bits—Miranda is a pretty private person) we were under the covers together, Miranda nestled in the crook of my arm. It was a little sweaty and sticky, but it was too nice to mind.

"I am a fool for saying this, but I can't believe I just hooked up with April May."

"What do you mean?" I asked, a little worried.

"Oh, I know that we're friends and that you're just a normal person. I think I've actually gotten to know you pretty well"—there was a hint of pride in her voice—"but you're still April May, y'know. Champion of our alien visitors, initiator of First Contact, initiator of the Dream."

"We did that last one together," I reminded her.

"Oh, April, we're all just satellites in your orbit."

That made me very uncomfortable.

"That's ridiculous, Miranda," I said seriously. "You're a genius. I can't believe I just hooked up with Miranda Beckwith."

That made her smile a whole lot.

"OH! I almost forgot." She raised up on her elbow, holding the sheets to her chest in modesty. "The most likely of everything is another code. There's an alternate numerical system that this looks like, actually, in which bars represent fives and dots represent ones. So one bar and one dot would be six. It's the Mayan numerical system."

"Mayan?" I asked, feeling a little light-headed. Suddenly I felt like I was cheating, though whether on Maya or Miranda I couldn't tell.

"Yeah, like the Maya, the Mesoamerican civilization?"

"Weird . . . ," I managed. "That seems like the strongest lead."

"Absolutely." And then she fell into explaining the intricacies of Mayan numerals to me. If she noticed my weirdness, she made no sign. I tried my best to pay attention as I stroked her hair and she explained how the Maya represented numbers in the hundreds and thousands.

July 12

> **@AprilMaybeNot:** This thing is happening. I'll be on CNN at 8 PM eastern.

There it is, the date you've been dreading. Don't worry, me too. There's been enough written about this to fill a thousand books, so I'm going to focus on the things that were part of my direct experience. You'll notice I haven't talked about international relations or even much of what was happening in my own country during all this. This is my story because, otherwise, it would be a forty-five-hour-long Ken Burns documentary.

At this point in the story, every Dream Sequence has been solved except for a secret one that only I have access to. People are working their butts off to try to make the hex code into something useful, but it just spits out random squiggles that clearly mean nothing. A group of people think that we're missing a key, a bit of code that might just be a few characters long that unlocks the whole thing. No one knows where that key might be except for me and my team. People remain in the Dream, searching fruitlessly. The Defenders' attempts to control the sequences have failed miserably, but they're doing OK at controlling the narrative. Petrawicki has a knack for diminishing the credibility of everyone who publicly disagrees with him. Most of his feed is half-baked conspiracy theories about anyone who has indicated that maybe things aren't terrible. Whenever I watch his videos or see him on TV, he seems delighted.

And me, I'm miserable. I can't solve the 767 Sequence, but I also can't bring myself to share that it exists. I'm rich and famous and suddenly I feel like I have no friends. The Som is somehow more popular than ever. People are rerunning every sequence in the Dream looking for clues to the key, and that's keeping everyone so busy it doesn't feel like we ever just hang out anymore. I've made everything weird with Miranda, Andy seems suddenly distant and frustrated but I don't want to ask why, and Maya and I were never going to be anything but rocky. Robin is the only one of the group who hasn't gotten weird with me. At the same time, though, he works for me, so I'm not sure if his friendship counts. If I stopped paying him, would he still be there?

All this frustration I have turned outward onto the Defenders. I spend most of my waking time reading their threads, countering their arguments, making videos, and fighting them on social media.

Jennifer Putnam convinced me, in my rage (and greed, but mostly rage), to go on TV and have it out in a one-on-one debate with Peter Petrawicki. This sounded like a terrible idea to me. He was better at talking than me, and when you put us side by side, I always looked like a kid.

But Putnam said that even if he scored some points, people who were bound to be on my side but didn't know about my side would join up. It was about reaching the most people with the message, and doing something the press could sell was the best way to do that.

Eventually, my hatred of Peter and my belief in Putnam (her advice had, after all, gotten me this far) got the best of me.

This is now mostly forgotten, but it was a huge deal then. We had established ourselves as the two sides of the argument, which had split roughly (very roughly) down established political lines.

We each had our little armies, and they really hated each other. My frustration with the entire idea that the Carls should be treated like a menace and an excuse for militarization fueled that rage on my side. On Peter's side, the rage was fueled by similar indignation with a healthy dose of fear on top.

We met on the most neutral ground we could find, CNN. It was a respectable show, as cable news goes, but still they spent a full week beforehand promo-ing our "head-to-head" as if it were a frickin' presidential debate. We both traveled to the studio in New York, where we sat at a fancy glass table in front of an extremely fancy wall and looked out at the lights and the cameras and the steel-beamed warehouse beyond.

TRANSCRIPT

Presenter: The sixty-four largest metropolitan areas in the world are being visited by alien technology, possibly alien life. But their intentions remain a mystery.

April May, the discoverer of New York Carl, and Peter Petrawicki, author of *Invaded*, have both been guests here on the show, but never together. The question is pretty simple: Are the Carls dangerous?

April, you clearly have never felt threatened by Carl, initially believing him to be some kind of modern sculpture.

With that nonquestion it was clear that it was my turn to talk, so I did the thing that everyone on these shows always did and ignored the prompt and said what I wanted to say: "If the Carls or their creators wanted to harm us, they would have no trouble doing so. They seem to be, by their very nature, passive." By this point I was surprised that I hadn't been interrupted, so I wasn't sure what else to say but was loath to cede the floor, so I continued. "They're so technologically advanced that we couldn't catch up in a thousand years."

That's when Petrawicki broke in. "Cheryl, you say the question is, 'Are the Carls dangerous?' I don't think that's the question at all. For me, the question is, 'Might the Carls be dangerous?' I'm simply saying that I don't know the answer to that question. I also don't know how hard it would be to fight them if we had to. I just think it's wise to not just sit back and assume the best of this technology that is not just passive. It's inside our minds and it's somewhere running loose in America."

This was a reference to the fact that Hollywood Carl's hand had still not been seen since it dropped off in front of Grauman's Chinese Theatre. None of the Carl hands in other countries (or in the US for that matter) had dropped off and run away; it was clear that all the rest of them had simply vanished. This was just another freaky mystery to puzzle scientists and scare Defenders.

In any case, the fact that Peter Petrawicki, who, when on the internet, never stopped shouting fake alarmist nonsense, seemed calm and reasonable threw me off guard. This wasn't the conversation I'd prepped for.

Cheryl, the anchor, took back over.

"There is a certain reasonableness to that, April?"

"I'm fine with practicing care, but the hatred and animosity that comes out of the Defenders movement—"

"You're fine with practicing care?" Peter shot back, interrupting forcefully. "You are the reason Carl woke up. You might have caused this invasion into our minds with your meddling. It's clear to me,

April. You said it yourself that you shouldn't have done that, that you should have let someone qualified make that call, but you didn't. You and your followers are just blindly tumbling forward without any regard for the safety of the people of this country."

Why was it always "this country" with this guy, as if the whole world wasn't in this one together? But I had already realized my misstep, so I got back on message.

"Here's what it comes down to. I think we have a visitor knocking on our front door and you want to point a gun at it."

"They didn't knock, dear, they walked straight inside without a word, and if that's a home invasion, then this is an invasion as well."

This was going badly. The presenter took back the reins. "Peter, April brings up a good point. What can we do, really, when faced with a technology that is so clearly superior to our own?"

"Figuring that out is not my job, that's the job of the commander in chief. All I want is for us to consider the threat, and not roll over at the first sign of a dominant life-form. Have we learned nothing from history? What happens when a dominant group meets an inferior group? Every single time, they're slaughtered and everything they have is taken away from them."

I actually found enough anger to interrupt here. "And you just assume because humans are terrible that other species are terrible too?"

"April, *I* don't think humans are terrible—"

I broke in, "You just—"

He cut me off in return. "If you'd let me finish . . . I don't think humans are terrible, I think we are strong and resourceful and if anyone can fight this fight and survive it, it's us."

> *April:* There is no fight to fight! You're inventing it, I don't
> even know why! Why do you spend your time scaring all
> these people?

> *Peter:* You really do think we're afraid. It's like you and I live
> in different countries, April May."
> *April:* Of course you're afraid, that's all you ever talk
> about, you—
> *Peter:* All we're asking for is a little common sense, and you
> come out and attack me! It's the same story over and over,
> regular people ask to slow down and exercise care and then
> suddenly we're "xenophobic" or "exophobic" or whatever
> other word you invented last week to help sell books.

I'd heard all this before, but I also knew that this line of argument
worked. If you tell people that they're being attacked for their beliefs,
then suddenly they want to defend their beliefs, even if they didn't really
believe them before. It's pretty amazing, really.

I had a thought for defusing the situation that I wanted to try. It was
vital that I didn't get sucked into defending myself from his last little
quip and, instead, go for the root of what he was getting at, which was
that there is a clear logical perspective and that it was his.

> *April:* Peter, you invoke the common sense of regular people,
> but there are lots of regular people who disagree with you,
> and they also think they're invoking common sense. We're
> all regular people, when it comes down to it.
> *Peter:* Not with your lifestyle.

I wasn't ready for that *at all.* I'd offered an olive branch and he
just whacked me with it.

> *April:* What?
> *Peter:* April, I don't think it's any secret that the life you lead
> isn't a common lifestyle.

April: I mean, nor you, right? We have weird lives, we're on TV,
   there are millions of people watching. None of this is normal.
Peter: Well, if you're going to be intentionally obtuse.
April: Are you talking about the fact that I'm a lesbian?
Peter: You say that, but you seem to only be a lesbian
   sometimes. Other times, not so much.
April: What? Why is this a topic of conversation?

The presenter, who was equally baffled, finally stepped in, "I have
to agree . . ."

And then, thinking that I would have to do this at some point
anyway, I did the dumbest thing possible. I stayed on Peter Petrawicki's talking point instead of moving to my own.

April: No, it's fine, he's right. This has absolutely nothing
   to do with this conversation, but I'm bisexual and that's
   just as regular as being gay or straight. A person's gender
   has never been a thing that influences whether I'm
   attracted to them and that's just as regular as being gay
   or straight.
Peter: Then why have you been lying about it for the last year?

The extent to which I had lost control of this conversation baffled
me. Here are a list of thoughts I had in the space of five seconds:

1. Sexuality is complicated and fluid (deeply off topic)
2. Being bi is normal, but . . . you know . . . (they don't know)
3. I lied because people like you are terrible! (accusatory)
4. It's only been six months, not a year! (not useful)
5. I lied because it was better for my career? (bad)
6. My agent told me to lie, it wasn't my idea! (only a little better)

But by far the most overwhelming thought, the one that kept me from mounting any useful reply was: *You walked right the fuck into his trap, you damned idiot.*

There were so many things that I might say, that I wanted to say, and then there was the overwhelming knowledge that I had fucked up almost comically, and all those things competing for my attention were like a flash-bang going off in my brain. It was so overwhelming that, to the outside observer, I appeared almost catatonic.

The most forgiving perspective—which, to be fair, lots of people had—was that I was a kid who had gotten in way over her head and that a bully had used that opportunity to take me down several notches. That outlook didn't make Peter look good, but it didn't really make me look great either. I wasn't on TV to gather sympathy; I was here to impress and change minds. Instead, my greatest victory of the day is that I didn't break down crying right then and there. I might have, but I was too shocked by my own incompetence.

The presenter mercifully pushed us to a commercial break, during which I walked out of the building without talking to a single person. I made it to the sidewalk before I started to cry, which was a feat of marvelous strength.

That interview aired on July 12, so I guess we all know what the next chapter's going to be about. Though I've got a juicy detail about that day that I've never told anyone, so if you're thinking of skipping, rethink.

CHAPTER THIRTEEN

I try not to regret any of what has happened to me in the last few years. I don't know if I'd be happier or if the world would be a better place if I hadn't involved myself (or the universe hadn't involved me), but that's OK. What I do regret is how I engaged with the Defenders. In the weeks and months before July 13, I distilled a diverse group of individuals down to a few of their beliefs. Those beliefs were based on fear, and so all my arguments began and ended with the same thought: *You're all cowards*. I didn't say those exact words out loud, but they heard them anyway. The people who supported Carl and supported me heard it too, and they *loved* it. They wanted me to say it all the time. Reasoned, caring conversations that considered the complexity of other perspectives didn't get views. Rants did. Outrage did. Simplicity did. So, simple, outraged rants is what I gave people.

Putnam couldn't have been happier, though of course she acted like she was miserable that I'd been dragged through the mud on cable TV. She told me that in the end it was good for me, because it created sympathy and made PP, as it was easier to think of him, look like a bully. No one else tried to spin the interview, though. Robin, Andy, Miranda, even my parents just told me that they loved me and that they agreed it was awful and that I would be OK and to just let them know if I wanted foot rubs or giant sugary coffee drinks.

But I didn't want love; I wanted to tear the Defenders apart. When I look back on that period before that abbreviated "debate" with Peter (if you could even call it that), I see a trajectory that, thank god, the universe did not allow me to follow. But I can imagine a reality in which the rest of this book never happened and I spent my whole life (or at least the next few years of my life) as a bitter, angry pundit arguing professionally with professional arguers.

Not that I wasn't also having fun. Ripping the Defenders' arguments to shreds and then reading all the comments agreeing passionately with me and electronically patting me on my cybershoulders was thrilling. It's so much harder to actually define yourself and work to imagine the best possible future than it is to tear down others' ideas. So I defined myself and my vision of Carl in opposition to the Defenders'. My path forward was the opposite of theirs and theirs was the opposite of mine. It distilled itself down until all that was left was the argument. And maybe, lurking just beneath that, the hatred.

It's so much easier for people to get excited about disliking something than agreeing to like it. The circle jerk of mockery and self-congratulation was so intense I didn't even notice I was at its center. It was so easy to get people to follow me, and in the end, that's what I wanted. It took no time at all for me to be just as bad as Peter Petrawicki.

I shouldn't have been so surprised when things started escalating. I mean, I knew people hated me. It was a real thing. Being recognized by fans is very different from checking out at the corner store and not knowing if the clerk is a Defender thinking about what a dirty traitor you are. I thought that I could only either run away from that or fight it, so I fought it. Fear is an even better fuel than anger. Also, it is even more destructive. Their constant attacks meant I never had to doubt my message. It must be right, because the people who disagreed with me were sooooo awful. The Carls were the perfect vector for disagreement because, through all of this, we still knew practically nothing about them. Governments were accused of hiding things because people just couldn't accept that those in power were exactly as lost as the rest of us. Human beings are terrible at accepting uncertainty, so when we're ignorant, we make assumptions based on how we imagine the world. And our guess is so obviously correct that other guesses seem, at best, willful ignorance—at worst, an attack.

Here's a quick overview of what happens when groups of passionate believers start to define themselves in opposition to others:

1. A simple message seems obvious to a large population, and those people can't understand what the opposition could possibly be thinking. They never or almost never engage with someone who holds those different beliefs, and if they do, it's in the context of the discussion, not in the context of, like, also being a human.

2. The vast majority of those people nod appreciatively and then change the channel and watch *NCIS* and eat the tacos that they made. It's their own recipe. They've developed it over years, and they like it better than any taco you could get at even a super fancy restaurant. They go to bed at 10:30 and worry a bit about whether their son is adjusting well to college.

3. A very small percentage get really riled up. They're angry, but they're mostly worried or even scared and want to cause some kind of action. They call their

representatives and do a little organizing. They're usually
motivated not just by agreement in the message but by a
hatred of the people trying to fight the message.

4. A tiny percentage of that percentage just go way the fuck
overboard. They get so frightened and angry that they
need to make something happen. How? Well, that's
simple, right? You eliminate the people who are actively
trying to destroy the world. If we're all really unlucky,
and if there are enough of them, those people find each
other and they confirm and exacerbate their own
extremism.

The bigger the Defender movement got, the larger that fourth
group became. Some of them were religious extremists who believed
the Carls were a symbol of the coming apocalypse or rapture or
whatever. Some of them were purely secular, deeply believing that
America and possibly the world was going to be destroyed if nothing
was done (no one was really clear on what that thing was, but NO
ONE WAS DOING IT!), and eventually they came to believe that I
was an active and informed participant in the government's (or the
Carls') plans to make humanity submit.

This is the first time a truly international issue had hit our newly
borderless world this hard, and no one knew how that might play out.
The conversation was international—we all knew that. The comments on my videos were in Hindi and Japanese and Arabic and
Spanish. We had a team of translators who would subtitle the videos
within a day or two of them going live, and the Som was now opera-
tional in more than twenty different languages. I saw this as an un-
ambiguously good thing. I felt very strongly that the Carls were a
globally unifying force. For the first time ever, humanity was literally sharing a dream. It felt more like we were sharing a planet than
ever before, and to me that felt like a gift given to us by the Carls.

I still believe the Carls were very good for the world, but obviously July 13 made that a lot more ambiguous.

The coordinated attacks in São Paulo, Lagos, Jakarta, and St. Petersburg killed more than eight hundred people and injured thousands. That the responsible group had managed to plan an attack in four different continents boggled the mind. This wasn't radicals making plans in back alleys; it was a growing, worldwide, borderless movement. In the US, it was the Defenders, but every culture had their own name for it, and they found commonality and connection in pop-up forums and anonymous chat rooms. They had convinced themselves that the Carls would be easy to destroy and that world governments were lying about their invulnerability. They also convinced themselves that tourists visiting Carls were not worth saving or protecting or whatever. Whether they saw it as a pilgrimage to a false deity or an act of submission to alien domination, it didn't matter; any positive connection to the Carls was a threat to the ideology they wanted to push forward. The Carls could not be seen as safe, even if they were the ones making the Carls dangerous.

The Carls, of course, were completely unhurt.

The attacks were synchronized at roughly 4 A.M. eastern time. That maximized crowds in Jakarta, Lagos, and St. Petersburg. It was still early morning in São Paulo, but they coordinated the time with the other attacks nonetheless.

At that exact moment, 4 A.M., when those bombs went off across the world, I awoke from the Dream, where I had been staring blankly at a 767, and shot out of my bed in fear and terror.

Was I somehow psychically roused? Had I sensed a great disturbance in the Force? Did Carl reach out to me through the Dream to tell me of the attacks? No. I had heard a loud CRACK from the direction of the sliding glass door that led to my little balcony. My blinds were closed, of course, so I couldn't see what had caused the noise.

My first thought was that someone had thrown a rock at it, but from eight stories below that would have to be some arm. Things had been getting heated with the Defenders; the messages were sometimes mean, sometimes threatening, and sometimes deeply fucking disturbing. I grabbed my phone as I got out of bed and slid it into my pajama bottoms. I flipped on the light, and as my heart rate slowly returned to normal, I went to look out the window.

At the base of the drapes, which hung all the way to the floor, if I had looked, I would have seen some little specks of glass mixed in with the Pop-Tart crumbs and dust. But I didn't look. I just drew back the drapes to see what may have made the noise.

Looking back on this behavior, it's depressingly dumb. Something has hit my window, and what's my plan of action? I've got it! I'll turn on the light and pull back the drapes in front of a glass door! SLOWLY!

Even with all the threats, it was still somehow inconceivable to me that someone would actually try to kill me. Harass me? Sure. Threaten me? Yeah. Sue me? If they could find a reason! But murder? That shit's for the movies. People don't *kill* people! I mean, they do, obviously, I've seen a newspaper. It says something, maybe, about how my mind works that I had received literal death threats but never considered that someone would try to kill me.

But now I was thinking about it, and two things happened simultaneously.

1. Something big (at the time, I thought it must have been a person) slammed painfully into my shoulder, knocking me away from the door.
2. The glass in my double-paned sliding glass door erupted out, spraying into the room and leaving a two-inch-wide hole.

I hit the floor hard, and the thing that had shoved me was gone before I could regain my wits. Little shards of glass lay all around the room. Having, by this point, figured out at least half of what was going on, I crumpled myself against the wall of my bedroom, too scared to cry. Someone had just tried to shoot me. Not, like, scare me, but actually put a bullet in my chest so that I could lie on the floor of my lonely apartment to die all by myself. And who the hell had shoved me? They had saved me, but they were also in my apartment!

And then I was no longer too scared to cry, and I cried. My blinds were still open a crack, and I was afraid that, at any moment, bullets would come flying through my window like a true war zone and if I was not backed against a brick wall I would be torn apart. But after about ten minutes of gasping for air between sobs, I convinced myself that I could sneak out of my bedroom and into the living room, where the windows faced a narrow alley, not the street.

So I half crawled, half ran out of the room. Once in my living room, I had access to a bathroom, a carpet, and the kitchen. Everything a girl needs! I did a cursory search, which uncovered nothing out of the ordinary. Clothes, carry-out containers, dirty napkins, maybe a damp towel or two. No sign of an intruder.

Should I call the cops? I thought. I mean, I definitely should call the cops. Someone was very probably trying to hurt me and maybe also there was literally a stranger hiding in my apartment right now?

But for some reason I really, really, really didn't want to tell anyone. Maybe I was being silly. *There is probably some reason for all of this that isn't attempted murder,* my mind was telling me. *So far attempted murder has never happened to me, so it seems like there must be some other explanation.*

And if it was real, other things were real too. Dealing with a police investigation and the reality that I could never sleep safely in this apartment again. And, oh god, my parents would have to know.

And Maya. I knew she'd never say it, but inside there would be that part of her thinking, *If only April had listened to me, this wouldn't have happened.* And I couldn't live with that. I couldn't live with any of those scenarios.

So, instead of the police, I called Robin.

"April," he said after one ring. Now . . . he never sounded put out (though I'd never before called him at 4 A.M.), but he seemed to positively have been expecting my call, which threw me.

"Were you expecting me to call?"

"Not expecting, but it is not surprising given the reports." Remember I had been dealing with my own crisis. By this point the São Paulo and St. Petersburg attacks were already being reported on American news. Someone must have called Robin from a less ridiculous time zone.

"What reports?"

"Oh, my."

"Oh, your what?" This was not how I was expecting the phone call to go.

"You should tell me why you are calling. I think that would simplify this conversation."

"I think someone's maybe just tried to hurt me. There is something very strange going on."

"Have you called the police?" His voice was at a pitch I had never heard before.

"That doesn't seem necessary," I half complained, half ordered.

"It does, though."

"Let's just . . . not have them involved yet."

"Would you be all right with me sending up the doorman?"

"Yes, I suppose that's fine."

"I will call you back momentarily." He hung up before I did.

In that moment, I had a thought. Whoever or whatever had hit me had to still be in my apartment. It wasn't in my bedroom, and I wasn't going to check the second bedroom . . . That room had a window overlooking the street and I didn't even know if the blinds were drawn. But it wasn't a huge place, and I hadn't actually looked very hard. So I looked under the couch and the chairs. Nothing. So I turned them all upside down. There was this weird black, meshy fabric covering the bottom of one of the chairs. It had been carefully and exactly cut along one side.

My phone rang. Robin. I muted it.

I slid my hand into the tear and ripped the fabric off the chair.

There, stretched out across the full width of my living room chair, wedged in place in the wooden frame, was Hollywood Carl's right hand.

CHAPTER FOURTEEN

BANG BANG BANG!

"Ms. May, are you all right?" The voice was muffled through the door.

My heart, having stopped beating completely, exploded. I gasped and looked back toward the door, then immediately back at Carl's hand, which had not moved.

"I'm fine!" I yelled, not sounding fine.

"May I please come in and have a look around?"

I was doing everything in my power not to look away from the hand. It was unmistakable. Three times the size of a man's hand, made of that mix of silver shine and matte-black armor. It was beautiful. I wanted to touch it, but I was terrified.

"False alarm! I'm an idiot!" I screamed into the underside of my very nice living room chair.

"Still, it wouldn't hurt for me to have a look around." Through the door I heard no indication that he was going to give up.

"I'm not wearing pants!" I was wearing pants.

There was some quiet murmuring, and then I realized he was talking to Robin on his cell phone.

"Could you please call Robin back because he is not letting me take no for an answer, and I do have a key."

Reluctantly I looked away from the hand in my chair for a moment to call Robin. When I looked back, it was still there, splayed out, holding its place in the base of the chair. Did it even know I had found it?

I interrupted Robin as soon as he started talking, "Everything is fine, call off the troops."

"Not everything is fine, and my primary need right now is to see that you are safe. There is a reason why you are not letting me fulfill that need, and I need to know what it is."

I looked at the hand, thinking that if Carl wanted to hurt me, then my entire life was a lie, so it couldn't be possible. "I am safe, Robin, I promise."

"Are you aware of the situations in São Paulo and St. Petersburg?" News from Lagos and Jakarta hadn't reached the US yet.

"I am not."

"There have been terrorist attacks on the Carls. Many people are dead. April, I'm afraid that you are a target as well."

Fuck fuck fuck fuck fuck, I thought.

"Fuck," I said. "Oh god." And then a lump rose in my throat but I didn't make a sound. This was too big, and it sank in for real that someone had definitely, absolutely tried to kill me just now. Rather than blowing up New York Carl, they had thought maybe a scalpel would be better than a cleaver. I felt like I was going to throw up. What if I had died? I reached under my shirt to feel my own skin, warm and soft and as fragile as air.

I looked down at the hand again and noticed for the first time something gray and dull in among the silver and black. Wedged between two of the armor plates was a jagged piece of something. I reached in and pulled it out: a shard of metal, a fragment of a bullet. I held it in my hand, cold and innocuous as a penny.

"Are you OK, April?"

"Not particularly, no." I tried to keep my tears out of my voice, but I failed.

"It's a lot, I know. I can hardly believe it's true. Please, I'm on my way to you now. Please let Steve in to check on you, I will be there soon."

"No, Robin. I'm safe, I promise. I . . ." I couldn't tell him about the hand. "I thought there was someone in my apartment, but I just saw it. It's a giant rat, and now there's a terrorist attack and I feel so silly. Please, I want to go back to bed, let's talk in the morning, OK?"

"OK, I'll let Steve know." He sounded drastically unsatisfied, but he still hung up.

Carl's hand had not moved, though it seemed unmistakably alive.

You know how when you're trying to get some stuff out of your car and there's, like, one too many things to bring them all in in one trip? You keep trying to figure out how to hold something slightly differently so you can save yourself the extra time. So you put some stuff down and consolidate some bags and you think you've got everything, but then you look down and realize that the cat food or the soda from lunch or the picture frames are still sitting there and you've got no way to pick them up.

There's a moment when one extra thing just breaks the whole process. If only you didn't have that thing, this would be a situation you could easily manage. Well, that's the way my mind felt in that moment. Except instead of one too many world-shattering, life-altering unpleasantnesses, there were like five too many to hang on to. Every time I spent time concentrating on one, some part of my brain would notice another lying in the trunk of my brain car and flip out with frustration and impotence.

I know a lot of people were feeling that way that day, but I'd like to think I had a couple of extra worries, and that might explain my behavior over the next twenty-four hours.

So, like any good, barely adult human, I flipped out and threw all of my angst groceries back into the brain car and gave up on trying to figure anything out. Instead, I concentrated on what I knew. Carl's hand hadn't been seen in months, and there it was, right in front of me. I was April May, Documenter of Carl Activities, so it was time to *document*.

I flipped my phone around and turned on the camera. The hand spun around suddenly, got its fingers under itself, and shot out at me before I had the video started. I staggered backward with a yelp that I'm glad no one else heard. My heartbeat thudded in my ears.

"OK! OK," I said as I put my phone back in my pocket. It peeked out from behind the couch, and then came out as slowly and carefully as a stray cat.

This was all excellent distraction from the fact that a real human person who existed in the world had tried to kill me. It was much more important that Carl, or at least some part of him, had saved me. And so:

1. Carl was alive.
2. Carl knew who I was.
3. Carl had at least two desires.
    1. That I not die.
    2. That I not take any pictures of his disembodied hand.

With my brain at 25 percent power, all I really wanted was to thank Carl, or Carl's hand. I reached out to it, and it approached me. It walked on all fives, each finger thudding on the thin carpet covering the wooden floor.

"Thanks for"—I felt a little silly talking to it but kept going anyway—"uh, everything, I guess. But mostly, just now, for literally taking a bullet for me. I guess."

The hand bowed. I mean, maybe. It flattened itself against the floor a bit and then stood back up.

"Uh, can you understand me?"

Nothing happened.

"One tap for yes, two taps for no. Can you understand me?"

Two taps.

"WHAT?!" I literally screamed. The hand stood there in front of me, looking rather smug. "Are you messing with me? Did you just make a fucking joke?!"

Nothing.

"OK, so you can see me and apparently hear me and possibly understand me and also apparently mock me. Correct?"

Nothing.

"Can I touch you?"

Nothing.

I know only "yes" means "yes," but it was a robot hand in my apartment and it's not like I had invited it over.

I reached out to it, to feel it, and it let me. I touched it. It felt different now. Not like touching Carl, that weird way it left all the heat in my hand. It just felt hard and very, very slightly warm. Carl also had always been completely immobile, but the hand was so clearly alive. Even when it wasn't moving, it had movement in it. It had life to it. Compared to the immobile statue that was Carl, it felt so much more complex and carefully crafted. Every joint as supple and nimble as my own hands.

We don't generally look down at a human hand sliding over a keyboard or stroking a pet or punching buttons on a remote control and think, *What a marvel!* but it truly is. Humans have yet to create something so delicate and intricate as our own hands. But Carl's hand was every bit as careful and nimble as my own, and a great deal stronger, it would seem.

I pulled my phone from my pocket and Carl skittered away again.

"I'm just calling Andy," I said. "You know Andy, right?"

So I punched him, number two on my speed dial after Robin these days. The phone rang once before noise exploded in my ears. I threw my phone across the room, screaming. Once it wasn't right up against my ear, I could hear it clearly.

> . . . *ship on my way to Mars, on a collision course. I am a satellite, I'm out of control. I am a sex machine ready to reload like an atom bomb about to oh oh oh oh oh explode* . . .

Queen, "Don't Stop Me Now."

"You're blocking me!" I accused the hand, panting from my freak-out.

Nothing.

"Look, I don't know what you want and I'm not going to know unless you tell me."

Nothing.

I grabbed my computer off the coffee table and sat on the floor with it a foot away from where the hand had taken residence. The Wi-Fi signal was strong, but every website timed out.

"Well, what am I supposed to do then!"

As you might have expected by this point, nothing.

"Can I tell anybody?"

Two taps.

"Was that an actual response?"

One tap.

"THIS IS REALLY HAPPENING!"

Nothing.

"Are you from outer space?"

Nothing.

"Have you heard about the Carls in St. Petersburg and São Paulo?"

Nothing.

"Can I tell anyone you're here?"

Two taps.

"Can I tell anyone you saved me?"

Two taps.

"Can I at least tell Robin?"

Two taps.

"Would you stop me if I tried to tell someone?"

Nothing.

I must have asked the hand a thousand questions and the only information I got out of it was that I was not, under any circumstances, to share that it had visited me. No one could know; no one could see it. I felt, of course, tremendously obliged to keep this promise because if the Carls did have some kind of massive plan, I sure didn't want to mess it up—also because I had built a whole life around believing the Carls were good—also because of the whole life-debt thing.

But that also meant not telling anyone that I had been shot at. This line of inquiry, of course, led to no response. The hand did not appear to be concerned about my safety. Possibly, it thought it could guarantee it. How was I supposed to tell anyone that I'd been shot at without breaking this promise?

Also, what was I going to say to the superintendent about the blown-out doors in my bedroom? And how was I supposed to clean up the rest of the glass without getting shot at again? That is not a normal thought, but it was a thought I had. Maybe there were bigger concerns.

As time somehow kept moving, the various sizes of various concerns were starting to seem less relevant. All my worries, from terrorist attacks to almost dying to whether I should clean the glass on my floor, somehow all seemed the same size. I realized I was crashing down from my high. My body had been in fight-or-flight mode for at least an hour, and exhaustion was kicking in hard. I reached out to the hand and wrapped my hand around its massive index finger.

"Why did you save me?" I asked the hand.

It didn't do anything.

"OK, I won't tell anyone." It looked to me as if maybe, just a tiny bit, it relaxed. Without thinking, I scooched toward the hand and curled myself around it, and it settled a bit into my embrace. I was asleep in seconds.

I don't want to have real dreams, so I just wander the city all night. The whole world is waiting for the key, searching fruitlessly even though I'm the only one who can get it. But I still haven't let Miranda or Maya share what we know. We're lying to the whole world. My fear and my mood have followed me into the Dream. I walk into an arcade, like from the eighties. There are tons of stand-up video games and pinball machines.

The puzzle sequence in here must be delicious. I spot a quarter on one of the machines—that's probably where the sequence begins—but I don't play. I go to the girls' bathroom. It's dirty and there are local band posters all over the wall, but none of them make any sense. My brain can't turn the letters into words. This tends to be the case when you get off track. It's a sign that you aren't in an important part of the puzzle. It's like the Carls couldn't be bothered to create the detail of every little spot.

I go into the dirty stall and sit on the toilet and cry until I wake up.

CHAPTER FIFTEEN

I woke to distant shouts.

Reality crashed into me. Someone bombed Carls all over the world. Someone tried to *kill me*. They looked into the scope of their rifle, saw me, and pulled the trigger. And Carl's hand, it was here, and it saved me. And where was it? I shot up off the floor and searched every inch of my living room and kitchen. Then I stood outside of my bedroom door, but I couldn't make myself go in. I gave up. I never went into either of the bedrooms again. In my heart, I think I knew the hand had departed as sneakily as it arrived.

I was still in my pajamas, which was fine, but my feet were cold. Some clothes were in the dryer and I grabbed the first socks I could make a pair out of. I remember very specifically that they were *Purrletariat* merch, Maya's comic. Soon, each of my ankles sported an adorably illustrated cat saying, "Eat the Rich, Steve."

I could hear people shouting in the street below, but again, I couldn't go look out the window, so I turned on the news.

The news media is almost always in a bizarre frantic resting state. During these rests it tries to make distant and vague threats seem up close and menacing in order to give you some reason to watch their advertisements. Here's a hint: It's not really "news" until they stop running ads. There were no ads this morning. The July 13 attacks were real news and everyone knew it. The fact that America was spared (though you, unlike anyone back then, now know that there was a planned attack, it was simply thwarted—well, I guess not *simply* thwarted) created excellent opportunities for rampant, useless, baseless speculation.

Occasionally they would show images of 23rd Street, which was packed with people whom the police were incapable of controlling. Most of the people in the crowd came to show that the world stood in solidarity with Nigeria, Russia, Indonesia, and Brazil. Others were protesting the continued threat Carl made. Analysts on television were saying terrifying things about a strategy terrorists sometimes used: Do something inflammatory and then, once the inevitable crowd formed, strike again with much greater impact. Since America hadn't been part of the attack, and Americans are incapable of considering that evil people would coordinate a massive attack and *leave us out of it*, everyone assumed something else was coming.

As I watched the news, a thought leaked into my mind. The world was tearing itself apart; people were dying. The noise in the street threatened to become a riot if a bunch of Defenders showed up. It was easy for me to blame all this on Peter and people like him. But ultimately, wasn't the source of it all Carl? Wouldn't those people still be alive if Carl hadn't showed up? Wasn't I as biased and irrational as the Defenders? Clinging to my unquestionable belief that Carl was here to bind us together, not to divide or destroy us? Seeing only the evidence that confirmed my point of view and not the evidence, right here in front of my eyes, that Carl was undeniably disruptive?

I realized that there was no way for that not to be in my brain in my next TV interview, though certainly I wouldn't mention it. And that's when I realized that I wasn't supposed to be watching the news about Carls; I was supposed to be *on* the news about Carls. And then I panicked a bit. Why hadn't anyone called me?!

I grabbed my phone and saw a fairly simple explanation: It was off. I tried turning it on . . . out of batteries. Oh god! Robin was probably having a fit. EVERYONE was probably having a fit! Why wasn't anyone at my house? And worse, both my chargers and my other phone were in my freaking bedroom. OK, computer then. At the very least I had to tell everyone I was OK.

I popped open my laptop. It seemed that my connection to the outside world had been restored. As expected, I had about five hundred new emails—TV producers, Robin, Andy, Miranda, Maya, parents, brother, everyone. Notifications from the Som were out of hand.

Here's what was not expected: I had replied to many of the emails.

That was confusing enough that I didn't understand it at first. I read the email Miranda had sent, and then I read my reply, and I tried to figure out who it was from. It sounded like me, though it wasn't complicated, basically just letting her know I was OK and would need some time before I did anything publicly.

My first thought was that Robin had, in a panic, impersonated me. Then I saw a whole conversation I'd had with him about why I wasn't answering texts and that I needed time to process and would be in touch soon. I'd told him to start a list of people interested in talking to me and it would be late morning before I could take any interviews. Andy's insistence that we make a video was responded to similarly. A message to my parents and brother told them not to worry and that I was safe and being looked after and the whole thing was just so terrible and I would call soon and thank you for worrying about me, but again, I was fine.

There was no response to Maya's email.

It is possible—I do not think this is what happened, but it is possible—that I woke up several times and answered those emails and then fell asleep between sessions (they were spread out over several hours) and was experiencing some kind of post-traumatic amnesia. I certainly would not have questioned the emails' validity if I had been any of the recipients, and if I had been awake, I probably would have sent extremely similar emails. But I had not been awake.

I read all of my sent and received messages and found no hint as to their origin. I did my best to imagine Carl's hand curled over my phone or computer typing out emails, but I figured I couldn't dust for fingerprints or anything. In the end (and until just now, actually), I just pretended I'd sent the messages. I was suddenly living a number of rather large lies, and this one seemed pretty inconsequential. I was numb to oddity. I emailed Andy telling him I wanted to do a shoot down in the street in the next few hours and told Robin to start scheduling for Skype-ins starting at noon and ending at four and that things would be weird but he had to just simply not ask any questions. Also, could he bring me something TV-worthy from Top Shop and an iPhone charger?

Having an assistant is awesome for when you are terrified to go into your own bedroom because of last night's attempted murder!

Before showering I finally tweeted something:

> **@AprilMaybeNot:** Sick with sadness. I have misplaced my hope. Let's be together today, and remember our humanity not our brutality.

And then immediately after:

> **@AprilMaybeNot:** Just a few people did this. In a world of eight billion. I am trying so hard to remember how few of us are truly evil.

I don't think I actually felt any of those ways, but it seemed on-brand. Those seemed like the kinds of things April May would tweet. In reality, I felt numb and I wanted to work. I wanted to write and talk and figure out how the Defenders were responding and start up the counterarguments immediately, even if I was finally questioning my own faith that the Carls were only here to help us. It was easier to act than doubt.

The police and government, at that point, were still searching for information on several disconnected bombers, we had no real information, and so the vacuum was being filled by lies, guesses, and assumptions. At least I refused to give in to that impulse.

Humans are terrible at believing reality. The things I tweeted about July 13 were absolutely true. These attacks were the work of such a minuscule number of people, a number so small as to be inconsequential. And the number of people hurt and killed, on a global scale, wasn't a huge deal either. More people died in car accidents on July 13 than in those bombings. But these are things you can't really say in the face of tragedy.

We are irrational beings, easy to manipulate if you're willing to do whatever it takes. That's exactly how terrorists convince themselves that murder is worthwhile. And the wound it left, it was larger than those lives lost; it was a wound we would all have to live with forever. The purity of my feelings for Carl was gone and I would never get it back.

CHAPTER SIXTEEN

Here's a weird thing. You remember July 13, and I sure hope you remember September 11, even if you weren't alive. But we've pretty much all forgotten June 28. June 28, 1914, to be exact, probably the weirdest day in recorded history. Here's what happened.

The guy who's next in line to the throne of the Austro-Hungarian Empire, which was this huge politically important country (second largest in Europe by size, third by population), was visiting Sarajevo, which is now in Bosnia but was then part of that massive empire. A lot of folks living there didn't like the Austro-Hungarians for complicated reasons that we don't need to get into.

A group of young guys have decided they want to kill this prince, who has, in his wisdom and bravery, prepublished the route he's going to be taking through Sarajevo in a literal open-topped car (note to world leaders: Stop doing this). These twenty men line up at various places along the published route with various devices and strategies for assassination. One of them jumps the gun a little bit and runs out of the crowd with a small bomb. He throws it at the prince, but the bomb doesn't detonate for several seconds, so it ends up exploding near a different car and injuring several people but not killing anyone.

Everyone disperses, the heir to the throne gets swept to safety, and none of the other would-be assassins get to try their hand at assassination.

That's a weird day already, right? Well, it gets much weirder.

The parade, of course, is called off and the prince is safe. But then he decides, in his wisdom and bravery, that he wants to go visit the people injured in the bombing at the hospital. The driver takes what is likely to be the worst wrong turn in history and then, realizing it, puts the car in reverse. It's 1914 and cars are very new and glitchy, so the car stalls in front of a deli where one of the foiled assassins, Gavrilo Princip, just happens to be standing.

Princip steps forward, pulls out his gun, and fires two shots. One hits the prince, who by now I hope you've figured out is Archduke Franz Ferdinand, in the neck. The other hits his wife, Sophie, in the belly, killing her quickly.

An aide, trying to hold closed the hole in the neck of his prince, asks him if he's in pain. The archduke says, "It is nothing." He repeats this—"It is nothing . . . It is nothing . . ."—over and over until he falls unconscious and then dies.

It was not nothing. The assassination of Franz Ferdinand touched off a cascade of terrible decisions and reckless diplomacy that ended in the deaths of more than sixteen million people.

Keep that in mind if it seems like the following events are improbable. Sometimes, weird things happen that change the course of history . . . and apparently they happen to me.

Andy looked like he'd slept a good thirteen minutes. He was untidy and quiet, and I could definitely smell him as he adjusted my lapel mic.

"You OK, dude?"

He looked at me like he was just realizing I was there before moving his eyes back to his work. "Yeah, fine. I'm fine."

"I don't think you're fine."

He snapped out of it a bit then. "Fuck, April, of course I'm not fine. What the hell are we doing?" He didn't sound agitated. He sounded tired.

"We're going to go out there and try to make this a little better for everyone. I need to believe something myself."

"Do you have any idea what you're going to say?"

"I have a couple ideas." I'm not sure I did, but I felt pretty sure that something good would come to me. "Is there anything you think I should say?"

"Aside from that the world is awful and how the hell did we come to this?" He sank down into the sofa. I hadn't told Andy about the shot, I hadn't told him about Carl Jr., and I hadn't seen any sign that it was still in my apartment. If it hadn't left, it was in one of the rooms I wasn't going into.

I looked down at Andy, understanding for the first time that his eyes weren't just puffy with lack of sleep. I realized I hadn't cried yet. That was messed up. I thought about just crying right then—it would have been easy, just relaxing a mental muscle and I would have been gushing. But then I thought (for real), *Nah, April, save it for the camera.*

Gross.

Out loud, I said, "All those people out there, they're defying the police and the terrorists to stand with Carl. To stand with us. To simply say, 'The world is not awful,' that's what we need to go down there and do."

"April, on the news, they're saying there might be more attacks. Look at all those people down there! No one's checking backpacks! I almost had a panic attack just getting into your building!"

"I spend all my time on the news, it's their job to scare you. I watch it firsthand all day long." I will say this for myself: I wasn't giving Andy a pep talk because I needed him. I could've gotten someone else to hold the camera. Hell, I could've gone down there with a selfie stick and it would have been great footage. I wanted him to do it because we were in this together and I wanted him to feel that way. I felt as if I was telling him the truth. I was just giving him a dose of reality because I thought it would make him feel better to do something great on a terrible day. I was kinda right, I guess.

I guess.

"Remember when I called you in the middle of the night to go look at a weird sculpture? I did that because I thought you wanted something and I could help give it to you. But, Andy, you are so much more than I thought you were then, and I'm so much less. I don't need you to help make me famous, I need you to help keep me sane. There's nothing more dangerous outside that door than a Halsey concert." He had his eyes closed, but I could see the concentration in his face. I don't know if he was concentrating on keeping his mind in the present, on facing his fear, on not crying, or on not saying things that he wanted to say to me but knew he shouldn't. In any case, it was clear that he was working hard. "Let's go down there and make the world a little better, OK?"

Andy was shooting on a DSLR, about the size of a teakettle, with a big, heavy wide-angle lens on it to help him get good shots even in close quarters. With the mic receiver and preamp assembly, it was about a three-pound rig. Ten years ago, a setup to get similar-quality video and audio would have weighed at least thirty pounds.

Another nice thing about wide-angle lenses: They don't show shaking as much. That's good when you're getting jostled around by a crowd . . . or just shaking in terror.

Jerry the doorman was worried as well. "April! I have to advise you not to go out there right now."

What fantastic advice.

"We'll be fine, Jerry, it's more of a party than a protest." I was nervous, but Andy was green and sweating.

"April, I'm responsible for your safety when you're in this building, but once you're out there there's nothing I can do." His paternalism was cute up to a point.

"This is what I do, Jerry. You are awesome. We'll be back in five or ten minutes, I promise."

We pushed through the revolving doors, me ready to start talking, Andy with the camera already rolling.

I turned around immediately and started walking backward into the crowd of people, speaking just above normal volume. You've probably seen this video, but it feels like part of the story, so I'm telling it:

"April May here on 23rd outside Gramercy Theatre, the residence of New York Carl, where the impromptu response to what will undoubtedly come to be known as the July 13 attacks is one of solidarity, hope, and friendship. Only a few stragglers of the Defenders movement have showed up to continue their outrageous protest of a clearly benign presence in our cities." People are starting to take notice, they almost all recognize me, and they're giving us a bit more room to move. I'm moving toward Carl, I want to see if I can get him in the shot, but you never really notice how wide streets are until they're filled with people.

I think for a second now, walking forward instead of backward, using my "April May" clout to clear a bit of a passage.

"Hey, April!" I hear called from the crowd. It's a young guy with a sign that reads "If This Is Humanity, Bring on the Invasion."

"Hey, handsome!" I respond. *He'll have a story for his friends*, I think.

I turn back to the camera and continue walking backward toward Carl.

"On this truly terrible day the world mourns. In our mourning we

241

have to remember that this was not done by an evil world or an evil species, it was done by a few individuals. Yes, the level of sophistication and organization is terrifying. Their goal is to be terrifying, and they have succeeded. I'm scared. Of course I am. But a few fools who killed themselves and others for some unfounded ideal that took hold in their broken hearts—I'm not afraid of them, I'm afraid of their fear." That was one of the lines I had prepped. I look around, people are staring now, they've formed a circle around us and it's getting quiet. "These people." I look around as Andy pans the camera. "This demonstration!" I shout, and everyone shouts, and it's beautiful and we're all doing it together and it feels so good. People have their cell phones out, recording me as I record them—the scene is covered from every angle. "This is what humanity is, solidarity in the face of fear. Hope in the face of destruction. If the Carls are here for any reason"—and amazingly Carl comes into view right when I say this, towering above the crowd just a few yards away—"then maybe they're here not to learn about us but to teach us about ourselves. I am learning more every day and I am learning now that even . . ."

A chorus of cries distracts me, but it's way too late for me to do anything. Someone has flung themselves out of the crowd just a few feet behind me. You can hear some of the cries distinctly on the video—"April!" "Stop him!" "Watch out!"—but it is mostly incomprehensible shouts of alarm.

He's clearly visible on the tape; he looks like just some white guy. Jeans, blond hair, medium height, white T-shirt, khaki jacket. He pushes his way out of the crowd and springs right for my back with a six-inch-long knife held up in his fist. I couldn't see any of that, though.

I didn't really react in any way until I felt the knife hit me, which is when I screamed. That scream is so loud and awful on the tape that we had to cut it out of the video. Lav mics are really good at picking up only the noise from the person they're clipped to, so it's just straight raw scream with very little of the background excitement. I only heard it one time during editing and I can call it back to memory at will. If I think about it, I can still feel a little echo of the knife slamming into me, just between my shoulder blade and my spine. The knife cut through my brand-new suit coat from Top Shop the first millisecond and brushed past my shoulder blade the second. It felt like being punched full force by a heavyweight fighter. The ripping of the skin didn't even register over the feeling of the blade hitting my ribs. The pain shot up and down my back from my neck to my tailbone and then down my arms for good measure. The next moment, the weight of my attacker crashed into me, knocking me forward and down to my hands and knees.

Andy was recording at 120 frames per second just in case. That lets you play the video in slow motion if you need to. You would have been able to see every bit of what happened if Andy had held the shot. He didn't, of course, but here's what the camera saw:

Half a second after he sees the guy running toward me, Andy's lifting the camera up over his head, thinking not about cinematography but about attack. At first all you can see is sky and buildings and crowd, but as the camera comes down, lens first, you can see the literal moment that changed history. One second, the guy is rushing me and pushing the knife into my back, the next he goes limp. Not just limp—he loses all structure. All the power he has held tight in his body collapses. In the instant before the camera smashes his face, his skin goes two shades darker. His body crashes into mine, knocking me forward, but he's no longer putting pressure on the knife, which wiggles a little in my back. The camera captures itself slamming into the guy's bizarrely distorted face and then everything goes black.

From the perspective of the cell phone cameras that surrounded us, it's a lot clearer. The guy crashes into me, knife in hand. The next instant, he's a sack of liquid slamming into my back, and the next, Andy crashes the camera down on his face. I didn't ever upload one of those wide shots to my channel, but there are plenty of videos around of it. His face, already bloated and distorted and dark, splits open under Andy's camera like a soap bubble popping. The black mass that squirts and oozes out of the split skin is clearly not blood. I collapse onto my hands and knees, the shape of the body slumping off me onto the ground. In only one video did the camera owner keep his wits together enough to film me rising from my hands to stand. The knife is just sticking there (it turned out to be lodged between two of my ribs), blood starts seeping through my shirt, but the white suit coat is nice, thick wool, so at this point, it doesn't look more than torn.

The crowd seems to be made mostly of screams. Some people stand perfectly still; others run. The running and the screaming at the center of the crowd causes panic in every direction. It's a miracle no one died in the stampede. I feel the warm gel sliding down my back as Martin Bellacourt, my own little Gavrilo Princip, lies lumpy on the ground, very, very dead. I turn around to look at the body and it's barely recognizable as a human. It looks like a bunch of dirty, wet, stained clothes on the street.

I look from the body to Andy and then to Carl and back to Andy. I'm in shock—well, not literally . . . yet. The pain is there and it is intense, but it's like someone else is feeling it. Andy looks at the camera, covered in the dark gel. He shudders, suddenly pale, and drops it to the asphalt.

"Are you OK?"

"Yeah, I think I'm fine." And then I add, "Though it feels like . . . like there's a knife in my back." I turn to show Andy, which sends a new wave of pain up my neck and down my back. This is a new, fresher, sharper variety. I flinch, which makes it worse. I feel the

knife wiggling around—moving my left arm in any way is excruciating.

"Oh my god. April, there's a fucking knife in you," he says. And
the wiggling knife, which was only ever an inch deep, falls out of my
back, clattering to the ground.

"It seems as if you are wrong!" I say, my head spinning as a fresh
warm stream of blood starts pouring down my back. "Oh, Andy, this
does not feel good." We both look down at the knife on the ground, a
little bloody but almost pathetic for all the damage it ended up doing.

It was a little thing. The cheap black plastic handle was designed
for the blade to fold into it. There's a picture of it online if you want
to see it—it seems even more pathetic in its little evidence baggie.
The blade is just a little wider than my finger. Turns out your ribs are
really tightly placed in your back, I suppose to protect against this
sort of thing.

Andy was staring at me, horrified. I guess that's understandable.
I wanted the camera, I wanted to finish the video, so I was like, "Can
you grab the camera for me?"

"No! What?! April, you've been stabbed. You need to sit down."
And then he shouted, "WE NEED SOME HELP OVER HERE!"

This did not seem like a good plan to me. "We came down here
for a reason. I've got like half a line left," I said weakly. I was starting
to feel dizzy, and suddenly every inch of my skin was covered in sweat.

"No, April, lie down, you're going to pass out." He was walking
toward me with his arms out, ready to catch me.

"NO ANDY GIVE ME THE FUCKING CAMERA!" And with
that final effort I was unconscious.

I came to about twenty seconds later on the asphalt in Andy's
arms. A news crew had made their way to us faster than the cops or
the paramedics.

Anyone watching Channel 7 news at that moment, or any other

television station anywhere within the next week, was treated to an image of Andy sitting on the ground hugging my unconscious body, calling out for help through his tears and trying to wake me up. The blood had stained a circle in my coat around my back, and Andy was pushing his hands on it. It's all very dramatic. On replay they tended not to show me coming to, preferring the simplicity of the bits where I'm completely unconscious and passive.

They also didn't show the part where the NYPD arrived and verbally tore the whole TV crew a brand-new set of holes.

My mouth tastes bitter, and I'm still seeing stars, but I'm conscious by this point.

"Andy, thank you. I'm sorry." This is a whisper while two cops start asking him questions.

Andy's answering their questions; one cop has a notepad out. He's telling them our names and what happened, and then he's trying to explain the gunk that's all over us and the stained pile of clothes that used to be Martin Bellacourt, which he's unsurprisingly failing at.

Then he just freaks out. "Look, Officer, I understand that you're doing your job, but she's been stabbed and I don't know what to do. Could we please get some help?"

Then I pipe up, nearly shouting, "I concur!" which causes a fresh wave of stars in my vision. I have no idea why I can't ever shut the fuck up. That's what I should've named this book.

I Have No Idea Why I Can't Ever Shut the Fuck Up: The April May Story.

Anyway, that actually works, and the cops let the paramedics through. There are four, possibly eight, possibly sixteen of them, and they are all very nice.

"Hello, ma'am, I'm Jessica, this is Mitty, we're paramedics, and we're going to have some questions for you. It's very important that you answer truthfully."

Jessica's rattling off questions that she's obviously asked a million times before: "Where does it hurt, ma'am?" "Well, mostly the hole in my back where the knife was." "Are you on any drugs?" "No." "Are you allergic to any drugs?" "No." "Can we cut these very expensive clothes off of you?" "Well, I've already bled all over them anyway." "Does this hurt?" "A bit." "What about this?" "AAAAGGHGHHHH!!!"

During all this, Mitty's laying me on my right side on the gurney, taking my blood pressure, shining a light in my eyes, asking me if I can feel and move my fingers and toes and then pinching my fingers and toes, after which he says, "Good cap refill in all extremities," and I reply, "That sounds like good news!"

They both laugh.

In a matter of moments I am being loaded into the ambulance.

"Hey, can I have a second with my friend?" I ask Jessica.

"Yeah, sure."

"Andy!" I call out.

He runs over from where he's been talking to the cops. "Yeah?"

"Look, this is going to sound shitty and the first thing is making sure I'm OK, but I think I'm OK so . . ." And I was honestly embarrassed to say it, which I guess is good. "We need to get out in front of this. We need to be the bigger voice, the better voice, or else this will just be another thing they'll blame Carl for." And at that moment, I look over at Carl. Still standing impassive, regal, powerful, oblivious, and untouchable, even missing a hand.

"As soon as the cops are done with me, yeah, I'll get on it."

"No, the cops are going to take that footage and sit on it. You need to give me the card."

He considers this for a moment and then realizes I am probably right. "Dang, girl, you are shockingly lucid for a person with a hole in them. What about the last line?"

"Let's just do it now."

He flips on the camera and pops out the mic cable since the EMTs removed my mic with the rest of my clothes. Andy hates using the built-in mic, but he hates accidentally recording something with no audio considerably more.

After locating a piece of clean shirt to wipe the lens clean, he squats down, only a foot or so away from my face, better for the built-in mic to pick up good audio. "Rolling."

In the shot, you can see that I'm lying on my side on a gurney. The ambulance is in the background, and you can see Mitty and Jessica milling about. I'm a mess, and there are still streaks of the Bellacourt goop on my face. The only thing I'm wearing on my upper body is a blanket. It's a pretty kick-ass shot.

I drop back into my presenting voice, strong and bold, even though it hurts. "As I was saying, even on this most terrible of days, even when the worst of us are all we can think of, I am proud to be a human."

Andy popped out the card and handed it to me under the blanket. I slipped it in my pants pocket.

CHAPTER SEVENTEEN

We're not supposed to be curious." This was Jessica, in the ambulance on the six-minute drive to the hospital, talking loudly over the siren and the rumble of the road. I was on my side, facing Jessica. Apparently they didn't want me lying on the wound.

"Explain," I replied.

"Well, there are a lot of things paramedics aren't supposed to do. One is wonder what happened. Mostly, I don't care, but even when I do, I can't. My job is to keep you as healthy as possible on the way to the hospital. And, well, we're supposed to be extra uninterested if the person in the back is, um, recognizable."

"Oh. Well, hello, I'm April May, you may have seen me in such YouTube videos as 'April May and New York Carl.'" Talking hurt, but not that much more than breathing did.

"I figured as much." I liked Jessica, with her big, thick-framed glasses and bright red lipstick. If I'd had to guess, I'd say she was maybe a couple of years older than me. She was checking my blood pressure and breathing constantly.

"Am I going to be OK?"

"Interestingly, that is another thing we're not supposed to talk about. If I say you are, and then you aren't, you could sue me."

"Oh. Well . . ." I thought for a second. "If a person were in your ambulance with exactly my symptoms, would you be concerned about their future ability to be alive?"

She smiled. "I would not be." The blood pressure cuff hissed out its air, but she left it velcroed on my arm.

"That is pleasant to hear."

"Do you want anything for the pain?"

"No, it hurts, but I'm OK. Actually, if you want to do me a favor, could you look in my blazer pocket and see if my phone is in there?"

"Yeah, it was, I already got it. Do you want me to call someone?" she asked as she pulled it out. "Oh. Damn, girl, you have like eight billion text messages."

"So, checking the phones of the patients in your ambulance is not on the list of things you're not supposed to do?"

She made an endearing embarrassed face. "Now that you mention it . . ."

"Don't worry. Uh, can you just text Robin? Just tell him that I have very minor injuries and what hospital I'm going to and to spread the word to friends and family. And tell him to bring a laptop."

I gave her my passcode, and as she tapped out the text she said, "You're going to Bellevue, by the way."

"Oh, neat!"

"Neat?"

"Yeah, it's such a pretty building, I've always wanted to check it out. Though maybe I could have found a less painful way of getting there."

She finished the text, and I heard the little whoosh noise of it flying off to the nearest cell tower and relaxed a little.

"Bad news, though, you're going to the ugly building."

"Figures. I suppose now I should talk to my parents."

"I mean, I don't mean to pry, but you've also got quite a few texts from a Maya who seems extremely concerned."

I let out a long, slow groan.

"Never mind! Sorry. None of my business."

"No, it's fine. Just text her that I'm fine, it looked worse than it was. Send the same to my parents, tell them I'm going to Bellevue."

Two more whooshes.

I shifted slightly on my side. "Whoooooa," I said, suddenly dizzy again.

"Sorry, I shouldn't be having you talk so much," she said as she started pumping up the blood pressure cuff again. "What are you feeling?"

"Just dizzy. Also my mouth feels like it's packed with dryer lint, I feel a little like I might puke, and I'm suddenly very sweaty. But that might just be being half naked in the back of a truck with a cute paramedic girl."

"Good lord, they're going to put you on morphine just to keep you quiet. Your blood pressure is low, but not dangerously. The pain is probably what's pushing you toward passing out. Do let me know if you're really thinking about puking, though."

"It does hurt quite a lot. More when I breathe."

"Well, don't stop breathing."

"I like you, Jessica."

"I like you too, April May. Now shut up." She moved around to sit behind me, lifted up the blanket, and placed the cold circle of a stethoscope on the injured side of my back.

After a few seconds she said, "The main concern is that your lung might be punctured, but I'm seeing no signs of that."

"What would that feel like?"

"I have no idea, no one's ever stabbed me in the back. Now seriously, be quiet."

I tried to work up some spit to lick my lips because they felt super dry. My tongue came away tasting sweet, like I'd been wearing grape-flavored lip gloss or something.

"Can I have some water?"

Jessica handed me a bottle, saying, "Go easy on it, you don't want to start coughing right now."

New York ambulances can never really go very fast since there's nowhere for the traffic in front to go. Luckily, you're always pretty close to a hospital. The weirdest thing about being in the ambulance (aside from being half naked under the blanket and having just been stabbed) was the steadiness of the siren. You hear sirens all the time, but they're always either coming or going—getting louder or quieter, and pitch-shifted by the Doppler effect. You never just hear a siren steadily for a long time. I guess Jessica and Mitty did, but it was one of those familiar but slightly off things that stuck in my head. That's what I was thinking about when we took the last turn before we arrived at Bellevue and the siren turned off.

"Can you do me a favor?" I suddenly asked.

"Probably not."

Moving my arm as little as possible, I carefully reached into my pants pocket and pulled out the flash card. "This is extremely important. Can you take it to the check-in desk or whatever and tell them to hold it for Robin Vree?"

There was a long pause. The ambulance was stopping in front of the ER and I could hear people talking outside. She grabbed it and tucked it into her uniform just as the ambulance doors opened, and she launched into a monologue, directed at the hospital doctors: "Twenty-three-year-old female, shallow stab wound to the left upper back between shoulder blade and spine, third and fourth ribs possibly fractured. No sign of spinal damage or lung puncture. Wound is packed but still bleeding. Blood pressure one twenty over eighty, cap refill good, no sign of internal bleeding . . ." It went on like that for a while. And then pretty immediately I was swooped into the system. X-rays, pain meds, shots, swabs, stitches.

CHAPTER EIGHTEEN

A lot of people came to my hospital room over the next couple of days. The first (that I remember, at least—I was on pain meds for some of the time) were a couple of guys from the NYPD.

"Ms. May, I'm Officer Barkley, this is Officer Barrett, we need to ask you some questions about your attack."

"I don't actually know that much, but I'll do my best."

"What were you doing when you were attacked?"

This didn't seem particularly relevant, but they were police, so I just told the truth. I was there shooting a video about the July 13 attacks and also about the demonstration going on on 23rd. Did I think it was a dangerous thing to do? Yes, but I wanted to do it anyway.

We went through the details of the actual event: the thousand-pound fist of the knife going into me; the body collapsing on me; the weird, disgusting, formless body dead on the ground.

"Do you know what happened to your attacker?"

I was talking softly, unusual for me, but taking deep breaths felt like being stabbed all over again. "Something very odd. I know Andy didn't kill him, though I think he would have been happy to. Whatever happened to that guy was not normal."

"Your friend Andy. His camera was missing its memory card."

"Oh god!" I said. "That's awful news!" And now I'm lying to the police. To my ear, it sounded not at all convincing. "It must have been in there when he was filming, he's not an amateur."

"You don't think it's possible that there was never a card in the camera?"

I felt like I was on treacherous ground here. I decided to keep all the doors open.

"It doesn't seem like the kind of mistake Andy would make, but maybe. Sometimes when a DSLR gets jolted, the card slot can open and the card can fall out." And then, for good measure, I added, "We need to find that card! It's not like we can reshoot that video! That was a once-in-a-lifetime chance!" I'm talking louder now, the pain suppressed by the adrenaline of lying. It was absolutely terrifying.

"Ms. May, given the circumstances, aren't there more pressing concerns than your video?"

"You have your jobs, I have mine."

They went over the whole thing with me again and told me that I was going to have to write a witness statement as soon as I was feeling up to it.

"Considering the circumstances, we're posting a uniformed officer at your door."

That gave me something to think about—two murder attempts in less than twenty-four hours, and the police only knew about one of them. I got to think about that, and how Carl had saved me, and how he hadn't saved a bunch of other people. I got to think about those things all by myself and for maybe just a little too long.

I haven't told you a ton about my parents. It's not that I don't like them. The opposite, actually, they are just massively supportive, sweet people. It was almost a cliché at the School of Visual Arts (where Andy and Maya and I went) that *no one's* parents wanted them to be there. It's a ridiculously expensive school, so a lot of the students are children of doctors and lawyers and investment bankers, and not many of those parents see art school as the best path to long-term success. But when my classmates swapped horror stories about the battles they had to fight to get their parents to shell out for school, or just simply allow them to pay their own way, I really didn't have much to contribute.

My parents saw I was passionate about something and did what they could to help me get it. I mentioned before that my parents own a company that manufactures and sells machines that milk cows. They fell into this after spending a summer interning on a small dairy farm after they graduated from school with degrees in political science. They thought the systems the farms used looked impractical and inefficient, and five years later, their company was supplying half of Northern California's small-scale dairy farms with upgraded systems. By the time I went to college they were selling to most of the northwest US and had a warehouse filled with equipment tailored for small dairies that they sent all over the world. They'd hired people to do the day-to-day work and were semiretired.

I think, since they didn't really know how they had become successful, and it certainly didn't have a ton to do with their education, they figured I should just do whatever. It had worked for them. They still owned the business, and I guess they "ran" it or whatever, but most of their time since I went to school was spent helping to run local nonprofits and traveling around to see bands they were into. Some parents worried about their children squandering their inheritance. I worried about my parents squandering it before it got to me.

They were just very happy people. Maybe I'm so snarky because I was just bored with how pleased they always seemed to be. Though not bored enough to ever actually do anything traditionally rebellious.

Here's an example of how supportive they were: When I called them from the hospital, they did not immediately fret or cry or ask me how I could have put myself in such danger, which would have been the normal response. We got through the initial report of what the doctors said (I was fine, though a couple of my ribs were cracked), they said their "We're so glad you're OKs," and then . . .

"Robin says he got your note and everything's being taken care of." This was my mom.

"My note?" I was confused.

"The note you left at the hospital reception desk."

I hadn't left a note; I'd left a memory card. My dad picked up the conversation, not giving me a chance to figure it out.

"He also says not to call or text anyone about that stuff. You shouldn't be stressing right now."

"Um, OK?" Why on earth had Robin gone through my parents?

Mom started again: "He was very adamant. He says it's being taken care of and he'll see you soon. So you won't call or text anyone?"

"I mean, I might." Lying to the police was one thing; my parents were too sweet for duplicity.

My dad: "Robin said he needed you to confirm verbally that you would not call or text anyone but us."

"This is very weird."

"We trust him, though, right?" my dad said.

"He seems like a very nice boy," followed my mom.

"He is indeed, and no, we're not dating."

"So?" my dad again.

"OK, I won't call or text anybody."

We talked for another twenty minutes, and they barely even brought it back around to how I had been stabbed in the back due to my own stupidity.

"Concentrate on getting well, we'll be there in the morning," Mom said. They were cutting their vacation short.

"I love you guys."

"We love you too," they said simultaneously, and then we hung up.

I was a little shocked that I hadn't seen Andy or Robin yet. I kept expecting them to walk in the room and it kept not happening. What I learned later was that as I lay there in bed, there had been a mad rush to keep our footage safe and secret while both the NYPD and the FBI attempted to find and control it.

Andy had gone back to his apartment, where he had seen a succession of uniforms asking him where his footage was. They couldn't legally search his apartment, but apparently there was a pretty good chance they were listening in on our phone conversations and text messages. Of course, Andy didn't have the footage, Robin did, and thus far, Robin hadn't been a person of interest.

I knew none of this. I knew that what had happened to Martin Bellacourt was horrifying and impossible, but I wasn't processing it as newly weird. Carl was a space alien, so weird was done with. As far as I was concerned, we were already at peak weird.

Hundreds of people had been killed in terrorist attacks, so while I assumed the fact that someone had tried to kill me was going to be in the news, I didn't think it was going to be front page.

And I thought that as the day stretched into evening and I started to wonder why no one had come in to tell me I was being discharged. And then a tall guy walked into the room with an earpiece and an intensity of awareness and readiness that I had never seen before. After taking in the room, he came up to me and said, "Ms. May, I'm Agent Thorne, and the president will be here shortly."

That was all the preparation I got. About five seconds later, another agent walked in, followed promptly by the president, a third agent, and a young woman in a suit. The president was wearing a blue blazer and white silk blouse. Her gray hair swept over her shoulders casually.

It was intensely surreal. There was a bit of that "Oh my god, they've got three dimensions and a size and a shape and I'm seeing a person with my own eyes that I have previously only seen through the eyes of cameras" feeling that you get with any famous person. That's a weird thing, and it's a very interesting and complex experience.

I had had that several times in my life by this point. But there was something much more impressive about the president. I mean, I was a big fan of hers, so there's that. She and I shared a lot of values and goals, and she had done so many things that I respected and was amazed by. My appreciation for her was and remains very deep, and while I could hang with any Hollywood celebrity and not be intimidated by their status, this was a very different thing. I was intensely intimidated, and yet, at the same time, there was a frailness to her.

I don't mean any particular physical frailty, of course. I simply mean that she was very much a human. Just bones and organs and stuff, like the rest of us. That became very real as she moved in to shake my hand. Firm, practiced, her skin rougher than I expected.

"April, it's wonderful to finally meet you, I'm sorry it's not under better circumstances. How are you doing?"

I wanted to ask her why she was here, but that seemed rude, so I just answered her question: "I'm fine. They say I can go home tomorrow, really just a scratch and some broken ribs. I'm more emotionally messed up than anything, to be honest."

"You're wondering why I'm here. Well, April, first, where is the footage from your attack? Everyone seems quite certain that it exists, and yet lots of people have failed in trying to find it."

"You're here for . . . my footage?" I was astounded.

"Among other reasons, yes. As I said, you have a way of being at the center of things, April. I am not holding that against you, and I hope it's clear that we are friends, but there are a number of fast-moving parts right now that need to be either slowed or harnessed, and there is a lot of concern that the footage that was on that camera is one of them." She was efficient as ever.

"You aren't making a ton of sense to me," I said.

"Be that as it may, I need your footage."

I was caught off guard and did not really know how to handle it, so I stalled.

"It's starting to feel a little bit like I need to know what will happen to me if I don't get you the footage." I said "get" instead of "give" to make it clear that I didn't have it.

"Nothing, April. To me, you, whether you like it or not, are a member of the press. It would be an extraordinary step for me to take information away from you or bar it from being broadcast. That would be the sort of thing that requires lawyers and judges, and I have neither the time nor the desire to go that route. But I can, as the president of the United States, ask you to do me a favor."

"Oh, maybe it would be better if I understood why?"

She seemed to think about this very hard for several seconds before she launched in on me. Her face got hard; her voice became darts.

"April, we are aware that someone tried to kill you last night. We believe it was the same man who tried to kill you this afternoon. Whatever possessed you to *not report the shooting* and then to *walk out of your building unguarded*, I'm. Not. Asking. Maybe it was the foolishness of youth, maybe it was more than that. But when you walked out of that building, you created a new history that we have to live in now."

She did not say this as something I should be proud of, more something that I had to live with. The dart hit its mark.

"This new history is one in which the alien technology that we've come to know as the Carls allowed hundreds, if not thousands, of people to die, and then, today, clearly and intentionally killed a man rather than allow harm to come to you."

"Well," I said, and then paused for a long time. "Wait, you think Carl killed that guy?"

"April, Martin Bellacourt's bones and organs and blood—everything except his skin—are now, as far as our best people can tell at the moment, grape jelly."

Long pause . . .

"Grape jelly?" I asked.

She did not respond. I thought back to the ambulance—to the grape-flavored lip gloss. My stomach turned, and then a wave of anxiety washed over me and sweat prickled out over my entire body.

"What are they?" I asked quietly, unable to stop myself.

"We don't know, April."

Her strength was so comforting, so calming, that I finally asked her the question I hadn't even been able to ask myself: "Are they bad?"

"April, I don't know." I caught a tiny glimmer of uncertainty in her eyes before she went on as confident as before. "What I do know is that we don't just have a space alien, dream-infecting robot visiting every city in the world, we have a space alien, dream-infecting robot killer. I want very much to frame this correctly and be a voice of reason. However, I feel strongly that you or one of your"—she searched for a word—"posse . . . are right now working on a video that, while probably very good, will not necessarily have all the nuance the US government is looking for right now. So, please, if you could, allow us to analyze your footage and do not release anything for at least twenty-four hours."

"Certainly there are already other videos out?" I wouldn't have been surprised if someone was livestreaming at the time.

"There are, but it's blurry cell phone footage. No one on scene had a camera as nice as yours. Please, just do this for us."

"And after twenty-four hours we can post our video and you won't want to review it or stop us from posting it?"

"April, I'm not a fool. I've seen the internet, you can't contain information anymore. Plus there's the whole First Amendment. It's one of the bigger rules."

"I'll get you the files right away," I said. "Where should they be delivered?"

"Here," she said.

"Right here?"

"I would rather not leave without them."

I took out my phone and called Robin.

"Robin, I need you to make a copy of Andy's footage from today and bring it to me in the hospital."

"Are you sure?"

"The president is here. We made—" I looked her right in the eyes as I said it. "We made a deal." She smiled at me.

"I'll be there in twenty minutes," he said.

I hung up.

"We have twenty minutes," I said to the president of the United States of America.

"Well, we have some other things to discuss. I've talked to your doctors and they said you could go home, but I was wondering if you could stay an extra day so that I could come by with the press tomorrow? They'll ask you a few questions, mostly they'll take pictures and video of me walking in and talking to you. I have to be shown being active right now or everyone will say, 'Where is the president at this Time of Need! Probably playing shuffleboard or having her period!' It's not my fault I like shuffleboard so much. I always say, add up all the time every other president has spent golfing and tell me that my shuffleboard habit is bad for America."

I laughed.

"What?" she asked.

"I don't know. You're"—I felt dumb as I said it—"really a person, aren't you."

"Oh, April, of all people I thought you would know what this is like. But I understand. The charisma of office, they call it. It's hard to see past it. Indeed, I work to cultivate it. It's part of the job."

It struck me then how very much she was indeed quite like me. As if, maybe, there was real kinship that I might have with this person who was more a symbol than a human.

"So what do you say?" she said.

"Yeah, so you're coming by again tomorrow?"

"I'm doing a number of things in the city." She meant New York. "Because it's where you were attacked, it makes more sense for me to be doing events here." Then, without even pausing for breath, she changed the subject. "April, I'm going to debrief you personally. This would normally be done by someone else, but since we have a little time and I used to be in intelligence, I'm happy to do it myself.

"Your attacker's name was Martin Bellacourt. He was acting alone in the sense that he did not have financial or logistical support, but he was part of the coordinated attack and was in contact with the other terrorists. If you're looking for a motive, which I applaud you if you aren't but it will be hard not to, I don't know that I can help you. He had criminal convictions for domestic violence and had been living alone for years. Initial reports are that his online rants weren't very coherent, but he was clearly an angry person who felt he had no control over what he saw as a decaying world.

"We don't know much about Carl, but we do know that he is able to do things that are far beyond human ability. The wholesale chemical conversion of Bellacourt's body definitely falls into that category, and so legally this will be classified as a homicide by Carl. It does seem a very odd thing to do, but when a person is killed in our society, we have a process, even when that homicide is clearly justified. We will have to do that here. We have decided to act as if New York Carl is a person with free will, and the law will treat him as such."

"What does that mean?" I asked.

"It means that there will be a hearing and a judge will decide whether the state will bring charges against Carl. If he is indicted, that means that there will be a trial. Anytime a person is killed by another person, it is a homicide, but it is not murder unless it was intentional and inexcusable. This seems like a clear case of justified homicide and we expect any judge in America would rule that way.

"I want you to understand that this is simply the process, and not an attempt by us to make New York Carl some kind of scapegoat."

"Is it just that?"

"It is mostly that"—she paused—"but also, April, I apologize but I have to ask, are you in communication with the Carls?"

"What?"

"Do you have a way to communicate with them? Or, less specifically, do you know anything about them that is not broadly known?"

"So you don't know either," I said.

"Know what?"

"Why he saved me and not all those other people."

"No, I don't, April. I'm sorry."

"Neither do I," I said, honestly, avoiding the earlier question that might lead to an awkward conversation about the giant robot hand / roommate I had recently acquired, and the slice of the Dream that I had but no one else did.

"Please, April, don't hold anything back here, we need to know."

So whom do you side with in a situation like this, your new best friend, the most powerful person in the world? Or the space alien who saved your life yesterday?

After a lengthy pause I decided to split the difference, "I have a different dream."

She did the thing where she didn't say anything so I would say more.

"In every other dream, no object ever moves unless it is moved by someone in the Dream. But in my dream, there's an airplane, a 767, that lands in the city. We think it's the final clue, the way to unlock the whole thing. I'm the only one, as far as we can tell, that has access to it. So we've kept it a complete secret."

She looked spellbound. "You did the right thing," she finally said. "Are you actively working to solve this sequence?" I was almost surprised to hear her using the correct nomenclature.

"We are, but we haven't gotten very far. Many of the sequences are very hard to solve if you don't have very specific knowledge."

"We have code breakers who may be able to help. But, April, when this sequence is solved—I have to say this very clearly—do not take action on what you discover without consulting us first."

"I think I have learned that lesson by now."

"I would also think that, but please promise."

"I will not take action if we solve the sequence without first talking to you," I said. That seemed like a safe promise to make. As much as I liked the idea of being an important piece of this, I recognized that I wasn't trained to be the emissary of my species. "But," I added, "can I come along in whatever journey this ends up being?"

"Yes, April, I would love to have you there. Now, is there anything else you know that you have not told us?"

"No." And then quite surprisingly I started to cry. "I feel like I should know, but I don't. How did I get in the middle of all this?"

"I'm sorry, this is going to be a difficult thing to live with. Whenever you're blaming yourself for being alive, for being the only one who was saved, please remember how deeply, deeply thankful I am that you are alive. I have seen you as an ally from day one, and I honestly am upset that this had to be the circumstance of our first meeting. Is there anything else you want to tell me?"

It felt like a neon sign spelling the word "LIAR" was glowing beneath my skin of my face.

"Thank you for your visit and for being so kind," I said, my voice quivering.

"Well, if you think of anything, you have my number."

Remarkably enough, that was true.

She continued. "You have a tremendous future in front of you, and it's going to be a joy to watch it."

Tremendous future, eh? Well, she wasn't wrong.

Robin came in just after the president left. He had been held back by Secret Service, who had taken the flash drive he'd brought for them.

"Andy is on his way to pick this up." He held up the memory card.

"Tell him to edit now, but that we can't upload until tomorrow."

"How are you?" Robin asked.

I thought about this for a second. With Robin, I felt like I owed more than just a casual assessment of my bodily integrity.

"I think I'm OK?" I said. "I mean, I can't figure out if I'm fine or terrible. Someone tried to kill me, Robin."

"I know." He looked past my bed out the window, letting the silence hang.

"Thank you for not telling me what an idiot I am."

"I figured you already knew."

"I do."

Robin started fishing around in his bag for his laptop.

"You want to hear some tweets?"

"Oh god, I don't know, do I?"

He smiled a pained smile. In a moment, his laptop was open and he was reading me replies to the tweet I'd posted that morning. It now had more likes and retweets and replies than anything I'd ever posted.

Having Robin read you comments and tweets is the best possible way to read them. He has a great voice, amazing enunciation, and, of course, he skips the awful ones.

"Courtney Anderson says, 'We're all thinking of you, April. You have so much faith in humanity even on a dark day like this. Thanks for sharing that strength.'"

That felt good enough that my eyes got a bit misty.

"This person's just sent you like twenty-five of some sort of hug emoji," Robin continued. Then, after another moment, "Oh, you'll like this one, SpidermanandSnape says, 'I've been watching the news all day, but this tweet is the only thing that matters to me right now. BE OK APRIL MAY!'"

After a pause he continued. "This one is from the Som. CMDRSprocket says, 'Everyone is just wedging arguments they were already having or babbling about things we don't know. Thanks for just being a human.'"

"Yeah, that one . . . ," I said, getting sleepier.

He kept reading to me until well after I was asleep.

Andy was there when I woke up. He seemed, as he had lately, burdened. But even more so now. He sagged into the chair next to my bed, still the skinniest kid I knew, but now somehow with a great weight in his posture.

"You're OK?" he said when he saw I was awake, seeming legitimately concerned.

"I'm OK. They say I'll be 100 percent in a few weeks."

"But on the inside too?"

"I think so. For now."

That question, asking how I was really doing, was not a nontrivial effort for Andy Skampt. He wasn't the kind of guy who asked other people how they were feeling. But then again, it's not every day that your best friend gets assaulted right in front of your eyes. As I was thinking these things, Andy broke a silence that I didn't realize had formed.

"April, did I kill him?"

Suddenly I was back in the moment, looking down at the stained pile of clothing, oozing and seeping.

"No. No. The president told me, Andy, it wasn't you." And then something, for the first time, clicked in my brain.

"Andy, you were terrified." He was shaking a bit, his head in his hands. Not crying, just quivering. I could picture him covered in the sticky goop that was Martin Bellacourt, standing in the middle of the street, a couple of yards away from Carl, looking absolutely alone.

Andy looked at me like I'd just put my own knife inside him. He whispered, "Jesus, April, of course I was terrified." I realized that he'd thought it was an accusation, that I was questioning his bravery.

"No, I mean, just to go out there, you looked like you were gonna hurl. But when that guy dashed at me, you . . ." I started crying.

Not, like, polite tears running down my cheeks as I eloquently told Andy how touched and amazed I was that he had been the first and only person to actually rush to defend me. Ugly crying. Painful gasps and sobs. Wailing. Andy, the goof, the weedy little clown, had raised his prized camera rig over his head and torn a man's head off his shoulders for me. Yeah, a structurally compromised man, but still.

I thought all those things, but instead of saying them, I made big, huge, horrible noises that doubled me over and pushed me into the fetal position, my back searing with pain, which made me cry out even more loudly. Andy stood to push back my hair and tell me it was going to be OK. The moment he touched me, I grabbed at him like I was drowning, I pulled him down into the hospital bed and covered his clean button-down shirt with my tears and snot.

"You fucking beautiful moron, that was the bravest thing I've ever seen. You saved me. You saved me. You saved me." I knew it wasn't technically true, but I think he understood what I meant. I think you do too.

The next morning *everyone* was in the hospital. My parents, Jennifer Putnam, Andy, Miranda, and Maya. For a very brief moment, Jessica the paramedic even popped in to say hi. And as much as they were all definitely there to see me, they were all there at the same time because the president was coming by to do her press thing. The president's twenty-four-hour video moratorium meant that we had some free time to prepare and (dare I say it) relax in the few hours before she showed up.

I got to hang alone with just my parents for an hour or so, which was welcome. They were doing everything they could to hold it together and not show me how freaked-out they were (which they, of course, failed at). It didn't really occur to me until then that I had been making decisions that would affect them so deeply.

They babbled on about Tom's honeymoon and their weirdo neighbors and did everything they could to make it feel like a normal parent-kid chat. You know what they didn't do, though? They didn't, not one single time, say, "What were you thinking?!" Not because they knew or because they understood—I really don't think they did. They didn't ask that because I sure as hell didn't stab myself in the back, and when a radical extremist stabs someone in the back, the only person at fault is the radical extremist.

"But you got to hang out with the president, though!" my mom said, trying again to turn the conversation away from the part where her daughter almost died.

"Yeah, I mean, you also are going to get to hang out with the president," I reminded her.

"But that's not the same, she came to see you because of something you did!"

"More like something that was done to me."

My dad continued Mom's thought: "I think you know that's not the whole story, hon. We're very proud of you, April, for taking this opportunity to say kind and thoughtful things even when being kind and thoughtful isn't easy right now."

"It's just the identity I built up, it's not even really me."

They both smiled at me like idiot puppies, and then my mom said, "April, you're not building a brand, you're building yourself." Dad's eyes were misty as he added, "It's so easy to forget, with everything that's happened this year, that you're only twenty-three years old."

"Ugghhh," I said, because that was my line. They just both smiled like idiots.

A while later, Robin came in to introduce me to a stylist, Vi, who was going to make me look nice for my photo op. I am aware that I am an attractive person, but there was a time when I hated having power over people because of it. That's one of the things I loved so much about Maya. Unlike anyone else I had ever dated, I think she had to get to know me before she started thinking I was hot. And that was really hot.

Ever since Carl, I had been doing more with my face, but mostly I was styling for legitimacy, making myself look older and more professional. I had become very intentional about the way I looked, and I did not just want to look beautiful; I wanted to look serious and important. Beautiful was good too, though, because if people like looking at you, they will end up listening to you almost by accident. This is fucked up, but it's true. Like, it isn't just a coincidence that Anderson Cooper can knock a hole in your heart with his steely blue eyes. I decided early on in this process that there wasn't any reason to not play the advantages I had to play.

But as the stylist set up her little trifolding mirror and huge tool-box full of magnificently expensive beauty products, she asked me how I wanted to look, and I honestly couldn't think of anything. I didn't feel like that woman I'd seen on the news clips. And I couldn't go elegant or glamorous—I was in a hospital gown. I was starting to feel intensely self-conscious because this was going to be my first appearance since the attack. My first anything, really. It was going to be everywhere and this was an extremely vulnerable position. Was I going to be in the bed? Was that what the president wanted? Was the goal to make me look weak? I think Robin saw my distress.

"April," he said, "what do you want people to feel when they see you?"

"That the Defenders are creating a climate that encourages extremism and that the stuff I've been saying is the only thing that makes sense?"

"Really?"

"Yeah, I mean, that's been the goal so far, right?"

"Um"—he turned to the stylist—"Vi, could you excuse us for a second?"

Her eyes got a little big, but then she said, "Yeah, sure," and left the hospital room.

"April," Robin continued seriously, "this is a whole new narrative. What do you think the main question people are going to be asking themselves is?"

"Why did the attacks happen? Why did someone want to kill me?"

"No, those are certainly on the list. But after this news comes out, the first thing the world will think when they look at you is why did Carl save you and not the hundreds of other people who died yesterday."

"Oh." I looked away from him. "Oh," I said again, because I didn't know what else to say.

"What is the obvious answer to that question?"

I felt too weak to believe my answer, but it was the only one I could come up with, "Because I'm important."

"There are two reasons why you might be so important, and neither of them are good."

I thought about it for a second. What would I think if I found out this mysterious force had taken its first-ever clear action and it was to kill to protect one girl in New York?

Either:

1. I was important to their plan, and their plan was to help humanity, in which case some people would start seeing me as a messiah. Or . . .
2. I was important to their plan, and their plan was to hurt humanity, in which case I was the worst kind of traitor that had ever existed.

He left it unsaid but continued. "You need very much to be neither of those things right now. You need to be what you really are, a hurt human being in the hospital."

"But, I don't mean to be a dick about this, but is that going to put me in the strongest position?"

"It might or it might not, but it's definitely the safer choice, and I think you owe it to a lot of people right now to make some less risky decisions." He said this very confidently and without the castigation that he could easily have put there.

He let his words hang in the air as he walked to the door and opened it, apologizing to Vi the stylist as he let her back into the room.

"Just freshen me up a little bit," I told her. "If you can make me look young, that might also be good. Basically, I'm feeling terrified and vulnerable and weak"—I turned to Robin—"and I think the right thing to do is be honest about that."

Fifteen minutes later Putnam walked in. "She'll be here in less than half an hour," she said, obviously referring to the president. "And what the HELL was the stylist thinking?! Is she still here? You look like a fourteen-year-old orphan."

"It's all right, Jennifer," I said.

"No, it's fine, there's plenty of time to fix it."

"No," I said, getting annoyed, "that's not what I'm saying. This is what I asked for."

"To look weak?"

"No, to look how I feel. To look like a human when everyone is going to want to make me a symbol."

"But, April, you need to be a symbol. That's what you've always wanted to be. This is a huge opportunity, maybe the biggest one you'll ever have. You need to make an impression. It's the president! You need to look good!"

"What do you want me to look like, a movie star in a hospital bed? A hero?" And then I was suddenly, actually angry, but I kept my voice low. "Like the Messiah or like Judas? Which one will sell more books, Jen?" I had never called her Jen before. I don't know that anyone had.

Her face was unreadable for a fraction of a second before she spoke.

"Oh god, April, I'm so sorry, I honestly do forget sometimes how extremely savvy you can be. It's not often that someone is a step ahead of me, but you're absolutely right. You have every right to be angry with me, I hadn't thought about it fully. I just wanted you to look good."

Textbook Putnam. As soon as she'd understood she wasn't going to win, she agreed with all the vigor and flattery she could muster.

"No, it's all right," I snapped. "It's just been a stressful day."

"Is there anyone you want to talk to before we get this show on the road?"

"Um, I actually have no idea what this show is going to be, so maybe someone to explain that to me?"

"Ah, yes, there will be a representative from the White House to go over all of that with you soon."

And there was. Five minutes later a young woman in an extremely well-tailored suit told us all what to expect, how to behave properly and not make fools of ourselves and avoid having the Secret Service tackle anyone.

For ten terrifying, mostly silent, awful minutes after that, my parents, Andy, Jennifer, Maya, Miranda, Robin, and I twiddled our thumbs in my hospital room, waiting for word. A soft "ting" from Jennifer's wrist signaled an incoming message. She looked at her watch and said, "She's arrived."

"Oh holy fuckballs," my mom said. Everyone laughed. It was cute watching them all freak out. I was nervous, though, not about the president but about the cameras. I would have to be clever and also respectful and also somehow find a way to humanize myself. It was going to be a delicate balance and my brain was turning to mush.

I definitely had to pee, but it was too late for that.

Two guys with that "I am obviously a Secret Service agent" look about them came in and analyzed the room, not seeing people as people but as potential threats to be categorized and monitored. One of them left; the other stayed by the door.

Then came a small camera crew: one photographer, one videographer, and one sound guy with a boom mic. They crammed themselves into the far side of the room. Then the president walked in. I heard the shutter on Andy's camera open. Good ol' Andy.

She spent a bit of time schmoozing with my parents, with Andy and Robin and Miranda and Maya. They were all beaming. Then she came over to my bed.

"April, how are you feeling?"

"They say I should be able to go home shortly," I replied, not sure if we were just going to replay our conversation from yesterday.

"You had a pretty close call there."

I thought of several cute, clever things to say and discarded them all immediately in favor of, "Very. It's so unreal, that someone would do something like this." I was directing the conversation, a habit that was hugely difficult to break. But also one that the most powerful person in the world is used to dealing with.

"It's nice that you have friends and family with you." She gestured to the quiet line of bystanders. I felt immediately guilty and did my best to pretend I didn't know why. "And know that the thoughts of the American people are with you as well."

"Thank you, Madam President." We shook hands again, and then the cameras were off.

"That's it?" I said.

"That's all they'll need. Pretty ballsy trying to direct the conversation."

"Habit! I'm sorry."

She laughed. "Sorry to run so quickly, but it is a busy day, as you might imagine."

"Of course," I said, and then she began her good-byes, and in less than a minute she was gone.

There was a general buzz in the room after she left. Everyone was already putting together the stories they'd be telling about this moment for the rest of their lives. But also, the twenty-four hours was up, so Andy was busy poking the video live on his phone. It was public in seconds. The whole thing, my speech as I walked in the crowd, the one or two screams as Martin pushed through to get at me. The moment he smacked into me, his skin going a few shades darker as he turned into a glob. The camera crashing into him. Then there was about fifteen seconds of audio with no video footage, before the sounds of scuffling, yelling, and running all faded. And then me, on a stretcher saying, "Even on this most terrible of days, even when the worst of us are all we can think of, I am proud to be a human."

It was the best video we'd ever made by a pretty long stretch. And as federal agencies had already begun to indicate that Carl was responsible for Bellacourt's death, it came at a good moment for me. The pictures of a concerned president bending over my hospital bed did good for me as well. We were right, more than right. This was the moment the Defenders lost the war. They couldn't be perceived broadly as a legitimate movement when a little girl was lying in a hospital bed after someone tried to stab her in the back. It was all out there now.

Of course, that made them all the more desperate. Those who truly believed I was a traitor to my species weren't going to stop believing it, and if the only way to take me down was a direct attack, that was their new tool.

CHAPTER NINETEEN

Everything was pretty grand in the days after the attack. Which is an absolutely awful thing to say, but I had no responsibilities. Indeed, the less I did, the more I (and my ideas) were talked about. I had my own surrogates now, and they were out there preaching my message. I got to convalesce (though I wasn't even that badly injured) while the Defenders lost every important argument they managed to get themselves into. Also, things were bound to get weird between Miranda and me even if I hadn't almost been assassinated a few nights after we hooked up. But at least this way I could pretend like any weirdness was due to the tremendous weight of the knowledge that real people wanted me dead badly enough that they would actually try to get it done themselves.

There were a couple of sour points, of course. I couldn't go back to my apartment and I had no idea what had happened to Carl's hand. I'm sure there was a safe way to go back but I couldn't. And a nice thing about being almost murdered is that people let you get away with irrationally refusing to ever return to your apartment. So I didn't let anyone go there, and I didn't go there myself. This way, no one would need to know that my bedroom windows had been shot out. At least, no one except the US government, which seemed to be letting me keep that secret for, I'm sure, their own reasons.

Andy had long since gotten a nice place in Rose Hill, bringing Jason along with him, I guess that made it easier to keep doing their podcast. After the hospital, I went to temporarily live in their guest bedroom. After about a week, when Robin found me a new place, I realized I had absolutely no desire to live on my own, so I just stayed at Andy's. Moving in with my dorky best friend and his dorkier roommate wasn't how I had planned to use my newfound, ludicrous wealth, but it worked.

The other big rough patch was that I had continued to utterly fail at solving the 767 Sequence. I was so frustrated that I resented falling asleep. But still, every night I circled the plane, I climbed the engines, I walked on the wings and tried to break the windows. I read everything I could find about airplanes. Ultimately, I knew the hexagons, which I'd painstakingly memorized and copied down to show Maya, were the code we needed to solve, and we just couldn't crack it.

Maya handled me like the delicate flower I was. Even though I'd fucked up tremendously and done the exact thing she'd told me not to do (and hooked up with Miranda, which she still didn't know about), she was nothing but nice. Basically, I knew the warning signs and was aware that, while things were going OK in this fight, I was headed into a bad brain place, seeing the catastrophe that was me through what I imagined as Maya's perspective.

I felt like the only way to escape that was to make some kind of overture, like sending her flowers or writing a big long apology letter. Of course, all those things seemed deeply inadequate, so instead, I made a decision.

I went to Club Monaco and dropped $1,200 on a new jacket,

Hello, everyone. I'll be honest with you, I'm pretty messed up right now. I was not badly injured physically, but I, and I think many of us, are feeling psychologically injured right now. I have a couple of broken ribs and a dozen stitches. But dealing with the reality that someone would want . . . [Here I have to work through the emotions, and I'm not acting] . . . to kill me . . . and to succeed in killing so many others who did nothing besides show excitement and interest in our visitors . . . that is a far deeper wound.

Of course, right now, the Defenders are disavowing these attacks. That is proper, and I honestly think that the vast majority of them would never condone this kind of action. But when the rhetoric is so inflammatory, so enraged, it is not surprising that some people would work together to take matters into their own misguided hands.

In my own less intense way, I have indeed done that very thing.

Since early July it has been fairly clear that all the puzzle sequences in the Dream except one have been uncovered and solved. The code has been compiled and seems complete except that it is asking for a password of some kind and no one knows where to look for it. Well, since before that was the case, I have known that there is a puzzle sequence in the Dream that only I have access to. I have been working on this sequence, which we've been calling the 767 Sequence, for over a month now, and frankly, I've gotten nowhere. The reason I've failed is that I wanted to solve this mystery alone. I wanted to be the hero that you all remember. I wanted to hold on to my fame and my exceptionality. And, because of that, I slowed down the process of us solving the Dream. If I hadn't locked away the information I had, maybe we would have solved the Dream a month ago. Maybe we would have come through this faster and safer. Maybe . . . [And then the video cuts to the next line because I didn't want to finish that sentence.]

I am also fully aware that Carl saved my life. The government has released a preliminary report that my attacker, Martin Bellacourt, died instantly when the inside of his body was apparently turned into grape jelly. And though this sounds like joke, we've all had to come to terms with it as a reality. As this was clearly the action of New York Carl, the New York grand jury will be deciding whether to indict Carl. I fully support these legal proceedings and have faith that Carl will be cleared of charges.

For those of you who have been active Dreamers, we now have one final puzzle to solve. I have put everything we know about the 767 Sequence in the Som—my posts are linked in the description. The Carls obviously intended for us to solve these mysteries together. I am sorry I spent so much time selfishly sitting on this information. I know not all of you will forgive me, and I don't have any reason to expect you to. But I hope you will believe that I deeply, deeply regret hiding this.

And that was that. Within an hour of that video going live, I read this thread in the Som:

I don't know if this is anything, but you know what that hexagon layout reminds me of is my grand-dad's accordion. I don't know how many buttons an accordion has on it, but I think they were laid out like that.

> Bump for interest . . . anyone play an instrument like this?

> > Hey! Yes, I've got my dad here, he plays concertina and accordion and he says (and I'm quoting because I don't understand any of this): "It's called the Wicki-Hayden note layout. No matter what button you're on, if you go to the right, that's a whole step up, if you go up and to the left that's a fourth up, and down and to the right is a fourth down. The closest button directly above is a full octave jump."

By the time that third reply happened, this comment had floated its way to the top of the thread and accordion and concertina players all over the world were chiming in. They were quickly deciphering what it would sound like if the honeycomb bits I had brought out of the Dream were played with the red hexagons representing pushed buttons. Within a half hour after that, it was clear that, though no one could say for sure what key it was meant to be played in, the hexagon patterns on the side of the 767 were a representation of "Call Me Maybe" by Carly Rae Jepsen. Carl has amazing taste in music.

Andy and I went on a research blitz, learning everything we could about the song and about CRJ, master of pop music.

Once I had all the words to "Call Me Maybe" memorized (I already knew most of them), I pulled the curtains of Andy's guest room and got in bed. It was only early afternoon, but I was exhausted (as usual) and needed to see what I could do with this new information. Getting to sleep was not easy—I wanted so badly to make it happen. I knew that literally the whole world was waiting to see what would come of this, and I was the only person in the world who could tell them.

So I cleared my mind and let my exhaustion take over. And then I did that another twenty-three times until it finally stuck and I found myself in the lobby of a fancy office in a fancy office building. A solid thirty minutes after that I was standing in front of a 767, singing in my thready, slightly off-key voice:

> *I threw a wish in the well*
> *Don't ask me I'll never tell*
> *I looked to you as it fell*
> *And now you're in my way*

And this was not actually that weird until I got to the chorus, which is so exquisitely crafted that it is very difficult to sing without getting pretty into it. The good news is that you're always the only person in the Dream, so no one is around to see you dancing around a 767 singing, *"BEFORE YOU CAME INTO MY LIFE I MISSED YOU SO BAD, I MISSED YOU SO BAD, I MISSED YOU SO SO BAD."*

My injuries didn't follow me into sleep, so while back in my real body lifting my left arm above my head remained a goal I'd be working toward for months, in the Dream I could get down like the spry twenty-something I should have been.

And then I finished, and I was pretty sure I got through the whole song without missing a word (though I definitely missed some notes), and I started to hear a soft hiss. Then, louder, came the noise of electric or hydraulic motors as the bays containing the landing gear opened and the massive wheels came down, from the wings and the nose of the airplane. They touched softly down on the grass of the plane park and immediately looked as if they'd been there forever.

I was in.

Or, at least, I was into the very small rooms that stored the airplane's wheels. In my studying 767s, I knew that these wheel bays were big enough for a person to be inside, until the wheels came back in, in which case a person would be very lucky not to be crushed. A number of people had climbed into the forward wheel bay to attempt to hitchhike. This, it turns out, is a fairly good way to die. But that did mean it was possible to climb into the wheel bays, which I proceeded to do immediately. I went up into the forward wheel bay first, because I knew that there was actually a port in there that led to the avionics bay, the room where all the plane's controls were. And from there was another port that led to the interior of the plane. Both of these ports, however, are not just doors, I knew. They're sealed and need special tools to open, but I figured that was my best bet for getting all the way into the plane. Once in the landing gear bay, I saw a remarkable spaghetti mess of tubes and cables. If I were an engineer at Boeing, I'd have a fairly good idea what I was looking at. But I was not, so in the dim light coming from the open hatch, all I saw was a big scary mess.

But spotting the hatch in the ceiling of the bay wasn't a problem. It was marked mostly by the nonexistence of tons of tubes and wires. It was basically the only flat surface on the ceiling. Opening the hatch, on the other hand, was not so simple. It was fastened in place with dozens of flush bolts. Instead of normal Phillips or flathead screws, they were just flat, like the head of a tack.

I dug my nails as deep as I could get into the hatch, but it was so obviously fruitless that I didn't even keep trying.

I crawled around in the bay for a little while longer, looking for . . . anything, I guess, but it all just looked like a mess.

I went back to the hatch to scratch at it a bit more because, I dunno, maybe I had received super strength in the last twenty minutes. This time, though, I noticed the texture of tiny raised letters on the handle. In the dimness of the light the letters were tough to make out—at least that's what I thought at first. Finally I realized that it was not that they were hard to see; they were simply not letters. They were there, but they were just a bunch of lines and circles that my brain couldn't form into words.

It was just the thing that happens when you're off track and the detail of the Dream begins to fade. But how could that be? I'd sung the song and it worked! This had to be it!

"AAAGGHHHH!" I screamed my frustration into the empty room. That didn't help. I aimed a kick at a collection of pipes on the wall, thinking to wake myself up in frustration. I mean, it's not like I had *nothing* to report back to the rest of the world. But if they had succeeded in bringing me a clue, I was loath to come back telling them it was a dead end!

So I only kicked enough to make a satisfying thud, not enough to wake myself up.

The air was stale and oily in the bay, so I decided that maybe there was something I had missed on the outside of the plane. Maybe the secret was in one of the other wheel bays.

I circled the plane again. I yanked on every single thing I could yank on and several I couldn't. I climbed into the other wheel bays and found nothing compelling or useful.

Frustrated, I just started walking away from the plane.

A few blocks down the street I turned to look at that massive machine. I'd spent hours in the Dream staring at it, so I didn't expect to see anything new. And I didn't, but I did feel my heart suddenly jump into my throat before I began running full speed back to the plane because I'd figured it out.

Back in the forward bay I had to let my eyes adjust for a few minutes before I could see the tiny engraved shapes on the handle again. They weren't the indecipherable scribble of "on the wrong track" dream writing; they were the lines and dots of the Mayan numerical system Miranda had taught me at that hotel in DC. The same system that, I was now certain, represented the number six on the tail of the plane.

I could absolutely have punched myself in the face and looked up the system with Andy, but I wanted nothing more than to do this on my own. After months of people all over the world co-solving sequences, I wanted to be more than the vehicle through which this final sequence was solved; I wanted my name on that goddamn Wikipedia page!

So I sat there and tried my damnedest to remember what Miranda had told me. The dots were ones and the bars were fives. So two bars with one dot was an eleven. I was pretty sure about that. Two dots, that was just two. This was simple—the Mayans knew what was up!

So I had a sequence of numbers: 11, 2, 7, 19, 4, 4, 12. Now, what the hell was I supposed to do with those numbers? Well, to the side of the door were seven dials, each numbered one to nineteen. Good lord, was it that easy?

I set each of the dials to the corresponding number, and actually had to dodge as the hatch fell down into the wheel bay. My foot slipped and I tumbled down out of the open hatch. My head slammed into the landing gear on the way down. I awoke in Andy's apartment.

"FUCK!" I shouted.

Andy screamed from the other room, "Are you OK?" and then ran into the room.

"Yes! I'm great! I just— FUCK! I got into the plane. Then I

solved the next step in the sequence, it was the Mayan numbers Mi-randa told me about, they were printed on a hatch in the landing gear bay. I was opening the hatch and I fucking fell and hit my head and woke up!"

Andy laughed like a madman.

"Shut up!"

"It's pretty funny, April. You bagged your first clue and finished it off by slamming your head into a wall?"

"I slammed my head into a landing gear, thank you very much. I need to go back there! And god only knows I can't get to sleep now!"

I rolled over and picked up my phone, which, of course, was set to Do Not Disturb. There was a text from Maya: *Thank you so much for that video. It was really good.*

That was a good feeling. A calming feeling.

"It's OK, April," Andy said. "You're the only one who can access this. There's no time constraint."

I sighed. "I know, I just . . . Goddamn it, y'know! I was almost there!"

"Well, you were almost to the next clue. I don't mean to harsh your buzz, but there's bound to be more."

CHAPTER TWENTY

It was a couple of weeks later and I was sitting in the cockpit of the 767 pushing buttons, trying to make the plane do something. Life had slowed down for me. When everyone you know (including the president of the United States) is telling you the same thing, eventually you listen. Also, being almost murdered twice in one day and then spending weeks dealing with constant dull, aching pain does inspire a little bit of self-reflection. Not only did I have to actually think about the danger I had placed myself in, I also found myself thinking for the first time about the fact that I could and also *would* die someday.

I was trying very hard to settle into my new, more "behind the scenes" life. I was still a household name, but I was mostly staying off-line at the moment. The world knew I was the only one who could work on the key, and that meant I (and the whole team) was super active on the Som, but I wasn't doing interviews or press events or even making videos. I made Robin take my social media passwords away. If I wanted to tweet something, I had to send it to Robin, who would edit it and make sure it was a good idea before it got tweeted.

He would post some relevant stuff on various social media to keep my profiles alive, but I was trying to read books and watch television shows and work slowly and methodically on the 767 Sequence. I had a huge portion of the world helping me, and it was a lot of pressure, so that was a good distraction from my deep, aching desire to leap back into the fray.

I was addicted to the attention and to the outrage and to the rush of being involved in something so huge, but more than any of that I was just addicted. After the attacks, things calmed down. People were, somehow, less freaked-out because we were all more on the same page. People had started to feel comfortable with the Carls, as if they'd just always been there and always would be. Basically, I wasn't really needed. But addiction isn't necessarily about the specific thing; it's about mental reliance, it's a bug in your brain software, and even with the support of some truly remarkable people working to keep me in line, I never went cold turkey. Even after the apps were off my phone, I would go to twitter.com using its browser.

The 767 Sequence was giving up none of its secrets. Once I got into the avionics bay, getting into the plane wasn't another sequence; it was just opening a hatch. But the interior of the plane had turned out to be massive and completely normal. Going back and forth between the Dream and the Som had provided a wealth of data on the plane: what year it was made, what model it was (did you know planes had models?), and even a fair guess at which precise plane it was modeled from. I had spent hours on the in-flight entertainment system, become quite familiar with the cockpit using a flight simulator, and interviewed pilots, mechanics, and flight attendants who worked on 767s. All to no avail.

Anyway, that's what I was doing when Robin shook me awake. This was pretty not-normal for Robin. He seemed visibly flustered in his pressed maroon dress shirt sitting on the edge of my bed in

Andy's spare room. Andy and Miranda were standing behind him. This was pretty dang weird.

"April, I have some important and bad news."

Gathering my wits, I said, "That sounds bad. And also important."

His lips made a thin line. That wasn't good.

"The Defenders have solved the 767 Sequence."

"That's not possible," I said, feeling relieved. "I'm the only one with access to it."

"Apparently, access isn't necessary. Miranda?"

Miranda began, "I hadn't been paying enough attention to the code. It's complete, it turns out. If you compile it, it's a complete program. It does, however, ask for a key."

"Isn't the whole code just keys?" I asked.

"In a manner of speaking, yes. We could tell that the code was useless until we had it all. So every piece was as important as every other piece. But now it seems like we do have it all, and it's asking for a password of sorts. We think that password is what you're working toward in the 767 Sequence."

"But if that's true, then how could the Defenders have it?"

Robin took over again. "We don't know, we just know that they've solved the sequence and are taking action based on that information right now. We don't know what they're doing, but we know they're doing it."

"Did they release a statement? They might just be baiting us into freaking out." I was pretty much fully out of my sleep haze now, but I still couldn't really believe the conversation we were having.

"No, I heard it directly from Peter Petrawicki." He looked almost sick as he said it.

"Why would he tell you that?"

"He didn't." Suddenly no one was making eye contact with me. "He told his agent."

"His agent is at your agency?"

"His agent is Jennifer Putnam."

A lot of things happened in my mind simultaneously, none of them good. I said, very slowly to Robin, who was doing his best to meet my eyes, "Jennifer Putnam is *my* agent."

"She is also Mr. Petrawicki's agent."

"Continue," I said, my voice sounding unfamiliar to my own ears. I didn't even realize how angry I was until I heard it.

"She took him on shortly after you," he said. "She was aware of the significance of the Carls before anyone else in the industry and felt that she had an obligation to scoop up related clients. I had a fight with her about it, I told her that his perspective was nasty and danger-ous. She told me we weren't in the business of deciding who was right and wrong and threatened to fire me and legally prevent me from working with you."

"How long have you known about this?!" I almost shouted.

He could have explained, I could see he wanted to, but I hadn't asked him to explain, so he just said, "Months."

"Months," I repeated. "So the whole time Putnam was trying to get me to do an in-person with Petrawicki . . . those months? An in-terview that was always going to have a better outcome for a profes-sional debater than a twenty-three-year-old graphic designer? But what does that matter because either way the money was going into Putnam's pocket?"

I was silent for long enough that Robin's mouth opened to speak, but I cut him off, quietly now. "The months during which *Mr. Petra-wicki* was dog-whistling his support of extremists who would go on to murder hundreds of people and try to murder me? But hey, gotta look out for the agency, so let's just keep our heads down and serve our clients? Those months?"

"April, I'm so sorry, once I started not telling you—"

"GET OUT!" I screamed. I was surprised to find that I wasn't crying. It felt like I should be crying, but there wasn't anything but anger there.

Robin's mouth pressed closed and his face contracted. It looked like he might cry, but he just stood up from the bed.

"If you need me—"

I interrupted coldly, "I'm sorry, I'm not being clear, you are fired."

In the silence that followed, Robin turned and walked out of the room.

I wanted to do nothing more than curl up and go back to the Dream. Back to my dream that Carl had made just for me. But Peter Petrawicki had solved the sequence, and he had done it without the Dream, which meant that I could too.

"That was pretty uncool, April," Andy said.

"What?"

"Robin has never done anything except help you. He's been there all day every day for the last six months and he's never even asked for a thank-you. And I'm not sure he's gotten one either."

"Never done anything except help me? Peter Petrawicki created a movement that tried to *kill* me. A movement that succeeded in destabilizing the whole PLANET, Andy! God, we don't have time for this. They've solved the sequence, we need to figure this out."

Andy sighed. Then he turned around and started walking out.

"Where are you going?" I asked, more accusatorial than I intended.

"I don't know, April." He turned back to me. "I'm going to leave. I don't know if I'll be excited to see you here when I get back."

"Well, then I won't be here," I retorted.

He looked at Miranda and then he looked at me. "Have fun, you two." The look on his face was something I didn't think Andy Skampt would be capable of. It was corrosive, disgusted, and also very tired. He walked out the door.

I want to tell you that I understood this then, but I didn't. I didn't get it, that we had spent weeks on the road on that book tour, the three of us, and that Andy had suddenly stopped seeming like he was that into me. And that we were all working so much, so maybe I didn't notice when Andy and Miranda had been spending more and more time together. That he was funny and smart and so was she and that Andy was afraid to make a move, probably because he had spent years perfectly aware that if he had made a move on me our friendship would have been over. And then I got lonely and bored one night and fucked it all up for him. But, no, I had no idea.

Miranda came over, her sympathy outweighing her discomfort, and sat on the edge of the bed.

"It's just a very high-stress time."

"It is more than that," I replied.

She leaned over to wrap her arms around me, which of course made me feel horribly trapped.

"I need to call Maya," I said stiffly.

Miranda sighed. "I understand," she said.

"What?"

"Nothing," she said, looking tiny. She was older than me, taller than me, smarter than me, and terrified of me.

"Just about the sequence, she's our expert. We can't just let the Defenders win this."

"OK, April."

I knew she didn't believe me, and looking back, she was absolutely right. I didn't want to hug Miranda. I didn't want to have a girlfriend. I didn't need another thing to worry about. I did need to talk to Maya. But she was also a convenient wrench to throw into this relationship because throwing wrenches into relationships is what I did.

I got out of the bed. I had started thinking of it as my bed, but that feeling had suddenly evaporated.

"Miranda, can you stay here and work on making sure you have the program ready to run if I can get the password?"

"It's ready to run now." And then she added, "I think," in a manner that was most unlike her. I was used to her being ridiculously sure of everything.

"Well, I need it ready to go the moment I have the key. Is there a way to email me a file or website I can input it into if I don't have you at hand?"

So, yes, I was offhandedly asking this beautiful genius who wanted nothing more than to be a part of this to compile a bunch of code for me that would make her unnecessary to me. Did she know that? Oh, absolutely. Did she do it anyway? Of course she did.

"Yeah, I can work on that."

"I need to go for a walk," I said, leaving "alone" implied, and left Miranda there without another word.

I exited Andy's building on 26th and just started walking. I called Maya immediately and explained the situation. I realized I was pissed at her too, because the Defenders wouldn't have been able to figure any of this out if I had just kept the 767 Sequence a secret like I initially wanted to. It was a dumb anger, and also not a helpful one. I tried not to throw that in her face because I needed her.

"How could the password be outside of the Dream?" I asked.

"We don't know that it is. The sequence may lead you to another part of the Dream that is public. Clues have been skipped by brute force before," she replied.

"Why did it have to be a Defender?" I asked in frustration, knowing that the question wasn't helpful. "They're like maybe 2 percent of the humans in the world. How did they figure it out before the rest of us?"

"That's actually a really good point, April," Maya said.

"It is?"

"Yeah, I mean, it could just be a coincidence, but it could also be one of two other things. One, they knew that the information would be passed along and they're just fucking with us. Or, two, it's something different about the way they think, about the way they see the Carls, that helped them uncover the password."

"Oh, so it helps to be a xenophobic, delusional conspiracy theorist?"

"Maybe, yeah."

I had just arrived in a park I didn't recognize. People lounged on grassy green hillocks. There were basketball courts and old guys playing chess. Very NYC.

Maya continued. "What do the Defenders obsess about that you don't?"

"Um . . . me? That I'm a secret space alien? They want me to do a DNA test, they don't think my parents exist. Either that or I'm a traitor to my species. Or that the Carls have been using me all along and that I was chosen specially and duped into being their shill. There are reams of conspiracy theories, Maya. I don't read them because it freaks me out."

"They think that you were chosen by the Carls, and you don't?"

"Right. It's ridiculous to think that they picked me out of eight billion humans on the planet. Like I was the only person lovable and gullible enough to be their missionary."

"April, really?"

"Really what?"

She didn't reply, sensing we were on treacherous ground, so I just continued talking.

"OK, yes, Carl saved me. He didn't save anyone else," I said, conveniently leaving out that I had *also* been saved from an assassin's bullet by Hollywood Carl's right hand. "They gave me a dream that no one else had access to. I get it, I'm . . ."

I couldn't finish that sentence.

"Yes, you are."

"God, that gives me the fucking creeps. The Defenders were spouting that from day one and I hate that it's true."

"You hate that you were chosen by an alien race to be their envoy? That they think you're special enough to give unique knowledge to, and to keep from being currently dead?" She said this somewhat mockingly—like, of course I loved being special.

"Yes, OK! I hate it!" I was suddenly angry. We had made it to the treacherous ground and now we had to deal with it. "I hate it now and I hated it the first moment I thought it. I hate that they saved me and let all those other people die. I hate that the weight of this bullshit situation is all on me!" My volume level had increased, but it was Manhattan—people screamed into their phones all the time.

"I'm sorry, you're right. I'm sorry I didn't think of that." She paused. "But it's not just you, you've got help. You've got good friends. Good people. I love Andy, of course, and Miranda and Robin seem lovely."

There was no way I was going to get into the weeds of my day thus far, so I just said, "I don't know that I do, Maya."

"Oh, April." She sighed.

"Yeah. I sure do know how to fuck shit up."

"Yeah, you do," she agreed.

Those words should have been extra weight on me, but for some reason they made me lighter. The silence hung for a while. For that one moment, I forgot that I was at the center of a swirling storm of political intrigue and I was just a shitty ex-girlfriend. It was kinda lovely. I laughed.

"OK." I headed back to the topic at hand. "So the Carls really did choose me and they really are treating me different than everyone in the rest of the world. How could that help the Defenders solve the 767 Sequence?"

"I don't know, April," she said, a little dejected. I didn't know why, possibly because we had gotten close to talking about something else and, again, I didn't let it happen. "I think the Carls, maybe they didn't pick you because of who you were but because of who you could become."

"That's a nice thing to say, though I don't know that I love who I've become."

"Maybe you're not done yet."

I didn't respond to that.

"April, I've never stopped being obsessed with . . ." And then she paused.

I waited patiently, silently for her to finish that sentence.

But then I couldn't because I had solved the 767 Sequence.

"Obsessed with me!" I said.

"No, that's not what I mean. I mean, I thought I could detach from this whole weirdness, but after you left, I just threw myself in. I lied when I said I just liked the Dream. I needed to keep being a part of it. I thought I was better than you, but I was exactly as obsessed, just in a different way."

I let her finish because it was important, but it was also agonizing.

"OK, but that is also not what I meant. I meant *the Defenders* are obsessed with me. They have a thousand conspiracy theories, Maya. They know everything about me. Every move I've ever made, every poster in the background of every video. Everything public I've ever done in my life!"

"And?"

"Row six," I said. "I sat in it that first week when I was flying out to meet Jennifer Putnam and do that late-night show. I got upgraded because someone was in the seat I'd been assigned, but they'd been assigned it too. It was my first time in business class. It was a 767. It was row six."

"Six like the Mayan number on the tail of the 767?"

"Yeah, and my little TV was broken. Or, I thought it was broken. It had a bunch of weird code on it!"

"Weird code like . . . ?"

"Weird like hex code."

"But how would the Defenders get their hands on that? How would we?"

"BECAUSE I FUCKING TWEETED IT, MAYA! GOD-DAMN IT!"

CHAPTER TWENTY-ONE

There were people looking at me, which wasn't great because I was pretty recognizable. I moved as fast as I could, with my back and shoulder still stiff and twinging, back toward Andy's place but then, instead, popped into a coffee shop on 12th. It was a cute place with a couple of bars and a few two-tops. About a half dozen student-looking people were drinking their lattes in front of their laptops.

"HELLO! My Name Is April May and I Need A Laptop Computer Right Now," I said.

I had bet correctly, and there was indeed one person, a guy in his late teens or early twenties, who was not just willing but honored to give me his computer.

In a moment I had my tweet up:

> **@AprilMaybeNot:** On my way to LA and got bumped to business class. My little plane TV is broken though, so I want the money I didn't spend back!

That was a simpler time.

The little plane TV indeed showed code that I now instantly

recognized as hexadecimal. Was that the passkey? It was a lot of characters. So I popped it into its own window and started typing it out. As soon as I was done, about five minutes later, I emailed it to Miranda and Maya, which hopefully wasn't going to cause any drama.

The Key?

I think this is the key, though I don't know what it is or what to do with it.

Then I texted them both separately, *Check your email.* Maya wrote back first, *It's hex, I've converted it, would you like to guess what it is?*

> **Me:** *The lyrics to a song?*
>
> **Maya:** *Last night they loved you, opening doors and pulling some strings, angel.*
>
> **Me:** *Of course it's Bowie*
>
> **Maya:** *Hell Yes*

Miranda replied back with the same information, except to say that she had also inputted it into the latest version of the full code compiled on the Som. *I'm sending you the result right now. It is not complicated, but April, let's talk about this.*

It wasn't complicated; it was an address in New Jersey and five words, "Only April. No One Else."

Until that moment, I had fully made up my mind to call the president as soon as we were sure we'd cracked it. It wasn't even a question in my mind, we had the procedure down and I was going to do what I'd been told. I was tired of making big decisions and I was especially tired of screwing everything up when I made them.

But now I was being told to do something else, and while I'd made up my mind what to do, it hadn't stopped me from fantasizing about what might be waiting for me at the end of this road. My secret heart said that it was a face-to-face meeting with the intelligence behind the Carls—rather, the entity that I had come to think of as Carl in my head. The thought of that meeting happening between Carl and Peter Petrawicki made me want to vom. That's not actually accurate: It made me angrier than any other thought I had ever had.

I was being asked to do one thing by the president, who had been honest with me, who had trusted me, who was the absolute personi-fication of authority. And then there was Carl. Carl who changed my life, who *saved* my life, who let everyone die except me. Carl the mystery. My mystery . . . my identity.

I logged out of all my accounts and thanked the guy for his com-puter. He wanted a photo, we took one, I told everyone else who had gathered to watch that I was in a bit of a rush but thanks for watching my videos! Less than half an hour had elapsed.

Miranda wrote again, *Are you going? If you're going, just let us know.*

But I didn't think I'd been given a choice, or maybe I didn't want to think I'd been given a choice. I finally felt fully comfortable with what I'd become. Did I know the Carls were good? No. I thought they were, I hoped they were, I *felt* they were. But I didn't know. What I did know is that I'd chosen my side, and my side had chosen me.

My phone rang—it was Maya. I didn't pick up.

Then it buzzed with a text: *I plugged in the key, I saw what it said. You can't go on your own.*

I didn't respond, but she didn't stop.

April, maybe you can go on your own, but don't do it right now. Let's take some time.

But the Defenders were already on their way, who knows what mess they would cause. She didn't give up: *APRIL JUST CALL ME, TALK TO ME.*

The phone rang again, I put it on mute. I was doing the thing I had to do, there wasn't any point, but I did keep my eye on the three little dots that told me Maya was writing something to me. It finally came through as a wall of text.

> *You're so caught up in this, you have no idea. To Miranda and Robin, you're so much more than a person. They've never known an April May that wasn't famous. Have either of them ever said no to anything you've ever told them to do? Listen to me, April. In those relationships, you have all the power. Too much power. I've watched you with them, they idolize you. That's how fame works. It sucks. No one you meet from now on is ever again going to feel normal around you. Both of them feel like it's a privilege just to be near you.*
>
> *This is just something that happens, not something you did on purpose. But when they let you do these . . . frankly dangerous things, that doesn't mean that they're agreeing it's a good idea. They just can't say no to you. April, I hear you. But please trust me. Do not do this. I am telling you not to do this because I love you.*

I read the whole thing through four or five times. Maya had never said "I love you" to me, she knew it would scare me off. Not responding felt like it would be one of the greatest betrayals I could commit. I didn't respond.

CHAPTER TWENTY-TWO

Are you sure this is it?" the driver asked. I didn't need to check my phone because I'd been studying this very spot on Google Street View on and off for the last thirty minutes. I'd even found a real estate listing. It's a warehouse. It's not currently occupied. It's for lease. If you would like to lease it, that would run you around $15,000 per month. It was, it turned out, a pretty big warehouse.

"Yep! Thank you!"

I didn't know whether to be relieved or worried that there was no sign of Peter Petrawicki and whatever camera crew would be following him around. Speaking of cameras, I didn't have one. What I did have was two phones and my ever-present "just in case" external battery.

I thought for a long time about what Carl wanted. The message said "Only April," but that seemed clearly about people's physical presence. Carl usually seemed to want me to bring an audience with me wherever I went. And feeling certain that whatever was about to happen would be historic, I made a call that was both deeply foolish and genius.

I went full livestream.

Facebook's system had gotten so good that it could handle pretty much infinite viewership these days. Worst-case scenario, I figured, I would crash it. Best-case scenario, I'd beat the record for the most-viewed stream of all time and share one of humanity's greatest moments with the largest live audience in history.

"This is April May, and I am pleased to announce that I have solved the 767 Sequence. For those of you who haven't been following, for a while now we've known that all of the Dream Sequences have been solved and that the world is awaiting the solution of one final sequence that only appeared in one dream."

While saying all that, I walked from the curb up to a chained fence gate.

"I don't know why I was the only one who had this dream, just as I don't know why New York Carl saved me from Martin Bellacourt on July 13."

I carefully kept the camera pointed at myself to minimize the clues of my location. The warehouse was big, three stories, made of wood, with large, mostly boarded-over windows and a few huge loading-bay doors. Wood lay strewn around the base of one of the walls. In between me and the door were both the fence and a parking lot that was being reclaimed by persistent little grasses.

"After solving the 767 Sequence, we were given a password, which, when inputted into the code generated from the rest of the Dream Sequences, directed me here. The Garden State. The message was very specific that I should come alone, so that is what I've done."

I was poking at the fence now. It was capped with barbed wire, and the chain at the gate was tight and secure. I began walking along it, thinking aloud to what was now a massive audience about how I was going to get in.

But then, after I turned the corner, I spotted a cut in the fence.

At this point, I decided to tell some truth. Not all of it or anything, but some.

"However, we received word, not long ago, that another group had decoded the sequence and that they were on their way here as well. This is why I have, I'll be honest, rushed into this trip a bit. I promised some people that I wouldn't do it like this, but as we can see here"—there were still bits of chain-link fence scattered around in the overgrown grass—"I am not the first here."

I crawled through the slit in the fence and started walking up to the building. Along the way, my voice got quieter. I knew some of the Defenders must be nearby, possibly already taking part in whatever weirdness Carl had in store.

I had thought a lot about what the endgame was, and, I'll be honest, my dream was that it was some grand prize. Not, like, a new car or a million dollars, but some gift only the Carls could bestow. Immortality, my own spaceship, world peace. And there was a feeling inside of me that, if I didn't get there, some ignorant, awful exophobe would be taking an all-expenses-paid trip to the Carl home world to show off how utterly awful humans are. I didn't say any of this out loud, mostly because I knew it was a pipe dream to think anyone could ever guess what the Carls were up to. But also because I had made a pledge to myself to completely ignore that the Defenders even existed when speaking publicly.

Instead, I talked in low tones about how we solved the 767 Sequence and all the people who had helped—the accordion players, all the people who knew Mayan numerals, the engineers who had taught me about the inner workings of a modern 767. And, of course, Maya, whom I had decided to give credit to for helping me uncover the final clue. It was she who had told me to get into the mind of the Defenders, after all.

As I got closer to the warehouse, I noticed a human-sized door to the side of one of the giant loading-bay doors. It was hanging loosely; one of its hinges had been pulled out of the doorframe and a pile of clothes lay in front of it. That seemed like the simplest point of entrance, but also the most dangerous. Still, I felt time pressing on me, so I approached it. The clothes in front of the door looked dirty and wet. I was terrified. My heart was fluttering and I suddenly had to pee. Sneaking into an abandoned building is scary whether or not you're alone and have been previously hunted. I believed and still believe that most of the Defenders wouldn't hurt me physically, but I had seen already that most was not all. Then again, I had already started the livestream and the numbers were ticking up.

And then I smelled grape jelly. It was in the clothes, seeping around the entrance to the warehouse. Who had it been? Peter Petrawicki?

"Oh god," I said, unable to control myself. I pointed the camera away as fast as I could. "I think . . . ," I said, and then paused to calm myself. "I think someone tried to go inside but Carl didn't want them to. I think . . . I think they died."

I couldn't bring myself to say more than that. I didn't even want to think about it, so I was silent as I stared at the doorway, doing my best to not look down at the mess at my feet. Carl had zapped them the moment they tried to walk inside, and now it was my turn. But Carl had told me to come here, and trusting Carl was who I was now.

I did my best to tiptoe around the mess and into the warehouse.

It took my eyes a solid moment to adjust to the darkness of the warehouse. The room I had entered was massive and empty. Dust floated inside the slices of light that fell through the few windows that hadn't been boarded up. Papers and leaves littered the concrete floor; a few bits and bolts of metal shot through that floor that I assumed were used for whatever manufacturing had once been done there.

"Well, it appears to be a giant empty warehouse," I said quietly to the livestream, feeling a bit let down. The entire lower level of the building was one open space, and there was nothing in it. There was, however, a metal-slatted staircase that led up to a second level that appeared to house some offices with windows that overlooked the warehouse floor.

"I'm going to go up these stairs to check out the offices."

The stairs clanged as I walked up them. I kept a tight grip on the railing with my left hand while broadcasting my progress with my right. The connection had remained solid—I was broadcasting in HD to the whole world.

My personal phone, the one I wasn't using to livestream, buzzed in my pocket. I dug it out as fast as I could and saw that it was Miranda. Wasn't she watching? Didn't she know I couldn't take a call right now? I was contemplating answering the phone when I heard it, playing off in the distance.

"Do you hear that?" I asked the livestream.

I'll stick with you baby for a thousand years, nothing's gonna touch you in these golden years.

It was the first sign of anything unusual inside the warehouse, and boy, did it seem like a solid clue. I stopped paying attention to anything. "That's the song. It's 'Golden Years,'" I said to the stream, and I started walking faster. By now, my audience was a couple million people strong.

I half expected the stream to die, whether from supernatural intervention by Carl or the sheer load on the world's servers, but apparently it held. The music kept getting louder.

A text notification popped up from Miranda: *April. Get Out Now.*

I saw the notification fly up over my screen, but my brain refused to accept it. What was she getting at? I looked up and I was already there anyway. A little office to the side of the catwalk. There was a desk, and from it came Bowie's voice.

I waited for the magic to happen, for my reward, and then another text appeared: *Run*

And still, I stood there.

> *Don't cry my sweet, don't break my heart. Doing all right, but you gotta get smart.*

As I stared dumbly, another text arrived: *It was faked. It's not real. It's the wrong place.*

I turned just in time to see the huge metal door behind me slam shut.

> *There's my baby, lost that's all. Once, I'm begging you, save her little soul.*

You know I'm a damn fool.

CHAPTER TWENTY-THREE

*This chapter is going to contain some graphic violence. I
will tell you when it's coming. I will not be offended if you
skip it.*

I immediately shot myself at the door, but it didn't budge. I
slammed on it, shouting, "WHAT THE HELL!"

There was no response.

Faintly, over the sound of "Golden Years," I heard footsteps rac-
ing off down the catwalk. I didn't understand how any of this was
possible until I saw, on the floor next to a filing cabinet, six large
empty plastic jugs of Welch's grape jelly. That achieved what I assumed was the desired effect: making me feel like a damned idiot.

"Well," I said to the livestream, panting with fear, "things have
taken a turn for the worse. I have been informed that this was a hoax,
and not real, and now I have been locked in a warehouse in New
Jersey, and, Miranda, as I'm sure you are watching, please call the
police and send them to me because I am stuck in here. Also, if

they could arrest the dickholes that just kidnapped me, that would be grand."

I searched around the room for a bit and came up with nothing that could maybe be used as a pry bar. I slammed the door with the desk chair a couple of times, then with one of the metal drawers from the desk, but that barely even dented the door.

Eventually, I got tired of hearing "Golden Years," so I tried to turn off the little music player that it was tinnily streaming out of. No matter what buttons I hit, it did not turn off.

"In every town around the world, each of us must be touched with gold. Don't cry my sweet, don't break my heart, I'll come runnin' but you gotta get smart," David sang.

I left the livestream going as I did all this, occasionally commenting to it because, at that point, I felt pretty safe. I'd gotten word out to the world at large, and though I was pretty scared and extremely disappointed not to be meeting Carl or whatever, I hadn't smelled the smoke yet.

Another text came in from Miranda: *I'm so sorry. Oh god, April, it's my fault. The code had been tampered with. It was sitting on the Som in an open page, anyone could edit it and I just didn't notice that someone had.*

I texted her back, still streaming as I did it: *It's OK, I'm fine. If I wasn't such an impulsive ass, we would have figured that out. I made you rush.*

I put the chair back behind the desk and set up my phone so it could see me from a not-terrible angle.

"Well, I know most of you have already checked out, and I'm terribly sorry for wasting all of your time today. Hopefully, if it's all right with you, we can hang out until the cops bust me out of this creepy room. Because, let's be honest with ourselves, you're my best friend.

"Oh, not any one of you. And certainly not the ones I actually know and love. Not the ones who have tried to be my friends. Not my brother. Not my mom. Not any of the guys or girls I've led on, lied to, cheated on. You. You mass of humans who I know nothing about, you are my best friend.

"And you know why? Because you like me, and no single person's love can compete with even casual regard from a hundred million. That impossible, inhuman wave of support. Not inhuman because you aren't humans, inhuman because no human is designed to process it, to understand it. Fame is a drug, and as I sit here in this gross little smoky-smelling room, trapped by some unknown prankster, I know that earlier today I was . . . I was really mean.

"I was a bad person and I hurt a lot of the people who I care most about in this world because I am addicted to attention. I do things that are bad for myself, and my friends, and my health, and my world so I can get more power because I think I need that power to do good things. But then I just do stupid things instead. And I'm streaming live so I can't edit this or take any of it back. So thanks for listening. I really pretty much hate myself right now, thank you for being my friend."

Everyone in the livestream chat, which had now dwindled enough that I could actually read some of what was being said before it flew by, seemed receptive to my monologue.

I tended to keep one eye on the chat anytime I was streaming, and while you can't always read every word, you can get an idea of what people are saying, and if there's something they want you to see, people will copy and paste it over and over to get your attention. In among the well-wishes and kind thoughts, I saw a word I didn't expect popping up over and over: "Lyrics."

I scrolled up the chat to see what that was about.

> **Ginny Di:** What were the lyrics again? Touched with gold? I
> know that song, it's definitely not in there.

Then a few threads of support, then:

> **Roger Ogden:** I just re-listened like twelve times. It sounds
> like "In every town around the world Jesus must be touched
> with gold." But wtf? It's super hard to hear over April talking
> though.

"So some people in the chat are saying that the words to 'Golden Years' have changed? I'm going to stop talking so that you all can just listen."

We had proved, over and over again, that thousands of people solving a puzzle are a lot better than one. But good lord, was shutting up for five minutes hard!

My personal phone rang—it was Robin. I didn't want to answer because it would interfere with everyone listening. I just kept scrolling through the chat. They were transcribing the lyrics, which made it more or less impossible to read anything in real time. But then I saw this:

> **Lane Harris:** Guys, the lyric changes happened on
> Spotify's copy too! Everyone can hear them.

"Everyone, apparently it isn't just this version of the song. It's the same on Spotify. Go listen there, I'm getting a phone call."

"April, thank god. I'm headed to where you are. Miranda already called the cops to help get you out. Can you get out of that room?"

"What? Not as far as I can tell. I tried to bust down the door."

"I don't like you being stuck in there. On the stream you said it smelled smoky?"

"Yeah." And I had thought maybe it smelled like old cigarettes, but now that Robin had said it, it smelled like woodsmoke. Also, now that I was thinking about it, it seemed like the smell was getting stronger. But that was probably just natural anxiety at the thought of burning alive in an abandoned warehouse, right?

"Robin, I am now suddenly worried," I replied.

"Does it still smell like smoke?"

"Yes, it maybe smells more like smoke?"

"April, hang up and figure out a way out of that room, I'm going to call the fire department," he said in a demanding staccato.

I hung up and looked around the room.

There was a metal filing cabinet, on which was a terra-cotta pot that maybe once held some sort of life. The desk, which I could definitely not lift; the drawer I had pulled out of the desk, which now sat in the corner of the room; the desk chair; the little iPod thing; a bunch of empty jars of jelly. None of this looked particularly helpful. Whoever had decorated this place had skipped the traditional wall-mounted crowbar.

I looked out the window. It seemed maybe a little foggier out there. Or, I suppose, smokier.

In traditional April May fashion, I decided to turn my critical thinking skills over to the audience.

"Uh," I said, picking up the livestream, "I am a little worried that I am trapped in a burning building?" I laughed. "It's actually not funny, I don't know why I just laughed. It's getting smokier. Fuck. FUCK!"

I was saved from outright panic by Robin calling on my other phone again.

"Fuck, Robin, fuck."

He answered immediately, "April, is there any way you can get out of that room?"

That scared the shit out of me. "I don't think so?"

"Try, try very hard. I just got here. The fire department is on its way, they'll be here soon, but the building is on fire."

"How on fire?"

"Very, the police have been trying to get in, but so far they haven't been able to."

"There's a window in here, it's maybe a twenty-foot drop to the concrete floor below, that's all I've got."

"Let me get you on with a policeman." As I heard the rustle of the wind as he ran, I thought about how clean and efficient we were being about this whole thing. It was like we were scheduling a TV interview.

"Hey, I have the young woman on the phone," I heard Robin say, not directly into the phone.

"Hello, April?" a strange man's voice said.

"Yes?"

"How are you feeling?"

"OK, the smoke is . . ." I coughed, for the first time. And then I really started to panic.

"Can you see where the smoke is coming from?"

I took a look around the room, and for the first time it was thick enough that I could see it was coming from under the door. I told the cop as much.

"Stuff whatever you can in that crack. Your pants, shirt, whatever. The smoke is your enemy right now."

So I took off my hoodie and stuffed it in there. It made a pretty good seal.

When I was back on the phone, he said, "If you have anything else to wrap around your face, that might also help with the smoke." So I took off my shirt and wore it like a bandit mask. I couldn't tell if it was helping, but at least I was half naked now.

"April, listen to me, we're going to get you out of there. You're high in the building, which means the smoke will be thicker where you are than lower in the building. Can you get lower in the building?"

"I'm locked in a room, the door is metal and I can't break it down. But there's a window—it's like twenty feet off the concrete, though."

"April, go over to the door for me. Feel it with the back of your hand."

I did. I pulled my hand back sharply from the door. It wasn't searing, but the feeling of any warmth coming from it terrified me.

"It's . . . pretty hot," I said, trying to keep my shit together.

"OK, April, we are working on getting into the building, but the entrances are all blocked or burning. We are working on making new entrances. How is the smoke in there?"

"It is not good."

"April, when you break the window, a lot of smoke is probably going to come in through it. Which means that once you do that, you will have to jump out of it pretty quickly. When you do that, you will want to lower yourself by your hands over the edge and then drop. Land on your feet, but don't lock your knees. I'll talk to you once you're down there."

"When I break the window." I said. Not a question, just a confirmation.

"Yes." He did not try to convince me. He did not tell me that I needed to do it; he talked about it as if it was as natural a thing as taking my next breath. "Do you have something to break it with?"

I looked at the metal drawer I had removed from the desk still lying on the floor by the door. There was the pot too. It was a weird choice. Metal drawer or clay pot . . . which tool will I use to smash the window through which I will then hurl my body without regard for whether I can survive the fall?

But, like, I wouldn't actually have to do that, my mind told me. Carl would save me. He had saved me before. Two times. Where was he now? Where was Hollywood Carl's hand? Why had he let me come in here? A feeling of frustration welled up in me so intense that I almost screamed.

"April, are you OK?"

I coughed. "Yeah."

"Can you break the window?"

"Yeah."

"OK, just stay on the line, and when the smoke gets too thick, you'll need to break that window."

"How do I know when that is?"

He paused for a second, then said, "You'll know."

I looked out the window—it was so thick with smoke that I couldn't make out the far wall. There was, however, an occasional flicker of orange light.

I grabbed the livestream phone. I can't believe I was still streaming. The audience had now ballooned to well over ten million viewers. My largest stream to date! Turns out broadcasting your own ongoing attempted murder is a great way to get views. Also, probably doesn't hurt to do it in just your bra and skinny jeans.

I guess, unsurprisingly, I wasn't concerned with modesty at the moment.

I coughed a few times, but not uncontrollably, and said, mostly to distract myself, "Hey, everybody. How's the David Bowie lyric thing going?" The little iPod was still playing.

Comments flew by too fast to see. I scrolled up to pause them. The people who weren't being blandly sympathetic (or accusing me of faking this whole thing) assured me that the conversation had moved over to the Som, which was, of course, built for just this sort of thing. Some people had already tried touching Carl with gold. White gold, yellow gold, twenty-four-karat gold, nothing had happened.

I just sat there reading comments as the smoke built up, my eyes started to water, and my lungs started to burn. Occasionally I would answer a question or make a remark: "I'm too much of an attention whore to fake my own death" or "That's really nice of you to say, Parker." That kind of thing. Eventually, I moved behind the desk because I could feel the heat coming off the wall. The smoke out the window was a consistent orange, and I could barely go two breaths without gasping.

I picked up my personal phone. "Hey, policeman?" I hacked a half dozen uncontrolled coughs.

"Hey, April. The fire department is here now, but we still need to give them as much time to work as we can. When you break the window, the smoke will come in fast, so you'll need to move quickly." He said all this without pausing.

"OK," I replied, in a croak.

"OK, I need you to do that now. The smoke is your biggest enemy."

"OK, I'm going to jump out of a window now," I said, suddenly aware that those might be my last words.

"OK," the man replied.

So I stuffed both phones in my jeans pocket. I grabbed the desk drawer and slammed it into the window. Smoke started pouring into the room. My next breath was excruciating. It didn't feel like it contained anything except tiny needles, and the coughing fit that ensued made me involuntarily gasp in more smoke. I coughed more. I realized I wasn't getting any real air.

I thought I would have time to clean off the glass, but I didn't. I took my shirt off my face and placed it over the glass nubs sticking up from the window frame—some protection, at least. I plopped my right ass cheek onto the shirt and nonetheless felt the glass biting through the shirt, my jeans, and my skin.

But I was retching now. I rushed to get my body positioned to lower myself from my hands—to save those precious five feet between me and the ground—but then I just fell. Ungainly, and listing to one side, I fell into open air. I felt the sudden heat of the fire—the little room had been protecting me—but in those milliseconds before I slammed into the ground, I could see the smoke begin to clear.

I hit, left foot first, then left arm, then my head slammed against the concrete. Somehow, this wasn't enough to knock me unconscious. I continued to cough, my lungs still filled with the evil particles of smoke. But now when I gasped, it didn't get worse. My brain could tell that I wasn't suffocating anymore, and so it moved to the more pressing issue of the screaming pain coming from my arm and leg.

The smoke was so clear down here that I could see the fire . . . It was licking every vertical surface in eyeshot. Several sensations screamed simultaneously through the fog of my concussion, but my leg was the loudest. I raised myself on my good right arm, getting myself into a rough sitting position. I looked down. The lower part—above the ankle—was very broken. Blood was already starting to soak through my pants.

"This Is God Damn Bull Shit!" I shouted.

I realized that everyone, seeing only the darkness of my pocket on the livestream, heard me say those words. Even now, I was still thinking about the audience.

I reached into my pants pocket, pulling out both phones. "OK, I'm OK—I mean, not OK. I'm badly injured, but I'm not dead yet. Let's hold on to the fact that I'm not dead yet." I could feel the heat beating on me from every direction, but more from the top and the right than from the left. So I started to move myself in that direction. There was a loud and persistent roaring filling the warehouse.

And then I had the dumbest thought that I'd ever had in my life. "Everywhere around the world! Guys. Not just one Carl at a time. Every Carl. At the same time."

Very me of me to assume that no one else had figured this out yet. But I had something no one else had, an audience. Bigger than the Super Bowl. Bigger than Neil Freaking Armstrong.

The stream view count read more than seven hundred million viewers. What *can't* you do with an audience that big? Well, sometimes . . . nothing.

I could hear the policeman shouting my name from my other phone. I picked it up and coughed a half dozen times before saying, "I broke my leg, but the air is much better down here."

"Can you move?"

"Not easily," I half yelled over the noise of the fire.

"Just move toward the back wall. There is less fire there."

"My new favorite kind of fire," I said, and the cop actually laughed.

At that moment, a call came in from Miranda. OK. That had to be important. "I'm getting another call, be right back," I said to the emergency response professional who was trying to save my life.

"Things are not good here," I said.

"I know, April, I'm watching. Maya is here."

"I know what we need to do. We need every Carl to be touched with gold simultaneously. Like with the iodine, but every Carl at the same time. In fact, I don't know why I'm telling you, I should be telling them."

I picked up the livestream phone. "Hello, I don't know if this will help me. Maybe it will, or maybe it's just the best chance we have of getting this last step done, but if you are near a Carl, or know someone who is, could you touch that Carl with a piece of gold? Just some jewelry will do, we think. I'd really like to know how this ends before . . . well, you know."

I picked up the phone Maya was on again and said, "OK, well, that's something at least."

"You're actually one step ahead of us for once," Maya said.

I laughed, then coughed.

"Miranda decoded the actual code with your passkey. It's just the atomic symbol for gold sixty-four times."

"Well, Carl clearly wanted to get his point across, I guess."

"April, there are a lot of places where the Carls aren't publicly accessible. There are fifteen Carls in China, and they've been under military guard for months. You can't just walk up to one and put a piece of gold on it."

I didn't know how to respond to that. Carl had sent us our instructions, but we were too damned stupid to allow ourselves to comply. Maybe in a few years, after treaties were signed, everyone would get on board and try it out, but probably not. Probably the Carls would just sit there forever, waiting for the Earth to get its shit together enough to do this one stupid, simple little thing.

I turned back to the livestream, moving in close to the mic so they could hear me over the roar of the fire. "Hello again, look, I'm not going to say this is hopeless. But there are sixty-four Carls in the world and a good 20 percent of them are under military guard. If the goal is to touch all of them with gold simultaneously, I honestly think we are being tested. The Carls want us to work together, they want us to be human together, to take a risk together, to make a choice together."

I took a break to cough.

"I'm stuck in a burning building. But more than that, I'm stuck on this planet with you. And honestly, I'm glad. I've been exposed to a lot of awful people in the last few months, but I've met so many more that are amazing, thoughtful, generous, and kind. I honestly believe that is the human condition. And if the Carls are testing us, this final test is the hardest to accomplish. If you pay attention, there is only one story that makes sense, and that is one in which humanity works together more and more since we took over this planet. Yeah, we fuck it up all the time, yeah, there have been some massive steps backward, but look at us! We are one species now more than we have ever been. People fight against that, and they probably always will, but could there be any time in history when what Carl is asking us would be more possible? Asking dozens of governments to take the same action simultaneously with an uncertain outcome? Or at least asking them to allow their citizens to take that action?"

More coughing.

"I don't know. I think maybe if we can't do it right now, with eight hundred million people watching, we won't ever be able to do it. So let's try to do something together. Thank you. Thank you for doing this together."

And then, I did something no sane creator would ever do. At the peak of my audience, I ended the stream.

Then I picked up Miranda's call again, yelling, "I think that will help."

Maya said something into the phone then, but I couldn't hear over the noise the fire was making. It was starting to feel hard to breathe. I was gasping even though the smoke wasn't so bad. The heat, I thought, or maybe shock. In fact, though I didn't know it then, the fire was consuming all the oxygen in the building.

It was so hot. So blazing hot, but there was no escape. It felt like it was coming equally from every direction simultaneously. And since trying to move with a compound fracture was no fun, I just sat still.

"Is Andy there?" I shouted, suddenly wanting to talk to him.

"No, he's currently holding one of my earrings against New York Carl," Miranda said.

"You guys. I'm sorry. I'm going to leave it at that."

And then I hung up to call Andy.

"Are you OK?" he answered.

"No, is anything happening yet?"

"No, April . . ."

"I know, Andy. There's nothing you could have done. I know that you're going to be mad at me forever, and that's OK, but don't be mad at yourself forever. You were right, and no one could have stopped me."

"Don't fucking give up, April." His voice was shaking.

"I'm not going to," I gasped, and then Andy shouted in what sounded like shock or fright.

"Are you OK?" I said.

"It's the hand . . ." And then there was a loud pop.

A fraction of a second later, from above me came a thundering crack. The roar of the fire had been a constant weight on my mind, but this dwarfed that noise. I looked up, still somehow thinking maybe . . . maybe now I would be saved. Through the veil of smoke above came a rushing tumult of fire and wood.

And this is the part you might really want to skip if you don't want the gore because a burning wood beam, probably several thousand pounds, fell through the space that was also occupied by my head. It entered just above my hairline on the right side. It hit with so much force that it didn't even knock me out of the way. It slid through me like a knife dropped into a glass of water.

The beam broke through my skull, taking a small hunk of brain.

Then it tore off the right side of my face.

It missed my torso by inches, and then slammed into my right leg just above the ankle. Those things hurt more than anything I had ever experienced. But then, as the flame expanded and the skin of my bare torso began to cook, I learned that it could get worse.

I remained conscious for a few terrible seconds after this, so I had a little bit of time to finally and without a doubt understand that I was going to die.

I understood it, but there was no acceptance in that understanding, only bitterness, terror, frustration, and hatred piled on top of the pain. I screamed and then it was all gone.

CHAPTER TWENTY-FOUR

I was in the lobby where you arrive in the Dream. That slick, modern office building. Carpet tiles, familiar music, reception desk, all of it exactly the same. Except at the desk, instead of the sleek little robot, stood Carl. I'd gotten used to seeing him with just one hand, so the fact that he had two stood out. His helmeted head almost scraped the ceiling. He was menacing, maybe because my mind was expecting danger, maybe because I had just watched my body get ripped apart, maybe because Carl had torn my world open and I knew it could never be put back together again or because so many people had died on July 13 and I wasn't one of them.

Maybe it was just because Carl was actually pretty scary-looking.

I looked down at myself, afraid of the burns and wounds I expected to see, but it was just me. I was wearing a silk blouse and a tight black skirt, like I was about to go to a nine-to-five at some corporate PR company.

"Carl?" I said.

"Your body is very badly damaged." That tremendous suit of armor didn't move, but the voice was clearly coming from it. It was a loud, clear tenor. If I had to guess gender, I would say male, but I'm glad I didn't have to guess. The voice bounced around the hard walls of the office.

"So, then I'm not . . . dead?" I was surprised.

"Not this moment."

That wasn't super comforting. I wanted to follow the logical course of the conversation, to find out what had happened and what was going to happen now, but I also was talking to Carl, and I had been imagining this moment for so long that I just skipped ahead and blurted out, "Why did you come here?"

"Three questions."

"What?"

"It is a tradition in your stories. Also, your body will likely not keep working for long without intervention." That certainly raised a question, but I wasn't taking the bait.

"Why did you come here?" I repeated.

"To observe." I waited for more, because, I mean, that had been my guess all along and it was a bit unsatisfying.

"Can you elaborate on that? Or does that count as another question? Does *that* count as another question?" And then, since I am so good at First Contact scenarios, I concluded in a frustrated whisper, ". . . Crapballs."

If Carl reacted to my mini freak-out, he did so internally.

"We had to see how you react to us. There was no way to know without contact. This is the beginning of a process." And then, to save me from my fear that I'd used all my questions, he said, "You have two more questions."

I wanted to ask very much what that process was. Had they been through this before? Were we dangerous? Were we being studied like ants? Like wild gorillas? Or like fungus?

But I had a more pressing debate happening in my mind. I wanted so badly to ask about myself, about why I had been singled out and saved so many times. But while epiphanies are temporary, I had learned this lesson too many times too recently. As much as this was about me, it was also about more than me.

"How do we measure up?" I asked, seriously, and with conviction.

"I don't understand," Carl said.

"You came to observe us, to test our reactions. Did we pass your tests?"

"I don't understand," Carl said again.

I struggled to rephrase the question. "Humanity, what do you think of us?"

"Beautiful," Carl replied.

We sat inside of that moment for a very long time. I thought maybe he would say more, but he didn't.

"I suppose that's something."

I figured any questions about where Carl was from or how he got here would be more or less useless without a lot of context and also probably advanced degrees in physics. So I caved and again, one final time, made it all about me.

"Did you choose me for this?" I asked.

And then I am at the 23rd Street subway station. My MetroCard is in my hand. The station is empty, it's late—I know when this is. It's the night I met Carl. I walk up to the turnstile and swipe the card. It flashes red. But I used this MetroCard dozens of times after this night. I'd never even thought about that. But my dream body turns and leaves the station even though my mind is already freaking out. The walk sign is on, so I cross 23rd. A taxi's horn blares at me as if I shouldn't be crossing the street. I look up. The taxi has a green light. I have the walk light, but the stoplight across 23rd is red. The walk light shouldn't be on . . . If the stoplight is red . . .

I came back to the dream lobby. The truth slammed into me

hard. Carl, or the Carls, or some related intelligence had stopped me from getting on that train. They had turned me around and sent me back, even going so far as to make sure I didn't walk down the wrong side of 23rd.

"Since then? You . . . you chose me before I even made the first video?"

"We did."

There was a long pause. I stared up at Carl, realizing I was crying with the weight of it. There are billions of people on this planet. Literally nothing made me special.

"Why?"

"Your story just started, April May," Carl replied. And then the dream ended.

CHAPTER TWENTY-FIVE

Hello, everyone. I'm Andy Skampt. April asked me to take over and finish, because, well, she wasn't around during this part of the story. I don't love doing this, but I understand why she wants me to do it, so here I am.

I've read this whole book and signed off on it. I think April has done a pretty great thing here. I think the book helped her, and I think it will help the rest of us too. Though, to be honest, it seems like this kind of stuff is easier for her now.

Anyway, let's take it from the point where I'm standing on 23rd, holding a golden earring onto New York Carl's hip, talking to April and realizing rapidly that I am unnecessary because about fifty other people have rushed to the scene to add their jewelry. I step away to hear April a bit better. I am feeling a lot like I'm 100 percent responsible for what's happening to her right now. Like, if I hadn't walked out on her, she would not now be dying of smoke inhalation in a warehouse in Hoboken.

It is the worst feeling I've ever had, and April is telling me to stop having it. It's emotional enough that I'm 100 percent uncomfortable relaying it to you.

So I'm walking away from Carl and the growing group of people around him, and April is talking to me. And then I hear a couple of people shouting exclamations of various sorts. I turn around, and I see Carl's missing hand, as big as a trash-can lid, skipping down the street at full speed. I mean, I say full speed, but I don't know how fast a full-speed hand is. It's going fast.

People leap away from Carl as they see it. All of the dozen people who have gotten their hands in, holding their trinkets to his surface, scatter, shouting in alarm.

The hand weaves between the bodies, still moving at speed when it slams noiselessly into place right onto New York Carl's right wrist. Everyone is either running away or just staring blankly. I realize that no one is holding any gold to his surface, so I run over with Miranda's earring and push it as hard as I can into Carl's belly.

Before I can even register that I've hit the surface of the robot, his right arm shoots up and the hand makes a fist like he's grabbing onto a point in space above his head. This took a long time for my brain to understand, and it helped that there was plenty of footage of it happening released later. But once my brain latched onto it, it's clear what happens: Carl grabs onto a point in the universe, and then yanks himself into the air. Fast. Fast enough that a vacuum is left behind and I'm sucked into (and through) the space where Carl was just standing. A massive CRACK sounds, and I fly into a bank of pay phones shoulder first. I'm later told that the crack I heard was a sonic boom. Carl left at faster than the speed of sound.

So now I'm standing there, nursing a sore shoulder, wondering what's happened. We've obeyed the final clue in the Dream. It appears that everywhere across the world, people held a piece of gold to every Carl simultaneously. And now he's gone. But April is still trapped in the building. I call Robin.

"Andy . . ." He's frantic, crying.

"Carl is gone, maybe he's coming to help."

He has a really hard time saying this next part. "The roof. It's caving in."

I don't know what to say to that, so I just say, "Carl is coming. Maybe he's already there."

"OK, Andy," he says, and I know exactly what he means . . . which is that I'm deluded and he knows what's actually going on, which is that April is dead.

God, this is hard to write.

After April made her plea, citizens all over the world rushed their Carls. The Carls in China and Russia that had military guards were each the scene of a mini riot. Only one person was killed, when a soldier in Chengdu opened fire on a growing crowd. Somehow, instead of scattering, the crowd closed in and the soldier stopped shooting. It had all happened in minutes. I maintain that it would have been impossible to pull off at any future moment.

The instant New York Carl took off, every other Carl in the world just disappeared. Physicists bent over backward trying to explain how every Carl was, in fact, just one Carl. They had already been through this once with Hollywood Carl's hand. Now it seemed 100 percent confirmed.

Everyone stopped having the Dream the moment Carl came to life. People who were having it at that moment just stopped having it. Most of them didn't even wake up. Sometimes people dream about the Dream, of course, but it seems to be over.

And then, we waited for them to find her body.

Weeks passed, and they didn't find anything. April's family came to see us all. I don't know if it made it better for them, but it made it worse for me. It was bad enough blaming myself for my best friend's death; I didn't want to think about how I'd destroyed these people's lives too. The experts on the news, because of course this was international news, said that a body can't burn up completely in a fire like the one at the warehouse, it wouldn't get hot enough, so that's very good.

They wanted to get me on the news to talk. Me or Maya or Miranda or Robin—none of us would do it. For the first week, the press was outside my building, so I just stopped leaving. Jason would go downstairs and pick up my Postmates orders. I just sat in my room reading Twitter and waiting for news.

There wasn't news, just people talking about all the things we already knew. Eventually, we each got our own separate letter of condolence from the president, and that somehow made it feel OK to mourn, even if we weren't sure what we were mourning.

A few weeks had passed the first time I got a call from Robin.

"They found the guys," he told me after we exchanged bland pleasantries.

"I didn't see anything online."

"It's not out yet. I've been keeping in touch with the NYPD, and they let me know they're going to be making arrests today." He didn't sound happy or sad or triumphant. He sounded like he was telling me about new shoes he bought at Dillard's.

"Who are they?" Somehow I thought maybe this would help me understand.

"There's three of them. They met in an anonymous chat room. One was a coder, one was a dope, and one was smart, committed, and really wanted to kill April or stop her or just make his mark on the world. The coder was bragging about how he could modify the code to spit out anything if the key was entered. Once the Defenders found the key, it became an open secret in their chats, and the lead guy told the hacker to go ahead and do the thing he was bragging about. He scouted the warehouse and gave him the address. Once the modified code was up, he and his follower friend just waited at the warehouse, and honestly, I think they were surprised when April showed up. The leader started the fire and ran. He bragged about it once in one of the chats, and another Defender from the chat called in a tip. That's all it took for the FBI to track them down. They don't know if they can charge them for murder because they haven't found a body."

The two guys who were there ended up getting maximum sentences for kidnapping, false imprisonment, arson, attempted murder, conspiracy to commit murder, and a bunch of other charges. Not murder, though.

I stayed quiet while he made the bland report.

"I'm glad they caught them."

"Yeah."

"One of the last things April said to me was that she was OK with me being mad at her, but she didn't want me to be mad at myself," I told him.

"Yeah," he replied.

Peter Petrawicki came away scot-free because he didn't actually have anything to do with the kidnapping. But the attack on April and the disappearance of Carl was pretty much the end of the Defenders movement. It pushed it over the edge in a way that July 13 somehow didn't. Maybe it was the removal of Carl as a visible threat, or the end of the Dream; maybe it was the dirty, duplicitous way they conspired to kill April; maybe it was April's livestream, which peaked at more than a billion simultaneous viewers.

Whatever it was, within a month of Carl's disappearance, even Peter Petrawicki was distancing himself from the Defenders movement, saying it had grown into something he could no longer respect. A worm is a worm is a worm. He moved to the Caribbean and is now apparently working on some skeezy-sounding cryptocurrency start-up.

The scariest of the bunch didn't go away, of course. And the conspiracy theories abounded. No one could explain what had happened to our minds to make the Dream possible, and if people could find a reason to be scared, they would be.

In only a month, our group had shattered. I don't know if it was because nothing was holding us together, or because we repelled each other with our guilt and grief (or both of those things), but suddenly Miranda was back at Berkeley, Robin was back in LA, and Maya was on some kind of pilgrimage, avoiding sleeping in the same place for more than a few days. Only I stayed in New York. I had the dumbest feeling that I wanted April to be able to find me. I wanted her to know where I was. Also, I knew the best thing for my mental health was keeping some semblance of stability in my life. It worked well enough and this way I wouldn't have to cry in front of Maya or Miranda all the time, which is mostly what I did when I saw them.

But not many days went by without Robin, Miranda, Maya, and me corresponding via a group text that we had never let die and that, yes, still contained April's number.

People keep asking me to speak at things, I sent one day.

Do you want to? Maya replied.

Good god, no. They never tell me what I'm supposed to say. I just don't know what I'm supposed to talk about.

You have a lot to talk about, Andy, Miranda wrote.

They don't actually want me, they just can't get April.

It was a long time before Maya replied, *I've been reading April's books. She's got a biography of Rodin that starts out with this line: 'Fame, after all, is but the sum of all the misunderstandings which gather about a new name.' I think she read that line a lot of times. Carl was always a canvas on which people would project their values and their hopes and their fears. April is going to become that now.*

Am I supposed to do something about that? I replied.

No, I just think we should be aware that, now that she isn't around to say things, people are going to be putting words into her mouth. I know you're keeping your eye on Twitter already.

It was true. I would occasionally put people in their place when they misquoted April or said she believed or would have done something that she didn't believe or wouldn't have done. Maya was right about this one and I knew it.

This isn't over, huh.

No, it's going to be who we are to the world forever.

So should I go talk to the University of Wisconsin?

Can you tell them something that will make them feel better?

It took a really long time for me to settle on, *Not yet.*

That's OK, her reply came quickly.

But then I started thinking about what I would say if I did say something. I wasn't ever going to go get grilled on cable news, but maybe I could sit down with someone for a public conversation or give a short talk. I couldn't put it on our YouTube channel—I felt an odd sense that that was a sacred space that had to freeze in time the moment April died.

Once I started thinking about what I would say, it was a very short step to actually writing it down. So that's what I did. I gave a lot of different talks that year, but I always ended with what I wrote that night:

> A year ago, I watched the world fall in love with
> my best friend. We thought it would be fun, we
> thought it would be silly, but then that love tore her
> apart and put her back together different. April and I,
> alone in a hotel room, plotted to change her from a
> person into a story. It worked. It worked because it
> was a great story, and one that fit her. We did not

know that she would actually become it. The most insidious part of fame for April wasn't that other people dehumanized her; it was that she dehumanized herself. She came to see herself not as a person but as a tool. And if that tool wasn't being used, sharpened, refined, or strengthened at every opportunity, then she was letting the world down. April was a person, but we all convinced her that she was both more and less than that. Maybe she did that to herself, maybe Carl did it to her, maybe it was me or Peter Petrawicki or cable news. But near the end, even I forgot, most days, that April May was a human being. As she said to me once, she was, like all of us, as fragile as air.

I don't know what happened to April. But I do know that she was a person. She just wanted to tell a story that would bring people together. Maybe she didn't do it perfectly every day, and she made so many mistakes, but I don't think any of us are blameless when we all, more and more often, see ourselves not as members of a culture but as weapons in a war.

Her message is clear to me—it will never leave me now. We are each individuals, but the far greater thing is what we are together, and if that isn't protected and cherished, we are headed to a bad place.

I was still miserable after I wrote it, I was crying and wrecked, but I felt like it was something. I wrote back to the University of Wisconsin, saying I would like to give a thirty-minute talk, and they worked with my schedule. I called Robin to ask if he wanted to be my booking agent. He said, "OK."

I'm tempted to say that Robin took it the hardest, but I don't want to start a grief competition. He had quit his job and isolated himself, so I was happy to give him something to do, some way to bring him back to something. He blamed himself more than any of the rest of us. Of course, we all blamed ourselves. If we had just been a little smarter, a little faster, a little more convincing . . . But Robin knew that it was his news—and also his betrayal, however slight—that pushed April to that building.

I don't want to say, "The worst thing was not knowing," because it definitely would have been worse if they had dug April's broken, burned body out of that building, but we all felt useless. In a way, the whole world was in this weird limbo. April was a superstar, and now either she was dead or she wasn't and no one knew. Her Twitter became a monument. The last tweet she sent Come watch me on Facebook Live. Big things happening.—had become the most-liked tweet in history. I thought more than once about how petrified April would have been to have such a shitty last tweet.

As the time passed, no one really knew how to move on. I traveled around, eulogizing her over and over again in different places. Speaking to humans was so vastly different from tweeting or even making videos. Even if it was a five-thousand-person room, it was a minuscule audience compared to the viewership of anything I might put online. But this way we all had to sit in the same set of thoughts for over an hour. The connection felt very good. And I found out that I was good at it. Her parents came to a few of my talks.

As the weeks ticked by, it seemed increasingly possible that we would never know what happened to April, and that the Carls were done with us.

I remember the first day when none of the major news stories were about April May or the Dream or the Carls or the trial of her killers. The Chinese economy was collapsing because people had taken on debt to bet on the stock market; Apple was releasing its new VR rig; there'd been a rash of robberies at research laboratories, and during one a bunch of monkeys escaped and ran all over Baltimore. Someday, April May would be something that happened once. That's what she was so afraid of, and when it finally started happening, I was surprised to feel relief.

A couple of months after that, I was sitting at my desk writing some emails about financial management of my now ludicrous fortune when there was a knock at my door. That was actually pretty weird because no one could get into the building without being buzzed in. Maybe it was a neighbor's package.

Then my phone pinged. I grabbed it on the way to the door and then froze when I saw the lock screen.

April May

Slide to Reply

I have no idea how long I stared at it, but I do remember finally opening it with my heart in my throat.

Just two words.

Knock Knock

Acknowledgments

I have never done this before, so even finding out that it was possible was a bit of a journey for me. For that I have several hundred thousand people to thank. First, John Green, who is my brother and who kept saying that being an author is not some impossible job and it's a real thing that real people do to enough people who weren't me that eventually I believed him. My wife, Katherine, who just kept loving the things I wrote in ways that I believed and that made sense to me. Phil Condon, who helped me realize that writing was a thing I was good at in large part by helping me understand the parts of my writing that were bad. Guy Bradley, who once told me that, if chemistry didn't end up being my job, writing might. And a number of people who, over the last four years, said something like, "Send me what you have and I swear I will be honest about whether it sucks." Those people included: Patrick Rothfuss, Hugh Howey, Amanda Hoerter, and Jodi Reamer at Writers House.

But, maybe more important than any of that, I could not have written this book if I had not been taken on a weirdly remarkable journey into Tier 3 fame by a bunch of very cool and very supportive people who like my videos, tweets, re-blogs, posts, and podcasts. In a very real way, Nerdfighteria created this.

I had to do a lot of really interesting research for this book, so

ACKNOWLEDGMENTS

thanks to Sarah Haege, Megan Rojek, and Lauren McCall, who attended the same school as April, Maya, and Andy and let me hang with them for a day to understand what their lives were like. Thanks to Phil Derner Jr. of NYCAviation.com for talking to me for a solid hour about the bowels of the Boeing 767. Thanks to Jessica and Mitty for DM-ing with me about ambulances and first-responder protocols. Thanks to Kevin Gisi, who helped me figure out what's possible, impossible, and *really* impossible to do to Wikipedia. Brent Weinstein and Natalie Novak are longtime friends who are also Hollywood agents, so I guess I should both thank them for the insights they provided me and apologize for all the things I said. Also thanks to @cmdrSprocket for naming *Slainspotting* when I asked on Twitter for a good podcast name about TV deaths.

I also set out to do something difficult and scary in writing about a lot of characters who have very different life experiences than I do, so I want to particularly thank the people who read through this manuscript to help me avoid my own biases and to more accurately represent people who aren't like me. For that, I am extremely grateful to Ashley C. Ford, Amanda Hoerter, Mary Robinette Kowal, and Gaby Dunn.

Thanks also to my parents, who are just like April's parents in that all they want to do is help me feel happy and valuable and are great at biting their tongues when they think I'm doing something ridiculous. And to my wonderful friends and coworkers in Montana and elsewhere for being so supportive and comforting and comfortable.

Before I started this I also didn't really know what editors do, so I'm so grateful to Maya Ziv for holding my hand every step of the way and helping me not freak out over problems big and small. Maya's advice and ideas were so deeply valuable to this project. Also, thanks to the valedictorian of my high school graduating class, Mary Beth Constant, who by some marvelous fluke of the universe was also the copy editor for this book. You saved my butt so many times. And of course, thanks to all the people at Dutton who helped make this book a thing and helped get it into the hands of readers.

I also want to thank every single person who ever says, "You have to read this book!" to a friend. I don't care if it's this book; I just want people to remind each other how wonderful books are. Particularly, thanks to the people who work at bookstores who do that every day—professionals who can help you find books you will love and are, get this, even better at that than computer programs.

About the Author

Hank Green is a vlogger, entrepreneur, science communicator, and probably some other things. His company, Complexly, has produced videos that have been viewed more than two billion times on channels like SciShow, Crash Course, and Vlogbrothers. He lives in Montana with his wife and son.

You can follow him on Twitter or Facebook @HankGreen.